Million Dollar Inheritance

By Marlené Carter

ISBN:

Lyfe Publishing

Publishers Since 2012

Published by Lyfe Publishing LLC

Lyfe Publishing, www.lyfepublishing.net

Library of Congress Cataloging in Publications Data

Anderson, Gerald C. Sr.

Million Dollar Inheritance / Marlené Carter

ISBN:

Amara Mackleroy (Fictitious Character)-Fiction

Seattle, Washington—Fiction

Million Dollar Inheritance—Fiction

Printed in the United States of America

1 2 3 4 5 6 7 8 9 10

Book design by Aionios Designs

DEDICATION

Glory to God and total thankfulness to all the family and friends who encouraged and helped me make this novel possible.

Characters

Amara Mackleroy-protagonist and journalist for the magazine

Terrance Riley-Amara's boyfriend and Seattle Police Officer

Remington Walters (Remy)-Amara's good friend and co-worker

Jackson Mackleroy-Amara's father and lawyer

Cora Mackleroy-Amara's mother and teacher

Rolanzo Dumont-Terrance's godfather and shipping magnate

Dora Lee Dumont-Rolanzo's business assistant and wife

Cian Molloy-Seattle Police Detective

Casey Athy-Amara's college nemesis

Mr. Athy-Casey's father

Mrs. Athy-Casey's mother

Divya-Amara's childhood friend

Pradeep-Divya's husband and business owner

Samesh-Pradeep's friend and Pradeep's company VP

Connor-Ella's father

Sydney Palmer-Seattle Police Officer

Ella-Little girl at the lending library box

Gerard-Thief

Omar-Divya's first husband

Nasir-Omar's best friend

Nasira-Omar's arranged bride and good friend

Chapter 1

Amara and Terrance followed the stream of wedding guests across the lush lawn to the oversized reception tent. The coveted invitations had been sent to select friends of the bride and groom; Rolanzo Dumont, a semi-retired international shipping magnate and Dora Lee, his assistant for over thirty years. The wedding and reception were held on the luxurious grounds of Rolanzo Dumont's Seattle estate.

Amara Mackelroy happened to be one of those special guests. It didn't hurt that her current boyfriend; Seattle police officer Terrance Riley, had a close relationship with the groom. Amara wrote investigative pieces for Net, a popular Seattle magazine. It was her dream job, and she loved it. She was also one of the reasons the groom was still alive. He'd probably call her a meddlesome woman, which was partially true. She helped the police identify the killer bent on revenge against the Million Dollar Club members, where Rolanzo serves as club president.

Amara fingered the fine curls at the nape of her boyfriend's neck as they made their way to the reception tent. A gentle breeze ruffled her auburn curls carefully styled for the occasion. Her royal-blue, silk-chiffon tiered dress complimented her date's navy suit. Terrance clasped her hand and guided her to the reception tent.

They'd been dating for nearly one year. Amara's inquisitiveness and obsession over the murders of Million Dollar Club members nearly ruined their relationship. She couldn't help it. Her desire to ferret information about important issues sometimes overrode her common sense. Everyone who knew her understood she was guilty of sticking her nose where it didn't belong; especially when it involved someone she cared about.

1

Dimples creased her cheeks as she admired the grandeur of the reception area. The bleached canvas of the oversized tent gleamed in the brilliant sunlight. The band played an old school selection by Earth, Wind and Fire as guests made their way across the manicured lawn from the outdoor wedding ceremony to the reception.

Terrance gave Amara's hand a tug when she paused to take in the splendor of white linen clothed tables, topped with gold rimmed bone china plates, atop matching chargers, classic gold flatware, and gold-rimmed, crystal champagne flutes.

Fresh cut pastel pink and cream roses adorned the center of each table in cut crystal vases. Their floral scent intermingled with the savory aroma of grilled salmon, steak, and chicken. An assortment of delectable mini cakes, cheesecakes and fruit tarts were gracefully arranged on linen clad tables. It took all of Amara's willpower not to swipe her finger across the curtain of chocolate that flowed into tiered bowls. A mound of skewered, juicy, red, hothouse strawberries sat in an oversized crystal bowl beside the fountain.

This wedding was the event of the season. Rolanzo Dumont spared no expense to make this day spectacular for his new bride. Neither Rolanzo nor Dora Lee had married before. Amara thought they'd had some type of professional understanding. Their conduct was always above reproach. When they announced their engagement, everyone wondered why it had taken so long for them to commit to one another.

Amara had become acquainted with the self-made multi-millionaire when she was in middle school. He'd come to their home to see her father, who'd been a prosecuting attorney. Rolanzo was accused of using his freighters for human trafficking. Her father referred him to one of the best defense lawyers in the city. Once Dumont was acquitted of all charges, her father successfully sued the company where the lie originated for millions.

2

They'd crossed paths again when Ralph Simpson, a deranged surgeon set out to kill all the members of the exclusive Million Dollar Club. It was later discovered he'd been hired to murder only Rolanzo Dumont, but Simpson had gone off script and sought revenge against all twenty-one club members for the death of his only daughter.

The case quickly became personal for Amara when Simpson kidnapped her uncle, a member of the elite club. She and her good friend Remy began their own research into the murders. Her relentless pursuit put her in the crosshairs of two killers: Ralph and his brother, Gerald.

But, all of that was in the past. She could enjoy this joyous event without having to worry or constantly look over her shoulder. Ralph Simpson was dead, and his brother Gerald was in prison.

Amara would be the first to admit she'd become obsessed with the case. Like a dog with a bone, she'd refused to let go. Even after Ralph Simpson threatened her life, kidnapped her uncle, and his trusted Russian sidekick attacked her mother.

Terrance continued to guide them through the throng of guests to their table positioned close to the head table. Amara's attention shifted to the head table where members of the wedding party were being escorted to their seats. She noticed the groom's best man and his wife were missing from the entourage. Their absence confirmed her suspicion regarding the best man's wife. She was the missing Russian heiress, presumed dead. Pastor Wainwright, Rolanzo's first cousin and his wife Winnie had taken their place.

She glanced at Terrance and hoped one day they'd be sitting at the head table of their wedding reception. She was crazy about him and the feeling seemed mutual. Her reverie was interrupted when she spotted a familiar face at a far table. Contempt appeared on her honey toned face like a beacon. Her hands clinched involuntarily.

Terrance leaned close and whispered, "Are you all right?"

Amara masked her irritation with a wobbly smile. "Yeah, sure!" It amazed her how attuned he was to her. Her ex-boyfriend of three years had been the exact opposite. She promptly discarded thoughts of that jerk.

Terrance glanced toward the far table where single guests were seated. He decided not to press the issue. Amara would tell him later.

Each time Amara surveyed her surroundings, she noticed something new. "This is such a beautiful reception. Mr. Dumont spared no expense to make this day special for his bride," she gushed.

"Dora Lee put up with Rolanzo for thirty years. He's lucky she agreed to marry his crusty butt," Terrance wisecracked.

Amara giggled and asked, "How well do you know Mr. Dumont?"

He looked away. "Rolanzo is my godfather," he whispered. Amara's eyes widened. "I've finally left you speechless! Wonders never cease," he teased. Terrance had made it a point not to tell people Rolanzo was not only his godfather, but also his legal guardian after his parents were killed in a tragic accident when he was thirteen.

Amara bumped his shoe with the toe of her sandal and smirked. The questions about his relationship with his godfather would have to wait.

A guest at their table raised her finger to her lips and pointed in the direction of the handsome man standing in front of the bride and groom's table holding a microphone. The speaker, a member of the Million Dollar Club, was sharing a funny story about the happy couple.

As toasts were made, Amara considered the person she'd spotted earlier. When she turned to get a better look, the woman was taking photos of other guests, which was against the rules. "No-she-didn't!" Amara hissed.

Signs were posted throughout the venue warning guests they'd be asked to leave if they violated the couple's wishes. Famous actors, musicians, politicians, and several prominent people from different countries were in attendance.

Amara watched the guest absently tuck loose strands of blond hair behind her right ear and expose a wireless ear bud. When she bowed her head, Amara could see her lips moving. Was she speaking on the phone? Amara leaned over and whispered in Terrance's ear.

He turned, made eye contact with the woman, and motioned for her to cease whatever she was doing. She immediately removed the earbuds and slid them inside her small clutch purse.

As the servers began to set plates of food in front of each guest, the guest stood. She was taller than Amara remembered. Slight curves had replaced the angular planes from her college years. Blond tresses curtained her face as she bent to gather her belongings. She flipped her hair over one shoulder and straightened the elegant oyster-hued silk suit. Spiked heels stuck in the grass and caused her to wobble before she righted herself and disappeared through the nearest exit.

Terrance caught the attention of the man with the security company logo emblazed in blue on his polo shirt and pointed at the guest's retreating form. The man pressed his hand against his ear and spoke quietly into his earpiece as he followed.

Terrance whispered he'd be back. The determined expression on his face as he exited the tent prevented Amara from joining. She knew her absence would draw unnecessary attention to the situation.

As the meals were served, guests made their way to one of the three bars for something stronger than iced tea. A low hum of conversation and clinking of silverware against plates was complimented by a selection from the band positioned at the far end of the tent.

Amara bit into the grilled salmon and fought the urge to moan. The fish was delectable. When Terrance hadn't returned, she grew concerned. Amara dabbed her mouth with her napkin, stood, and left the tent.

Chapter 2

Terrance and the security guard were positioned on either side of the guest. Her agitated voice grew louder as she attempted to shove past the guard. Big mistake. He pointed his finger at her purse and held out his hand. Her long blond hair swished from side to side.

A member of Dumont's security team approached. The woman was blocked on all sides. Dumont's security looked like a pro linebacker. He was tall, muscular, and scary. He held out his oversized hand.

This time she didn't resist. She dug into her purse and slapped the phone into the palm of his hand. He pointed at one of the many signs that warned photos of the guests were not permitted and phones/cameras would be confiscated and returned once the photos/videos were deleted. In smaller, bold print it read, "This is private property. If anyone disagrees or chooses not to abide by the rules, we advise you to NOT enter the premises." Without a word, he deleted the photos of the wedding guests, returned the phone, and escorted her off the property.

"Hey!" the woman shouted as she stumbled to the sidewalk. Her crystal blue eyes blazed as yelled threats of a lawsuit at the security team.

The large man from Dumont's security stepped in her direction. His stern expression staunched further outbursts.

Amara winced. If the woman continued, it was not going to end well.

The woman clamped her mouth shut, slammed her phone into her purse, and stomped away. The only sound was the clickity-clack of high heels that pounded angrily against the cement sidewalk as she strode away.

Terrance turned to Amara. "That's the same woman you eyed earlier. Do you know her?"

Amara couldn't mask the contempt she felt. Yes, she knew the conniving, two-faced cow. She was the cause of her loss of the *Seattle Post Intelligencer* internship during her sophomore year in college.

Amara sighed and replied, "Yeah, I know her. We'd competed for the same staff position on the *Seattle Post Intelligencer* during college. Her name is Casey Athy. She accused me of plagiarizing an article I'd submitted and got me kicked out of the internship program."

Amara took a deep breath; surprised at her anger over an incident that occurred well over six years ago. "I explained I hadn't plagiarized anything. I even provided all my research notes, but it was futile. Casey's father was an editor at the paper."

She coughed to hide the depth of her despair. "I didn't stand a chance. They'd already selected Casey and thanked me for participating in the internship."

Amara brushed her hands together for emphasis. "It later dawned on me I never had a chance. Though I couldn't fathom why she felt the need to falsely accuse me."

Terrance pulled Amara close and kissed her forehead. "I've read your magazine articles and they're good. You write with passion." Amara leaned into him and soaked up his praise. Terrance turned her toward the reception tent. "Let's head back inside. I didn't get a chance to eat and I'm hungry."

Their table was empty. The other guests were either on the dance floor or socializing with friends at their table. A server brought fresh meals and iced tea. Amara fed Terrance some of her fish while he speared a piece of steak with his fork. She licked the garlic butter from her lips and gave a satisfied grin.

"Delicious," she whispered. Terrance grinned and pointed at the salmon. "Not bad, though my steak is better." Amara waved away his comment and finished her meal.

Terrance led Amara to the dance floor. It was a slow song, and he held her close. His lips nearly touched her ear as he whispered, "I'm glad we found each other." Amara tilted her head and gazed into his eyes. Her voice was silky and low when she replied, "Me too."

Chapter 3

Seattle homicide detective Cian Molloy was a bit disoriented when the corner of a cold, blunt object poked his bare shoulder. His wife called his name the second or third time before he grunted, accepted the phone, and pried his eyes open.

The red digital numbers on the bedside clock read four-zero-zero. Being awakened that early was never a good sign. "Hello," he said, his voice thick with sleep.

The urgent tone on the other end caused him to sit up straight. His wife yanked the covers, turned her back in his direction, and easily fell asleep. After twenty years, she was used to the drill.

Molloy dressed, rushed to the garage, and sped to Schmitz Park. He was intercepted by a police officer who guided him down a dimly lit, tree-lined, dirt path. Molloy rubbed his hands together to ward off the early morning chill as he joined the officers.

"We received a call from two men jogging along the trail. They're delivery truck drivers and work various shifts. They admitted to trespassing. Apparently, they've been doing it for months. Since the trails are so popular during the day, they chose to jog together at dawn before the park opened."

The joggers were conversing with a patrol officer a few feet away. The men were dressed in long, spandex leggings and sleek fluorescent running jackets. Bright orange cable knit skull caps covered their heads. One runner fidgeted, while the other spoke in a hushed tone.

Molloy was escorted further down the path. The officer pointed at the joggers' heads. "See, they have lights strapped over their caps. You know, like miners use."

The detective smirked as the officer shrugged and directed the detective's attention to a large wooden tree trunk that was sawed down the center and painted to resemble an alligator. It was a popular site for photos; especially with tourists.

Molloy focused his attention on the CSI detectives. They'd erected lights, roped off the area, and begun the arduous task of processing the crime scene. Bright lights illuminated the body of an alabaster skinned woman dressed in a light-colored suit. The victim, who appeared to be in her late twenties or early thirties, was sandwiched between the split trunk fashioned to look like an alligator's mouth.

The victim's expensive suit was covered with grass stains and patches of dried mud. Strands of blond hair fell limply on either side of the tree trunk. Bulging eyes stared vacantly into the starless night. A braided welt was imprinted on the victim's neck; welts scarred both wrists. Her nails were chipped and filled with dirt. Dried blood mixed with mud caked her bare knee caps. Mud coated the victim's expensive high heeled shoes. One was missing a heel.

Had the victim been running to escape her captor, tripped and fell, or was she shoved to the ground? The ligature marks on her neck were from something woven together. A rope or belt, maybe?

Molloy acknowledged the medical examiner with a nod. The ME's delivery was succinct as he reported, "Rigor has started to set in. She's been dead approximately five to six hours." As the ME's assistant carefully moved the body to prepare her for transport, the detective spotted what looked like a small purse beneath her torso. Unlike the victim's clothing, the purse was pristine. His gloved hand opened it; empty. Where were her phone, identification, keys? Molloy ran gloved fingers along the inside of the purse and felt something protruding behind the lining. He motioned to one of the CSI detectives and handed him the purse. "There's something inside the lining."

11

The CSI detective processed the purse before carefully making a neat slit in the lining. Gloved fingers removed a white sealed envelope, the size of a small greeting card. Molloy glimpsed the carefully printed block letters on the face of the envelope. The letters, written with a felt tip pen, formed a name. He read it and cursed aloud.

Molloy examined the surroundings along the dirt path. Shadowed outlines of tall birch and evergreen trees coupled with thick vegetation were on either side. Nocturnal animals scurried away from the squelch of radios, bright lights, and muted conversations between detectives and police officers. He sighed as he watched the ME's assistant lift the victim, encased in a protective black bag, onto the gurney.

Schmitz Park consisted of fifty-three acres of trails, trees, plants, and fauna. The killer or killers could have hidden the victim's body anywhere in the dense woods or thick vegetation which might have taken weeks to find. He believed the killer's intent was to have the victim's body discovered quickly. If that was the case, why had the killer removed her identification? None of it made sense. Molloy headed over to the two witnesses.

His attention briefly returned to the envelope as he approached the two joggers. Once the CSI gathered forensic evidence from it, he'd read whatever was written on the enclosed note.

The first witness raised his hands as if to avoid physical blows. "We only found her. I have no clue who she is." He pointed to the police officer who'd questioned him. "Like I told the officer, we didn't see or hear anyone during our jog along the path."

"We find the early morning jog peaceful. It's a perfect way to end our shift before we go home and get some sleep," the other runner chimed in.

Molloy read their statements and asked both witnesses a few more questions before he left them with the officer. The wheels of the gurney rolled up the hill and squeaked slightly when it halted at the van. As the van door opened, the detective squinted into the predawn darkness and whispered, "Who are you and how did you get here?"

The name written on the envelope disturbed him. He could feel an oncoming headache. This person had that effect on him. He didn't relish having to question her. It would only cause undue hardship in the future.

"Damn," he hissed and headed toward the CSI detectives who continued to comb through possible evidence and process the crime scene.

Chapter 4

Amara Mackelroy's mouth felt as if it was filled with cotton when she awoke early the next morning. She'd had a few too many drinks, and they'd danced until well after midnight. The party at the wedding reception was in full swing when they left for Terrance's house.

The room was darkened by closed wooden shutters. After months of remodeling, the interior of the house was finally completed. Gone were the sheets of plastic that hung from the ceiling, partitioning rooms, and the incessant dust on every surface.

The fact Terrance welcomed her decorating ideas made her feel part of it all. He claimed the house had good bones and just needed tender loving care. The truth was her boyfriend seemed oblivious to the fact his childhood home had been stuck in the 80s.

His parents hadn't changed anything since they'd purchased the house over forty years ago. She'd fought tooth and nail to get rid of the dated chintz patterned sofa and matching chair encased in protective plastic that stuck to her thighs the few times she'd been forced to sit on it.

Walls separating the living room, dining room, and kitchen were removed and was now one huge, open space. She'd taken down the flowered wallpaper in the kitchen and dining room and chose soft earth tones. Amara encouraged Terrance to update the kitchen appliances that were decades old. Her boyfriend admitted the house seemed larger, more modern, and airier.

She'd left his oversized, solid oak furniture in the master bedroom untouched, but brightened the walls with cream colored paint, and replaced the dark curtains and flimsy plastic blinds with wooden shutters that blocked out light when he worked shifts.

Terrance reached out and pulled her close. He kissed the back of her neck and whispered, "I know I said it yesterday, but you looked really pretty at the wedding."

She turned, balanced her head on the palm of her right hand as her elbow rested on the pillow. She lifted a brow while suppressing a smile. "Oh, just yesterday?"

Terrance sputtered an explanation. She cut him off mid-sentence with a kiss and quipped, "You didn't look so bad yourself."

He laughed and pulled her with him as he got out the bed.

Amara spied the time and was glad it was Sunday. They'd planned to have brunch with her parents after church. She quickly padded to his closet, retrieved her clothes, and rushed into the spacious master bathroom. Though she'd never tell him to his face, Terrance Riley took way too much time. Twice as long as she. She removed a clean washcloth from the towel warmer and pushed a button that had her exact desired water temperature and spray setting programmed.

Dressed in a tangerine wrap dress and matching sandals, Amara exited the bathroom as Terrance quickly entered and shut the door. Luckily the house had two bathrooms. She'd apply her makeup and style her hair in the guest bathroom.

Amara brushed mascara on her long lashes and wrestled auburn curls into a neat bun at the nape of her neck. It took her years to embrace the unusual color and curly texture of her hair. She'd been teased mercilessly in elementary school. Not many African American girls had natural auburn, spiral curls that hung down their back. If she never again heard *Tomorrow*, the theme song from Annie, it would be too soon. Her fingertip spread gloss on full lips. She tilted her face and spread moisturizer on smooth, honey toned skin.

"Wasn't the wedding nice?" Amara asked on the way to church. Terrance cut his eyes in her direction and grunted his assent. His fingers gripped the steering wheel in anticipation for the real question she desired to ask. "So, I'm guessing the wife of the best man is the missing Russian heiress. Was the best man Mr. Dumont's cousin?"

Terrance sighed and replied, "The best man is Rolanzo's younger brother, not his cousin. His wife is from Moscow, Idaho; not Moscow, Russia."

Amara gave an exaggerated eye roll and tutted, "Uh, huh…" Though shocked to learn Rolanzo Dumont had a brother, Amara was certain the wife was the Russian heiress presumed dead a decade ago.

She'd researched the heiress during Ralph Simpson's killing spree several months ago. Initially, she'd believed the missing woman's husband had funded the murders of several Million Dollar club members. Now, she wasn't so sure. She'd looked so unhappy and abnormally thin when she'd been married to her Russian husband. At the wedding, she seemed happier and healthier than she had in the dated internet photos. Amara guessed the heiress was the real reason for the strict photography rules, though she'd never know for sure.

Though Rolanzo and his younger brother shared the same gray eyes and long lashes, his brother was several inches shorter and shades lighter. Rolanzo was tall with sinewy muscles and lithe like a runner. His brother was stocky with the muscular physique of a boxer or wrestler.

She glanced at Terrance. The taut jawline and fingers clutched around the steering wheel a bit too tight prompted her to stop asking questions. Amara turned up the radio and sang to a gospel song. Terrance bobbed his head and joined in.

A church usher led them down the carpeted aisle to the pew where Amara's parents sat. She leaned over, kissed her

16

mother's cheek, and squeezed her father's shoulder. Her mother grasped Terrance's hand and whispered hello. Terrance smiled and greeted Amara's parents before shifting his attention to the front of the church as the choir prepared to sing.

Amara spotted Pastor Wainwright off to the side in a dark suit. He sipped from a bottle of water and clutched a worn Bible in his left hand. He looked rested after presiding over his cousin's wedding last night.

Once the service was over, Amara looked forward to having brunch at her favorite restaurant. She and Terrance followed her parents to the parking lot.

Chapter 5

The foursome entered The Skillet; a popular restaurant located in Capitol Hill. Oversized potted plants dotted the walkway to the entrance where a large cast iron skillet hung near the door. They were escorted to a table with retro green bench seats. Amara shoved the menu aside and announced, "I know exactly what I want!"

"Chicken and waffles," Terrance said. Amara nodded. He and her parents followed suit. Conversation revolved around the Dumonts' wedding. Amara and her mother Cora rehashed the designer outfits worn by famous guests. Popular singers, actors, and actresses had been part of Dimly's entertainment company before Ralph Simpson murdered him. He'd also been president of the Million Dollar Club and Mr. Dumont's close friend. They discussed professional athletes and dignitaries sprinkled among the one hundred guests.

Terrance sat up straight when he spotted a familiar face enter the restaurant. He waved to catch the man's attention.

Molloy acknowledged the wave with a slight nod and headed to their table. His demeanor and stride made it apparent this was not a chance encounter.

Terrance wiped his mouth and excused himself. He met the detective in the middle of the restaurant and followed him out of the restaurant.

Amara attempted to stand, and Cora's palm pressed against her thigh, pinning her in place. She frowned as Terrance and the detective left the restaurant. She pointed at the pair seated at an outdoor table. Their heads were bowed as they conversed. "Mom, I need to go out there! Did you see the way they turned to look at me? They're talking about me!"

Jackson balanced his fork on the side of his plate. "Mari, if they want to include you in their conversation, they'll invite you." Her father picked up his fork and pointed the tines in her direction. "I'm sure they're discussing police business. Eat your food, Pumpkin." He took a healthy bite of his waffle to emphasize the point.

Amara pouted and was about to debate the issue further when her father's prediction proved correct. Molloy reentered the restaurant and approached the table.

His expression was apologetic as he addressed Amara and her parents. 'I apologize for interrupting your meal. I just need a moment with your daughter. Amara, may I speak with you?"

She stood, as did her father. Jackson had worked with Molloy for several years when he'd been a prosecuting attorney. Amara motioned for her father to sit down. "I'm fine, dad," she declared and followed the detective through the double doors out to the patio area.

Her lips formed a sly smile when she overheard her mother chide, "Jackson, you are as bad as your daughter. We both know she gets her inquisitiveness from you. Stay right where you are. She'll call if she needs you."

Amara was too far away to hear her father's response. She wondered what she'd done to garner Molloy's attention or more likely ire on a Sunday afternoon.

When they joined Terrance, she gave the detective her full attention.

"Amara, there was a homicide on the west side of town. The victim is newspaper reporter, Casey Athy."

Amara jerked back as if he'd struck her. She'd seen Casey less than twenty-four hours ago! Though she didn't care for Casey, she'd never wish her harm. "I'm sorry to hear about her death, but why are you telling me? What happened?"

19

Molloy exhaled and explained, "Her body was discovered early this morning by two joggers on one of the trails in Schmitz Park. Someone, most likely the killer, sandwiched her body between the trunk of the large tree that's painted to look like the jaws of an alligator."

Amara knew the location. She'd had her photograph taken at the tourist attraction several years ago. How was this connected to her?

Molloy removed his cell phone and held it for Amara to view. "We found this in her purse."

Amara stared at the photo of an evidence bag that held a stark white envelope with her name printed in neat bold letters. Her voice was high pitched when she inquired, "Why is my name on that envelope? What's going on?" She looked into the detective's emerald green eyes and fought the urge to demand he get on with it.

"The envelope was hidden inside the lining of the victim's handbag. We discovered the purse beneath her body." The detective explained Casey's wallet, phone and whatever else she may have had inside the purse were missing. She'd been identified by her fingerprints.

"For whatever reason, the killer wanted to delay the process of her identification, even though her body was placed in plain sight. We believe Casey tried to flee and perhaps put up a fight."

Amara peered at the photo once more and asked, "What was inside the envelope? Why was it hidden in the lining of the purse and addressed to me? I haven't spoken to Casey since our college internship with the *Post Intelligencer*."

The detective's head snapped up; his eyes focused on Amara's face. "That's why I'm here. I need to know your history with the victim. I wasn't aware you two were in the internship program."

Amara closed her eyes as she contemplated how much information to share. Terrance nudged her shoulder and gave an imperceptible nod. She plunged into the plagiarism incident and explained they hadn't spoken since their junior year in college. "The Dumonts' wedding was the first time I'd seen Casey in years."

The detective swiped at his phone screen to another photo. "This was found inside the envelope." He held up a picture of a beautiful Indian woman. It was clear the photo had been taken without her knowledge.

Amara placed a shaky hand over her mouth and gasped. She turned to look at Terrance. "Remember the friend I told you about from India? That's her; Divya. Why would Casey have a photo of Divya?"

The detective squinted and waited for Amara to continue.

"Divya and I were best friends in elementary through middle school. Her parents sent her to India during the first three years of high school. We kept in touch the entire time she was away. She returned during our senior year. What does she have to do with this?"

The detective leaned forward. "Are you still in touch with Divya? What can you tell me about her?"

Amara tongue felt thick as she answered, "No, we didn't keep in touch."

Molloy leaned back in the chair and motioned for Amara to continue.

"Casey attended high school in Redmond. Divya and I went to Franklin High School. Casey and I attended undergrad at U-Dub; University of Washington." She shrugged and added, "I'm not sure if Divya attended college. If she did, it wasn't right after high school. Divya worked at a health food store for a couple years." Her voice was quiet as she admitted, "Our friendship

21

didn't withstand the test of time. After she returned from India, Divya hung out with a different crowd."

Molloy slipped his phone into his jacket pocket.

Amara quirked a brow. "You're holding back detective, what aren't you telling me? Was there a note or something written on the back of the photo? Why was the envelope addressed to me?" She took a deep breath and confessed, "Since I haven't had contact with either of them in years, I'm not sure how I fit into all of this."

Molloy's expression was pinched. It was his turn to decide how much to reveal. "Come by my office tomorrow after work. I'm in the process of investigating a lead. I should have more to share by then." He stood and thanked them for their time.

Terrance accompanied the detective to his car. The clouds had turned dark, and a fine mist began to sprinkle the tops of the outdoor tables and umbrellas. Amara tucked herself further beneath the umbrella and watched Terrance and Molloy. She wished she could hear what they were discussing.

Terrance returned and pulled her to her feet. "Your hands are freezing and it's drizzling. Let's go inside,"

Deep in thought, Amara remained quiet as Terrance guided her inside the restaurant. She sat down and looked longingly at her cold waffle and remaining pieces of chicken.

Her mother signaled the waitress and requested the couple's food be reheated. The waitress smiled and carried their plates into the kitchen. Amara's father leaned close. "What was that about?" He looked from Amara to Terrance.

Amara didn't respond. Once Terrance made sure no one was in earshot, he quietly filled them in.

Cora blinked rapidly and sat back hard against the cushioned bench seat. "Even though Casey did my baby wrong, I'm sorry to hear about her death. Wasn't she at the wedding?"

For years Amara had purposely avoided reading Casey's articles. Now she wished she had. Was she investigating something or someone that caused her death? How did Divya fit into all of this? Amara flinched when the waitress placed her plate on the table.

Knife and fork in hand, Amara paused when her mother prodded, "Sweetheart, I asked you a question. Are you okay?" Amara shook her head as she cut into her waffle and took a bite. Her stomach roiled and she suddenly felt ill. She excused herself and hurried to the bathroom. Cora followed.

Amara leaned over the basin and took deep breaths to tamp down the nausea. She splashed cold water on her face while her mother rubbed her back. The gentle, circular motion calmed her.

"Do you want to tell me what's going on?" her mother prompted.

Amara leaned against her mother and got her emotions under control. Her mother, a svelte woman, with short, salt and pepper hair, handed her a tissue. Amara dabbed her eyes. "It's as if my past has returned to haunt me," she sniffed.

"You know how tight Divya and I were. When she returned from India, I was treated like a pariah; it hurt. We'd been best friends since second grade. The Divya I'd known and loved was gone. In her place was this glamorous young woman. I was still a nerdy girl with braces who chose books over fashion and most boys." She tossed the tissue in the trash and added with a laugh, "No matter how hard you tried."

Cora cupped her daughter's face. "I also remember you made new friends and continued to pursue your dream while Divya's life seemed to lack direction. I believe she got married."

Amara nodded. Though her mother was right, she felt hollow and bereft. She'd learned of Divya's marriage from a mutual friend's social media site. "Let's go back to our table. I'm sure Terrance is worried," she said and headed to the door.

Cora's voice was soft as she placed a hand on her daughter's shoulder. "Don't let your father's nonchalant attitude fool you. He's worried as well."

Amara pressed her lips together and fought the impulse to cry. Shoulders straight, head erect, she led the way to their seats.

Terrance clasped her hand. "Are you alright?"

She nodded and sipped her lukewarm tea. Jackson caught her eye. "It's going to be all right Pumpkin. We'll get to the bottom of this."

She raised her mug in her father's direction. "Thanks Dad."

Chapter 6

The drive to Amara's apartment was quiet. Theories and speculations swirled in her mind as she considered Molloy's news. Divya had ended their friendship abruptly and Casey caused her integrity to be questioned. Not to mention she'd lost the coveted staff position at the newspaper. Those experiences had been the darkest times in her life.

Amara tried to focus on the information she'd received from Molloy. There were many unanswered questions. Why had Casey addressed the envelope to her, enclosed Divya's photo, and hidden it? There had been several opportunities for Casey to speak with her at the wedding, but she hadn't. Why?

Casey got what she'd wanted. In time, so had she. Amara loved writing investigative and trending articles for Net magazine and the pay was far better. Also, her blog was doing well. She might not reach as many readers as Casey, but her readership continued to grow.

"We're here," Terrance announced. Amara looked through the windshield, startled they'd arrived at her apartment. She sat in the car and stared at her apartment.

Terrance's hands gently cupped her face. "Do you want to talk about it?"

She tilted her head upward to prevent tears from falling. "This entire situation has evoked painful memories. I need time to digest it all," she confessed.

Amara aimed a finger at her chest. "I'm a better writer and Casey knew it. I guess she had to lie to save face since her grandfather and father had worked at the paper."

Terrance cut off the engine.

Eyes closed; Amara rested her head against the seat. "As for Divya, the end of our friendship was unexpected and I took it hard." She considered the letters they'd exchanged throughout her friend's stay in India. It surprised her how something that occurred several years ago still affected her.

Terrance wiped a tear from her cheek with the pad of his thumb. She grabbed a tissue from the glove box and blew her nose. "If I'm being honest, we'd both changed. The girl who went to India was a shy, chubby girl who wore matching polyester tunic and pant sets sewn by her mother. Her long hair was always in a thick plait that trailed down her back, to her waist. Even though Divya was shy, she had a wicked sense of humor. She spoke English and Hindi fluently. I enjoyed our deep conversations about our different religious beliefs and her culture."

Terrance kissed her. He tasted of maple syrup and coffee. She stared at her boyfriend, grateful for his concern and understanding. She unbuckled her seatbelt and got out the car. He watched until she reached the door, turned, and lifted her right hand, fingers splayed, palm faced out, before going inside.

Amara heard Terrance's vehicle back out the parking slot and drive out of the apartment complex. She placed her leftover meal in the refrigerator and sat on the sofa. Discussing Divya with Terrance triggered other memories. Divya was the oldest sibling in her family and cared for her younger sister and brother while both parents worked long hours.

Divya had declined invitations to school sports and activities. After a while, the invitations ceased. Amara remembered Divya's kind, beautiful mother who had taught her how to wear a sari. The silky fabric draped over her body made her feel grown up. Divya's mother made chai tea, and Amara fell in love with it.

Eyes closed; Amara remembered what happened a few months later. Divya's mother severed the friendship. To this day, she had no idea why.

Divya was sent to India to live with relatives. Surprisingly, their friendship hadn't ended. In fact, they became closer. The letters they'd exchanged cemented a shared vow to remain best friends despite their separation.

Amara recalled her excitement when she received one of Divya's letters written on crinkly, thin blue international stationary folded into an envelope with its international postmark.

Divya complained about the terrible humidity, mosquitos, and the need to shower several times a day. She joked about her aunt's terrible cooking and described the new acquaintances at a school she barely tolerated. The last line in every letter Divya wrote was she missed her best friend and was ready to return to Seattle. It took three years for that to happen.

Chapter 7

Amara changed into jeans and her favorite college sweatshirt. Her feet slid into lamb's wool slippers as she ruminated over her relationship with Divya.

She padded into her living room and slumped against the sofa cushions. Eyes closed; Amara recalled the elation she felt at the sight of her best friend. Divya was at her locker, spinning the dial left and right to the combination of numbers scrawled on a white slip of paper clutched in her left hand.

She'd raced down the hall and pulled Divya into a tight hug. The sentiment wasn't reciprocated. Instead, her best friend's arms dangled limply at her sides. Divya's expression was one of boredom or worse, irritation. It went downhill from there.

Weeks of avoidance make it perfectly clear Divya had no desire to remain friends. When she'd mustered the courage to ask Divya what caused their friendship to deteriorate, the question remained unanswered. Amara jumped when her phone rang.

"Hey baby, I'm just calling to make sure you're okay," her mother said. "I know you took the end of your friendship with Divya hard. You two were thick as thieves for so many years."

Amara didn't trust her voice to speak. It would be humiliating if it shook or worse, she cried.

"There's something I need to tell you about Divya's mother," Cora confessed.

Amara stilled. She'd known her mom visited Divya's mother. Her mom refused to discuss what transpired during the visit. Finally, Amara would learn what happened.

"Divya's mother caught her daughter smoking weed. Divya told her you'd supplied the drug." Her mother further explained Divya was seeing an older guy who was not Indian and a high school dropout. "Divya confided you'd introduced them, and they secretly met at our house while I was at work."

New tears stung Amara's eyes as she listened to the terrible lies.

"After that, Divya's parents felt they had no choice but to sever the friendship and send their daughter to India to live with relatives." Amara's mother harrumphed and added, "For all the good that did."

Amara was stunned. Divya had lied and implicated her! Why? She'd been so shy and sweet natured. Hadn't she? Amara cleared her throat. "Thanks for telling me mom. Her actions make sense now. I guess the big question is, why did she continue to write me the entire time she was in India?"

Her mother sighed. "I don't know, sweetheart. Maybe she wanted to know if you knew the truth. Perhaps you were a connection to her old life. Who knows? I just don't want you to get hurt again."

Amara wouldn't allow that to happen. It had been years since they'd spoken. She thanked her mom, ended the call, grabbed her laptop, and began an internet search on her old classmate. Her search was interrupted by a phone call from Remy, her co-worker and good friend. Their friendship was cemented when they'd investigated and helped solve the Million Dollar Club murders.

His voice sounded upbeat. "Hey, I didn't get a chance to talk to you at the wedding. I've been to some lavish weddings, but I must admit, Mr. Dumont knows how to throw a party. My date and I didn't leave until three in the morning!"

Amara murmured something incomprehensible and continued to type. Remy paused. "Uh, what's going on? You didn't even give me crap about my date, who I must admit was gor-ge-ous!" He sang the last word for added emphasis and waited for a retort that didn't come. "Now I know something is wrong, what's up?"

Amara inhaled deeply and told him what transpired during brunch with Detective Molloy.

"What?! You must be in shock! What does it all mean?" Remy asked.

Amara rubbed her temple with her free hand. "I don't know. Right before you called, I was researching Divya."

"I'm on my way over. Together we might get to the bottom of this." His earnestness caused Amara to smile.

"I appreciate and welcome your help. The truth is, I'd be terrible company. Let's research separately and discuss what we find tomorrow at work. I'll supply the coffee. Would you mind reading the last articles Casey wrote and see if there's a connection?" Amara heard the tapping of computer keys over the phone and smiled.

"I'm due to meet with my favorite detective after work tomorrow. I'll fill you in on any information I get from him," she said and ended the call.

Amara placed her phone on "do not disturb" and got to work. She discovered her old friend had remarried. Divya's first husband was extremely wealthy from Dubai. According to their social media sites, they appeared very happy, in love and travelled all over the world. He'd died in a freak accident while water skiing with friends in the south of France. They had no children. Amara discovered Divya owned property in several countries. Her late husband was the only son and heir to his father's vast fortune.

One of the gossip sites insinuated Divya returned her late husband's palatial family home in Dubai to his mother and two sisters. Another suggested Divya married for money and didn't get along with her mother-in-law or his sisters, although in photos, they seemed quite chummy. Which statement was true?

Chapter 8

Amara was surprised she hadn't uncovered any businesses owned by Divya. She was heavily involved with several charities and orphanages in Dubai while married to her first husband and later Mumbai. She discovered photos of Divya at an orphanage in India, and an article where she posed with inner city children at a literacy center in Seattle.

Amara's stomach rumbled. She stood and stretched the kinks from her shoulders and neck. It was well past dinnertime. Fortunately, her mother had the foresight to box her leftover brunch of chicken and a waffle.

Amara turned on the oven as she flexed the muscles in her legs and fingers. When she checked her phone, there was an encouraging text from Terrance. She typed a quick reply.

There was also a text from Remy. Her fingers clutched her phone tight after she read the three-word text; "I found something." The message had been sent two hours ago! It was close to ten o'clock. Amara placed her food in the oven and glanced at the clock once more.

Before common sense prevailed, she typed, "U up?" Amara looked at the new text, did a little happy dance, and immediately called Remy.

He picked up on the first ring. "What took you so long?" he teased.

Amara snickered. "You are such a smart ass. What did you find?" She heard the tap-tap of computer keys in the background.

"Your *buddy* Casey was one busy beaver." Amara rolled her eyes. "I know you're rolling your eyes. Stop it." Amara snorted in reply. Remy read from his computer screen. "Okay, here it is. She was writing an exposé on Divya but get this; the focus wasn't on her. It was on her second husband, Pradeep. He's a prominent businessman with companies in India, California and right here in Seattle."

Amara was intrigued. The oven timer dinged. She placed the phone on speaker, and turned off the oven. Remy's voice blared through the speaker as she removed her dinner from the oven. He filled her in while she cut into the warm dough of her waffle.

She'd read about the twenty-year age gap between Divya and her current husband, Pradeep, who had two adult children. The fact he was a successful businessman and owned a women's cosmetic company didn't surprise her. What surprised her was his reputation.

Remy broke into her thoughts when he added, "Casey wrote a grisly piece about one of Pradeep's skin products. She described women's faces peeling, rashes, and boils due to his contaminated face creams."

Amara's fork stopped in midair. "Ew, I'm eating!" she cried.

"Why are you eating so late?" he asked.

She skirted the question with one of her own. "What else did you learn from Casey's articles?"

Remy perked up. His voice grew animated. "I have a friend who works at the paper." Amara sighed and rolled her eyes once more. "Stop it Mackelroy! Anyway, my friend..."

"Female of course," she interjected.

"As I was saying, my friend told me Casey wasn't doing well professionally."

Amara bit her bottom lip to prevent callous words from escaping. The woman was dead. It was best to keep quiet.

"According to my source, these articles on Divya were her last chance to prove herself and keep her position. My guess is while investigating Divya, she learned about the shady deals involving her husband."

"Interesting. Well, you're right about one thing. Divya was wealthy before she married her second husband," Amara replied.

"According to my research, Pradeep lives in their palatial mansion in Mumbai. If they have children together, they've done a great job of keeping them out of social media," he added.

This strengthened Amara's assumption that the couple lived separate lives in different countries.

He stifled a yawn. "It's late and I need to get some sleep. Don't stay up too much longer," he chastised. "See you at work."

Amara smothered a yawn, ended the call, and headed to bed.

Chapter 9

Concentration eluded Amara as she stared at her office computer screen. Her current article for the magazine was more of a lifestyle piece. She felt slightly offended Matt had given her the assignment. It was early and the rest of the staff hadn't arrived.

She yawned and made her way to Remy's desk. He stared at the dark circles beneath her bloodshot eyes. "Didn't get much sleep last night, huh?"

Amara gave a tired smile. In fact, she hadn't. "Is it that obvious?"

Remy leaned back in his chair. "If I didn't know better, I'd swear you'd partied a little too hard over the weekend," he joked.

"I spent most of Sunday researching Divya." I went to bed shortly after talking with you, but couldn't shut my brain off." She plopped down in the chair beside his desk. "Why had Casey involved me?"

Remy schooled his expression to hide the concern her words evoked. She'd been obsessed with the Million Dollar Club murders. If the serial killer hadn't been murdered by his own brother, he might have succeeded with his promise to kill all twenty-one members of the exclusive club and her.

"Amara, don't go down that road again," he warned. "Consider your health." She'd lost a great deal of weight and nearly lost her boyfriend over the case.

Curls cascaded over her face when Amara ducked her head. Her obsession with the Simpson murders nearly cost her everything; including the lives of family members. She couldn't, wouldn't allow that to happen again. Unshed tears glistened in her eyes.

When their eyes met, she saw something unfamiliar in Remy's blue eyes. Concern, pity, remorse? Amara exhaled and stood. "You're right. I need to get a handle on this. I hope my meeting with Molloy will shed light on what's going on."

Remy tilted his head and hoped she was being honest with him; more important, with herself. Time would tell. "You're my friend and I care about you. Just be careful, okay?"

His caring words washed over her. She gave a quick nod and returned to her desk. Amara got to work as staff members entered the office.

At the end of the day, Matt, Remy's older brother and owner of the magazine, came from his office. He stopped short, surprised Amara and Remy were still working.

He knew about Casey Athy's death, and the evidence Detective Molloy discovered. Matt tucked his hand inside his front pant pocket and stared at the pair. "You two are working late."

"Yes, I'm preparing for my interviews with the four students, their parents, and members of the neighborhood watch, regarding the vandalism of the lending library box," Amara said. She checked the time on her phone. It took all of her willpower to hide her exasperation as she grabbed her satchel and hoisted it over her shoulder. "I'm headed to a meet with Detective Molloy. The station is closer to the office than my apartment, so I decided to stay a bit late and work on the magazine article."

Matt quirked a brow. "How well did you know Casey Athy?" Amara told him they'd attended college together. Matt leaned his shoulder against the partition and eyed her. She could tell he had something on his mind and braced herself for a lecture or barrage of questions.

"Okay, let me know if you need anything." He turned to Remy. "I'll see you at dinner tonight."

Remy avoided his brother's stare and fought the impulse to groan. Matt had become overprotective ever since he and Amara had gone to Mr. Dumont's cabin to warn him of a possible attack. The same cabin was set on fire hours later. The men responsible for the fire broke into Amara's apartment and attempted to break into his.

"I'll be there," he grumbled. Do I need to bring anything?"

Matt ignored Remy's tone. "Just your appetite," he replied cheerily. He turned to Amara. "If you need anything to prepare for your meeting with the detective, let me know."

She adjusted her satchel and replied, "I'm not sure what Molloy plans to tell me. It's all a bit unnerving."

Matt headed to his office. "Call if you need anything. Otherwise, I'll see you tomorrow."

Amara promised she would and followed Remy out the door.

The traffic was heavy on I-5. She was grateful to have the extra minutes to ponder what Detective Molloy planned discuss. Deep in thought, she zoomed past her exit. "Get it together Amara!" she chastised.

Chapter 10

Amara felt a rush of adrenalin when she entered the detective's suite. She had no idea what he'd tell her regarding Casey or Divya. Her attempt at a smile faltered when his green eyes met hers. Normally they sparkled with energy; today, they appeared tired. He placed the file he'd been reading on the desk and gestured to the chair she'd nicknamed TC for torture chair.

She glowered at the simple piece of furniture that was drastically different from its ergonomically friendly brothers and sisters. No human should be subjected to the type of torture this chair offered. Its bland, beige surface was as hard and imposing as its owner.

Molloy once confided he'd swiped the chair from one of the interview rooms several years ago when they'd left the old headquarters. It had been intended for the dump. Anyone who sat in it understood why.

When she hesitated, Molloy cleared his throat. The corner of his lip quirked as his eyes shifted to the chair.

Although Amara perched on the edge of the chair, the slope of the seat caused her bottom to slide until it filled the unyielding surface. No matter how many times she adjusted her sitting position, the outcome was the same. Her rear end would go numb.

Impatience added to her discomfort. Fortunately, idle chit chat had never been the detective's forte. On this occasion that trait worked to her benefit. When he rested his hands on top of the folder she asked, "What did you learn?" Amara mentally berated herself for the high-pitched timbre of her voice.

The fingers of the detective's right hand raked through his thick, unruly, mane. Tired, green eyes latched on to hers as he replied, "I don't have good news."

Amara groaned louder than intended.

Molloy waved his hands. "Now, now; don't jump to conclusions. I should have said, I don't have a lot of information regarding Ms. Athy's case." He opened the file on his desk.

"I spoke with her parents this morning. They acknowledged Casey's position at the newspaper was tenuous. The exposé she was writing on Pradeep's career and marriage to Divya would solidify or end her employment at the paper." The detective picked up a soft, leather-bound book.

Amara immediately recognized the worn, camel brown cover and frayed yellowed pages. It had belonged to Casey. She carried that book everywhere when they were interns.

"Casey's parents provided the journal she used to write notes regarding her articles. It has drafts of the articles on Pradeep and Divya. Apparently, the journal was a present from her grandfather who'd worked in advertising at the same newspaper several decades ago."

Amara knew Casey constantly wrote notes on the yellowed pages. She intertwined her fingers to fight the impulse to yank the journal from the detective's grasp and read it. "Does the journal indicate why the envelope was addressed to me and what she'd planned to do with it?"

Molloy nodded. "According to her research, Ms. Athy learned you and Divya were once close friends. She wanted to question you about Divya...except..."

Amara leaned forward. "Except what?"

Molloy shook his head. "Except she wasn't sure if you'd agree to speak to her. According to her journal, she'd planned to leave the envelope where you'd find it during the wedding reception. If that failed, it would be delivered to your office. Casey believed the photo alone would provoke you to reach out to her." He smirked. "I guess she knew how nosey you are."

Amara didn't respond. She waited for Molloy to continue.

He relaxed in his chair and added, "Mr. Athy told me about the plagiarism allegation."

She shrugged. "You already knew about that. What aren't you telling me?" Her eyes held his unwavering stare. When he didn't answer she admitted, "It's true I haven't spoken with Casey since the internship incident."

Amara shifted topics. "Casey was escorted off the premises at Dumont's wedding reception by security. She violated the rules and took photos of guests. She'd attempted to send the photos to someone, possibly a person on the newspaper staff. Casey also spoke to someone on the phone during the wedding toasts." Her forefinger shot up. "Before you ask, no, I didn't speak to her. I kept my distance while Mr. Dumont's security and Terrance handled the situation. When Casey was escorted from the premises, she became belligerent."

Amara tapped her upper lip. "When Casey left, I thought it strange she walked in the opposite direction of the valet stationed at the entrance. I'd assumed she'd used the valet service provided for the wedding guests." She stared at the leather-bound journal and asked, "Did you find her car?"

The pages of the journal fluttered when Molloy placed the book on his desk. "No, we're still searching for Casey's phone, wallet and vehicle." His finger gently tapped the cover of the journal. "I haven't had a chance to read the entire journal. I presume she was unable to leave the envelope once she was escorted off the premises."

Amara considered the detective's rationale. "I disagree. Casey had several opportunities to give me the envelope if she'd wanted to." She raised a finger and added, "Though, it would have been difficult since the envelope was hidden in the lining of her purse."

Molloy gave a slight nod.

The real question remained; why had she hidden the envelope in the first place? Was she frightened, had someone threatened her? Had a wedding guest been a threat? If so, who? Casey had an opportunity to interact with her when she'd joined Terrance outside the reception tent. Instead, she'd acted as if they'd never met.

Casey was already seated when she and Terrance entered the reception tent. When Terrance signaled for her to end the call, she could have made her intentions known. Yet, Casey made no move to acknowledge her with a nod or wave. She chose to leave the tent. It was all very strange.

Molloy's voice refocused her attention. "Were you listening young lady?"

Amara cheeks flamed with embarrassment. She'd been so busy unraveling the sequence of events at the wedding reception, she hadn't heard.

Molloy pursed his lips. "I asked if you knew why she hadn't approached you at the wedding or on the grounds after you joined Terrance and the security guards?"

"I was pondering that very question. She could have pulled me aside while guests entered the tent and made their way to their assigned seats. There'd been a hundred guests at the reception. The process took time."

Molloy's head dipped in agreement. He'd attended Dumont's wedding as well.

Amara added, "Another option was to place the envelope on my seat or on the table. That didn't happen."

Molloy stroked his chin. "There's an interesting entry in the victim's journal. Her research uncovered Pradeep's unsavory business practices. I confirmed his skin care line is under

41

investigation for tainted face creams. I also learned Pradeep and his second wife reside in separate households in different countries. I haven't had the chance to research his wife's assets. We received Casey's phone number from her parents and are checking with the carrier to learn who she contacted or spoke with prior to her death. As I said, except for the envelope in the lining, Ms. Athy's purse was empty."

Amara chose not to divulge the hours she'd spent researching her old classmate. She knew about the charities Divya was involved with and the couple's living arrangement. Her involvement in her husband's business or if she had businesses required more research.

Amara knew Divya had amassed considerable wealth from her first marriage. The calls Casey made before her death might prove important. Had she been lured to the park to meet with someone? A source maybe? If so, how did she get to the park? Where was her car?

Molloy stirred. He'd stopped talking. His stubby finger lightly tapped the cover of Casey's journal.

Amara stood to leave. "Thank you for the update."

"Not so fast, young lady." He made a looping motion with his forefinger next to his head. "I see the wheels turning in that mind of yours. I don't want you snooping around Divya and putting anything about this case in your blog. Casey's murder is still under investigation as well as Divya and Pradeep. We'll get to the bottom of this."

"I know I'm wasting my breath, but I need for you to allow the police handle this," he groused. He waved off her anticipated rebuttal. "I mean it, Amara. You know what happened when you got obsessed with Ralph Simpson's case."

Amara's nostrils flared with indignation. Why does everyone keep reminding me of my obsession with the Ralph Simpson case? "Of course I do, detective," she snapped. "I also know Remy and I may have saved Rolanzo Dumont's life, and Simpson's violent rampage was stopped. Gerald Simpson's participation in his brother's death was also uncovered." She pointed at her chest and fought to keep her voice steady. "I believe I helped put Gerald Simpson in prison!"

Detective Molloy's green eyes flashed. "Yeah, and you almost lost your life in the process!" He waved his hand in a shooing motion. "I've got work to do. Thank you for stopping by."

He watched Amara head to the door and sighed. He couldn't deny she and her family suffered during Simpson's killing spree. Amara set her sights on Ralph's brother Gerald, and dug until he'd lost control, broken into her apartment, and tried to shoot her. Molloy rubbed his temples and snarled, "Amara, you are one of the few people who can give me a headache."

Amara coughed to mask the laugh that tickled the back of her throat. When she spoke, her tone was conciliatory. "Okay, I'll be careful and promise not to write about this in my blog or contact Divya or her husband." She paused and raised a hand. "But, if Divya reaches out to me, I'm going to talk to her."

The detective glared at her. "If she contacts you, your first call better be to me." He pointed his forefinger at his wide chest for emphasis. He knew Amara was right. If Divya was involved, it was only a matter of time before she contacted her. She'd want to know what Amara knew.

"I appreciate your filling me in on the details about the journal and interview with Casey's parents. You didn't have to reveal as much as you did."

"Don't make me regret it, young lady. Someone murdered Casey and she involved you. Somehow, Divya, Pradeep and our victim are intertwined. This is a dangerous situation. We don't need any more victims."

43

Amara couldn't deny the envelope with her name printed in bold letters had involved her. "I promise to be careful," she replied. Amara rubbed her backside. "When are you getting rid of that Torture Chair?"

Molloy snickered in response.

Amara hurried down the hall to the bank of elevators. Distracted with thoughts of her conversation with Molloy, she rushed out the elevator and collided with Terrance.

"Whoa!" Terrance warned as he clasped Amara's shoulders to steady her.

Amara yelped in surprise. "Oh! I'm so sorry. I just met with Molloy and wasn't paying attention."

Terrance gave a devilish grin. "I gather by your smug expression; the meeting went well."

Amara slipped her arm through his. "If you have time for dinner tonight, I'd love to tell you all about it."

Terrance checked his watch. "I'm off in about thirty minutes. I can come by your place and we can head out to dinner." Amara smiled and gave his arm a quick squeeze before exiting the station.

Terrance watched her leave before he returned to his desk.

Chapter 11

Her phone rang as she pulled onto the street. "How was your meeting with Molloy? What did you find out?" Remy asked.

The excitement in his voice made her smile. Amara plunged into the details of the meeting.

When she'd finished, Remy asked, "Don't you think it's strange she didn't talk to you at the wedding as intended?"

Amara slapped the steering wheel with the palm of her hand. "Exactly! I asked Molloy the same question. Did you have a chance to research Pradeep further?"

He lowered his voice. "I'm still at my brother's house...mandatory dinner is about to begin. I'll do a bit of research later."

"That's fine. I'm going out to dinner with Terrance. I'll talk to you soon!" She disconnected the call and merged with the interstate traffic.

Amara had just enough time to change clothes and style her hair before Terrance arrived. The evening temperature had dipped. She adjusted her turtleneck sweater and was glad it wasn't raining. Her phone signaled Terrance was at the door.

He gave her an appreciative once over and leaned in for a kiss. "You look great." Terrance double checked her door locks and took her hand.

"You look fine yourself!" she declared. He kissed her hand and led her to his car.

Terrance and Amara sat at a table next to the expansive picture window of the Tilikum Place Café. The space needle was in the distance. Amara loved the homey feel of the restaurant where the specials of the day were written on a wide, framed blackboard on the far wall. They sat close together in the high-back, dark wooden chairs to be heard over the din of conversations.

Amara shared her discussion with Detective Molloy. "What bothers me is Casey had several opportunities to give me the envelope or at least speak to me and chose not to. Why?"

Terrance's shoulders lifted. "Good question. I saw her look in your direction when you joined us outside the tent. If you hadn't told me, I wouldn't have known you two were acquainted. Her body language didn't reveal that at all."

"My point exactly!" she huffed. "Something isn't right." She looked around and lowered her voice. "According to Molloy, Casey's journal revealed she'd planned to give me the envelope at the wedding. For whatever reason, she chose not to."

The waitress returned with their drinks, two bowls of onion soup, and their signature beet salad with spinach and lemon ricotta. Amara broke the cheesy crust of the soup.

Terrance speared lettuce and a chunk of tomato with his fork. "What do you plan to do?"

Amara spooned more soup and blew on it to give herself time to think. She didn't want Terrance to worry. Her obsession with Ralph Simpson's case had nearly ruined their relationship. Amara vowed never to allow herself to become that invested again.

She laid out her plan about researching Divya and her husband Pradeep.

Terrance lifted and brow. "How deep is Remy tied into this?"

Busted. She avoided his intense stare.

"Uh, huh," he said.

Amara's response came out in a rush. "He knows I had a meeting with Molloy and has done a bit of research on Casey's articles. I asked him to research Pradeep as well. I plan to focus on Divya."

She leaned forward. "My mom called last night. She told me about her meeting with Divya's mother before she was sent to India." Amara explained what her mother revealed. "She lied to cover her bad behavior! Plain and simple. I was the patsy!"

Terrance intertwined his fingers with hers. "Are you up to researching this?"

She sat up straight. "Yes. If nothing else, I'm curious. Divya and I haven't been friends since she returned during our senior year in high school. I'd seen her a couple times at the health food store where she used to work after we graduated. That was before she became rich and famous. Other than the obligatory hello, we never engaged in conversation. I'm sure it would be awkward if I saw her now."

Amara ate her soup. Eyes closed, she relished the pungent flavors of the soup and cheese. She opened her eyes. "Let's enjoy the evening," she suggested. "That's enough talk about Divya and Casey."

Terrance turned his head toward the door and cleared his throat. "I'm not so sure about that."

She stared at her boyfriend. He tilted his head in the direction of the entrance. When she turned, her breath caught. "This can't be happening," she groaned.

Divya stood at the door with two other women. She was more gorgeous than Amara remembered. The trio were dressed in designer outfits and conversed in rapid Hindi. Amara returned her attention to Terrance and her dinner.

Terrance took her hand. "Do you want to get boxes for our dinners and leave?"

Amara picked up her fork. As she stabbed a lettuce leaf, she shook her head. "We were just discussing her; now she's here. How's that for coincidence?" The quiver in her voice betrayed her true feelings. She fell silent and concentrated on her meal.

Terrance managed a discreet look before cracking the melted cheese of his soup. Amara had grown quiet. He needed to get her mind off Divya. He tried to get her to talk about her new article. When she didn't readily dive into her article as usual, he sipped his water and fell silent.

Amara watched Divya and her party follow the hostess to a far table in the back of the restaurant. As the seconds turned into minutes of silence, Terrance pointed his spoon in Divya's direction. "How much energy do you plan to expend on them?" he asked. Terrance set down his spoon and tucked an errant curl behind her ear. "All I ask is that you don't allow this murder and your quest to learn more information take over your life."

Amara took a sip of water and replied, "I promise to never allow myself to fall into the trap I did with Ralph, but I can't shake this."

As her thumb pointed to the back of the restaurant, she hissed, "Casey had hidden an envelope in the lining of her purse with that woman's photo and my name written on the outside before she was murdered."

Amara sighed deeply and fought tears. "Why me? Other people knew Divya and they're probably still friends. She's with two of them now."

It was time to lift their mood. Terrance leaned forward as a slight smile played on his lips. "You'll get a kick out of this story. We had a case where a man got trapped in his car."

Curiosity got the best of Amara. "How, what happened?"

Terrance spoke in a low, conspiratorial tone which caused Amara to lean closer. "Apparently, he broke into a car he claimed was his. Though the cars were the same color, make and model; his car was shabby with faded paint. It certainly didn't look like the pristine car he'd broken into."

He had Amara's full attention. "The actual owner came out and found this strange man in his car. Each time the guy tried to unlock the door and escape, the owner used his remote to lock the door, preventing the trespasser from leaving until the police arrived. Can you imagine?" He mimed the man unlocking the door and the owner locking it.

Amara giggled. "The owner is lucky the thief didn't break the window."

Terrance made small talk until they finished their meal. When it came time to leave, Amara fought the urge to look in Divya's direction. Terrance took her hand and led her from the restaurant. "Want to come over for a while?"

Amara planned to research Divya and her husband, but considered her promise. "Sure, I don't have to be at work until noon tomorrow. Matt assigned me a new article to write. I'm interviewing four children; their parents and a neighborhood watch group about lending library boxes built by students and placed in neighborhoods around the city. One of the library boxes has been repeatedly vandalized. The neighborhood watch group hopes to discover who's responsible and why."

The credits of the movie scrolled across the television screen as Amara's head rested against Terrance's shoulder. Terrance moved carefully in order not to wake her. He could tell she hadn't slept well the night before. He also knew there was nothing he could do to prevent her from becoming obsessed with researching her childhood best friend.

He considered talking to Remy, but recalled how she stopped speaking to her coworker the last time Remy chastised her for becoming obsessed with Ralph Simpson.

Terrance reconsidered and texted Remy. Perhaps the two of them could work together and make sure she didn't get too invested. Terrance snorted. Fat chance, he thought as he typed the text. No harm in trying. Remy's response was immediate.

Remy shared the same concerns and promised to keep tabs on Amara during their research, and contact him if he thought she was getting too involved. Terrance thanked him and placed his phone on the table.

Chapter 12

Amara awoke in a strange bed dressed in an oversized cotton t-shirt. Her heart raced until she recognized Terrance's bedroom. How had she not awakened when he undressed and tucked her in bed? Her arm extended to the far side of the bed. It was empty and cold to the touch.

She sat up, smoothed tangled tresses into place, and swung her feet onto the floor. Her breath caught when she peeked at the clock on the night stand. It was eight in the morning! Her breathing calmed when she remembered her noon interview with the four students. It was a training day for the teachers and students had the day off from school. Though it still felt like a puff piece, she was slowly warming to the article.

The students who'd built the boxes had done their homework. They'd coordinated and gained authorization from city officials and home owner associations before placing the lending library boxes in different neighborhoods around the city.

A retired carpenter donated wood, chicken wire, as well as his expertise. The four students; two boys and two girls, ages eight to eleven, constructed the boxes and painted them vibrant colors.

The library boxes contained books donated from organizations and neighborhood residents. The books ranged from classics to graphic novels. These young people were doing great things. Two of the boxes were placed in inner city neighborhoods, the other two in the suburbs. All the library boxes were flourishing, except one. It had been repaired three times during the past month. The students wanted to remove the box, but the residents formed a lending library box watch group.

Amara coordinated with the watch group leader. The group had narrowed the time frame of the vandalism between midnight and three a.m., as well as specific days of the week. The group planned to discover who was responsible for the vandalism that night and agreed she could join them. She'd ask Terrance to accompany her.

She hoped her magazine article would not provoke further vandalism on the remaining library boxes and books.

Amara took a shower, combed out her tangled curls and wound them atop her head in a stylish, messy bun. Clear gloss covered her full lips. She checked her eyes, relieved they were no longer bloodshot, as she brushed on mascara. She dressed in clothes she'd stored in the closet during her last visit; comfortable jeans, long sleeved top and running shoes. She made a final inspection in the bathroom mirror and headed to the kitchen.

"Good morning, sleepyhead," Terrance teased as he popped a piece of warm pastry into his mouth. Amara took a moment to admire her boyfriend's handsome features. She loved his smoldering, intense brown eyes, high cheek bones, small, button nose and skin the color of hot cocoa. She was rewarded with the slight dimples that appeared when he gave a genuine smile. His close-cropped curls were damp from his morning shower. She was surprised he wasn't in uniform, but dressed casually in jeans, polo shirt and high-top basketball shoes.

Amara poured herself coffee and warmed one of the apple turnovers in the microwave. She took a seat and pecked him on the lips. Her tongue swiped across her lips. "That was very sweet," she purred.

Terrance chuckled and drank the last of his coffee as he stood and placed his dishes in the dishwasher. "What do you have scheduled for today?"

Amara reminded him of her interview with the four students at noon. She pointed at his clothes. "Are you off today?"

He shook his head. "I'm working on a community project with Molloy."

Amara licked her sticky fingers and asked, "What kind of project?"

When Terrance explained the detective's involvement with a mentorship program for at-risk young men, she nearly choked. She'd known Molloy several years and never knew he volunteered to help troubled teens. Terrance snickered, "I'm guessing by your expression I surprised you."

Amara sipped her coffee. "That's putting it mildly. Detective Molloy continues to astound me."

"You and me both." He wiped down the counter and added, "I'm looking forward to helping and checking out the program. It's connected with the county. He's volunteered for years and has a few success stories."

"I'm impressed! It's important to give back to the community. To whom much is given, much is expected," she recited.

She tore her gaze away from his dazzling smile. "Hey, just a reminder, I'm joining the neighborhood watch group tonight. They're trying to discover who's destroying the lending library box and books at one of their locations. Would you like to join me?"

Terrance wagged his forefinger side to side. "No thanks. I do enough of that at work. I'll let you have all the fun this time."

"Ha, ha. Gee, thanks," Amara deadpanned.

"Take some coffee and don't forget the donuts!" he joked.

Amara rolled her eyes as Terrance headed to the door. "I've got to meet Cian, are you ready to go? I'll drop you off at your apartment on the way to the station."

The early morning sun shone bright as she waved goodbye to Terrance. Amara entered her apartment and glanced at her watch. She had a few hours before her interview with the students and neighborhood watch crew. Though she wanted to research Divya and Casey, she decided to use the time to do laundry and clean her apartment. She gave herself one hour to brave the Seattle traffic and arrive at her destination on time.

Hands on hips, Amara surveyed the clean apartment. Her clothes were washed and put away. The alarm on her phone dinged as she grabbed her satchel. She headed to her car, removed the camera from the trunk, and placed it on the passenger seat. Her phone GPS began to recite the directions to the neighborhood. Amara grabbed her sunglasses from its compartment and drove out of the apartment complex.

The neighborhood was peaceful, with large birch trees on either side of the road. Manicured lawns and the community park across the street made it difficult to imagine any type of vandalism.

The library box was positioned close to the curb across the street from the park. She'd arrived early and decided to photograph the box and check out the area before her interview.

She parked several feet away and slung the camera strap around her neck. It swayed and bumped against her chest as dried birch leaves crunched beneath the soles of her sneakers. Amara halted in front of the box, painted purple with bright yellow trim and snapped several photos.

The freshly painted box gleamed from its recent repair. The structure resembled an oversized birdhouse. Suddenly, puffy clouds blocked the sun and the shaded area felt chilly, even though she'd worn a long-sleeved shirt.

Peals of laughter echoed from the park as children played on apparatuses under the watchful eyes of their parents. There were no houses near the box or park. The closest home was halfway down the block.

The distance between the box, park and houses was a two-edged sword. The box's location was convenient for children to check out a book after playing at the park; but the distance from the houses and wooded area made it an easy mark for vandals.

Amara crossed the street and snapped photos of the heavily wooded area adjacent to the park. It would be a convenient location to hide. She imagined the woods at dusk and decided she'd need to ask someone to accompany her when she returned that night.

Amara had to admit the students' perseverance was admirable. She pondered why this box continued to be targeted. The fact that the lending library box was in the students' neighborhood hadn't escaped her.

She picked up her camera and refocused her lens across the street on the titles displayed through the chicken wire. There were books for kids of all ages. Some looked brand new. "Nice," she murmured and snapped more photos.

The crunch of leaves beneath bike tires caught her attention as two children approached. They looked to be between the ages of seven and nine. The clunk of their bikes as they hit the pavement were muffled by the fallen leaves.

Two books spilled from the pink wicker basket affixed to the girl's bike. The little girl carefully brushed the cover of the books with her small hand. She gave one book to the little boy, who raced to the box and peered inside. Amara grinned when the girl joined the boy and thumbed through the books. "It's here!" she squealed.

Amara peered through her lens as hot pink polished fingers folded over the spine of a book. She snapped a few photos of the backside of the girl as she waved her book in the air. "My favorite!" she exclaimed. Amara spied the cover of the book through her camera lens. She knew the book well. It had been one of her favorite series in elementary school. Maybe her assumption of the girl's age was accurate.

The little boy shoved her aside after she placed the book she'd brought inside the box. Several inches shorter, he balanced on the balls of his sneakered toes and grabbed the spine of a thin, paperback book with a glossy cover containing masked Samurai warriors. Her camera clicked softly.

Amara watched the small boy step away and stealthily place the new book on top of the book he'd brought. The little sneak hadn't replaced the book he'd taken.

The girl gave him a pointed look as his tiny fingers clasped the edges of both books.

Amara was certain their fragile pages would fold and tear under the constant pressure of the little boy's tight grip. The girl, older and taller, pointed at the extra book, then the library box. He held the book high in the air and proceeded with slow, robotic movements. The girl snatched the book from his grasp.

"Hey," the little boy whined. "Give it back! I can do it myself!" He grabbed the corner of the book and tugged hard. He raced to the library box and shoved the book inside. A triumphant grin spread across his round face.

The pair turned in unison and checked the door to the box to make sure it was properly closed.

Amara snapped another photo of the two children as they faced the box. They were dressed in jeans, with safety helmets that matched the colors of their bikes. A pony tail fell to the girl's waist in a rivulet of dark, shiny waves from the back edge of her pink helmet.

Amara crossed the street and introduced herself. She held up her camera and explained she was writing an article for a magazine. The kids were excited and asked if they could be in the article. They explained how much they loved the library box and were allowed to ride their bikes to the site once a week to return a book in exchange for a new one. Amara asked a few more questions before they grew bored and raced to their bikes. She was careful not to take pictures of their faces as her camera shutter clicked several times.

The duo waved and picked up their bikes sprawled on the sidewalk. They placed the books inside the wicker basket, jumped on their bikes, and pedaled away in unison. She photographed the backside of the two children as they raced down the sidewalk, and disappeared around the next corner.

Amara placed the cap over the lens of her camera and noticed how quiet it had become. A slight breeze ruffled her curls as she paused to look around. It felt as if someone was watching her. Her father had drilled the importance of being cognizant of her surroundings from an early age. Was it the vandals? Would they be bold enough to destroy the box in broad daylight?

Amara crossed the street and took in the immediate area. Intermittent shrieks of laughter from the children at the park wafted in the air. A couple passed with a stocky bulldog that strained its leash to sniff her shoes. She spoke as the couple strolled past. The couple greeted her with matching nods and continued down the sidewalk.

It was then she spied the shiny, black Maserati SUV parked beneath the shade of a large birch tree on the opposite side of the street. How had she missed its approach? Sun streaked through the branches of the nearby tree and reflected against the driver's side window.

Though tempted to uncap her lens and use her camera to take a closer look, she stared in the direction of the driver's side window. It was a man. His thick, dark hair was combed away from his wide, tan, forehead.

Why hadn't he parked near the houses down the road? He was alone in the vehicle. Amara turned, removed the lens cap, and acted as if she was photographing the lending library box. As deftly as possible, she snapped several photos of the driver and car.

She jumped when the car engine roared to life and the driver swiftly pulled away from the curb. As it passed, she photographed the license plate. The SUV halted at the stop sign and continued down the road. "What was that about?" she asked aloud.

Tucked safely inside her car, Amara transferred the photos to her phone and texted Terrance. Her fingers trembled slightly as she typed the message. Had the guy been watching her, the library box, or the two children?

Amara considered the two children. Both were Indian, as was the driver of the Maserati. Coincidence? Surely. It was a diverse neighborhood. Amara breathed deep to calm herself.

She drove around the corner to the park's parking lot and pulled into a vacant slot. The children, parents and members of the neighborhood watch would arrive shortly. She leaned her head against the headrest and closed her eyes. Was she making too much out of the man in the Maserati? The expensive car seemed out of place in the middle-class neighborhood.

Amara reasoned the man in the car had nothing to do with her, the children or library box. Perhaps he'd been waiting for someone. If that was the case, why was she breathing so hard?

She flinched when her phone rang through her car speaker. It was Terrance. "I got your text. What's going on? Did the driver seem threatening?"

Amara relayed her thoughts about the expensive car in the modest neighborhood. She told him about the two children at the lending library box. "Do you think there's a connection?"

His voice was calm. "No one knew you were going to be there, so I don't think it has anything to do with you. I can't say the same for the children. You'd texted they returned books before they took new ones every week."

Amara couldn't dismiss the feeling something wasn't quite right. She shrugged off the feeling and reasoned she was being paranoid.

Terrance interrupted her musings. "I called the station. I'm still with Molloy. I'll follow up on license plate once we're finished here."

Amara decided not to push the issue. "You sound upbeat. Are you enjoying spending time with the young men?"

The timbre of his voice revealed his elation. "I really am. I want to do this again. I believe I have something to offer. They are attentive and surprisingly respectful." Amara was pleased to hear he was having fun. "Dinner tonight? We can talk about our day," he suggested.

Amara agreed and checked her watch. It was close to noon. Time to interview the students and the neighborhood watch crew. She got out of her car and trekked down the dirt path to the park picnic table.

Chapter 13

Amara watched a robin perch on the branch of a tree while she pondered the interviews. The students were an impressive bunch; determined to make a difference. The oldest member of the group was a young man who attended the nearby middle school. He seemed comfortable in the role of group spokesperson, though all the children chimed in. Their excitement was contagious.

The young volunteers posed and mugged in front of the camera while their parents looked on with pride. Amara told the parents the story and the children's photo was scheduled for the next issue of the magazine.

The neighborhood watch group was a different story. She interviewed them once the students and parents departed. They consisted of two men in their forties and two women in their mid-thirties. Both women had young children. One thing was certain. They were serious about catching the culprit or culprits responsible for vandalizing the lending library box. Amara confirmed she wanted to join the group later that evening.

She jotted a few notes and reviewed the photos on her camera, pleased her article was shaping up nicely. As she headed to her car, she hoped they'd discover the identity of the vandal or vandals later that night.

Amara arrived at her office, grabbed her satchel, camera and hurried inside. As the office door closed, a black Maserati SUV passed unnoticed in the opposite direction.

She uploaded the photos she'd taken and hammered out an outline in minutes. A satisfied smile formed as the article unfolded on the computer screen.

Remy slumped into the vacant chair beside her desk. "How did it go today?"

Amara typed the rest of the sentence and turned to answer her friend. Why did his simple query feel like such a loaded question? She looked at Remy and paused.

She used her forefinger to draw an imaginary line from his newly styled hair to his designer leather shoes. "Hmm...You look different, what's up?"

Remy's face flushed. "We're talking about you. Just give it to me straight." He looked around. "No judgment here," he whispered.

She gave his shoulder a playful shove. "I hate that you know me so well." Amara told him about the children, the box, and the Maserati SUV.

Remy whistled. "Those SUV's run close to hundred thousand. Did you see the driver?"

"Yeah, kind of. The windows were tinted, but I glimpsed his profile. I also got his license plate number." She picked up her camera from the desk, scrolled through several photos and passed it to Remy. "I know it's kind of hard to see the driver. It was a man with tan skin and dark hair."

Remy returned Amara's camera and thought about Terrance's text the previous night. "Hey, do you want company on your stakeout tonight?"

"Only if it doesn't intrude on whatever you have planned," she cracked. She gave him another exaggerated once over. "New haircut; which looks great by the way, new shirt..."

"Okay, okay. My sister-in-law fixed me up with one of her girlfriends. We went to lunch. I should have caught a clue when she told me her girlfriend's best asset was her personality."

61

Amara laughed. "Was it really that bad?" Remy's grim expression indicated it had been. Amara's brows furrowed. "When did you have time to go on a date with this woman and what happened to the gorgeous blond you took to Mr. Dumont's wedding?"

Remy shook his head. "It wasn't a real date per se. Like I said, we met for lunch this afternoon. The woman I took to the wedding is a flight attendant and currently working a flight to Paris," he explained. He gave a crooked grin. "She has a layover in Paris this weekend and I plan to join her."

It was Amara's turn to whistle. "Dang Remy, I'm so jealous! Hide me in your luggage, please!"

Remy snorted. "No way, dear friend. Terrance would kick my butt."

Amara laughed heartily as Remy returned to his desk.

The hours flew by. It was time to go home. She turned off her computer, grabbed her satchel and camera.

Remy waited for Amara. It had become his habit. As usual, they were the last to leave. Something about the scenario she described with the SUV made him uncomfortable. He was familiar with the neighborhood and a Maserati would have been out of place.

He hadn't had a chance to fill her in on his research of Pradeep. He'd tell her later during the neighborhood watch. "What time do you want to get together?" he asked.

Amara checked her watch. "I'm scheduled to meet up with the neighborhood watch crew at the park around ten. The area has a lot of lights, which I think will illuminate the location of the library box. Terrance turned me down." She raised a finger. "Though he did advise me to pack plenty of coffee and donuts," she joked.

Remy mimed holding a mike. "So, Officer Mackelroy, do you plan to apprehend the scoundrels vandalizing the library box when you catch them in the act?"

Amara laughed and shoved away his hand. The opportunity to release some tension felt good. She hadn't been able to shake her unease about the Maserati.

Remy interrupted her musings and announced, "I'll see you around nine thirty. Do you want to ride together? I can fill you in on what my research about Pradeep."

Amara agreed.

Remy suggested they meet at her apartment. He gave an exaggerated eye roll and griped, "I'm having dinner with my brother's family."

"Poor baby. I'm having dinner with Terrance and plan to return to my apartment. See you then."

Chapter 14

As Amara drove to Terrance's house, her thoughts returned to the mysterious man in the black SUV and the two children. Was he watching them or was it just a coincidence? She tapped her steering wheel and considered the magazine article. It was turning out to be an interesting piece.

Since she couldn't write about Divya and Pradeep in her blog, she'd write about the power of children's desires to improve their community. The four students identified a need and made it happen!

The picture of the two children facing the library box was wonderful. They were so cute in their pink and blue bike helmets. Since she didn't have the parent's approval, their faces were not shown. Amara planned to leave a couple copies of the next issue inside the lending library box once it was published.

She turned up the radio volume and sang along to a song by Jill Scott. The traffic moved smoothly, and she was able to relax and enjoy the drive.

Amara knocked on the door and heard a voice call her inside. She spotted the backside of her boyfriend in the kitchen with a dish towel draped over his left shoulder. He looked good in his jeans and polo shirt.

Terrance caught her checking him out and returned the favor. "Something smells delicious!" she announced before giving him a kiss.

He wrapped one arm around her waist and pulled her close. "It's a new dish I'm trying. I want it to be a surprise, so I won't tell you what it is." He kissed her once more before he returned his attention to the large pot.

Amara washed her hands at the sink and removed bowls and glasses from the cabinet to set the table. Her fingers trailed the bright colored flowers on the ceramic bowls that once belonged to his mother and grandmother. They were old-fashioned, but in great condition.

"I ran the license plate of the SUV. It's leased to a corporation," Terrance said.

Amara fought the urge to bombard him with questions.

"It's based out of India. The corporation has companies in Seattle, California and overseas."

She straightened the flatware. "Isn't that Pradeep's company?"

Terrance fingers tightened around the spoon handle as he continued to stir the sauce. "Yep. I don't think the car at the park was a coincidence. You may have been followed."

Amara's curls swayed to and fro. "Me?! No way...I would have noticed the car earlier. I didn't see it until I finished photographing the box and children."

Terrance eyed Amara. "Did he follow the children?"

Amara sat down at the table. "No, he continued straight when the children turned right at the corner."

Terrance switched off the burner and carried the pot to the table. He was quiet as he placed the pot on the metal trivet.

Amara retrieved the bowl of rice and cornbread from the newly renovated quartz counter. The delicious aroma floated in the air. "You made jambalaya! It smells scrumptious! When did you have time to do all this?"

Terrance sat across from her and bragged, "I'm a man of many talents."

Amara inhaled the spicy aroma once more. "Yes, you are." She listened as her boyfriend shared his experience with the group of young men.

"It was a great!" he exclaimed and spooned rice and Jambalaya into bowl and passed it to Amara. "They're a cool group of guys. Molloy's group consists of six young men, ages ranging from thirteen to seventeen. I gotta tell you, he's totally different around them."

Terrance grinned. "Molloy's still a hard ass, but he listens and is respectful. That respect goes a long way. Those guys trust him and are open and honest. His no-nonsense attitude contributes to their willingness to be themselves." He tasted the jambalaya and pointed his spoon at the bowl. "This is good!" Amara agreed and prompted him to continue with her free hand.

"Some of those guys have had tough experiences; loss of a parent, mistreatment, abandonment, drugs...A couple of them were forced to live on the street and make money any way they could, to include burglary and petty theft. Overall, they seem to have direction and are taking control of their lives."

Terrance's excitement was contagious. "Wow! Do you think you'll go back?" she asked.

Mouth full, he nodded. "A new group is arriving next week. I plan to meet with a couple of them. I'm not ready to handle a big group like Cian, but I think I can mentor one or two guys. I'd have to arrange time off with the sergeant, but it's doable."

Amara smiled bright. "I think you'll be a wonderful mentor." She ate a spoonful of jambalaya. "Mmm! This is very good. If you keep cooking like this, I'll have to come around more often," she kidded.

"This recipe is definitely a keeper." They continued to talk about the program throughout dinner. Amara helped clear the table and washed the pots and pan while Terrance loaded the dishwasher and cleaned the table and counters.

"Don't forget I'm meeting with members of the neighborhood watch tonight. Remy volunteered to go with me."

Terrance tucked away the dish towel. "Glad to hear it. After learning about the car, I was going to volunteer to come with you."

Amara made Terrance laugh when she shared the story about Remy's sister-in-law fixing him up with one of her friends.

"What happened to the blond he brought to the wedding?" he asked.

Amara wiggled her eyebrows. "She's a flight attendant and he's meeting her in Paris this weekend."

"That sounds nice. I'm surprised you didn't beg to tag along. I remember you telling me about the trip to Paris with your parents." Amara blushed and didn't reply. Terrance wagged a finger. "You did ask him!"

"I begged to hide in his luggage," she confessed.

Terrance pulled her close and whispered in her ear. His voice was velvety, the foreign words sexy.

Her eyes grew wide. "You speak French?"

"Oui! I know a little somethin'-somethin'. I took French in high school and one semester in college to impress an international student. She dumped me and I dumped French."

Amara covered her mouth to stifle a laugh. "Oh, my goodness! No, you didn't."

Terrance looked sheepish. "I did."

Amara laughed hard. Once she caught her breath, she began to speak flawless French.

He raised a brow. "Now I'm impressed. I know you didn't learn that from just one visit. What's your story?"

Amara gave a one shoulder shrug. "My mother is fluent and taught me."

He rolled his eyes. "Of course! She was a high school teacher. Does your dad speak French?"

It was Amara's turn to roll her eyes. "Have you met my dad?" He laughed and Amara joined in. Tears appeared from laughing so hard. She swiped a napkin from the table and blotted her eyes. She gave her boyfriend a quick kiss. "I need to go home and change. Remy is picking me up and we're meeting the neighborhood watch group at ten. Thank you for dinner. It was delicious."

Terrance walked her to the door and folded her into his arms. "Be safe and text me when you get home from your stakeout. No matter how late."

She caressed his face and promised she would.

He watched until her car backed out the drive. Worry lines creased his forehead as he shut the door. He pulled out his phone and gave Remy a call. He wanted to make sure she stayed safe and didn't do anything impulsive. Remy promised to keep an eye on her.

Remy knocked on her door at nine thirty. Amara was dressed in black jeans and a black turtleneck sweater. Her massive curls were held in place with a thick black headband. "Are we going to burglarize someone's house tonight?" he ribbed.

"Shut up," Amara snapped. She pointed at his outfit and mocked, "You can't talk about me. You're wearing the exact same thing!"

He fingered his soft, black, cashmere sweater. "You're such an easy target. I couldn't help it." Remy held up a thermos. "I brought coffee!"

She lifted a baggie filled with cookies. "They're not donuts, but I baked them fresh. They're the ready-made kind you pop in the oven."

Remy licked his lips and removed a warm cookie from the bag. Amara grabbed her jacket, and camera and followed Remy as he headed down the steps munching on a cookie.

Chapter 15

Remy steered his red Mustang into one of the slots at the park, while Amara stared at the path that led to the park. It looked ominous in the moonlight. She'd seen light poles during her earlier visit. Why weren't they on? Amara inched closer to Remy as leaves rustled along the wood line. The shadowed trees seemed taller and scarier at night.

They trudged along the path and Amara noticed several of the protective sheaths over the bulbs were cracked. The lights had been knocked out. They had to illuminate the pathway that snaked to the park with lights from their phones.

She breathed a sigh of relief when the trail opened to a well-lit park. Her neck and shoulder muscles relaxed at the sight of empty swings, monkey bars, and a tall slide next to the picnic area. They turned off the lights from their phones and made their way to the pine wood picnic table with matching bench seats.

A noise in the vicinity of the tall slide caught their attention. A group of teenagers watched from their perch atop of the bright yellow, plastic structure. Their fingers clutched the necks of beer bottles as they glared defiantly in their direction.

Before either could utter a reprimand, the sound of heavy footsteps on dried leaves shifted everyone's attention to the park entrance. Four members of the neighborhood watch emerged wielding bright flashlights. Their beams focused on the teenagers as they leapt from the slide and scattered in the direction of the wood line.

The leader of the neighborhood watch group sported a baseball cap with the Seattle Mariners logo. His deep voice boomed and echoed throughout the park as he called out the name of each teenager. They'd scattered to the thicket of trees at the far side of the park.

The adults made their way to the picnic table. Amara raised a hand in greeting and introduced Remy, and the group leader introduced the other three members.

"I guess you guys know those teens," Amara prodded. She purposely left out the fact they were underage and carried open bottles of beer.

A petite, olive-complexioned woman shoved her hands deep inside the pockets of her denim jacket and sighed heavily. Her dark, thick hair was held in place with a dark blue barrette. "Yeah, one of those hooligans babysits my girls. I think I might have to find someone new," she lamented. "It's a shame. The girls really like her."

Amara studied each member as the group leader cleared his throat. He wore jeans, a checkered flannel shirt and sported a ginger-colored goatee. He was a tall, sturdy built man. She could imagine him with an axe, chopping down trees.

The other man was a slender Asian man whose serious dark eyes seemed to catalog everything in the vicinity. He'd been relaxed and jovial when they'd met earlier.

The second woman was a tall, slender, chocolate-skin toned woman with thick cornrow braids that trailed down her back.

The group leader handed Amara and Remy oversized flashlights and everyone a walkie talkie. The flashlights would come in handy if they were forced to leave the park and traverse the dark path to the library box. Amara gripped her flashlight a bit tighter than necessary.

The petite woman explained the procedures as she separated everyone into pairs. The beam of her flashlight swept over the park, indicating where each team would be positioned. "If you spot the vandals, don't leave your partner or attempt to confront or stop them," she warned. "Use the walkie-talkie to let us know if you notice anything out of the ordinary."

She pointed to the man with the ginger goatee. "He'll call the police. The local police station is a few miles away. There will be a patrol in the area tonight. Let the police handle any situation. If the vandals attempt to run, don't chase them. Try to take a photo and we'll provide that to the police as well."

The group tested their walkie-talkies and headed to their designated positions. Amara shivered and zipped up her jacket. She wasn't sure if it was the cool spring night or excitement.

Remy walked beside Amara and stage-whispered, "This is exciting!" Amara poked him gently with her elbow. "Ow!" Remy complained loudly. Amara shushed him and he chuckled. Leaves rustled beneath their feet as they trudged across the grass to their shadowed position several feet from the picnic table. The park felt eerie and desolate as they waited.

Two hours passed. Amara checked her watch for the umpteenth time and shifted her weight to the other leg. It was midnight. She was about to suggest they leave when Remy nudged her arm and pointed to the right.

The silhouette of a lone figure meandered through the tree-lined boundary into the park. The dark figure skirted the boundary of the playground and remained close to the wood line. When the person was forced to walk across the grass to get to the path that led out of the park, the moonlight illuminated a crowbar gripped tight in a gloved left hand.

Amara snapped several photos while Remy whispered into the walkie-talkie to report the lone figure. The leader of the group phoned the police and in a matter of seconds, a patrol car sped down the street and screeched to a halt. Two officers jumped out and raced across the grass. The lone figure turned and sprinted to the wood line.

Remy and Amara watched as the culprit was intercepted by two additional police officers who'd emerged from the woods. One of the officers began to shout commands. The offender dropped the crowbar and raised gloved hands. The police officer collected the crowbar while the other escorted the person to the waiting sedan.

Leaves rustled in the darkness as sounds of running footsteps echoed from the east side of the wooded area. The bright beam from the officers' flashlights exposed two silhouettes as they fled deeper into the woods. The officers gave chase.

One of the officers barked a command for the two people to halt. Minutes later, four figures emerged from the wood line. The police officers escorted two people who looked to be middle, possibly high school-aged boys.

The patrol officer asked the leader of the neighborhood watch if he recognized the youths. He slowly approached and shined his bright flashlight in their faces. The boys blinked and shut their eyes tight. He grunted in disgust and signaled for the woman with the cornrows to approach.

As the woman neared, she nervously flipped long braids over her shoulder and called the boys by name. Her focus remained on one of the boys a beat longer. Her voice broke when she called his name a second time.

The boy's head was bent; eyes trained on his expensive basketball shoes.

A red painted fingernail pointed in the direction of a skinny, dark-complexioned boy. "That's my nephew and the other hooligan is his best friend." She shook her finger and admonished, "Wait until I tell your mothers about this!" The boys groaned in unison.

As the police escorted the boys to the sedan, the woman faced the group and held out her hands in a pleading gesture. "My sister works two jobs and is really strict." She pointed in the direction of the police sedan and added, "That boy is her only child. Her husband is a long-haul truck driver." She turned.

"Excuse me. I'm going to see if the officer will release those two to me."

The group watched her jog in the direction of the police sedan. Amara hoped the boys would be released.

Relief shown on the woman's face as she marched both young men back to the group. Their heads were bowed and they remained silent.

Amara almost felt sorry for them. They'd gotten off easy. At least until their parents got a hold of them.

The leader of the group turned and thanked Amara and Remy for their help. His eyes seemed to glow in the dim light as he focused on Amara. "I trust you won't put their names in your article."

Amara raised a hand. "This will be a cautionary tale. No names required." The group relaxed as Amara and Remy expressed their gratitude for being allowed to take part. They headed to his car while the rest of the group remained huddled together in the park. Amara looked at her friend and drawled, "Well, that was awkward."

Remy pulled out the lot. "That wasn't quite what I expected. The question remains, why were those guys vandalizing the box? Did they have something against the group that built it or were they simply bored?"

"Good question," Amara replied. "Since they've vandalized the box more than once. I think it might be a bit of both." Amara snapped her finger and added, "You know, one of the kids who helped build the boxes is in middle school. He may be the connection. Jealousy perhaps?" She shrugged and added, "I get it. One of the kids has a strict mom who works a lot and his dad is on the road most of the time. The mom wants to keep her son safe and probably doesn't allow him much freedom while she's at work. That's a lot of responsibility for one kid, especially if he doesn't have a younger sibling to torture."

"Or have a younger sibling to torture him!" Remy joked.

"Oh, are you speaking from experience?"

"Yep. Matt was the good, obedient, older son. I was the little terror always into something. He took the blame for my misdeeds more times than I can count."

"I'm an only child, so I can relate to the young man's plight. Both of my parents worked and it was boring and lonely. Even when my aunt, who's only five years older, lived with us. She basically ignored me. Her room and friends were off limits. I hung out with my parents a lot. When they had to work, they made sure I had outlets and wasn't stuck at home all the time. You know the saying, 'It takes a village?' I was blessed with a village of caring adults who checked on me daily and sometimes invited me over for cookies or just to hang out. When my mom had a conference or appointment after school or in the evening, her good friend who lives a couple houses down the street, would drive me to dance lessons or writing classes at the youth center. I was fortunate."

"I was too," Remy confessed. "My parents traveled a lot and our nanny made sure we did our homework and took us to baseball practice, karate and ballroom dancing."

Amara stared at Remy in shock. "You took ballroom dancing?"

"I can dance a mean waltz and tango like nobody's business," Remy said. The thought caused Amara to laugh aloud. Remy joined her.

Amara jogged up the steps to her apartment and waved while Remy waited for the front door to close. He devoured the last cookie in two bites and drove away.

Amara bumped the door close with her hip and locked it with her free hand. She set down her purse and camera on the table, removed her jacket and shoes and headed to the kitchen. Within minutes, a cup of hot chamomile tea steeped on the counter while she sent Terrance a text. It was close to one in the morning. When he immediately texted back, she smiled, aware he'd waited up for her. She picked up her cup of tea and walked barefoot to the bedroom.

Chapter 16

Amara slapped the snooze button on her alarm clock one last time before she forced herself from her comfy, warm bed. She'd take a quick shower and skip breakfast to make it to work on time.

She grabbed a breakfast bar and filled her thermos cup with coffee. Brown liquid sloshed onto her clean kitchen counter. "Darn it!" she groused and swabbed the counter with a paper towel. Thermos in one hand, she grabbed her satchel and slung it over her shoulder on the way to the door. Amara jerked open the door and yelped when she nearly collided with the man who blocked her doorway. He was a tall man, smartly dressed in a dark suit. His ebony hair slicked back. He looked like a federal agent.

The fact he was Indian set off alarms in her head. Her hand slid inside her satchel and gripped the canister of pepper spray her father had given her for protection. Her free hand closed the front door. It was too early for a cordial visit; especially by a stranger. "Who are you and what do you want?!"

The man smiled pleasantly. His orthodontically straightened teeth were chemically bleached white; a stark contrast to his gingerbread complexion. "Are you Amara Mackelroy?" he asked. He spoke with an accent. British perhaps.

"I asked you first!"

He seemed unfazed by her terse tone. The same jovial expression remained. It was as if he couldn't quite close his mouth to cover oversized, bleached white teeth. He identified himself as a private detective who was investigating a case for a private citizen.

When Amara asked the name of the case or client, he evaded her question and asked her identity once more. When he slipped his hand inside his jacket, Amara allowed her satchel to slide down her arm to the ground. Her eyes never left his as fingers clasped the cylinder inside and flipped the top of her pepper spray. She considered running back inside her apartment, but feared he'd follow or force his way inside. She felt unsafe in the man's presence, even though he smiled like a Chesire cat.

"I don't know why you're here or what you want, but you need to back up now!" Her heart pounded hard against her chest as she angled her body and stood in a fighting stance. He was way too close. This was not a game. Her eyes never left his as he continued to smile and raised both hands in surrender. Why hadn't his expression changed?

"I can see I've gone about this all wrong." He stepped back and held out the business card he removed from his jacket pocket and introduced himself.

Amara took care to grip only the edge of the card as her eyes remained on the uninvited visitor. Her opposite hand held the cannister, poised to spray him in the eyes if he so much as flinched. When his hand drifted inside his coat, she spoke in a loud, authoritative tone.

"Every move you make is being recorded and sent to my boyfriend who's a cop." She jerked her head upward as her phone began to ring. The man's eyes flitted to the small camera positioned above her door. She smirked and tilted her head to one side.

His hand fell away from his pocket as he stepped back. "I'm terribly sorry I startled you. I just have a few questions..." He stuck his hand into his side jacket pocket once more.

Amara extended her arm with her palm faced out and fingers extended as she shook her head. "Uh-uh. It's six-thirty in the morning. I don't know you. Please leave now!" Her voice grew louder with more confidence than she felt.

The doors on either side of her apartment opened and two men stepped onto the small landing. "Is there a problem here?" The man was built like a Mac truck. His loose tank top exposed tattooed muscular arms and torso. His thighs were the size of tree stumps. He worked at the jail as a guard and was friends with Terrance. The other neighbor was wiry and towered over the visitor. The visitor held up his hands once more and apologized. He mumbled something about it not being a good time and promised to return when it was more convenient. The heels of his dress shoes clip clopped against each stair as he swiftly made his way down the cement steps.

Amara exhaled and thanked her neighbors. The men nodded and returned to their apartments. Shaky fingers gripped her phone as she removed it from her pocket and recorded the car license plate. She remained at her door until the vehicle was well out of sight. Amara glanced at the card. The name wasn't familiar. She bent to retrieve her satchel and tucked the card inside. Amara took care to double check the locks before heading to her car. She locked the car door and leaned her forehead against the steering wheel. After a few calming breaths she lifted her head. "What in the world is going on?"

Amara's phone rang as she pulled away from her parking space. It was Terrance. "I saw the recording. What happened? Who was that dude?"

"I don't know. I opened the door to leave for work and he was standing there. He knew my name!" Her voice rose. "When I asked him to identify himself, he just stood there with a stupid grin on his face. Once I revealed he was being recorded, he gave me his card and finally introduced himself.

"Yeah, I know. I'm already running a check. He looks Indian. Have you been researching Divya or Pradeep?"

Amara bristled. "What? No! I haven't had time to research Divya or her crooked husband. You know I've been working on the article about the library boxes! I was with you yesterday evening and out with Remy and the neighborhood watch group past midnight!" Her voice grew shrill with each word.

"I know baby. I'm sorry. This whole situation has me rattled. First, the guy in the black Maserati, now a guy shows up at your house unannounced first thing in the morning. I'm worried."

Amara's voice quivered. "Me too. Did you learn anything more about the guy in the Maserati?" She sniffed and took the exit to her office.

"Hey, hey, don't cry...I'm sorry about what I said. Why don't you stay at my place tonight? We can go to your apartment after you get off from work and pick up some clothes and whatever else you need. We can also research information about your visitor. I'll follow up on the information on the Maserati and the visitor's license plate."

Amara was relieved by his offer. The guy creeped her out. "Okay, sounds good. I gotta go."

Remy looked up from his computer monitor. He playfully checked his watch and joked, "Late night with a bunch of hooligans? You'd better watch the company you keep."

When he saw her red-rimmed eyes and worried expression, he jerked his head in the direction of his brother's empty office. Matt was at a dental appointment and they wouldn't be overheard by the staff. He guided Amara to one of the empty chairs in front of the desk and sat in the chair next to hers. "What's wrong? Has something happened?"

Amara told him about her early morning visitor. She played the video from her surveillance camera and carefully removed the man's card from her purse. Remy immediately walked behind the desk and began to type on his brother's computer keyboard. The search engine whirled and several photos of a handsome man with curly black hair appeared.

Amara stood and walked behind the desk and stared at the computer screen. "The hair is different, but that looks like the guy," she whispered.

Remy skimmed the information on the screen and remarked, "He owns a private investigation agency. There are multiple offices in the U.S. and abroad." His fingers flew over the keyboard to another website. "This guy deals with the rich and famous. Let me check with a couple of my friends who've hired a private detective in the past. They might know him or something about his company." He printed two copies of the page that contained information and handed one to Amara.

Amara sounded weary as she thanked Remy. "I have one question. If this guy deals with high-end investigations for wealthy clients, why would he personally show up at six-thirty in the morning at my apartment? Why not send one of his investigators? It doesn't make sense."

Remy agreed and guided Amara out of his brother's office.

She slipped the card and sheet of paper into her satchel. It was time to get to work. Her article about the library boxes needed to be completed. She called the leader of the neighborhood watch and asked about the kids who vandalized the box. Her search on the private investigation agency and its owner would have to wait.

Amara glanced at the clock and shut down her computer. As suspected, the kids who vandalized the box had a grudge against the middle school student who'd helped build the lending library boxes. The young volunteer hadn't been very nice to his fellow students.

The three boys accused him of destroying their science project before the school science fair last month. Apparently, their group won the competition the year prior. Though their vengeance was aimed at one person, it affected the entire group that built the boxes and the neighborhood children who used the lending library box. This was a cautionary tale for sure.

The early morning visitor and late night at the park had taken its toll. She rubbed tired eyes and headed to the break room for a cup of coffee.

When she returned, Matt had sent a new assignment. She was to follow up on rumors of children being sheltered at night in restaurants and motels instead of being placed in foster homes. He provided the name of a caseworker she'd need to interview from social services.

Amara covered a yawn. It would have to wait until tomorrow. She was exhausted and an oncoming headache caused her to leave with the rest of the staff.

Remy headed to his brother's office. He needed to inform him about the private investigator who appeared at Amara's apartment.

Amara was relieved to see Terrance's car in the parking lot. She gave a tired wave.

He got out and brushed curls from her forehead before kissing her. "Are you okay?"

Amara forced a smile. "I am now," she confessed.

His arm slipped through hers as they walked to her car. He waited until she'd left the parking lot and followed her to the apartment. She quickly gathered what she'd need for work tomorrow. Terrance made sure her alarm was set and double checked the locks on the door.

Terrance trailed behind and made sure no one followed. When they arrived at his house, he suggested she park her car in the garage. Amara pulled into the garage and handed Terrance her duffle bag. He slung it over his shoulder and closed the garage door.

Amara felt his protective arm around her shoulder and relaxed. She made a bee-line to his bedroom, shed her work clothes, climbed into bed and was asleep in minutes.

Terrance picked up her clothes from the upholstered chair and hung them in the closet. He removed the man's business card from Amara's satchel and quietly closed the bedroom door.

In his office, he held the business card beneath the bright light of the desk lamp. As he examined the card, his cell phone buzzed. He'd phoned Molloy earlier and hoped the detective had new information regarding the uninvited visitor. He straightened in the chair. The detective didn't sound happy.

Chapter 17

Terrance ended the call and considered Detective Molloy's update. The man who had showed up at Amara's apartment was an impostor. The actual owner of the investigative agency was visiting family in London and had no idea of the identification of his doppelgänger. Molloy was confident the private investigator never visited Amara's apartment, though he couldn't deny her early morning visitor closely resembled the real owner of the agency.

The investigator assured Molloy he and his siblings were in London to celebrate their father's eightieth birthday. He'd sent a photo with a date and time stamp that verified his claim and promised to investigate the incident upon his return.

Terrance ran a hand over his hair. Why had this man gone to Amara's and impersonated the owner of the company? He held the business card under the light once more. The cardstock was flimsy; the ink cheap. Terrance was confident the ink would smudge if he rubbed his thumb over the face of the card. He placed the card in an evidence bag and sealed it.

He watched the video from Amara's security camera and saw the man touch the card with his thumb and forefinger. Hopefully the fingerprints would provide the impersonator's identity.

Terrance grabbed his keys, slipped out the house and phoned Molloy as he drove to the station.

Molloy lifted his head from the file he was reading when Terrance entered the suite. Terrance acknowledged one of the other detectives at the far desk, hard at work. Molloy pointed at the bag and asked, "Is that the card?" Terrance handed him the evidence bag. Molloy pushed a button and the bag was taken to the lab. "I asked for a rush. We should know something soon."

As Terrance entered the elevator, he was confident there was a connection with this guy and Pradeep's business in Seattle. He'd learned the Maserati was leased to one of Pradeep's employees. The car was expensive, so he guessed it belonged to one of his executives.

He made a detour to his desk and called Pradeep's company. A receptionist answered; her voice cheerful and professional. Terrance wasted no time and plunged into his spiel.

When he placed the phone onto the receiver, Terrance was more confused than before. According to the receptionist, the company didn't lease expensive cars. Their leased cars were energy efficient hybrid cars, not expensive SUV's. She explained the company maintained a strict policy that vehicles were intended for professional use only.

He did glean one piece of interesting information. As he'd assumed, one of Pradeep's vice presidents owned a black Maserati SUV. When he pressed for more information, the receptionist immediately transferred him to the vice president's secretary. The vice president's secretary though pleasant, refused to answer his questions. She transferred the call to her boss' direct line. Terrance ended the call when he heard the recorded message.

He perked up when he realized the voice on the recorded message sounded like the man who'd shown up at Amara's. He called the number once more and left a message.

Molloy called. The results were back from the lab. Terrance hurried to the detective's office.

Molloy waved a sheet of paper in the air. "One thing is certain; this man isn't the owner of the exclusive private investigation agency. In fact, he's...."

Terrance interrupted before the detective could finish. "He's Samesh, one of the vice presidents at Pradeep's company."

"Yeah, how did you know?" Molloy asked in surprise.

"Remember the Maserati that was at the park when Amara took photos for her article?" Molloy confirmed he had. "I learned the vehicle was leased through Pradeep's company. I called his company and asked about it."

He told him about the familiarity of the man's voice on the voicemail. "I was in the process of checking the rental car company to determine the name used for the vehicle Amara saw this morning at her apartment. It hadn't been the Maserati." Terrance leaned against the wall. "I'm sure he used a false name and I won't find out anything. The big question is, why is he snooping around Amara?"

"This is connected with the murder victim at Schmitz Park," Molloy said.

Terrance blew out a nervous breath. He'd considered the connection as well. Casey had gotten too close to Pradeep or someone in his company. "I agree, Cian. They're somehow connected." Terrance checked his watch and pushed away from the wall. "I'd better get going. I want to follow up with the car rental company. Thanks for fast-tracking the results on the business card."

Molloy dialed the number to Pradeep's office. "I guess I'll be paying Samesh a visit tomorrow," he muttered.

Chapter 18

The house was silent when Terrance returned. Amara was still asleep. There'd be no need to explain his absence or what he'd learned. Casey's murder and the link between Pradeep, Divya and possibly Samesh monopolized his thoughts. He wasn't sure how or why the three were involved, but he hoped to discover the answer soon.

What did this person who was bold enough to show up at her apartment unannounced, believe she possessed? Information, evidence? The fact it happened unsettled him. That meant the impostor watched beforehand and knew where she lived and the time she went to work.

The realization put him on edge. He considered the photos Molloy had shown him of the crime scene. The victim was dirty. The bruises on her wrists and ankles indicated she'd been bound. Her purse was empty except for the envelope in the lining. Had she implicated Amara before her death? Doubtful.

Why hadn't the killer removed the note or the entire purse? Had the two joggers interrupted him before he could search it? He needed to check with Molloy for the park surveillance footage the night Casey was murdered.

Terrance considered the photograph inside the envelope addressed to Amara. He removed his cell from his pocket and phoned the detective.

Molloy answered in his usual gruff manner.

"Cian, when you went to the victim's residence, did you notice if anything had been moved or tampered with? Also, did you see anything on the park surveillance footage?"

A long silence ensued. "There was a shadow of a figure walking down the trail. The person's face was shrouded by a hooded jacket. We didn't find any video recordings of Casey in the park.

The only people clearly recognizable were the joggers entering the park together. As for the victim's apartment, it had been ransacked. Someone conducted a very thorough search." Molloy believed whoever broke into the apartment hadn't found what they were looking for. There'd been open drawers and cabinets, and smashed glasses and dishes in the kitchen as well as a slashed mattress in the bedroom.

"Casey Athy was clever. According to her parents she'd dropped off her notes, journals, and laptop at their house the morning of Dumont's wedding. Not to mention the envelope sewn in the lining of her purse. Her paranoia paid off. I believe whoever broke into her condo was looking for her laptop and notes," Molloy said.

He shuffled papers. "I have an appointment tomorrow afternoon with Samesh. After I speak with him, I think I'll reinterview Pradeep. I was told he'd be in the office tomorrow as well."

Molloy assured Terrance he'd get to the bottom of what was going on. He'd also scheduled an appointment to interview Divya. Her personal assistant said Divya had been in Mumbai for two weeks and was scheduled to return the following day.

Terrance told Detective Molloy they'd recently seen her at the Tilikum Place Café with friends. He wondered why Divya's assistant lied.

The large pot clanked against the burner as Terrance set it on the stove. He placed leftover beef stew from a freezer bag into the pot. The serrated blade of the knife sliced through the loaf of sour dough bread while he mulled over the information Molloy had provided.

His heart ached for Amara. For once, her snooping was not the reason she was in this situation. She'd done nothing to provoke the extra attention. Casey's envelope addressed to Amara implicated her in whatever was going on. Had the killer known about the photo or Casey's relationship with Amara prior to her death? If not, what provoked the unwarranted attention?

Samesh was somehow involved. Was he acting on Pradeep's orders or alone? Molloy would learn more when he interviewed them tomorrow.

The scuffle of slippers on the tiled floor caused him to look over his shoulder. The oversized t-shirt pooled around Amara's thighs. He loved her soft, wild curls, which she'd piled high in a curly mass atop her head. Stray curls escaped her clip and framed her face. If he wasn't so worried about her, he'd guide her back to bed and forget about the stew.

Amara gave a saucy grin. "I know that look, you naughty boy."

Terrance chuckled as he set the knife on the counter and pulled her into a hug. He kissed her forehead and breathed in her soft floral scent. His teeth nipped her ear lobe as he growled, "You know me well."

She turned serious. "What did you find out from Molloy?"

Busted. He paused a beat to gather his thoughts. How much should he tell her? Terrance sighed, guided her to the kitchen table, and relayed what transpired at the station.

Her eyes grew wide. "Oh my gosh! He impersonated the owner of that agency! Who is he?"

Terrance told her about his call to Pradeep's office. "The big question is how deep is Pradeep's involvement and what does his VP think you have or know?"

Amara's brows knitted together as she speculated, "The guy looked a heck of a lot like the owner of the investigative agency. Do you think they're related?"

The corners of his lips turned downward as he replied, "No. The owner of the investigative agency is in London celebrating his father's birthday. The entire family is in the photo Molloy showed me. I think he used makeup and prosthetics to resemble the other guy. I haven't had a chance to find out what Samesh looks like and compare the two men."

Amara rubbed her hands together. "I can remedy that." She rushed to the bedroom and removed her laptop from her satchel.

When she returned, Terrance moved to the stove and turned down the fire under his stew. He gave her a sideways glance; his expression pinched. "You are so stubborn," he admonished.

Amara heaved a sigh, closed the laptop, and returned it to the bedroom. She knew his frustration stemmed from a desire to keep her safe. There'd be time to research later. The extra time would allow her to mentally put the pieces together based on what she'd learned from Terrance.

It was no secret Casey was especially close with her father. He'd been her confidant and ally throughout the internship. Casey spoke to her father every evening before she and Amara left the program. Based on the conversations Amara had overheard, they discussed everything. Nothing was off limits. Had she shared information with her father regarding the exposé on Pradeep and Divya? She'd bet the answer was yes.

"You're too quiet. What mischief are you planning?" Terrance asked.

Amara pointed at the pot. "Your stew smells wonderful and I'm starving. Let's eat!"

Terrance fought the urge to throw his hands in the air. The woman exasperated him to no end. At least she'd put away her laptop. He bit back the admonishment on the tip of his tongue and handed her a bowl of hot stew and a spoon.

Amara could tell Terrance was frustrated and a bit concerned about her plan to research Pradeep and Samesh. Had they assumed Casey provided evidence or shared information on whatever she'd been investigating?

Too bad that wasn't the case. She'd would have been better prepared to handle the onslaught of attention from Pradeep's company. Based on her research and what she'd learned from Remy, Pradeep seemed shady. Not to mention his company was under investigation. If the photos of his tea plantations and condition of the workers in India were accurate, his humanitarian skills had much to be desired. She couldn't imagine workers, including young children, being treated so inhumanely.

Remy had told her Pradeep and Divya's mansion in India was beyond posh. How could he live in the lap of luxury and not provide his workers with basic sanitation and proper facilities? According to the photos, they didn't have an adequate number of toilets, showers, or enough fresh drinking water. Many of his workers looked malnourished.

She tore off a piece of sourdough bread and dipped it into the stew and contemplated her next move. Tonight, she'd research the executive members of Pradeep's company to include his executive staff overseas. Tomorrow would be a good time to call Casey's parents and ask if they'd be willing to meet with her.

Amara looked up and caught Terrance staring at her. He looked pensive. What could she say to alleviate his anxiety when she shared his apprehension? All she knew was Casey addressed an envelope to her with a photo of Divya; her childhood best friend, hidden in the lining of her purse before her death.

Casey was murdered hours after being ousted from the reception. At no time had she shown recognition or a desire to speak with her. It was all very strange. Unless...unless someone at the wedding posed a threat. Amara looked at Terrance and smiled.

"Uh oh...I know that smile. Am I going to regret asking what you want?"

"I think one of the wedding guests posed a threat to Casey." She paused and allowed Terrance to absorb the implication. "Since you're Mr. Dumont's godson, I'm sure you could pull some strings and get us access to the guest list, or at least a peek."

Terrance rested his forehead against the palm of his hand. "You know Rolanzo and Dora Lee are on their honeymoon, right?"

Amara waved away his response. "Please! You know his head of security. I bet if you explained what's going on, he'd allow you, us to look at the guest list and photos." She pointed a finger at herself and Terrance.

She leaned forward. "Did you happen to see the wedding photos before they were erased from Casey's phone?!"

"No, I didn't." Terrance admitted.

"You are Rolanzo Dumont's godson. Surely that carries some clout. I know you've gone out of your way to help him from time to time," she cajoled.

Her singsong tone felt like a gentle caress. Terrance gave a lopsided grin. She was persuasive and cute. "Okay, okay, I'll give his head of security a call." He shook his finger in her direction and warned, "If he says, no, that's it. I won't ask Rolanzo when he returns."

It was the response she'd hoped to receive. "Thank you," she said and picked up her spoon to eat her stew.

When Terrance headed to his office to phone Rolanzo's head of security, Amara grabbed her laptop. She couldn't wait to research this mystery guy. Was he the same man she'd spotted at the park while photographing the kids and lending library box? Her fingers swept across the keys as she typed in the name of Pradeep's company. "Bingo," she whispered.

Her eyes shifted to the hallway in the direction of Terrance's office before she began to sift through the executive employees at the company. There were three VPs; one for each of Pradeep's companies and several executive staff members. She clicked on each name and read personal details and viewed their photo. She reached the photo of the VP for the Washington state company and stared at the photo. It was the man who'd come to her apartment that morning! "Private investigator my foot," she wisecracked.

Amara compared Samesh's photo with the owner of the private investigation company. He'd altered his features, but the eyes and slicked back hair were a dead giveaway. "What do you think I have? More important, what are you looking for?"

She hoped Casey's parents knew the answer to those questions. It wasn't too late to call the Athys. She pulled out her cell phone and dialed the number.

After the call, Amara placed her phone on the table and rubbed sweaty palms over her bare thighs. The call was more difficult than anticipated. Though Casey's parents were grieving, they'd agreed to meet with her. Amara replayed their conversation in her mind. It was as if they'd expected her to call. The realization alarmed her.

Terrance entered the kitchen holding the page she'd printed. "Is this the guy I saw through the security camera at your apartment? He looks different."

Amara took the paper with the photo and placed her hand over the man's nose and mouth.

Terrance examined the photo and nodded. "Yep, that's him. Minus the fake teeth and prosthetic nose."

She gave a sly smile. "I thought those teeth were fake. That explains why they appeared overly white, and a bit too large for his mouth. He kept smiling for no reason. The guy couldn't close his mouth over the oversized, false teeth." Amara giggled at the thought. "Even if he were upset, he'd have to keep that goofy, smile," she joked.

Terrance shook his head and chuckled. "You're sick," he teased. His remark caused Amara to laugh harder.

She pressed moisture from the corners of her eyes with tips of her fingers and became serious. "I called the Athys and asked if they'd be willing to meet with me tomorrow." Before he could interject, she continued. "It was as if they were expecting my call."

Terrance shifted his weight to the other leg. "I contacted Rolanzo's head of security. He wouldn't allow us to check the guest list without his boss' permission, but he agreed to give us copies of the photos."

"Does that mean we can visit Mr. Dumont's mansion?" Her eyes sparkled with excitement. Those photos might provide answers. If nothing else, she felt they might reveal the reason Casey hadn't given her the envelope at the wedding.

He looked smug. "Yep, in fact, he said we could come over tonight."

Chapter 19

Each visit to Rolanzo Dumont's mansion left her enthralled. The home, like its owner, was meticulously maintained and formidable. It reminded her of a fortress, belied by a manicured lawn, shrubs, and beautiful flowers.

They drove through the gated entrance around a long, circular drive. A young man directed them to the east side of the mansion. A member of Dumont's security waited patiently as they exited the vehicle. He was a large man, with long, intricate braids neatly bound with a black leather strap at the nape of his wide neck. The guard's strong arms and chest bulged from his fitted black t-shirt and matching cargo pants belted around a slender waist, pulled taut around thick, muscular thighs. He reminded her of a world class weight lifter.

Amara recognized him from the cavern she and Remy visited in the mountains several months ago. They'd arrived uninvited to warn Mr. Dumont his location wasn't secure and advised him to leave. When she'd been denied entry, she used her father's name and his previous association with Rolanzo Dumont to gain access. Luckily, Mr. Dumont had taken her advice.

"I see we meet again daughter of Mr. Mackelroy," he taunted.

Amara sighed heavily. What could she say? She'd used the tactic to gain access to Mr. Dumont when he'd stopped her and Remy for trespassing. Amara raised her head and met mud brown eyes filled with mirth. She remained quiet. This was no time to flex. She needed the information.

The guard chuckled low in his throat and led them through a reinforced steel door camouflaged with a brick façade. They trekked down a long, battleship gray hall, with walls devoid of décor. Rods of bright, motion sensor LED lights guided them. The sound of their footsteps reverberated against the cement tiled floor while mounted cameras tracked their movements.

They approached a steel door with a cypher lock and retinal scan. Mr. Dumont is serious about his security, she mused.

Seconds later the head of security emerged through the heavy steel door. Amara strained to peek inside as the door shut with a muted thud. The tip of a flash drive peeked through the man's fisted right hand. Amara turned her attention to the short, svelte man, dressed entirely in black.

He resembled his Tunisian brothers, the country from where his parents had emigrated over half a century ago. His dark, falcon-like eyes framed with bushy brows felt like pin pricks against her skin. His expression was predatory as if deciding whether she was friend or foe.

Amara fought the urge to stand more erect under his unwavering gaze. He reluctantly handed her the flash drive. When he spoke, his voice was low and calm with a noticeable accent. She wondered how many languages he spoke. She guessed many.

Dark eyes held hers as he announced, "I trust you'll keep these photos safe and not copy them. The guests who attended Mr. Dumont's wedding expect their privacy to be protected."

She closed her fingers tight around the flash drive as she murmured a thanks. When his eyes didn't stray from hers, she promised not to allow the flash drive out of her sight or make copies. His expression remained circumspect as he shifted his attention to Terrance.

Amara stepped back as Terrance moved forward. He seemed to tower over the diminutive man. As they shook hands, the older man showed remarkable strength when he pulled Terrance close. One hand held Terrance's hand while the other rested on his back. Amara could see the man's lips move as he spoke quietly into Terrance's ear.

Terrance straightened and stepped away once Dumont's head of security patted his back and released his hand. The older man turned, punched in the code, and disappeared inside the heavily secured room.

The same guard wordlessly escorted them down the hall in the direction of the formidable steel door they'd entered. Terrance flexed his fingers to return the circulation and clasped Amara's hand which had grown cold. The only sound was the echo of their footsteps against the cement tiles. The guard held the door open as the couple stepped over the threshold into the night.

Amara shivered as the cool night air ruffled her hair. The loud thud of the door as it closed caused her to jump and move closer to Terrance. She was sure the guard did that for her benefit; jerk. The message was loud and clear, "You got what you wanted; don't come back for any more information."

Amara waited to speak until they were inside the car. "You'd think he was giving up secret military codes," she joked. When Terrance didn't respond, Amara rotated the flash drive in her hand and stared out the side window.

She knew it was a big deal to receive the coveted photos of Dumont's wedding guests. It also wasn't lost on her she'd obtained copies of the photos due to her boyfriend's relationship with Rolanzo.

Once they were on the road, Terrance broke the silence. "When my parents died, I was still a teenager."

Amara turned to face him. She knew about his parents' deaths, but always thought he'd been an adult. He'd never elaborated and she knew better than to push.

"At the time of their death, both sets of my grandparents were no longer living." He smiled slightly as memories flooded to the present. "My mother used to tell me I was her miracle baby. She and my dad had been to countless doctors, but she couldn't get pregnant. Mom finally got pregnant when she was forty. Though Rolanzo was younger than my dad, they were best friends. He'd agreed to be my godfather and was present at my christening.

"When my parents died in a car accident, and I had no living relatives, the plan was to place me in foster care. Fortunately, my parents had the foresight to draft a will and an estate plan. The lawyer contacted Rolanzo. He became my guardian and I moved into his mansion. The first year was rough. I was thirteen, surly, and angry at the world. Rolanzo was patient. He gave me love, direction and made sure I was prepared for college and life. He also continued to pay the mortgage on my parents' house. He gave me the house after I graduated from the police academy."

Terrance took a deep breath. "That's why the house looked like it was stuck in the late 80s. My parents always talked about updating the interior but never got around to it. My friends would make jokes whenever they visited."

He shrugged and acknowledged, "It took me years to get rid of their belongings; to include some of the furniture. Rolanzo respected my decision to keep everything as it was before they died. He even hired a cleaning service to maintain the inside of the house. He'd drop me off at my old house and paid me an allowance to mow the lawn every Saturday and pull weeds from my mom's flower garden in the backyard.

At the time I didn't realize what I thought was a chore was actually cathartic. When I'd finished mowing the lawn, I'd go inside and sit in my dad's favorite chair or walk through the kitchen and recall the smell of my mom's famous chicken and dumplings or bacon frying for Sunday brunch after church, and feel like they were still part of me."

Terrance gripped the steering wheel; his voice low and scratchy as he explained. "Rolanzo taught me the importance of loyalty, diversifying my investments from the money I'd earned doing chores and ultimately jobs I held during high school and college. My mom and dad's life insurance paid for my college tuition. I wouldn't let Rolanzo pay." He shrugged and added, "I felt he'd done enough. But those investments...those investments I'd started as a teenager allowed me to renovate the inside of my parent's house."

Amara swiped away a tear. All those times she'd complained about the outdated décor and gaudy flowered wallpaper in the kitchen and guest bathroom. Had she known; the furniture would have been reupholstered and repurposed.

She brightened as a thought occurred. Amara would use the spare key he'd given her to his storage unit during the renovation. In the next couple days, she'd select a few pieces of furniture, have them reupholstered and surprise him. There was plenty of room for another chair in the family room and a couple pieces could go in the guest rooms. He'd kept his parents' and childhood bedroom furniture. He'd also refinished their old dining room table, removed the extra leaf, and placed it in the kitchen. "Terrance I'm so sorry I didn't...."

He cut her off. "I know. I wasn't ready to share that piece of my life. Although you knew my parents died in a car accident, I never told you I was just a teenager. Rolanzo is more than a godfather, he took over the role of father and Dora Lee loved me as if I were her son. They were there when I really needed them."

The knot in her throat prevented Amara from speaking. She rested a hand on his thigh and gave it a gentle squeeze. His hesitancy to change the inside of his house now made sense. The outdated oil painting of him and his parents that hung above the mantle came to mind. He also had several framed photos of his parents in various rooms throughout the house. She wouldn't be so quick to suggest further changes.

As Terrance pulled into his driveway, Amara's thoughts shifted to the wedding photos. It was going to be like searching for a needle in a haystack. She wished Remy could help. He knew many of the wealthy and famous guests who'd attended the wedding. Her eyes flitted in Terrance's direction. She'd need his input. He'd grown up in Rolanzo's home and most likely knew many of the guests. If he would weed them out, she could focus on the remaining guests.

Terrance had retreated to the bedroom. Amara was too excited to sleep. The short nap had energized her and she was wide awake. Her fingers trembled slightly as she plugged the flash drive into her computer. She couldn't wait to dive in and start the research. She wanted answers. Hopefully the photographs from the Dumont's wedding would provide answers. Amara nearly shouted with joy when she saw the guest list had been included as well.

She bit her bottom lip and began the tedious task of matching names with photos. It would be time-consuming, but she was tenacious and would figure it out. Amara was so absorbed in her research she jumped at the sound of chair legs scooting across the tile floor. A grin stretched across her face when Terrance sat beside her.

He gently tugged an errant curl. "I know you aren't planning to get much sleep tonight. Let's get to work."

Amara tapped her shoes against the tile in a happy dance beneath the table as they began comparing guests from the list with the wedding photos.

It was midnight by the time Terrance matched the last photos of guests he knew with names from the guest list. He stood and announced he was going to bed.

Amara thanked him, poured herself a cup of coffee and began sifting through names of guests Terrance hadn't known. She got through half the names before her eyelids began to droop. It was tedious work.

A yawn erupted while Amara saved her work, removed the flash drive, and cleared her search history before shutting down the computer. She placed the flash drive in Terrance's safe. If someone was following her, it wouldn't be wise to carry it around. She now understood why Casey hid the envelope in the lining of her purse. She tucked the laptop inside her satchel and stumbled in the direction of Terrance's bedroom.

Chapter 20

Amara pushed back her office chair and decided to call it quits after typing the same sentence twice. She was sleep deprived and had a slew of unanswered questions regarding Pradeep and his company. Her thoughts drifted to the two children who'd ridden their bikes to the lending library box. It was not the first time the pair had crossed her mind. Were they somehow involved in this? She was certain the man in the Maserati had been Samesh. Was it a coincidence the children were present? What caused him to turn his attention to her?

She checked her watch. Her meeting with the Athys was scheduled in a couple of hours. It was time for a break. Amara stood and grabbed issues of the newly published magazine. She'd drop off the magazines at the library boxes before her meeting.

Amara took pride in the article and wished she could see the children's expressions when they read it. As she closed the door of the last lending library box; three children raced to the box and removed a book and the magazine. Amara jogged across the street, and snapped a photo of the children with her phone. She zoomed in on the article as they faced the box and pointed at the glossy photos of the two children in the magazine.

The drive to the Athy's bungalow style home was uneventful. Amara pulled to the curb and parked. As she walked up the steps, the front door opened. A tall, slender, bespectacled man stood in the doorway. His blond hair had thinned and grayed, but the intelligent glint in his eyes remained. Casey had been tall and greatly resembled her father. They must be devastated, she thought.

Amara tamped down the sadness she felt for their loss and extended her hand. "Good afternoon, Mr. Athy, thank you for agreeing to meet with me." His handshake was firm, but not bone crushing like some of the men she'd interviewed in the past.

"The circumstances are unfortunate, but it's good to see you, Amara. It's been a while." Sadness filled his eyes and Amara averted her gaze as she stepped inside. The Athy's home was cozy and well lived in.

Photographs of their only child graced most of the walls and the top of a shiny black piano next to a corner window. Amara imagined Casey sitting by the window and playing pieces from one of her lesson books tucked in the bench seat.

The aroma of fresh baked cinnamon rolls and coffee filled the room. Amara pressed her hands against her stomach to squelch its rumbling. She'd been anxious about the meeting and hadn't dared to eat anything.

A petite woman with blond hair styled in a perfect pixie cut entered the room. She balanced a wooden tray laden with cups of coffee and plates of hot cinnamon rolls. Amara could tell she'd expertly camouflaged the puffiness beneath her eyes with makeup. She caught Amara staring and remembered to smile pleasantly.

Mr. Athy motioned for them to take a seat. Amara sat in the overstuffed chair and accepted a cup of coffee, a plate with a warm cinnamon roll, and napkin. She placed the coffee and pastry on the small side table next to the chair and thanked them for agreeing to meet with her.

"I am so sorry for your loss. As you both may know, Casey and I haven't spoken in years. I was surprised to learn about the envelope addressed to me."

The Athys leaned forward, soaking up Amara's words, accepting any information regarding their daughter's last hours of life.

"I saw her at the Dumont's wedding reception," Amara said.

The couple exchanged a glance. "Casey told us about the wedding. She knew you'd be attending and planned to speak with you," Mr. Athy admitted.

Amara met his gaze. "Really? She sat a few tables from me and never approached or spoke to me. I saw her leave and she didn't seem to recognize me." Amara shrugged and added, "If she did, she didn't say anything."

Casey's parents exchanged another look. It was as if they were silently communicating with one another. Amara recognized the look. Her parents did the same thing. She wondered if it came with being married over a long period of time.

"I assume you know she was writing an exposé on Divya and her husband Pradeep." Amara acknowledged she was aware. "She wanted to talk to you about Divya. She'd learned you two were friends in high school."

Amara's expression turned sour as she fought the urge to snort.

Mrs. Athy interjected, "We know you and our Casey didn't end on favorable terms after the internship. She regretted that greatly. Casey wasn't sure you'd speak to her, so she decided to take a chance and approach you at the wedding."

Amara wanted to explain the sour expression had nothing to do with her feelings regarding Casey. It had everything to do with the assumption she and Divya were friends in high school. Amara opted to stay on task. "Unfortunately, she didn't. I believe your daughter recognized someone at the wedding she considered a threat and hadn't wanted him or her to know we were acquainted."

Amara picked up the coffee mug and took sip. She needed something to settle her nerves. It was brewed just as she liked it; nice and strong. "Casey took photos of guests and attempted to text them to someone, which was against the rules. When she left the reception tent, she was intercepted by security. She was escorted off the property and we didn't have the opportunity to speak."

Amara took another sip and continued. "As for Divya, we were close friends in elementary and middle school. We didn't socialize in high school, though I saw her a couple times after we graduated. She managed the health food store in Renton several years ago. I believe she's married twice since then." The savory aroma of the cinnamon roll was distracting.

Mrs. Athy observed Amara's repeated glance at the pastry and gestured for her to indulge. "I made them fresh. Please have some."

Amara thanked her and took a bite. The warm, sweet, gooey texture calmed her queasy stomach. "This is very good; thank you, Mrs. Athy." The woman smiled as tears welled in her eyes. Amara put the plate down and asked, "Why didn't Casey speak directly with Divya?"

Mr. Athy adjusted his glasses. "She tried, but Divya refused to speak with her."

"What about her husband, Pradeep?"

Mr. Athy scoffed, "He sent one of his office goons to warn her not to contact him or members of his staff. If she did, they'd take legal action against her. In fact, Pradeep got a restraining order against Casey. He claimed she was stalking him and his children."

Amara rolled her eyes. "Please, his children are adults and don't reside in Washington state."

Mr. Athy brightened. "So, you've done a bit of research on Pradeep; good." His hand waved in the air as his voice rose. "He's crooked and up to no good. Based on what Casey discovered, I believe both his business and marriage are in trouble. Divya is the one with all the money, not Pradeep."

Amara rested against the flowered, chair cushion. That jibed with what she'd learned. "I guess that explains why she hid the envelope, but what information did she intend to learn from me?"

Mr. Athy stood and retrieved a flat, black, oblong object from a shiny green ceramic dish on a wooden side table. "I scanned her notes and what she'd written on her laptop about this exposé." His voice caught as he said, "I'm hoping you can learn what was so damning to cause someone to murder our child."

Amara spied the flash drive in his outstretched hand. Though she wanted to know what was on the flash drive, Amara feared it might put her life in greater danger. She clasped her hands together and shook her head.

"I think Detective Molloy should have the flash drive. He's investigating your daughter's case. Since the wedding, I've been followed and one of Pradeep's men showed up at my apartment unannounced, impersonating a well-known private investigator. He tried to ask questions, but I refused to engage. The police plan to question him." Amara pinched a piece of cinnamon roll and sipped her coffee. She watched Mr. Athy place the drive on the side table next to her chair. "What did Casey think was going on?" Amara used the napkin to wipe her fingers as Mr. Athy returned to his seat beside his wife.

His eyes slid to his wife as if to ask permission to reveal whatever they knew.

Mrs. Athy flicked her wrist as if to signal him to continue. She'd clasped her hands so tight in her lap, her knuckles were pale.

Mr. Athy breathed deep. "Casey believed Pradeep was mixing packages of synthetic opioids and heroin with his company's overseas tea shipments from India. It's also rumored he smuggled weapons and supplies for terrorist factions on his ships through Indian and U.S. ports."

Amara's eyes grew wide. "Have you shared this with the police?"

He confirmed he had.

"What are they doing about it?"

Mr. Athy's outstretched arms and less-than-hopeful expression answered her question.

"Detective Molloy is one of the best homicide detectives on the force." She jotted his name and number on a slip of paper. "Please give him a call." She pointed at the flash drive and added, "He's also the best person to handle the information on that. I recommend you give the drive to him. He can keep it safe and investigate any leads."

Mr. Athy adjusted his glasses. "I know Cian. He's crotchety, but good at what he does." He fanned the air and amended, "Except we want someone who's going to give this their undivided attention." He pointed in Amara's direction and said, "That person is you. I know first-hand what you're capable of. You're like a pit bull. You refuse to let something go once you have it."

The tremble in his voice caused Amara to fight the lump in her throat. She closed her eyes and took a deep breath.

Glassy blue eyes focused on Amara. "I've read your articles and know about your efforts involving the Million Dollar Club murders." He pointed at the black, oblong drive that sat beside her plate. "I'm begging you, for Casey's sake, take this drive and see what you can find out."

Reluctantly, Amara agreed. She picked it up from the table. It felt like a hot coal in the palm of her hand as she slipped it inside her purse and stood. Amara tamped down the desire to rush to the door and thanked the Athys for their time.

Mrs. Athy wrapped Amara's cinnamon roll in a napkin and handed it to her. Amara thanked her as Mr. Athy escorted her to the door. He looked up and down the narrow street before allowing her to depart.

Amara entered her car and locked the doors. She took a huge bite of the cinnamon roll before she cranked the engine. As she drove to Molloy's office, she replayed the meeting with the Athy's in her mind. Amara took another bite of the cinnamon roll and licked icing from her lips.

Before she could phone Molloy, Amara noticed the unmistakable black SUV three cars back and groaned. She stomped on the gas pedal and raced through the intersection, making a sharp left turn amid honks and tire squeals. The light turned red, halting the traffic behind her. Amara zoomed into a nearby parking garage and parked among similar looking cars. Her heart beat fast as she turned off her engine and contacted Terrance. "I'm being followed by the black Maserati!" she squawked.

"Where are you?" he demanded.

"In a parking garage." She slumped low in her seat and gave him the location.

"Stay put, I'm on my way."

Amara felt anxious as she waited for Terrance to arrive. The decision to drive to the police station might have saved her life. Less than ten minutes later, the screech of tires echoed in the parking garage. She spotted Terrance's car and pumped her brakes. He saw the red taillights and motioned for her to pull out and head to the station.

Amara entered the police parking garage. Terrance parked beside her. She got out of her car and asked, "Did they catch him?" He nodded, but his expression didn't calm her fears. "What happened?"

"We can't charge him with anything. The good news is the police kept him from following you. He knows we're aware of his presence and won't be so cavalier in the future."

Amara's shoulders slumped as she asked, "Was it Samesh, Pradeep's VP?" Terrance nodded once more. "Is Molloy in? I have something to give him." She held up the flash drive and filled him in on her meeting with Casey's parents.

"You're doing the right thing. Molloy is better equipped to handle the situation and investigate any leads."

Amara brows knitted together. "I hope this gets them off my tail and away from my apartment!"

Terrance looked away, unable to meet her gaze.

"What?!" she snapped.

"Someone tried to break into your apartment this morning. I saw it on the camera and scared them away. I took a photo from the video. The suspected intruder is an employee at Pradeep's company. The police are questioning him now."

Suddenly the weight of Mr. Athy's suspicions about Pradeep's involvement and his company bore down on her. Amara thought about Casey. During college, she never threw anything away while working on an article, not even note paper. Amara was certain Casey had scraps of papers and documents hidden somewhere.

"Casey has a storage unit somewhere. I need to call her father," she whispered. Before Terrance could protest, Amara dialed the number and spoke with Mr. Athy. Her eyes shone bright when she ended the call. "He's going to send me the information about the storage unit. He needs to find the paperwork and combination for the lock."

Terrance placed a hand on Amara's shoulder and inhaled deeply. He knew Amara was doing this on behalf of the Athy's request to investigate unofficially. "Let's go see Molloy," he said.

Chapter 21

Molloy stood when Amara and Terrance entered his office. "Are you okay?" he asked. Dumbfounded by his show of concern, Amara merely nodded. He pointed at two chairs before returning to his chair.

Amara handed him the flash drive and divulged what she'd learned from Mr. Athy. "I haven't looked at the information on the flash drive, but it must be very incriminating for Samesh to blatantly follow me. I guess he followed me from work."

The thought angered her. How long had he been spying on her? She'd been so careful. How had she missed him today? She'd surveyed her surroundings just as she'd been taught before getting in the car.

The black Maserati didn't blend in easily with other vehicles on the road. Had he placed some type of tracking device on her car? The thought sickened her. Did he know where Terrance lived? Probably. Is this guy desperate or just stupid? She guessed a little of both. Desperate people did stupid things.

She focused on the detective as he inserted the flash drive into his computer. She stood to look at the screen when Molloy signaled for her to stay put. She reluctantly sat down.

He grunted as he clicked the mouse and scanned the pages. "If this information is correct, Pradeep will go to prison for a long time." He checked his watch, picked up the desk phone and spoke quietly into the receiver. He hung up and said, "According to Casey's notes, there were drugs mixed in with Pradeep's last shipment from his plantations in India. A shipment of goods from India is scheduled to dock at the port this evening. We'll have eyes on the port and attempt to intercept it."

"I assume you didn't interview Samesh since he was following me. Were you able to interview Pradeep or Divya?" Amara inquired.

Molloy shook his head. "Both lawyered up and refused to speak to me. The VP's secretary claimed Samesh was meeting with a client off site. She'd made a point to show me the meeting on his calendar. We now know it was a ruse."

"Or he lied to his secretary," Amara interjected.

He waved in the direction of the computer. "If this information pans out, we'll have the evidence we need to pursue our investigation on Pradeep and perhaps Samesh. We have nothing on Divya; except the fact she's married to a scumbag."

Molloy thanked Amara and cautioned her to remain vigilant. She and Terrance left the office.

Amara turned to Terrance. "Do you think Pradeep will be arrogant or stupid enough to follow through with the shipment tonight?" She knew if the freighter was diverted to another port, it would take a lot of coordination, time, and clearance. Terrance interrupted her thoughts with a nudge.

"Did you hear what I said?"

Amara's cheeks flushed. "Sorry, what were you saying?"

Terrance gave a wicked smile. "I was saying I know someone who can provide the information."

Amara told Terrance she'd drive to his place. She wanted to continue her research on the wedding guests and didn't care to relive the interaction with Mr. Dumont's head of security. She'd had enough of him and the snarky security guard to last a while.

The house was quiet. Amara secured the bolt lock on the door. She positioned her laptop on the table, changed into comfortable lounging pants, and one of Terrance's sweat shirts.

She instinctively checked the exterior camera at her apartment from her phone before starting her research.

Amara continued the tedious job of matching the remaining guests' names with internet photos and pairing them with existing wedding guest photos. She'd already established a system to quicken the process. She reached the final name and was dumbfounded. The photo of the last wedding guest didn't match the internet photo of the name on the guest list. "Hello," Amara cooed. She snapped a photo of the unidentified gentleman who'd attended the wedding along with the photo from the internet and texted Terrance. "Please ask Mr. Dumont's head of security about these two men."

There were no photos of the man who'd been invited. Had the guest's invitation been stolen or compromised? She shivered when her thoughts ventured to a dark place. Was he still alive?

She texted Terrance once more. "Please have the head of security contact the guest who'd been invited. I want to make sure he's okay." She paused and typed, "I know it's silly, but I have a feeling something bad happened to him."

Amara waited for a response. She saw the little bubbles and knew Terrance was typing. The bubbles disappeared. Amara walked to Terrance's office in socked feet and printed a copy of the photo. She retrieved a magnifying glass from his desk drawer and examined the photo. The man who'd attended the wedding looked to be in his late thirties. He had a slim build and dark features. She'd been around Remy enough to recognize the suit was expensive, but not tailor made. It hung slightly off his lean frame. The tips of the man's white collared shirt had tiny frays. He hadn't shaved and needed a haircut. Though he resembled the missing wedding guest, there was no question he was younger. Perhaps that was the reason he hadn't shaved. He wanted to give the perception he was older. "Who are you?" she murmured.

Amara removed the memory stick from her laptop, gathered all her notes, photos, and placed them in the safe. A soft knock sounded at the front door as she locked the safe. Amara checked the safe, grabbed her phone, and viewed the visitors at the front door. Two men dressed in black suits with white shirts and skinny black ties waited patiently for someone to answer. They looked as if they performed clandestine work for the government.

I watch way too many spy movies, she thought. Socked feet noiselessly made their way to the control panel where she checked the alarm. It wasn't armed. She immediately set the alarm. Before she could query the visitors, one of the locks on the front door turned. Her heart felt as if it would jump out of her chest. Suddenly, the alarm blared.

Amara raced to Terrance's room for the pistol he kept in the bedroom. Though she didn't like guns, he had convinced her to go to the range and learn how to properly handle and fire them. She checked the magazine. It was already loaded. She pushed the magazine in place, pulled the slide back and used her thumb to release the safety. She stood at the edge of the living room, placed her feet in the stance he'd taught her, extended her arms, and aimed at the door.

Her breathing was harsh and erratic. Her hand began to shake. The sound of the alarm continued to resonate throughout the house. She was certain the intruders heard it. Amara blocked out the blaring noise and took a deep breath to calm her jangled nerves. She adjusted her grip and remained in her stance until the sound of an engine revving caught her attention. Amara flipped the pistol's safety and made her way to the window. By the time she peeked through the blinds the car was gone and a few neighbors were outside peering at the house. She rushed to the console and punched in the security code. The sound ceased and she inhaled deeply. "What in the world did you get me involved in, Casey?" she shrieked. Amara placed the pistol on the side table and bent to catch her breath.

Terrance burst through the door with one of Dumont's guards. Amara ran into his arms as he made shushing noises. Had she been crying?

She pointed at his pistol. "I did exactly how you taught me."

Terrance strode to the side table and checked the pistol to make sure the weapon was on safe and replied, "That's my girl." Dumont's guard stood close to the door and peered up and down the street. His phone chimed and he headed outside to answer it.

"Did you see them?" she asked.

Terrance removed the magazine from the pistol and ensured there wasn't a bullet in the chamber before he returned it to the gun safe. When he joined Amara he replied, "We didn't, but they won't get far. I was on my way to the house when one of my neighbors called me. He'd heard the alarm and provided the license plate number and make of the car to the police. It won't take long to track them down." He faced Amara and asked, "Are you all right?"

Amara closed her eyes and took a deep breath and nodded. Dumont's man returned. "We've got them. They aren't going anywhere. The police were notified. Amara heard a police siren in the distance. When she opened her eyes, Dumont's man was staring at her. Gone was the smirk and attitude. He was all business. She understood why he was part of Mr. Dumont's security team. Today he wore a navy leather strap around his braids with the same form fitted black shirt and cargo pants. He'd be considered handsome if he ever bothered to smile. Thankfully, he couldn't read her thoughts.

Terrance tucked an errant curl behind Amara's ear and said, "We took your advice and contacted the last guy you researched from the guest list." He grimaced and explained, "According to a police report, Rolanzo's guest died of heart attack the day before the wedding."

"No way!" Amara cried. "I don't believe that for one minute!" She was about to justify her statement when Terrance gently stroked her arms.

"We know. It appears the mystery wedding guest is involved. Rolanzo's head of security is checking and will let us know when they identify him. I'm sure he'll have information soon."

"Too bad they don't have the FBI facial recognition system," she quipped. Terrance and the guard exchanged a look. "Wow," Amara mouthed. It was time to be quiet. The guard's upper lip contorted in what could possibly be interpreted as a smile but looked more like a snarl. She wasn't sure; and at this point was too frazzled to care.

"I'm out," Dumont's man announced and strode to the door. Terrance followed. Amara leaned against the door jamb and watched as they shook hands. Dumont's man turned and met her gaze. She caught the glint of humor in his eyes as he shook his head and walked to his vehicle. It felt like being chastised by an older brother.

She silently berated herself for allowing the guy to irritate her. The roar of the SUV pierced the quiet as the he pulled from the curb and sped down the street.

Amara headed to the bedroom while Terrance went next door to thank his neighbor. He returned, rushed into the bedroom, and gathered her in his arms. They stayed in that position several seconds. "I'm not going to let anything happen to you. I love you Amara," he whispered.

Amara tilted up her face to his and replied, "I love you too." Her head rested against his chest as the steady rhythm of his heartbeat comforted her.

Chapter 22

Terrance slipped from the bed. Amara looked peaceful. He was glad she'd slept through the night. A sly smile creased his face. He was also pleased he'd been able to help her relax. He dressed quietly and tip-toed from the room.

The police were scheduled to question the two men who'd attempted to break into his house. He wanted to observe the interview. They'd tried to question them yesterday evening, but their lawyer appeared and ended the interview. He'd received word that one of the men agreed to speak with the police.

He'd need to do some fast talking to persuade the officers involved. Hopefully the footage of the two men attempting to break into his house would convince them. Terrance scrawled a note and placed it on the kitchen table before he rushed out the door.

When Amara opened her eyes, everything was a blur. She'd slept well last night. Her arm reached across the bed to Terrance's side. The sheets felt cold. Amara bolted upright in the darkened room. The bedroom shutters were closed and the house was quiet. She slid her feet into slippers and headed to the kitchen, where a note was propped against an empty coffee mug. Terrance would be out for a few hours and they'd go to brunch when he returned. It was Saturday and they hadn't made any plans.

Amara checked her watch. It was eight thirty. As she showered and dressed, an idea struck. Her hand trembled when she reached for her phone and checked the text messages. "Yes!" she exclaimed and punched the air. He'd sent it!

Keys in hand, she reread the text message from Mr. Athy. He'd provided the location, access code and lock combination to Casey's storage unit. Luck was on her side. Amara jotted a note to Terrance and rushed out the door.

Amara remained vigilant as she drove to the storage unit. She couldn't chance Pradeep's VP or one of his other henchmen following her. This solo trip to Casey's storage unit was impulsive and a bit reckless. She played upbeat music from her playlist to soothe her jangled nerves. Casey had been a packrat in college. Amara had no idea of the condition of the storage unit. The only thing she felt certain was there'd be papers or perhaps evidence to back up what Casey wrote in her journal. The fact Casey had hidden the envelope in the lining of her purse indicated she was either scared or suspicious someone was after the information or worse, her. Amara could relate.

When had Casey become paranoid? Was it before being served with a restraining order from Pradeep's lawyer or after? It was apparent he was hiding something. Now, she was on his radar. Sending those guys to Terrance's house was bold and foolish. What's more, they acted as if they thought no one was in the house, or didn't care. The latter unnerved her.

Amara clutched the steering wheel. There were so many unanswered questions. Had Casey discovered she was in danger too late? How had they coaxed her to Schmitz Park at night, after hours? Casey was smart and never one to rush into a situation. She'd always been cautious to the point of paranoia. Had she been taken by force? If yes, Amara knew Casey fought her attacker. If she wasn't abducted, where was her car? The police still hadn't located it.

Amara turned up her music and began to sing to one of her favorite songs by Kelly Clarkson. Based on Terrance's note, she had a couple hours to search before he returned. "Please let there be some type of order," she whispered.

Amara turned down her music, slowed at the gate of the storage facility and punched in the code. The large, metal gate creaked open. Her eyes shifted from the front windshield to the rearview mirror as she drove through the entrance. Once her car cleared the gate; Amara waited until the gate chugged along its rusty track and closed with a loud thud. Satisfied no one was behind her, she drove down the narrow lane to Casey's storage unit.

Overhead lights flickered in protest as she flipped the switch. Thank goodness the boxes were neatly arranged and stacked along the walls. Each box faced the center of the room; its contents written on the side panel with a thick, black felt pen. The neat block lettered script matched the one on the envelope Casey had addressed to her. The bright light attached to the rafter in the ceiling continued to flicker as she scanned the boxes. She moved several boxes before locating one tucked in the far corner labeled "Divya". Amara grabbed it and used the tip of her apartment key to rip the Scotch tape that sealed the flaps.

Though it was a sizeable box, the contents were several stacks of photos held together with bright colored rubber bands. Torn sheets of paper and note cards littered the bottom of the box. She picked up the first group of photos and slid off the band. The photos were of Divya, her two sisters-in-law and mother-in law-from her first marriage. The photos were not originals. Possibly copies from one of the gossip sites on the internet. They looked like they were taken somewhere in the Middle East. The backs of the photos were blank; devoid of any description or comment.

Amara placed each photo on the concrete floor and examined them. They were proof those gossip magazines she'd read got it wrong. The women were all smiles; arms draped around one another. She snapped copies with her phone and rewrapped the bundle. The next bundle contained photos of Pradeep and his adult daughter and son. There was also a photo of a little girl at the bottom of the stack.

Amara held it up to the bright light before setting it on the floor with the others. The little girl looked familiar. Where had she seen the child? Divya wasn't in this stack. She photographed each of the snapshots, replaced the rubber band and set them inside the box. The next bunch were of Divya and Pradeep. The couple looked anything but happy. In one, they pointed at each another in an accusatory manner. It looked like they were at a park with a lot of trees. In others, they stood inches apart, never touching. It was clear the couple wasn't aware they were being photographed. Had Casey taken these photos? "What in the world?" Amara whispered as she snapped copies with her phone.

Another stack contained photos of a large freighter and a mansion that looked like Divya's Mercer Island home she'd viewed online. There were pictures of a mansion that resembled their home in Mumbai Remy had shown her.

She stared at a picture of a man seated in a bright yellow dingy in the Puget Sound headed in the direction of the freighter. The man's profile resembled Samesh, Pradeep's VP.

"Gotcha!" Amara snarled. She quickly photographed the snapshots and returned them to the box. There were photos of Pradeep's office buildings in California, India, and Seattle. In one, Divya was surrounded by American children. Several photos of Divya dressed in a sari surrounded by Indian children were included. How had Casey gotten these photos? It was clear many were taken in India.

The last stack gave her pause. They were pictures of malnourished adults and children, standing in front of what could easily be described as a shanty with clothes hanging from protruding nails stuck in flimsy, plywood walls. Amara forced her hand to remain steady as she made copies. It was hard to understand how someone as rich as Pradeep allowed his workers to live and work in such substandard conditions. She returned the last bundle of photos to the box.

Amara collected fifty misshapen slips of paper and note cards written in Casey's blocked script from the box and placed them on the concrete floor. She snapped pictures of each before returning them and placing the box in its original location.

What had Casey planned to do with the pictures? Did the sheets of paper and note cards correspond to the photos? Nothing was written on the backs of the prints. Amara inspected the remainder of the boxes and found no others with Pradeep, Divya or his company name written on them. She turned on her heels and looked where she'd placed the box. Should she take it with her? The temptation was great, but not prudent.

These guys knew where she and Terrance lived. They'd tried to break in! No, the safest place for the box was inside Casey's storage unit. Besides, Mr. Athy hadn't given her permission to remove it. She wasn't worried. She'd done the next best thing; photographed everything and emailed them to herself, just in case. Amara turned out the light and pulled the rope to close the accordion style door.

Her lungs filled with the fresh, morning air as she slid the combination lock through the metal hole in the door. When she turned the dial, it reminded her of high school and seeing Divya for the first time after she'd returned from India.

As her car tires bumped over the rusty rail of the gate, she considered the box with the photos. Did any of those sheets of paper correspond to the photos? Who had taken the ones in India and places outside of Washington state? Why did Casey have pictures of Pradeep's children and who was the little girl in the photo she'd found at the bottom of the stack? Her research on Divya helped to identify most of the people in the photos. Amara wondered why Casey had photos of Divya's first husband's relatives. Was the young girl part of Pradeep's family? She knew Divya and Pradeep had not been married long enough to have a daughter that age, nine or ten years old. Could the child be Pradeep's?

Also, the child looked biracial. Possibly Indian and Caucasian, or African American and Caucasian. Pradeep's children were the color of sandalwood with thick, dark hair, long, narrow faces with brown eyes. In the photos, his daughter's eyes were sad; her mouth downturned. She wore a nose ring and her narrow face was framed with beautiful, dark brown, long, wavy hair. The brother was more handsome with a prominent nose like his father, a neat beard, and thick wavy hair that looked professionally styled. His dark eyes and expression were intense and serious. They both looked unhappy. Had they any fun as children?

The little girl was different. Her olive skin tone complimented the most beautiful large hazel eyes she'd ever seen. Long, ebony, wavy hair framed a round face and her smile was genuine. It was clear the photo was taken without her knowledge. She was gorgeous with perfect little features; much prettier than Pradeep's daughter. In fact, there was no resemblance to either of Pradeep's children. "Who are you?" Amara asked aloud.

Amara arrived at Terrance's house shortly before he returned. The note was in her hand when he entered the kitchen. He looked unhappy. Amara's smile quickly faded as she crumpled the note inside her fisted hand. "What's happened?" she asked.

Terrance scowled and leaned against the wall; arms crossed. Amara shoved the note into her back pocket and turned to fetch two water bottles from the refrigerator. He unscrewed the cap and sat at the kitchen table. His stare was accusatory. "Would you like to tell me where you've been?" His voice was dangerously low and even.

Amara fished the note from her pocket and placed it on the table before she sat. "I ran an errand. I left you a note," she replied.

He read the note without touching it and stared in her direction.

Her eyes remained trained on the water bottle as her fingers fidgeted against the ridges of bottle. "I got a text from Mr. Athy and went to Casey's storage unit," she explained.

Terrance looked so angry she imagined smoke coming out his ears like a cartoon character. She wanted to laugh, but knew better. This was one of those times she needed to hold her tongue and brace herself for the verbal onslaught. He didn't disappoint.

"Two guys tried to break into my house yesterday and you've been followed all over town! What in the world do you think you were doing going there alone?!" His eyes squinted. "You didn't drag Remy into your little escapade, did you?"

Amara slammed the bottle of water on the table with such force it sloshed in a puddle. "That's enough!" she yelled. "I didn't ask for this!" She pointed to the roof. "It was dropped in my lap. Someone I knew was murdered and had an envelope and photo addressed to me!" She held up one finger. "I gave the flash drive to the detective without looking at it!" She held up two fingers and continued. "I haven't contacted Divya or anyone else suspected in this case and no, I didn't enlist Remy to accompany me, though that probably wouldn't have been a bad idea. So, back off, Terrance!" Amara stood so abruptly the legs of the chair scraped against the tiled floor. She stomped from the room and retrieved her laptop and purse from Terrance's bedroom. It was time to go home. She passed by the kitchen table without looking in his direction.

"Amara," he called softly. She stopped, but didn't turn to look at him. "I'm sorry. I was worried. I saw you leave on the security camera and nearly lost it. You can't keep going off on your own. It's too dangerous. No one knew you were gone...What if..." He didn't complete the sentence. She turned and looked into sorrowful eyes.

She hitched her satchel higher on her shoulder. "I didn't want to worry you. You were gone. I'm guessing the police station. It's daylight, I have my pepper spray and left you a note!" Her voice rose an octave with the last word.

Terrance stood and shook his head. He slowly removed the satchel from her shoulder. "What in the world am I going to do with you? You scared the crap out of me." He clasped her hand in his and led her back to the kitchen table.

"What did you find out about the two guys?" she asked. She'd wait to tell him about the photos and the girl.

Terrance smirked; aware she'd shifted the focus to him. "They claim to be maritime private investigators looking into maritime crimes connected with Pradeep's company."

Amara frowned. "You don't believe them."

"Nope, neither did Molloy. They had badges and knew about Pradeep's shipment of teas arriving at the port this evening. The million-dollar question is, why were they trying to break into my house?"

Her brow quirked. "Why were they?

Terrance gave a loud snort and replied, "Their explanation was they'd received inaccurate intelligence regarding one of Pradeep's employees." He gave the name of an employee suspected of maritime crimes.

The name didn't sound familiar and she hadn't run across the name during her research. She wondered if Remy had. "Would you mind if I ask Remy about the name? He's the one who researched Pradeep."

Terrance nodded. "Right now, this is all being kept hush-hush. I had to do some serious finagling just to observe the interview."

"Who do you think these guys are?" she asked.

"I believe they are maritime private investigators. The big question is, who hired them and what had they hoped to find at my house? Who gave them intel about one of Pradeep's employees living here?" Terrance shrugged. "I don't believe they have permission to investigate on U.S. soil. Molloy is working that puzzle with some fed guy he knows."

Amara grinned and Terrance shook his head. She wasn't deterred. "You could ask Rolanzo's head of security. If this has to do with maritime investigative agencies, he'd know." She tilted her head to the side and added, "Most likely, he knows who these guys really are."

Terrance placed his head in his hands. When he looked up, his expression was dour. He exhaled loudly and removed his phone from his pocket. His eyes squinted in her direction as he pushed a button on his phone. "I hope I don't regret this," he grumbled.

Rolanzo's head of security instructed Terrance to send photos and video of the two men from the camera above his front door. The response was immediate. Terrance read the text aloud. "These guys are bad news. Though legit, they are foreign investigators who sometime work with Interpol investigating maritime crimes. Their agency is highly regarded, but known to bend the law for their client if the price is right." Terrance cursed under his breath.

Amara gave an I-told-you so, grin. "What's your game plan? You now know they have no problem bending the rules. My guess is they work for Pradeep." She removed her phone. "Take a look at these photos. I took them from a pile of photographs Casey had in a box marked, 'Divya'." She showed him the ones of Pradeep's VP in the yellow dingy heading to the freighter along with two photos of the freighter.

"This has something to do with Pradeep's shipment of goods. Why is his VP going out alone to the freighter in that dingy? Is he picking up or delivering something? It appears as if he's sneaking around."

Terrance examined the photos and released a tired breath. "I need to call Molloy. Let's take a ride," he said.

Chapter 23

As Molloy gave Amara another reprimand, she remained quiet and took it in stride. This wasn't the first time she'd been chastised by him and most likely not the last. When he finished, Amara showed him photos she'd taken on her phone.

"Look at the one where Pradeep's VP is in the dingy moving toward the freighter and separate photos of the ship. I don't know if they always use the same freighter, but dates on these photos are different and both ships have the same identification number. For whatever reason, Casey photographed the same freighter twice."

Molloy transferred the photos and notes to his laptop. When he returned the phone, his tone left no room for rebuttal. "Delete the photos!"

"Detective Molloy, please!"

His green eyes locked onto her eyes. "This is not negotiable! Someone attempted to break into your apartment and Terrance's house. You've been followed around town. Erase the photos or I will confiscate your phone!

Terrance leaned over and whispered, "Do it. He's trying to protect you."

Amara clutched her phone tight and weighed her options.

Molloy grew impatient. "Delete those photos now young lady!"

Amara huffed and did so. She knew the detective was right. This was not her fight. The professionals needed to handle it from this point. Plus, she'd already forwarded the photos and notes to her email.

"Have you found her car?" she asked. Molloy shook his head. "Do you know what kind of car she drove?"

The detective sat back in his chair; silent for several seconds. He leaned forward, clicked his mouse, and announced, "She drove a late model, white BMW coupe."

Amara knew she'd pressed her luck, but asked anyway. "What's her license plate number?" Molloy pursed his lips. Amara asked another question. "Are you still having police officers watch the port tonight?" He gave a curt nod.

Amara's gaze dropped to her phone. There was nothing more she could do. She stood and thanked the detective. Terrance joined her.

Molloy picked up the receiver and Amara overheard him ask for the Port Police Commander as they headed out the door.

Amara clinched her teeth together so hard her jaw ached. As they entered the elevator, her gaze remained focused on the two steel doors even though she felt Terrance's eyes on her. The only sound was the chime that dinged as they descended to the lobby.

Everyone seemed to forget she hadn't asked for any of this. It was dumped in her lap courtesy of Casey Athy and now Casey's father. His expectations were too high. She'd discovered the photos and now they were in the hands of the authorities. Mr. Athy knew his daughter's license plate number, but she didn't dare ask in Terrance's presence.

Once they were on the road, Amara broke the silence. "I'd like to stop by the Athys and give them an update. I feel like I owe them an explanation. Is that okay?" She fought hard to keep her voice even. Terrance's jaw rippled as he focused on the road.

He spared her a quick glance. "You're right, they do deserve an update. Why don't you call instead?" he advised.

Pick your battles, she thought and dialed the Athys number. It was picked up on the first ring. Amara explained what she'd found and the status of what was going on. Mr. Athy's voice sounded tired as he thanked her and ended the call.

"How did he take it?" Terrance asked.

Amara released a jagged breath. "As good as could be expected." she replied. Her voice quivered when she admitted, "I may not have cared for Casey, but I would never wish this on anyone or want her parents to suffer this way. It's terrible, Terrance." Her eyes glistened. "I hope Molloy gets to the bottom of this!"

Terrance shook his head. "If it were only that easy."

"What? What do you mean?"

Terrance explained, "This thing has many tentacles. One leads to Pradeep, another to Samesh. We have no clue how Divya ties into all of this."

Amara sat up straight. "Hey, can we drive by the port?" She placed her hands together in a pleading gesture and fixed the saddest expression she could muster on her face. "Pl-ease?" Before he could refuse, she explained, "I have a hunch and want to follow up on it."

She texted Mr. Athy and asked for his daughter's car license plate number. Her phone dinged immediately and the number appeared. Bingo! She avoided looking at Terrance as she tucked her phone away.

Terrance groaned. "Okay, what's your hunch?"

Amara wasted no time with a response. "Why were there photos of the freighter and Pradeep's VP in the yellow dingy? She had to be at the port to take those photos. Most of the people in Casey's photographs weren't aware they were being photographed. I believe there's a link between the port and Casey's accusation about drugs being mixed in with the shipments of tea." Amara snapped her fingers and asked, "Is there a way we can find out if that freighter was docked at the port the night Casey went missing?" She rattled off the identification number from vessel.

Terrance smirked. "Of course, you'd memorize the numbers on the freighter." He paused. "Okay, I admit, you have a point."

He pressed the button on his steering wheel, phoned his buddy who worked with the Port Police, and provided the numbers that corresponded with the vessel. Music filled the interior of the car while they were on hold. The port police officer's voice boomed through the speaker as he confirmed the freighter was docked at the port the night Casey was killed. Terrance thanked him as Amara pulled out her phone and began to scroll through a website.

Terrance continued to drive. "What are you looking for?"

"Would you mind if we check out the parking lots by the pier? I have an idea."

Terrance exhaled impatiently. "Do you know how many parking lots there are for the pier?!"

Amara was unaffected by his outburst. "Let's start with the Pier 91 lot. I have a feeling we're going to find Casey's car in one of these lots."

Terrance pushed the button on his steering wheel and Molloy's voice came over the line. He informed the detective of his plan. His buddy at the Port Police Department had already notified his Commander. He disconnected the call and headed to the pier.

Molloy agreed it wouldn't hurt to check it out. He instructed them to keep him posted. The Commander asked to be notified if they discovered anything and offered his assistance. Amara faced the passenger window so Terrance wouldn't see gloat.

Terrance showed his badge and was granted entry into parking lot D. Its 1,500-spaces seemed daunting. Terrance began the slow drive down each aisle. The Port police officer started at the opposite end of the lot. They kept in touch by radio.

They'd been at it close to one hour. Amara was about to admit defeat when they passed a white BMW. The license plate indicated the owner was an UW Alumni. "Stop!" she yelled.

Terrance stomped on the brake and placed the car in reverse. He stopped in front of a white BMW coupe. Amara jumped out the car. Flashlight clutched in his right hand; Terrance radioed the Port police officer and followed her.

Amara referred to Mr. Athy's text of Casey's license plate number. "This is it!" she cried. "It's Casey's car!"

Terrance cautioned her not to touch anything.

Amara slowly circled the BMW, and peeked through the tinted windows. Why had Casey parked in such a public place instead of directly at the pier? She must have known the freighter had docked. Had she intended to meet someone at the docks?

Terrance donned gloves and tried the door. It was locked. He shined the flashlight into the car as the Port police officer arrived. The officer called the Port Commander while Terrance phoned Detective Molloy.

"I'm on my way!" Molloy yelled into the receiver.

Another Port police officer and his K-9 pulled up. Twenty minutes later, Molloy arrived with Mr. Athy in tow. He'd refused to hand over the extra key fob and insisted on following Molloy. Though his face was flushed, Mr. Athy's expression was determined as they neared the vehicle. "That's her car!" he cried.

Amara heard the strain and desperation in his voice.

Molloy held out his hand and Mr. Athy gave him the key fob. As he stepped away, his fingers curled into tight fists while his eyes remained glued to his daughter's car. Amara wished there was something she could say to console him.

Molloy pushed the button to the key fob and the lights flashed and locks clicked. He donned gloves and opened the car door and trunk. Amara scooted to a position out of the way, but could see inside the car. There were scraps of paper everywhere. The state of the car reminded her of how Casey had been in college; a hoarder of materials that had to do with whatever she was writing about. Amara noticed a slip of paper with the vessel's identification number written in Casey's neat block script on the edge of the passenger front seat.

Terrance handed Molloy his flashlight. Scraps of papers, a paperback book, several pens, and an empty Styrofoam food container littered the passenger seat and floor mat. Amara was shocked when Molloy checked the trunk and found Casey's work identification badge, wallet with driver's license and credit cards along with Dumont's wedding invitation tucked inside the wheel well beneath the spare tire. Why had she removed them from her purse and where was Casey's key fob?

It gave Amara a bit of satisfaction to know the killer hadn't discovered her car and the items she'd left behind. Had the killer thought Casey gave the information to her! She began to put the pieces together. Casey must have set out to meet or spy on someone at the pier where the vessel was docked. Most likely the latter. She imagined the person of interest was likely Samesh.

If her car was here, how did her body get from the pier to Schmitz Park? Why was she muddy and bruised? There was no doubt Casey would have fought her attacker. She was fearless, strong, and had been on the college crew team.

Amara hadn't seen Casey's body, but assumed she'd been attacked from behind. The grass stains and mud must have come from the park. Except...what if it had come from the grounds at the port? There were grass, dirt, and trees here as well.

Before she could get a closer look, Molloy motioned for her and Mr. Athy to move away from the car. Amara moved, but craned her neck to see what else the police discovered. When glanced in Mr. Athy's direction, he appeared close to hyperventilating.

Amara stepped close and whispered, "Breathe deep. Don't worry, they'll get to the bottom of this. They're the best." She pointed in the direction of Detective Molloy, the Port Police officer, and her boyfriend.

Mr. Athy bent forward, rested his hands on his knees, and sucked in fresh air. When he stood, he released a ragged, harsh, breath.

Molloy coordinated with the Port Commander and requested CSI support and a tow truck. Amara hung her head, saddened by the turn of events.

The Port Police Commander requested copies of the surveillance videos of the parking lot for the night in question and the pier where the vessel had been docked. They'd be able to track Casey's movements and determine where she went, if she was alone, and if she visited the pier the night she was murdered.

The Port Police Commander contacted the captain of the vessel. Amara murmured, "Now we're getting somewhere." She glanced at Mr. Athy and noticed he was listening to the call and appeared more relaxed. His hands were unfurled and hung limply at his sides.

Amara's heart went out to him and his family. At least the investigation was gaining momentum.

Mr. Athy glanced in Amara's direction; his eyes held unshed tears. "You did this. Thank you," he whispered.

Amara was too choked up to reply. She gave a shaky smile and touched his shoulder. An idea struck her. She turned to Mr. Athy and asked, "We didn't find Casey's key fob. Where would she have put her key?"

Mr. Athy brightened and pointed at a place beneath the car. "She had a hide-a-key box. Casey was always leaving her key somewhere. Her mother had given it to her."

Amara motioned for Terrance to come over. Mr. Athy repeated what he'd said.

Chapter 24

There was a flurry of activity. Everyone moved with purpose. Detectives from the Port Criminal Investigation Division gathered prints and other forensic evidence. As Mr. Athy predicted, the key fob was secreted inside a metal key box attached to the rear wheel well on the passenger side.

Amara was captivated by the speed and thoroughness of the detectives. It reminded her of a symphony. Everyone knew their part and went about their task with ease. She inched close and eavesdropped on the conversation between Molloy and the Port Commander. Once the lines of jurisdiction were ironed out, Casey's car was towed to the station for further inspection.

Mr. Athy lifted his glasses and swiped at a single tear with the tip of his forefinger as he watched the tow truck with his daughter's car rumble down the road.

Amara felt helpless. There was nothing she could do to lessen his grief.

Terrance approached Mr. Athy. "The CSI detectives will continue to gather evidence that will help tell the story of what happened to your daughter."

Unable to speak, Mr. Athy looked away until he gained control of his emotions.

When they were inside Terrance's car, he turned to look at her. His voice reassuring. "The detectives have it under control." He squeezed her hand and whispered, "Well done."

Amara looked out the window as the sun began to set. It had been a long day. Her emotions warred between sadness and relief as she watched the Port Police officers and detectives disperse. Sadness because the discovery of the car wouldn't bring Casey back and solace in the fact that they now had a new point of origin.

Terrance explained Molloy would maintain the lead in the investigation.

Why wasn't Casey on any of the port security videos Molloy previously viewed? Had she encountered someone in the parking lot and never made it to the port? Amara made a mental catalog of everything she knew regarding the evidence thus far. Now more than ever, she wished she'd read Casey's notes before turning it over to Molloy.

At least she had Casey's notes and photos from the storage unit to comb through. She hoped they'd reveal what Casey had been working on. Terrance was right. This case had many tentacles.

It was clear Casey discovered something and paid for it with her life. The Port Police agreed to review the manifest and use their K-9 patrol to inspect the cargo containers filled with Pradeep's shipment. She'd overheard that some of the containers were offloaded the night prior. There was no doubt in her mind the missing containers were filled with illegal drugs. Would the K-9 be able to detect residual odor from the drugs?

How was Divya connected to the all of this? How involved was she in her husband's business affairs? The envelope addressed to her had Divya's photo inside, not Pradeep's. Also, if Pradeep was innocent, why had he obtained a restraining order against Casey?

She considered Pradeep's VP. He'd been at the library box, why? Had he known something about her and followed her to that location?

"Earth to Amara," Terrance chided.

Lost in thought, she hadn't heard a word he'd said. "I'm sorry, what did you say?"

"I asked if you want to go someplace for dinner. It's been an unusual day. We missed brunch and I don't feel like going home."

Amara agreed. If they went to his house or her apartment, she'd continue to obsess over the investigation. "When will Molloy review the security videos?" she asked.

"I'm certain it will be at the top of his list of things to do when he returns to the office."

"Do you think Casey was kidnapped at the port? Was she killed at the port and transported to the park?" Amara didn't give Terrance a chance to respond. She was on a roll. "If she was killed at the port, why would the killer go to the trouble of transporting her body and dumping it nearly fifteen miles away? Why kill her and leave her body at Schmitz Park?" Amara rubbed the back of her neck. "Casey was strangled right?" Terrance gave a tight nod. "How did the killer sneak up on her? I know she fought him or her."

Silence filled the vehicle.

"I see the wheels turning, what are you thinking?" Terrance asked.

Amara cleared her throat. "If she was in the vicinity of the freighter, why hadn't the Port Security cameras detected her presence? If the killer followed or discovered her snooping around the port, why didn't he just dump her body in the Puget Sound?"

"Ugh, that's harsh!" Terrance sputtered.

Amara shrugged. "It's true and you know it. There are cameras all over that place. Why would the killer risk being seen carrying her body when he could have disposed of her in the water?" She poked his leather dashboard with the tip of her finger for emphasis.

Terrance allowed a few seconds to pass before he answered. "I believe the killer didn't want her death connected with the port or freighter carrying Pradeep's shipment. Let's go with your assumption that she fought her assailant." Amara rolled her eyes. "Hear me out. Let's assume during the scuffle, she fell or was pushed down in the grass and dirt. Since she was already dirty, the park with dirt and vegetation was a practical alternate location."

Amara considered his theory. "Okay, they found her body on the alligator, one of the most popular tourist sites. He could have left her in the woods. I've been to that park. The vegetation is thick once you leave the trails. Her body wouldn't have been discovered for days, maybe weeks!"

Terrance brows lifted. "When did you become so morbid?"

"My ordeal with Ralph Simpson changed my outlook on certain people," she huffed.

It was time to change the subject. "Where would you like to eat?" he asked.

Amara forced the negative thoughts from her mind and suggested they go to Chan's restaurant. "I love their bibimbap and kimchi."

"That'll work. I like their steak tartare." They drove in companionable silence to the restaurant.

Chapter 25

Amara held her Styrofoam container of leftovers and raced to the car as Terrance unlocked and opened the passenger door. Thunder echoed in the darkness as it began to rain in earnest. She slid onto the passenger seat and closed the door.

Terrance cranked the engine. Amara removed napkins from the glovebox and handed several to Terrance to dry his face. She used the others on her face and hands. Heavy raindrops pelted the windshield as they bantered about the Seattle Mariners on the way to his house. Terrance slowed and pulled into the garage.

Amara retrieved a small umbrella from the back seat and ran through the chilly rain to the house. Terrance unlocked his front door and immediately sensed something wasn't right. His left arm shot out to prevent Amara from entering. His law enforcement instincts kicked in and his demeanor was all business.

A dim light illuminated the family room. He hadn't left on any lights. He removed his pistol from its holster and pushed the door open with the toe of his shoe. He used the door frame as a barrier and aimed his weapon in the direction of the shadowed person sitting in one of the high back chairs. Once his eyes adjusted, he lowered his pistol and exhaled sharply.

Rolanzo Dumont relaxed in the chair that sat close to the floor lamp; a book on his lap. His deep voice was calm. "I heard you've had a bit of trouble with a certain businessman."

"What the hell, Rolanzo!" Terrance screeched as he shoved his pistol into its holster. "How did you bypass my alarm system?" Terrance threw his hands in the air. "Don't answer that. I don't want to know!"

Rolanzo placed the book on the side table and smoothed his slacks as he stood. He was a tall man, with coffee brown skin and the most unusual gray eyes. Coal black hair was held in place with pomade; his unlined face expressionless.

Amara peeked at Rolanzo from behind Terrance. She would not want to meet this man in an alley. He exuded masculinity and danger. She'd never seen him with a hair out of place or clothes mussed. Even when she and Remy drove to the cave in the mountains to warn him of danger, his appearance was pristine. She knew firsthand that he was not a man to be trifled with. "Welcome back, Mr. Dumont," Amara called as she moved from behind Terrance.

Rolanzo acknowledged her with a tilt of his head. His baritone voice was smooth as he replied, "Amara." He made her name sound like an introduction to a song. "You may call me Rolanzo, you know."

Amara turned to close the front door. Regardless of what she called him; he'd always be Mr. Dumont in her mind. When Terrance and Rolanzo remained standing, facing one another, she wasn't sure what to do.

Terrance eyed Amara as she stood entranced a few feet away. Terrance ran a hand over his damp face. He motioned for Rolanzo to have a seat. He asked Amara if she would make them coffee.

She excused herself and went to the kitchen. She tried to act normal, but her eyes betrayed her disappointment. Why was Mr. Dumont there? Had he discovered something about his friend the police hadn't?

Rolanzo sat and spoke in Italian. "Talk to me. Someone impersonated one of my guests, who I discovered was possibly murdered. I want to know why."

Amara filled the coffee maker with grounds and turned it on. She tried to eavesdrop on their conversation, but it was useless. They'd switched to Italian. Another surprise. Terrance's speech was staccato, unlike Rolanzo's smooth diction, but he was conversing. Darn them both!

Terrance sat on the sofa across from Rolanzo and explained what they knew thus far. "We just returned from the port which might be the actual murder site of Casey Athy. As you know, she was asked to leave your wedding reception. We believe she photographed someone who was a threat to her. Most likely, the gentleman who posed as your wedding guest."

Rolanzo's eyes slid in the direction of the kitchen as he said, "Of course, Amara is in the thick of it."

Terrance leaned forward and rested his forearms on his knees. "She's the reason we found Casey's car in the Pier 91 parking lot. Molloy is going over the videos now. Her body was discovered at Schmitz Park on a popular tourist attraction. It's clear the killer wanted us to find her to derail any possibility of us connecting her appearance at the docks the night she was murdered."

Terrance lowered his voice. "Amara asked a pretty good question. She wondered why the killer hadn't simply thrown Casey's body in the Sound after he murdered her? Why take her fifteen miles away and stage her body on such a popular tourist attraction at the park? Why not hide her body in the thick forest of trees and vegetation at the park? She's right, you know."

The conversation ceased when Amara returned with a tray of three steaming mugs of coffee. She placed the tray on the retro coffee table and handed each man a mug before grabbing one for herself. She'd made out her and Casey's name, Schmitz Park, but nothing else. "Would you care for anything else?" she asked Rolanzo. He shook his head and thanked her for the coffee. She sat next to Terrance on the sofa and was relieved when they switched back to English.

"I don't like my special day being marred by the death of a good friend. I want to find out the identity of the impersonator and what he's after. Not to mention the maritime private investigators who attempted to break into your house. I've dealt with those rascals before. They're unscrupulous."

Terrance bowed his head to hide his embarrassment. He felt as if he was thirteen again, being chastised by his guardian. Rolanzo had advised him to upgrade his security, but he hadn't.

"Was your head of security able to learn what happened to your invited guest?" Amara asked.

Rolanzo steepled his fingers beneath his chin. "We're still working on it. I know the police are taking another look at it. He doesn't have family, which in this case worked in our favor. He hasn't been buried yet. Hopefully, we'll learn the true cause of his death."

"What was your friend's occupation?" she asked.

Rolanzo's gray eyes held hers a bit longer than necessary. Had she overstepped? Probably. She didn't care. People were getting killed while others tried to break into her and Terrance's homes. She needed to know what they were looking for.

"He was a maritime lawyer. He'd ended his law practice and purchased several freighters. A few years ago, he retired and sold the vessels. His wife recently passed and they had no children. When he wasn't traveling all over the world, he lived in his apartment on the Upper East Side of New York.

Ah, so this guy was rich, thought Amara.

As if he read her mind, Rolanzo nodded. "He was very wealthy."

Amara blushed and stood. "It was nice seeing you Mr. Dumont, uh...I mean Rolanzo. Welcome back. I hope you and Ms. Dora Lee had a wonderful honeymoon."

He gave a slight smile as she silently collected the coffee mugs and retreated to the kitchen.

Amara pulled out her phone, grabbed her laptop from the kitchen table and headed to Terrance's bedroom. It was time to do a bit of research while the two men talked. She wanted to go through the notes she'd photographed from Casey's storage unit. As she opened her laptop, she pondered Dumont's lawyer friend. If he lived in such a posh neighborhood, how did the man impersonating him gain access? It probably had a concierge and surveillance cameras. What had the cameras recorded during the timeframe he died?

Rolanzo stuck a thumb in the direction of Terrance's bedroom. "She is relentless. You've got your hands full with that one."

"Yep, and I'm crazy about her. I just wished she wasn't so darn inquisitive and as you aptly described, relentless."

Rolanzo laughed. "She's been that way since she was a child. She'll keep you on your toes. Hopefully that will avoid her from stepping on mine."

"Don't count on it 'Lanzo," Terrance wisecracked.

Rolanzo stood and prepared to leave. The two men embraced and Terrance walked the man who'd been like a father to the door. "Upgrade your security like I told you and change your pass code," Rolanzo advised.

Terrance looked sheepish. "Yes sir." When he opened the door, a member of Rolanzo's security team appeared to escort him to his SUV. Terrance glanced up and down the street before he closed the door.

Amara was typing furiously when Terrance entered the bedroom. She stopped and looked at her boyfriend. Her expression was one of amusement and admiration. "Italian, huh? What other languages do you speak?"

Terrance grinned as he sat on the edge of the bed, causing her laptop to move up and down from the extra weight. "Rolanzo speaks five languages fluently; Spanish, English, French, Italian, Russian and a bit of Mandarin Chinese."

Amara whistled. "How many of those languages do you speak?"

Terrance blushed. "All of them; just not fluently. When I moved in with Rolanzo, he exposed me to different languages and cultures. He'd speak a different language around the house and during dinner. His cook prepared dishes from those countries as well. Dora Lee took private lessons and is conversant in those languages."

He repositioned himself and leaned against the headboard. "Rolanzo's shipping business took him to distant ports in other countries. He wanted to understand what people were saying. Initially, he taught himself by reading foreign newspapers and watching their TV shows. Later, he took university courses and hired private tutors." The corner of his mouth lifted in a sly grin. "I'm sure he had a few lady friends to practice with when he visited their countries. I know he learned Russian from an older woman who lives in Moscow."

Amara's eyes widened. "That man never ceases to amaze me." She pointed at the laptop. "I was checking out the place where Rolanzo's friend lived." When Terrance frowned. Amara held up a hand and said, "I found the address from the newspaper and researched the layout of the building. It has top of the line security, a concierge, and doorman. An intruder would be hard pressed to enter the building undetected." She ran her finger over the touchpad and asked, "Do you think the killer might actually live in the same apartment building?"

"What?! Why would you think that?"

Amara pointed at her computer screen. "Here's the building layout. There's a front entrance and rear service entrance. The lobby and both doorways have cameras. The doorman opens the door and the concierge is positioned to view the entire lobby. If a stranger enters, the concierge would question the visitor, as I was initially questioned at Remy's apartment complex." She shrugged. "He could have lied, but the concierge is obligated to call the resident to verify the visitor before granting him access. That's not to say he couldn't slip past the concierge, but there are cameras and security in the building."

Terrance examined the layout. "I get the picture. Where are you going with this?"

"Rolanzo's men need to contact the security for the building and request video footage during the timeframe of Dumont's friend's death."

Terrance pressed his lips together. He was confident Rolanzo's men were doing just that.

"His men are on top of it. Good." Amara closed her laptop and stretched. There was no way she'd be able to continue her research with Terrance hovering. She also wanted to print out the notes from Casey's storage unit.

"I'm going to head home." When it looked as if Terrance would protest, she added, "It's time. The guys who came to your house were picked up and questioned by the police. Pradeep knows he's being watched as well as is his numbskull VP who came to my apartment. They'd be stupid to come to my apartment or follow me. I'll be okay. Plus, I've been checking my camera feed and no one has come to my door. I'll call you when I get home." She kissed him. "Thank you for keeping me safe."

Terrance knew it would be futile to protest. He walked her to the door and watched until she got into her car. As she backed out the driveway, he grabbed his keys and raced out the door.

Chapter 26

Amara checked her rearview mirror and surroundings as she drove home. She saw Terrance's car two cars behind and smiled. She'd played it safe and chose a route with less traffic.

There wasn't much research she could do on Casey's murder. Molloy was all over it and Terrance would be furious if she interfered.

The photo of the little girl she discovered in the storage unit niggled at her brain. She'd seen the girl before, but couldn't remember where. Amara parked her car, grabbed her satchel and duffle, and rushed up the steps two at a time. Terrance slowed and waited until her door closed.

She texted a thanks to Terrance and printed the notes and pictures she'd photographed in Casey's storage unit. She placed the printed pages on her carpet and carefully examined them. When Amara picked up the picture of the little girl, she remembered something! She grabbed her camera and reviewed the photos from the park and library box.

It was her! The little girl in the pink helmet! Who was she? Amara checked the time. It was too late to call the leader of the neighborhood watch. She'd have to wait until tomorrow. Perhaps he or one of the other members knew her. Amara tucked the photos inside a secret compartment in her satchel and laughed. She was as bad as Casey.

Her thoughts returned to Samesh. Had he been watching the little girl and intended to follow her?

The next hour was spent pouring over the notes from Casey's storage unit. They weren't dated or organized. Some were handwritten, while others were typed. She tamped down her frustration and carefully read through each note.

One thing was certain. Casey believed drugs were being transported with the tea and cosmetics from India. One note contained handwritten times and dates when the freighter docked at the pier. Amara stood and rolled the kinks from her neck and shoulders. It was time to do something else.

Duffle unpacked; she started a load of laundry. It was late, but Amara was too keyed up to sleep. She decided to call Remy. He'd provide a different perspective and she could discuss her theories.

When Remy answered, she heard a woman giggling in the background. Amara immediately hung up and texted an apology. She'd forgotten Remy was in Paris with his new friend. A smiley face emoji was texted with a promise to catch up on Monday.

Amara slapped her phone against her thigh and paced back and forth. What had Casey discovered that concerned the little girl? Was she related to Samesh or Pradeep in some way? Casey had included the girl's photo with Pradeep's children. What was the connection?

Amara jumped when her phone rang. It was a restricted number. Her finger hovered over the decline button momentarily before she ended the call. It was late and too much had happened. She also wanted to be able to sleep tonight. The phone rang once more from a restricted number. She allowed the call to go to voicemail. "What in the world?" she muttered. Though tempted to listen, she didn't. Not after finding Casey's car earlier that day. Had someone been watching them at the pier parking lot? Not to mention those international guys who'd attempted to break into Terrance's house.

She returned her attention to Casey's notes. They appeared to be random thoughts. Some sheets had a single word, random thought, or idea. One had the word "daughter" written on it.

One note alluded to an unnamed impostor while another contained a notation about an illegal shipment with a question mark. Several pages had diagrams without notations.

Amara set the notes aside and focused on the deceased maritime lawyer. He was just as Mr. Dumont described; a wealthy, well known attorney, and previous owner of a small freighter business. She reviewed a few of his cases. None seemed connected to Pradeep's companies. He'd opened his own law firm and practiced family law the past ten years.

A small article in the business section read he'd made a tidy sum on the sale of his ships to a private overseas company. Attempts to uncover the buyer proved unsuccessful. Had Mr. Dumont purchased the ships? According to what she could find, the year before his wife's death, they travelled the world. His social media page was filled with his travels and tributes to his deceased wife. "Why were you killed and why did that guy impersonate you?" she asked aloud. Amara yawned and collected the papers. She placed them in a neat stack on her kitchen table and went to bed.

Chapter 27

Amara and Terrance went to her parents' house for brunch after church. Her mother busied herself with reheating the breakfast casserole and mini quiches. Amara plucked a strawberry from the mixed fruit arranged on a misshapen platter she'd proudly made in elementary school.

She'd been distracted at church with thoughts of Casey's incomplete notes and drawings, the photo of the little girl, and the death of Mr. Dumont's friend. She doubted her father knew anything about the New York lawyer but planned to ask him after brunch.

She also intended to ask Terrance about the mystery man who'd crashed the wedding. There was no doubt Rolanzo knew his identity. He didn't tolerate people taking advantage or using him.

As if on cue, Terrance's phone rang. He excused himself and took the call. Amara forced herself to continue talking with her parents.

Terrance returned and rested his hand lightly on Amara's shoulder. "I'm sorry, I need to head to the station." He complimented Amara's mother and turned to her father. "Mr. Mackelroy, would you mind taking Amara home?"

"No problem son."

Amara tried to sound casual. "What's up?"

Terrance pressed his lips together. She knew that look. He couldn't say and would tell her later.

"Does this have to do with Casey's murder?"

"I'll call you when I can," he promised, and rushed out.

She moved the last of her casserole around her plate with her fork. Amara sighed and turned to her father. "Dad, I need your help with a law issue. Can we go to your study?"

"I'll sweep and wipe down the counters when I'm finished with dad," Amara called over her shoulder to her mother.

Jackson Mackelroy sat in the plush chair behind his desk. "What's going on?" He shook a finger in her direction before he continued. "If this has anything to do with Casey's murder..."

"Not exactly," she interjected. Her response was met with a raised brow. She fought the impulse to laugh aloud. It was the same look he used in court when he believed the witness wasn't being forthright.

"Dad, stop! We're not in a courtroom." She explained the situation regarding the death of Rolanzo's wedding guest.

"The police requested the ME to check the victim's body for signs of foul play. Dad, I'm not sure he died of natural causes. He lived alone and had no immediate family. His wife is deceased and they didn't have children."

Amara leaned close, her tone low, "He'd been a maritime lawyer." Before he could interrupt, she rushed on. "There's more!" She ticked off each fact using the tips of her fingers. "He quit his practice, purchased a fleet of ships, made a lot of money and was semi-retired."

Jackson removed his glasses and clasped his hands on his desk. She had his undivided attention.

"He started his own law firm a decade ago and practiced family law until his death." Amara saw the twinkle in her father's eyes and knew it was time to ask the favor. "Would you do some checking and find out what type of cases he tried in family court?"

"Yes, I can do that." He scribbled the information Amara provided.

She stood, walked around the desk, and gave him a quick peck on the cheek. "Thanks dad. I'd better go help mom."

Jackson waited until his daughter was out of the office and called a close friend who practiced in New York.

Amara put away the broom and wrung out the dish cloth as her mother entered the kitchen. She'd changed into a bright colored sundress. "You look pretty, Mom."

"Thanks, sweetheart." She pointed her thumb in the direction of her husband's study. "What was that about?"

Amara explained the conversation she had with her father. Her mother's displeased expression caused her to change the subject. "Did you know Mr. Dumont spoke five languages fluently and taught Terrance?"

Her mother raised a brow. "Yes, he'd drop by my class and we'd speak French."

"Get out of here! Really? You never told me that!"

"I don't tell you everything about my life, just as you don't tell me everything about yours," she retorted. Cora stared into her daughter's large brown eyes and automatically tucked an errant curl behind her ear. "Terrance is a nice young man. Are you two getting serious?"

Amara nodded. "I really like him." She blushed and confided, "I can see myself spending the rest of my life with him. He's so different from all my other boyfriends; especially Grainger. He respects my ideas and doesn't try to change me. Though he can be a bit overprotective."

She covered her mother's hands with her own. They were smooth and soft. Her manicured nails were trimmed short and painted a pale pink. "Plus, you like him."

Cora laughed and slipped her hands from beneath her daughter's and gave her shoulder a playful shove. "You've got that right! I never liked Grainger," she admitted. "He's a user and never fully appreciated you; only what you could do for him. I'm glad he found someone more compatible and married her. Good riddance I mean good luck to them both!"

Amara stared at her mother and laughed heartily.

Her mother turned serious. "Look, I know there was no love lost between you and Casey. I'm proud you stepped up and did the right thing. I'm sure her parents appreciate it. Cian Molloy is very good at what he does. Even though the man is so darn gruff, he's always had a soft spot for you. Ever since you were a little girl and would visit his office with your dad. You'd ask Cian hundreds of questions and he'd answer them. I respect that about him."

"I remember visiting his office. He was so imposing. But, you're right. He always took the time to answer my questions." She shook her head. "I know I get on his last nerve and he's wanted to wring my neck on more than one occasion."

"He'd better stand in line!" her mother joked.

Amara laughed and returned the conversation to Casey. "What else do you remember about Casey? How do you think Divya fits into all this?"

Her mother touched her wrist. "Hmm, Casey always wore a gold bracelet. I think it had a charm. You'd told me her dad bought it after her acceptance into the internship at the newspaper."

"Oh my gosh! I totally forgot about the bracelet! She showed it off to everyone. Wasn't there a diamond or her birthstone in the center, and her initials on the charm?" As her mother tried to remember more Amara slapped the counter. "Mom! You're brilliant!" She grabbed her phone and found a photo of Casey taken last month. There it was, a bracelet on her right wrist.

Amara phoned Terrance. It went to voicemail. She typed a text to him and Molloy.

"What bracelet? What are you talking about?" Molloy texted.

Amara didn't answer. She texted Mr. Athy next. He too responded quickly.

"Yes, she never took it off. It wasn't with her belongings returned by the police. Did you find it at the storage unit?"

"Oh, my goodness!" Amara whispered and typed a response to Mr. Athy.

Cora peered at Amara's cell phone and asked, "What's wrong?"

Amara showed her mother the text messages. She pocketed her phone and asked, "Want to take a drive to Schmitz Park?"

Her mother shrugged. "I'm sure we won't find anything after all this time, but it won't hurt to walk around a few of the trails." She patted her tummy and added, "I ate too much. A walk would be nice." She pointed at her sandals. "Let me change my shoes." Cora returned, called out to her husband, and grabbed her keys.

Chapter 28

Cora picked up the conversation where they'd left off as she drove. "You asked how Divya fit into this situation." Her eyes slid to Amara and returned to the road. "Divya lied in the past to shift the blame to you. Who's to say she hasn't done the same with her current husband?"

Amara thought about the photograph in which the couple was pointing at one another. The possibility caused her to shudder. What would Divya lie about? She'd been a widow before they married and was rich in her own right.

She doubted Divya ever had children of her own. Her second husband's children were adults when they married. If her research was correct, Pradeep's kids were reared by his parents after the death of his first wife. His daughter lived with her grandparents, not with him in Mumbai. Amara turned to her mother and replied, "That's a good question and I don't have an answer."

Cora glanced at her daughter and pursed her lips. "Are you taking care of yourself?"

Amara placed her phone on her lap. She knew her mother's question was code for, "Are you getting obsessed with this case?" Amara avoided the question and asked one of her own. "Mom, do you remember the last time we visited Schmitz Park?"

Her mother sighed. "Mari, what do you hope to find that the police haven't? It's been over a week since the poor child died."

She pointed at the clear, blue sky. "Actually, I just want to walk the trails at the park with my best friend."

Her mother parked the car and grabbed her sweater from the backseat. Cora switched to French. "Good answer! I don't believe you, but darn good answer. Is this about the charm?"

"Oui, Maman!" Amara replied.

Cora swatted her daughter's rear end and reverted to English. "I should have known."

The trails were crowded with noisy children, joggers, and couples strolling hand in hand. Cora pointed out flowers and plants for Amara to name. It was a game they played whenever they visited.

Amara dutifully recited their names. Shards of sunlight broke through thick branches like a beacon. The scent from the flowers and trees permeated the air as they strode along the damp earth of the trail.

Her mother pointed to a plant a few feet from the trail. Its leaves glittered from the shaft of sunlight. As Amara named the plant, her eyes widened. That wasn't all that glittered. The sun reflected on something that glistened in the dirt near the plant. She quickly tapped her mother's arm and pointed.

"Mom! No way! What's that?" she gasped. They were nowhere near the alligator landmark, located on the other side of the park.

Her mother shaded her eyes. "It's probably a bottle cap or shiny button someone lost."

Amara veered off the trail and removed her phone from her back pocket. She snapped several photos of the item embedded in the dirt. When she returned to the trail, Amara asked her mother for a tissue. She always kept a packet in her pocket.

Her mother tugged a tissue free from its fold, handed it to Amara, and followed her off the trail. They walked through the vegetation to the round, gold object.

Amara passed her phone to her mother, moved closer to the shiny object, and asked her mother to record her in case it proved to be something important. She stooped and used the tissue to dislodge the disc from the dirt. After Amara conducted a cursory search of the immediate area, her mother stopped the video and they returned to the trail. The sun had moved and the area became shaded once more. She held out the object in the tissue for her mother to see.

Cora stared at the muddy disc. "What is it?" she asked.

"I'm not sure." They moved back into the sunlight. When she flipped the gold disc over in the tissue, her breath caught. Though the surface was smudged with damp soil, she could see something engraved on the surface. The piece was badly scratched, but intact. There was no way to make out the writing without wiping away the dirt. It resembled the circular charm Casey wore. Hesitant to disturb the piece further, she asked her mother to contact Terrance.

His image appeared on the screen. Amara's words came out in a rush. "Terrance, I think I found something! It looks like a charm!" Her mother tilted the phone down so it focused on the object in the tissue. "There's something engraved on it, but I can't make out the writing without disturbing the dirt on it!"

"Amara what are you talking about? Where are you?" Terrance asked.

Amara took the phone with her free hand. "My mom and I are at Schmitz Park, nowhere near the alligator. Is it possible Casey was alive when she was brought to the park?" She swallowed hard and tried to get her breathing under control. "Wait! I'll have mom take a picture so you can see it more clearly!"

Cora snapped several photos of the charm and sent them to Terrance.

He stared at the photos. When he spoke, his words were rushed as he warned them to stay put, he was on his way. The call ended and Amara stared at her mother as she cradled the charm inside the tissue.

Cora felt a mixture of nerves and excitement. "It might be nothing, then again, it might be something big."

Amara asked her mother to send a copy of the photo to Molloy. She looked around the immediate wooded area for broken branches. She hadn't seen any blood on the ground when she picked up the small circular charm. But the murder took place last week.

Twenty-five minutes later, Terrance and Molloy jogged down the trail. Amara pointed in the direction they'd discovered the charm. "As you can see, we're nowhere near the spot where Casey's body was discovered. This trail is on the other side of the park." She handed Molloy the tissue.

He examined the charm without touching it. "Show me exactly where you found this."

Amara walked to the edge of the trail and pointed to the area. She showed them the video where she walked into the vegetation and removed the object.

Molloy wanted to chastise Amara for possibly contaminating a possible crime scene but couldn't. This might be evidence that belonged to his victim. "Okay, got it," he grunted. The detective dropped the charm into an evidence bag and informed Amara he'd send the piece to the lab. "I'll also contact Mr. Athy." Although his expression didn't match his words, he added, "It might be a coincidence."

"Except you don't believe in coincidences," Amara and Terrance chanted in unison.

Molloy's face flushed as he blustered, "Okay, okay...I'm going to head back to the station." He turned to Terrance. "I'll speak with the park manager and have him block off this trail. I'll let you know as soon as I get a confirmation. If it's what we think it is, we'll send out a K-9 unit and additional officers." He gestured at Terrance who was on his radio requesting a patrol. "Stay put until you hear from me."

Terrance was still dressed in his church clothes. He looped the badge that hung from a lanyard around his neck and walked to the entrance of the trail. He didn't have to wait long. The Schmitz Park manager arrived with signage and two orange cones to block the trail's entrance. Two patrol officers headed his way. The manager explained the access point at the opposite end of the trail would be blocked as well.

Though Amara wanted to stay, her mother guided her up the trail.

Amara gave Terrance a sad wave and peered at her mother. "What are the odds of that happening?!" she whispered.

Cora looked down the trail. "Extremely rare," she replied. Once they reached the car, Cora invited her daughter to stay overnight. Amara declined the offer. She wanted to research Divya and Casey a bit more.

Chapter 29

Molloy watched a tearful father lumber from his office. Mr. Athy confirmed the charm had belonged to Casey. Forensics would validate Mr. Athy's claim, though Molloy was certain Mr. Athy was right.

The detective watched the port video feed from the night Casey was murdered. Most of it was grainy. It was dusk when Casey pulled her car into the parking lot and got out. The video captured her walking toward the shuttle bus stop.

Four hours later, she appeared on video at the port. He could make out her long blond hair, light colored suit, and high heels as she walked alone near the pier where the freighter with Pradeep's shipment was docked. Casey looked around and ventured out of the view of the security cameras. Molloy cursed under his breath. It was apparent this wasn't the first time she'd visited the docks. She'd known how to avoid the cameras. How many times had she been there?

Molloy clicked his mouse and changed views. Several minutes later she reappeared. Her gait was unsteady. If he hadn't seen her minutes before, he'd swear she was drunk. She swayed and nearly fell. What had happened when she'd been out of the camera's range?

Molloy leaned forward and stared at the screen. A man appeared dressed in dark clothing and a baseball cap pulled low on his head. He'd come from the same direction as Casey.

The man grabbed Casey's arm as if to steady her and lead her away from the dock and moored ships. When they passed under the security lights, Molloy could make out Casey's face. The person who escorted her kept his face turned away. Casey's head slumped forward as the person tugged her along.

Molloy's fist pounded the desk as he stared at the video. The man in the cap kept his face hidden from the camera. Casey hadn't fought or attempted to flee. Had she known him? Molloy stared at the monitor hoping to glimpse the man's face when they reached bright security lights.

Suddenly, Casey rammed her elbow into her escort's stomach, turned to kick him hard in the groin. The man doubled over and she ran away. Her gait was unsteady and she lost her balance when the heel caught on the uneven pavement. Casey's hands shot forward as her body collided with the pavement. The injured man loped in her direction. Casey rolled onto her back and kicked off her shoes. She'd broken one of the heels. She scrambled to her feet and sprinted into the darkness, outside the view of the security cameras. The man paused to pick up the shoes and loped in the same direction.

Molloy clicked the mouse to view different vantage points. It was no use; they'd evaded the cameras and were gone. All that remained was blackness and the glare of bright lights from the docks. He tried the video feed from other port locations; nothing.

One thing was certain, Casey Athy was alive at the dock and had an altercation with an unknown assailant. Molloy returned his attention to the radio traffic from Schmitz Park. His phone rang. It was Terrance. He grabbed his jacket and headed to Schmitz Park.

The K-9 patrol headed down the park trail. Terrance could see the K-9 officer clutch a plastic bag with a piece of clothing. He removed the garment and allowed the dog to sniff before he released him from the leash and gave the command.

The dog scampered off the trail and was swallowed by vegetation. The sound of the K9 tearing through thick growth echoed a few feet away.

Terrance could make out the animal's head and tail as he reappeared in a small clearing. He held his breath when the K9 alerted on something in the dirt. The dog sat and waited for the handler to approach.

The handler made his way to his K9 and spoke words of praise, and carefully conducted a visual search of the immediate area. "There's something here!" he yelled.

Terrance watched as the handler collected a torn piece of cloth and gold bangle bracelet. He bagged each piece of possible evidence and continued to look around the area. "There's a set of large shoeprints over here!" the officer exclaimed.

Soon the park was filled with police officers. They discovered dried blood against one of the tree trunks near the location where the police dog alerted. They also made casts of the shoeprints from a pair of large, athletic running shoes in the damp earth. It was a miracle the shoe prints were still visible. The thick vegetation must have shielded it from the rain. Terrance stared in the direction where the K9 had alerted.

Somehow, Casey had escaped her abductor and run into the woods. He guessed by the blood on the tree; she'd been injured and hid behind it.

The attacker must have snuck up from behind and wrapped the braided cord around her neck. She'd died of asphyxiation, though it was clear she'd fought back. Terrance hoped the lab discovered forensic evidence that would help identify her attacker.

Terrance considered the new evidence. He turned in the direction Casey's body was discovered. The attacker must have carried her body to the other side of the park and placed her inside the alligator tree. Clever. Except it was dark and the killer was probably unaware the bracelet had fallen from her wrist.

Had Casey left the bracelet intentionally? If Amara hadn't discovered the charm, they'd never have found the actual location of the attack. Schmitz Park was huge! Even though the police swept the area; they'd focused on the vicinity where the victim's body was found. He ran a hand over his face. A needle in the haystack, indeed.

Terrance met Molloy on the trail as CSI arrived and took over the crime scene. After he'd briefed the detective, Terrance headed to his SUV. It was time to follow his godfather's advice and upgrade his security and change the code. He'd also upgrade Amara's alarm system. He wasn't certain Pradeep's people had stopped following her.

He considered the two calls she received from the restricted number as well as the voicemail. That couldn't be good. He wanted to listen to the voicemail.

Terrance went home and met with the security company his godfather used. Once they were finished, he drove to Amara's apartment.

Amara flung open the door. "What did you find?"

Terrance motioned the representative from the security company inside. "He's going to upgrade your security, starting with the locks on your door." The man quickly went to work. "He'll also upgrade your camera and install a new alarm."

Amara's lips puckered. "Did something else happen?" When Terrance didn't reply, she quieted and allowed the technician to complete the security upgrades.

Terrance saw her unease and whispered, "I just want you to be safe. Finding the evidence in the park this afternoon was incentive enough. I prefer to be overly cautious than caught unprepared. We don't know who we're dealing with. You've been followed around town and they were bold enough to send two men to break into my house. I'm a police officer, for goodness' sake!"

Amara exhaled and leaned against him. Terrance wrapped his arms around her as the technician finished. She knew he was right and didn't want to end up like Casey. She turned to face her boyfriend. "What's next?" she asked.

Terrance placed his hands on her shoulders. "We'll find whoever is responsible and put them away."

"I like the sound of that," she replied. Amara watched as the technician packed his tools and left. "He's not your regular security installer, is he?"

"Nope."

She knew by his tone not to ask more questions. She'd ask him about the charm and any other pieces of evidence discovered at the crime scene later.

Terrance gave her a quick kiss and handed her the new keys. "I need to get back to the station. I wanted to be here while the locks and upgraded alarm system were installed." He snapped his fingers and asked, "Did you listen to the voicemail you received last night?"

Amara shook her head and watched Terrance jog down the steps. She'd discounted the calls and voicemail. Her thoughts were on the new evidence found at the park. She closed the door and fingered the new keys.

Amara quickly forgot about the voicemail as she grabbed her laptop. She decided to focus her research on Samesh. Her father taught her the importance of knowing your enemy. Something from a book he'd read about the Chinese military general and philosopher, Sun Tzu. "It is more important to outthink your enemy than to outfight them." She typed in the name of Pradeep's VP. She knew he was at the crux of this chaos. It was time to learn more about this man and his life.

Amara stood and loosened stiff muscles. Her research revealed Samesh lived well beyond his means and wasn't ashamed to flaunt it. His annual income from the position he held at Pradeep's company would never cover the possessions he posted on social media. The expensive cars; a leased Maserati, a vintage Porsche, late-model Bentley, the yacht where he and his friends partied most weekends. Not to mention trips to France, London, India, Syria, and Bosnia on private jets. As well as the bevy of beautiful women of all nationalities that hung around him.

She had to admit, Samesh had great taste in women. Through his social media sites, she discovered he owned a home in Belize and a luxury condo off the water on 43rd street in Seattle. That alone was valued in the millions. He spent more money on his toys alone than he'd earn in several years.

Samesh came from an upper middle-class family and was educated at the University of Oxford. He and Pradeep had attended college together.

Amara decided to read Casey's articles on Pradeep for further insight. They weren't favorable. Her last story hinted he'd been involved in nefarious dealings. Though she didn't go into detail, it was easy to decipher her insinuations. Her photos exposed malnourished adults and children and their poor working and living conditions.

Terrance phoned while she made dinner with an update. Molloy had obtained video footage that proved Casey was alive at the pier. Of course, she was. Amara wondered if Molloy would allow her to read parts of Casey's journal.

She removed baked chicken from the oven and placed the pan on the trivet a bit harder than necessary. The detective's answer would be an emphatic no.

Amara activated her new alarm and made her way to the bedroom. Though it was earlier than her usual bedtime, the day's events left her exhausted. Tired fingers clasped spiral curls and bound them with a thick satin wrap. A weary sigh escaped as she slipped into bed. This Sunday had not been a day of rest.

Chapter 30

Amara glanced at Remy as he sauntered into the office whistling a familiar French tune. Showoff, she thought. He looked tan and relaxed as he sat at his desk. Amara lifted a brow as he continued to whistle *Je l'aime a mourir* by Cabrel. She knew the tune by heart because her mother used to play the song over and over. It was one of the ways she'd learned French, through songs.

She glared in his direction and asked him to knock it off in French.

Remy grinned and whispered, "jealous" in French. Several staff members stopped typing to observe the friendly banter.

Amara blushed at the unwanted attention and returned to typing.

Remy chuckled and muttered, "trouble maker," in French.

Amara sent him a message letting him know she had something important to share during lunch. He responded in French and asked to meet at their favorite Thai restaurant. She answered, "yes," and ended the message with the word, "smarty pants" in French.

Remy smiled and returned his attention to his new article.

At lunch Remy slouched in their booth and yawned. "I guess I'm a bit jet lagged." He focused tired eyes on Amara. "What did you want to talk about?"

By the time Amara finished, Remy was alert and sitting up straight. "I can't believe I missed all the excitement!" He leaned forward. "What happens now?"

Amara played with her chopsticks. "It's up to the detectives." Amara looked around the restaurant and added, "I think Samesh is dirty. He's living way beyond his income and flaunts it! There's no way he can he afford all the toys and travel on his income." Her voice was low as looked around the restaurant once more. "He was the one in the yellow dingy and I bet my paycheck he attacked Casey at the pier."

Remy shook his head. "What!? I thought Pradeep was the culprit?"

Amara's curls swished in front of her face. "Pradeep lives well within his means. We both know Divya is twice as wealthy as her husband. I focused on Samesh last night. I plan to check out Divya's businesses next. Plus, there's this young girl..."

"Back up. What girl? Who are you talking about?"

Amara explained the photo she discovered in Casey's storage unit and the pictures she'd taken at the library box. "They're the same girl! I'm going to contact the leader of the neighborhood watch today. He might know who she is."

The conversation halted when the waitress placed spicy chicken pad Thai noodle dishes on the table. Remy wasted no time and dug in. "I can check into Divya's businesses tonight. I agree with your theory about Samesh. Let me ask some of my friends about him. If he's hanging around with the rich and famous, I'll find out."

Amara's shoulders relaxed. She'd hoped he'd offer to help.

Remy squinted and pointed his fork in her direction. "You're making me nervous. It's never a good thing when you smile like that. What are you up to?"

"I'm just glad you're back and willing to help."

"Of course! You'd be lost without me," he bragged. "Plus, I've got the connections."

"True, true," she confessed. She leaned against the cushions. "Now, tell me all about your trip!"

Remy removed his phone and scrolled through photos. His voice was animated as he told her about the sites and places they'd visited.

Chapter 31

After lunch, Amara phoned the leader of the neighborhood watch group. He provided the number of a member who had daughters the same age as the young girl.

Amara was relieved the woman answered. She went through her spiel once more and sent the photo of the girl. She held her breath while the woman examined the photo.

"Ah, yes! She plays with my girls often. Her little brother is a terror," the woman sighed and added, "Sorry, I shouldn't have said that. He's a rambunctious boy and I have girls. I'm not used to that level of energy."

Amara listened intently as the woman continued. "Her name is Ella. She was adopted as a baby by a nice Indian couple. They're both doctors. As I understand it, they had a relative in India who gave birth to the little girl and couldn't take care of her. They were able to go through a quick adoption process since they maintain dual citizenship. Two years later she got pregnant and had their son."

Amara scribbled notes. "Do you know Ella's last name?" The woman provided the information and Amara thanked her.

The rest of the day dragged on. She checked her watch and shut down her computer. There was no need to stay late.

Remy followed suit. He was exhausted.

Amara waved at office mates and got into her car. Her phone rang as she drove home. Her father's deep voice boomed through the speakers.

"Hey, Pumpkin, how was your day?"

She told him what she'd discovered about the little girl from the photo found in Casey's storage unit. "She was adopted, Dad."

"Well, perhaps my information will prove helpful. The lawyer you asked me to research dealt with adoptions. In particular; foreign adoptions by parents residing in the U.S."

Amara's breath hitched. "Do you think he was somehow involved with this adoption?"

There was a pause. "I don't know, Mari. He facilitated adoptions of Indian, Chinese, Russian, African, infants and toddlers to American parents."

"Wow! Thanks, Dad!" she exclaimed and ended the call. Had this lawyer helped the family adopt Ella? If so, what was Samesh's interest in the girl?

This confirmed he'd been focused on the child when she'd snapped photos at the library box. "What do you think I know?" she asked aloud.

Amara entered her apartment and kicked off her shoes. Terrance was working late. She made dinner and contemplated her next move. It was time to call her mother for advice.

"Hey, baby," her mother answered. The happy lilt in her voice made Amara smile.

"Mom, I want to bounce something off you and get your perspective." Amara added spaghetti noodles to boiling water and took a seat. "Dad just phoned with information about the lawyer who died. You know, the one who was supposed to be Mr. Dumont's wedding guest. It turns out, he practiced family law and specialized in adoptions of foreign babies and toddlers."

"Your dad told me. Do you think there's a link between the lawyer's death and Casey's?"

Amara pulled the phone from her ear and stared at it. Was this her mother, all calm and talking about not one murder, but maybe two?

"Yes, I think it might be a possibility. It's the same girl in the photo I got from Casey's storage unit. I'm sure there's a connection, but I can't piece it together. That's why I called you."

Amara checked her noodles and poured spaghetti sauce in another pot. She crumbled frozen ground turkey into the pot while she waited for her mother to respond.

"Well," drawled mother. "It could be his love child."

"Mother!" Amara squawked.

Her mother tsked. "Stop sounding so pious. What do you know about this man?"

"I know that he lives well beyond his means and is a playboy."

Her mother thought a moment. "If that's the case, I highly doubt he'd want to support a child."

Amara needed to think this through. Her mother had a valid point. Would information about an illegitimate child be worth killing someone else over? She wasn't sure. "Thanks Mom. You gave me more to consider."

After dinner, Amara pondered her next move. What does Divya do with all her money? Does she work, own businesses? She didn't find any information regarding possible children. Her husband spent half the year in India at his Mumbai office.

Legs crossed; she opened her laptop. Amara navigated through different sites without success. It was time to try something else. She stood and grabbed her phone.

Amara needed to call Mr. Dumont about his wedding guest. She sighed and texted Terrance. A text was quickly returned. "Go for it."

"Dumont's residence," a nasal, female voice answered. Amara asked to speak with Mr. Dumont. She was placed on hold a few seconds before Rolanzo answered.

"Amara, what may I do for you this evening?" His deep voice resonated through the receiver.

She paused and forced herself to remain calm. "Good evening Mr. Dumont, I apologize for disturbing you, but I discovered some information I'd like to discuss."

"I'm all ears," he replied.

Amara began to tell him what she knew regarding the lawyer and the little girl. The line was quiet several seconds. "Hello, Mr. Dumont, Rolanzo, are you still there?"

"Yes, I'm here. It's just a shock. Today we learned the police discovered new evidence. My dear friend might have been murdered."

Amara sighed. "I'm very sorry. I know Detective Molloy is working on the identity of the person who attended your wedding under false pretenses. Do you know who he is?"

"Yes."

His icy tone caused her to switch topics. "Would you happen to know if your friend had anything to do with the adoption of a child born in India?" She gave Ella's full name.

"I'll have to do a bit of research." Rolanzo waited a beat and added, "Be careful. The people involved in this are dangerous. They killed Casey and most likely murdered my friend. I don't believe they'd think twice about adding you to the list."

Amara felt as if the air had left her lungs. "Th-thank you for your time," she stammered. The line went silent. Rolanzo had ended the call. Amara cupped her face in her hands and asked aloud, "What should I do next?"

When she returned to her research, Amara couldn't find what Divya did with her time or money.

She considered her conversation with Mr. Dumont and was glad she'd informed Terrance beforehand. Rolanzo considered her a busybody. Partly true; though her main goal was to ferret out information about Casey's death. Why had she been murdered? More important, what does Divya have to do with all of this? Why was Samesh so interested in Ella? Who are her biological parents?

She snatched a sheet of paper, jotted down four names, and drew circles and lines linking each circle together. In the center of the paper, she drew a large question mark. Was there a link between Ella, Casey, and Samesh, and now the dead lawyer?

Amara tapped her pencil against the notepad as she considered Pradeep's latest shipment. She grabbed her phone and called Terrance. "Hey, was contraband discovered in the shipment at the pier?"

His response was terse: "No." He explained he was busy and would call later.

She fidgeted with the pencil while she looked at the names she'd written. Someone ordered the contraband to be removed from the shipment before the authorities could inspect it. She drew another circle around Samesh's name.

Dora Lee watched her husband pace back and forth. "That girl is going to get herself killed. She's too damn smart for her own good," he complained.

His wife patted the sofa. Rolanzo strode over and sat down. She took his hands in hers. "Honey, Amara is a grown woman. You've known her since she was old enough to eavesdrop by her father's door. That child has always been inquisitive. It's a blessing and a curse. You warned her and that's all you can do right now."

He tried to speak, but was shushed with a passionate kiss. He wrapped his arms around his new wife as thoughts about Amara evaporated.

Chapter 32

Terrance stared at Molloy's computer screen. They'd discovered the identity of the man who'd pretended to be the dead lawyer at the wedding. Gerard was a con-man who'd done time for fraud, theft, and burglary. He'd impersonate guests at parties to scope out the residence and security systems, then return when no one was home and steal their valuables.

There was a warrant for his arrest in New York for six burglaries in Manhattan. He'd never committed murder or assault in the past. What had changed his modus operandi? According to the NYPD, the suspect had vacated his apartment last week. The apartment manager complained he'd left the place in shambles.

The police had a video of him in front of the lawyer's apartment and his departure from the service entrance. They'd questioned his landlord and neighbors, but he'd kept a low profile.

Terrance wondered if he'd met the same fate as the man he'd impersonated once the deed was completed?

His quick departure suggested someone was after him. The NYPD reported his apartment had been ransacked.

Terrance rubbed his eyes. It was late and he was ready to head home. He wondered how to tell Amara the news. If he didn't tell her, she'd eventually find out from someone else. He called her and asked to come over.

Amara checked the time. It was eleven o'clock. What was so important he felt the need to tell her tonight? She looked down at her lavender flannel pajamas and wondered if she should change. Amara removed the head wrap, fluffed her curls, and put on a little lip gloss. She didn't want to look a total wreck when he arrived.

"What's going on?" she asked when he arrived.

"We've identified the man we suspect impersonated the lawyer at Rolanzo's wedding."

"Who is he? Where is he now? Did he murder the Mr. Dumont's friend?" She took a breath, sat down on the sofa, and motioned for him to take a seat.

Terrance sat and shared what he'd learned. "Gerard is a small-time thief and burglar. We don't know if he's responsible for the lawyer's death, but he'd left his apartment in a hurry and someone broke in. The place had been ransacked."

He looked at her worried expression pulled her close. "Don't worry, it's only a matter of time before the police track him down."

"Why would a thief resort to murder?" she asked.

Terrance stared at his fresh-faced girlfriend in her cute flannel pajamas. Suddenly he didn't feel like discussing Gerard. He framed her face with his strong hands and kissed her passionately. "It's going to be okay. I just wanted you to hear the news from me."

Amara wrapped her arms around his neck and deepened the kiss. "Are you sure that's all you wanted?"

Terrance growled as he picked her up, carried her to the bedroom, and shut the door with his foot.

"Wait," she said. "You didn't finish telling me about the guy!" All talking ceased when he laid her on the bed and slowly unbuttoned her pajama top.

Chapter 33

Amara awoke with a warm body curled close to hers. She peeked at the clock on her nightstand and groaned. It was set to go off in five minutes. She shut off the alarm and ambled to the bathroom to get ready for work.

She kissed Terrance on his forehead. He mumbled something that sounded like, "Have a good day." Amara drank in the sight of his handsome face before she tiptoed out the room. The front door closed with a soft click as she headed out the apartment.

Terrance was awakened by muffled sounds from the living room. He sat up and checked the clock on the night stand. It was nine o'clock. Amara had gone to work hours ago. The mirror on the wall showed a red lipstick print on his forehead where'd she'd kissed him before she left. Terrance wiped it away, pulled on his pants and grabbed his pistol. He sent a quick text to the station and crept barefoot into the carpeted hallway.

Two men in dark clothing were rummaging through Amara's kitchen cabinets. The metallic click of his pistol got their attention.

"Police! Hands up, now!" he commanded.

The man closest to him stopped and immediately obeyed. The second intruder turned and ran to the door. As the door swung open, Terrance warned, "Stop right there or I will shoot!"

The man halted, turned, and faced Terrance; his trembling hands extended as high as he could reach. He looked young. Possibly in his early twenties. His shoulder-length hair was shaved on both sides.

A large man filled the doorway. Terrance took aim.

"It's me!" Dumont's man shouted.

Terrance kept his pistol aimed at the other two men, while Dumont's man bound the men's hands with plastic zip ties.

"Thanks," Terrance grunted. His focus returned to the men.

"Who are you and what are you two doing in this apartment?" he challenged.

The man with the hair shaved on both sides began to blubber, "Hey, I didn't sign up for this. We thought no one was home and..."

"Shut the hell up!" his partner snarled. He glared in Terrance's direction. "We have nothing to say to you. We want a lawyer."

Before he could question them further, two police officers clomped up the stairs and took the two men into custody. The officers recognized Terrance and motioned for him to put his weapon away. The squeal of tires echoed from outside the apartment as another patrol arrived.

The trespassers were loaded into the police sedans and transported to the police station. The officers took statements from Terrance and David, Dumont's man.

After the police departed, David pointed at the yellow puddle in the carpet where one of the trespassers stood. "Mackelroy's daughter is gonna be upset if she comes home to an apartment smelling like pee. You'd better take care of that."

Terrance swore under his breath, stomped to the kitchen, removed the box of baking soda from the refrigerator, and sprinkled an ample amount on the stain. His eyes turned to slits as he glared at Dumont's security. "What are you doing here?!"

David exhaled through his nose. "Your girl called Rolanzo last night about the wedding guest found dead in his apartment. She believed his death was related to the other murder and asked Rolanzo some questions." He shrugged and added, "Rolanzo thought she might be in danger. She's getting too close to something and someone doesn't want her to figure it all out."

Terrance's mouth felt dry. He'd gotten sidetracked and hadn't finished telling her everything he'd learned last night.

"Uh huh. So, he sent me to keep an eye on things. I saw them go in, but I didn't know you were here." He looked at Terrance's bare chest and gave a wicked grin. "I was going to wait until they left and follow them. When the door flew open and they hadn't left, my plan changed."

Terrance ran a hand through his hair and thanked David, who lifted his chin in response and jogged down the steps to his car.

As Terrance drove to the station, he phoned Rolanzo to find out what he and Amara discussed. When he arrived, Detective Molloy asked him to come to his office.

The detective reclined in his seat, holding a set of lock pick tools. "These were discovered in the pocket of one of the men you found in Amara's apartment this morning. I'm about to interview them. Want to listen in?"

After work, Terrance went home to change and drove to Amara's office. Remy gave a quick greeting. Amara's smile was wide as she stood and grabbed her purse. "This is a nice surprise." Terrance rarely showed up unannounced to take her to dinner. She felt special.

"Are you finished for the day?" he asked. He wore what Amara called his cop face.

She checked her watch and replied, "Yep, I missed lunch and can leave early!" Amara grabbed Terrance's hand as they walked to his car. When she glanced at his profile, her smile faded. "What's wrong?"

"Let's get something to eat and I'll tell you all about it."

Remy watched the couple depart. Terrance didn't look happy. "Uh oh," he muttered and continued to type his article.

Amara leaned her hip against the passenger door. She crossed her arms under her breasts and asked, "What's wrong and why are you really here? Did you speak with Mr. Dumont? You said it was okay to call him." Amara waited for Terrance to respond.

Terrance turned to face her; all pretenses dropped. "Let's talk in the car."

She hesitated a beat before opening the door. Hands folded in her lap. "We're not going to dinner, are we?" Terrance shook his head.

She pushed curls away from her face. "Judging by your expression, you have something you want to say. Let's hear it."

Terrance told her about the two men in her apartment. "You're asking too many questions and getting way too close to this case! Remember what happened with the Simpson murder case."

Amara inhaled sharply. It felt as if he'd slapped her. "Wait! What!?" Her shock quickly turned to anger. "Oh! So, because I called Mr. Dumont and researched people involved in this case, I caused two men I've never met to break into my home?! Is that what you're saying?!"

"Screw this and screw you!" she shouted and flung open the car door. She was tired. Tired of always having to defend herself, tired of people thinking it was okay to attack her at will. Enough was enough! Amara stomped from Terrance's car, not bothering to close his door. She slid onto the driver's seat of her car and sped out the parking lot without a backward glance.

Terrance leaned over, pulled the passenger door shut, and rested his head against the steering wheel.

Amara called Molloy and asked if she could come see him. Though he sounded distracted, he invited her to join him at his favorite deli near the police station.

Amara donned sunglasses against the late afternoon sun and to hide her red, puffy eyes. A slight breeze tousled her curly mane as she headed to the glass door of the deli. Molloy had already ordered two sandwiches, chips, and drinks. Amara sat down hard on the wooden chair and released an exasperated breath.

Molloy bit into his sandwich. Amara knew he wasn't going to make it easy for her.

She removed her glasses, unwrapped the Reuben sandwich, and bit into the dense, rye bread. She sipped her Coke and took another bite of sandwich. As she tore open the bag of chips she grumbled, "I guess you know someone broke into my apartment. Do you know what they were looking for or who they are?"

Molloy chewed slowly. "Both suspects had lawyers. I'm not sure what they were searching for, but I believe it has something to do with the young girl you photographed. The one who matched the photo from our victim's storage unit."

"How did you come to that conclusion?"

Molloy pointed a stubby finger in her direction. "You've been asking questions about her. You also had your dad check on that dead lawyer, the one who handled foreign adoptions."

Amara's eyes grew wide. How on earth does he know that, she wondered? Her dad must have tattled.

"Not to mention you were involved in finding the charm and bracelet we've confirmed belonged to Casey Athy."

"Again, what is it they think I possess and who are these men?"

Molloy lowered his voice. "You need to leave this alone. They believe you have information that is detrimental to Pradeep's company. The police responded to your apartment while Terrance and Dumont's man were there."

Amara placed her sandwich on the plate and wiped her fingers. "What information? Did my dad tell you I was asking about the girl? Yes, I know she's adopted. Have you learned the identity of her biological parents or who broke into my apartment?!"

Molloy shook his head and sighed. "Terrance told me you spoke with Rolanzo Dumont about the lawyer and young girl. As for the two suspects; you're not going to like what I have to say."

"Just give it to me straight."

Before he could reply, his phone rang. Molloy held up his forefinger in Amara's direction and answered the call. He pressed the phone tight against his ear as he stood, muttered an apology, and bounded out the door.

Amara watched as he strode in the direction of the police station. She picked up her sandwich but her appetite was gone. Her breath caught and she lifted her face to fight the tears. As the sun began to set, Amara made her way to her car.

At least it wasn't raining. That was one thing she didn't have to add to her dismal day. How had the day gone from great to awful so quickly?

Chapter 34

Detective Molloy was about to tell her something regarding the men who'd broken into her apartment. He said she wasn't going to like it. What had he meant? Terrance had ruined her day; what was a bit more bad news? Amara's fist pounded the steering wheel as she drove home.

What if the intruders' goal was not to take something, but to leave something? Her phone vibrated and she checked the caller's ID on the screen in her car. Amara declined the call. She was in no mood to speak with Terrance.

Amara parked in front of her apartment and jogged up the stairs. When she opened the door, her attention was drawn to a mound of white powder in the middle of her carpeted floor. It looked like baking soda. Had Terrance or the intruders spilled something? After changing out of her work clothes, she donned rubber gloves, grabbed the small broom used to sweep her car mats and swept up most of the baking soda. She absently vacuumed over the spot as her thoughts drifted to her current predicament.

She checked the spot. There was no stain. She ruminated over Casey and the dead lawyer as she continued to vacuum. Am I going to be the third victim? Her hand clasped the vacuum handle tight. She felt more anger than fear.

Terrance's attitude and their short discussion caused her to push the vacuum harder than necessary. She'd really tried to remain out of the investigation. Hadn't she? Before Amara knew it, she'd vacuumed her entire apartment.

She checked the locks and alarm system. Amara hated feeling paranoid and unsafe in her own home. She retrieved a ladder from her closet, positioned it in front of the first set of cabinets, climbed to the highest rung, and opened the cabinet doors.

Amara stacked dishes and glasses on the counter. Her gloved fingers felt unsteady as she methodically traced the inside the cabinet from top to bottom, side to side, to the bottom of the shelves.

Her index finger swept across a small circular disc the size of a pencil eraser. On tip toes, she peered inside the cabinet and caught sight of a round, brush nickel object tucked in the far corner. She tugged the disc from the particle board and examined it in the palm of her hand. Amara grabbed a sandwich bag and placed the disc inside. She followed the same process for each cabinet and located three identical discs. Listening devices. What on earth did they think she'd say? Amara nearly fell from the rung of the ladder when her phone chimed. It was Remy.

"Hey, is everything okay?" he whispered.

"Why are you whispering?" she asked.

Remy blew out an exasperated breath. "You know why. Mandatory dinner at Matt's."

Amara stifled a laugh. She could always count on Remy to cheer her up. She took a photo of one of the devices and sent it to Remy. "I sent you a photo. I found it in my kitchen cabinet."

Remy looked at the picture. "Let's meet at my place in a couple hours," he suggested.

Amara rolled her eyes. "Can't we discuss it now? Why do you think it was planted in my cabinet?"

Remy repeated his invitation and ended the call. She stared at the phone before sliding it into her back pocket and continuing her search.

Five discs were neatly stacked on top of each other inside the sandwich bag. There were no devices beneath her lamps, tables, or chairs. Terrance must have caught them before they could hide more. Who would want to listen to her conversations and what did they think she knew?

Her phone buzzed once more. She glanced at her phone and ignored the call. After a hot shower, Amara scrutinized her reflection in the mirror. She'd lost a lot of weight dealing with the murders committed by Ralph Simpson and the threats that spilled over to her family. She'd never been a skinny woman. Her voluptuous figure wouldn't allow it. But she enjoyed her new, slimmer size. It was surprisingly easy to maintain. She jogged regularly. Amara pursed her lips and smiled at the beautiful woman in the mirror.

Her mother called and invited her to dinner. Amara told her mother about the break-in at her apartment and Terrance's reaction. Cora's invitation to stay at the house was readily accepted. The plan was to stay at her parents' house until the current issue was resolved, which she hoped would be soon.

Amara dressed in jeans and one of her favorite soft t-shirts. She'd tamed the curls that spiraled down her back in ringlets. Her packed duffle bag with several changes of clothes and toiletries sat in the corner. The thought of her mother's pot roast made her stomach rumble. She'd only eaten half of her sandwich at the deli. Amara retrieved her duffle, laptop, and set her alarm. She double checked both locks and headed to her car.

Chapter 35

Terrance felt awful. He'd overreacted. Instead of calmly discussing the issue, he played the blame game. When would he learn? Amara was unlike any woman he'd ever dated. It was a challenge keeping up with her. To make matters worse, he'd allowed the fear of keeping her safe override his common sense. He checked his phone. She hadn't read any of his text messages and refused his calls. When he drove by her apartment, her parking space was empty.

His next call was to Amara's mother. Her line was busy. Amara was probably at her parents or Remy's discussing what a jerk he'd been.

Terrance slapped the steering wheel. He hadn't told Amara the two men who broke into her apartment were hired to place listening devices. They claimed to not know what information was supposed to be gathered. Both were interns at Pradeep's company.

They'd been informed a co-worker supposedly living in Amara's apartment had taken sensitive information regarding their face creams and leaked confidential information to competitors. The intruders refused to divulge their boss' name. He knew they worked at Pradeep's company and had picked the lock to gain access into Amara's apartment. She hadn't locked the new bolt lock or activated the alarm because he'd stayed overnight.

He considered Amara's discussion with Rolanzo. Was the little girl related to Pradeep or his VP? If yes, why had they stalked the young girl?

Several minutes later his phone rang. "I saw your call," Cora said. "I was speaking with Amara."

Her tone let him know she was aware of what had occurred between him and her daughter. Terrance took a slow, deep breath and released it before admitting he'd screwed up.

"Well, you'd better find a way to fix it. I'm not living with a gloomy child for the rest of the week!"

Terrance smiled. She'd gone to her parents; good. "Thank you, Mrs. Mackelroy. I'm ready to grovel if necessary."

Cora harrumphed and mentioned they were having pot roast if he'd like to join them for dinner.

Terrance was headed to the Mackelroy's home and thinking how best to apologize to Amara when Molloy phoned and asked him to come to the station as soon as possible.

"The two suspects who broke into Amara's apartment were hired by a programmer who works at Pradeep's company," Molloy said.

"What connection does this guy have to Pradeep, other than being one of his employees?" Terrance asked.

"Good question. I know you're aware of the suspects' story about stolen sensitive information supposedly hidden in Amara's apartment." Molloy rolled his eyes. "The employer who allegedly requested the devices be installed is here for questioning. I thought you might like to listen to the interview."

Terrance followed the detective to an empty room adjacent to the interview room.

A clean-cut Caucasian man with dark brown, wavy hair and hazel eyes sat in the interview room. He looked to be in his mid-thirties. Molloy entered and introduced himself. He wasted no time getting to the point. He explained the two suspects identified him as the one who hired them to break into an apartment.

The employer vehemently denied any collusion with the suspects. He stood, and informed Molloy he was leaving unless he planned to arrest him. The detective had no option but to allow him to leave.

Molloy's green eyes bore into the man's back as he sauntered out the room. He'd been clever. The police couldn't prove a connection between him and the two suspects. All the text messages and phone calls regarding the break-in were between the two detained suspects. But if this man was involved, Molloy would find out. There'd be a misstep and when it occurred, he'd be waiting.

Terrance met Molloy in the hallway. "What do you think?"

Molloy frowned. "I think he's lying. I plan to dig deeper into his background. He's involved with this case. I can't prove it yet, but I sure feel it."

Terrance glanced down the hall and watched the man leave the station. He walked out through the doors as if he hadn't a care in the world. "You may be right," Terrance said.

Molloy grunted and made his way to the bank of elevators. "Don't worry, we'll keep an eye on him."

Terrance headed to the Mackelroy's house. He knocked on the door and Cora answered. He was on the porch, eyes cast downward. She almost felt sorry for him...almost.

Her brow quirked as she stood in the doorway.

Terrance met her gaze and cleared his throat. He felt like a sixteen-year-old asking the parent of a girl he liked if she could go out on a date. "Good evening, Mrs. Mackelroy, may I have a word with Amara?" A few seconds passed before Cora stepped back and allowed him to enter. "Thank you," he said shyly.

"We're in the kitchen eating dinner. Have you eaten?" He shook his head. She patted his back and said, "Come have dinner with us."

Jackson Mackelroy's eyes brightened at the sight of Terrance. "Terrance, so nice of you to join us. Mari didn't tell us you were coming over!" He gestured to the empty seat. "Please sit down. There's plenty and my wife makes a killer pot roast," he bragged.

Terrance chanced a glance in Amara's direction. She continued to eat without acknowledging him.

The conversation was lively around the table. Terrance nearly forgot Amara was furious with him. Except for the fact she hadn't spoken to him. At least she hadn't been nasty or asked him to leave.

Once dinner was finished, Cora shooed the couple to the family room while she and her husband straightened the kitchen. Amara led the way.

Before they sat down, Terrance touched her shoulder. She glanced in his direction. "Amara, I'm sorry. I was wrong. I should have listened to what you had to say before I began making accusations."

Amara's lips were pressed together in a straight line. She was angry and hurt. The worst part was the break-in occurred *after* she'd left for work. To make matters worse, she hadn't asked to be involved in the case. The Athy's had asked her.

Terrance's eyes pleaded for her to understand and forgive him.

They sat down and Amara motioned for him to speak. "You came over for a reason. Say whatever it is you came to say." Her words were clipped and direct.

Terrance explained what transpired at the police station and passed on information about the two men who'd broken into her apartment. "They confessed to hiding five listening devices in your apartment," he said.

"You mean these?" Amara fished her phone from her pocket and showed him the photos.?"

Terrance stared at the photo and confirmed she was correct. His voice was barely above a whisper.

Amara went to her purse that hung on the coat rack, removed the baggie with the devices, and handed it to him. She slung the long strap of her purse across her body. "I'm going over to Remy's for a while. I plan to stay here a few days until things die down."

He'd been dismissed! His legs felt unsteady when he stood. Amara's eyes blazed with indignation. She was not going to make this easy. "Okay, I guess I'll go," he said.

Amara's training kicked in as she escorted him to the door. Though she thanked him for stopping by, her voice was flat, devoid of emotion.

He heard the soft click of the door as he walked to his car and sighed. She'd not said a word before she closed the door.

Amara took in a shaky breath and returned to the kitchen. It took all her willpower to prevent angry tears from falling.

"Hey Pumpkin, your mom told me what happened. I'm so sorry. What are you going to do now?"

"I'll stay here until the weekend. I don't feel safe at home right now. I met with Molloy earlier, but our meeting was cut short when he was called back to the station." Amara adjusted her purse strap and removed her phone from her pocket. She read the text from Remy and told her parents she'd be at his place for a couple of hours.

Her mother moved in close and tucked a loose curl behind her ear. "Don't be too hard on Terrance. He meant well."

"I'll see you two later," she said. Amara grabbed her jacket and texted Remy to let him know she was on her way.

Chapter 36

Remy whistled as Amara gave a quick rundown of events. "Dang, woman! You are a magnet for trouble," he teased.

Amara threw a paper clip and hit him in the chest. When he collapsed in his chair and pretended to be wounded, she laughed.

Remy was pleased he'd been able to coax her into a better mood. "You know you're going to forgive Terrance." He raised his hands defensively as if to prevent her from throwing another paper clip. He peeked around his hands. "I agree, he'd been a jerk. But it's no secret the guy is crazy about you." He tilted his head. "I think the feeling is mutual."

A blush crept up Amara's neck to her cheeks. "Okay, yes! The feeling is mutual. But right now, I'm really pissed at him. Terrance didn't allow any discussion or listen to what I had to say. He just showed up at the office, ready to chew me out! That was foul!"

Remy's head bobbed up and down before he deftly changed the subject. "So, you discovered the listening devices and these guys work at Pradeep's company. There's no doubt this is connected to the murders. Though, I'm not sure how the little girl fits into all this.

They discussed possible reasons Casey might have been murdered. Assuming it boiled down to money, the question was, whose money and why. Remy promised to research Pradeep further. Amara checked her watch and stood. She felt anxious. They were no closer to a solution than when she arrived.

"I plan to speak with Molloy and give Mr. Dumont a call later this week. Maybe they discovered something." She looked out at the Puget Sound and added, "I'm not sure what the detective will be able to share." Amara held up three fingers. "We know there's a connection between the girl, Pradeep, and his VP. The questions are, how, why and the importance of it all."

Remy walked her to the door. "Be careful," he cautioned.

Amara promised she would. Paying extra attention to her surroundings, she drove directly to her parents' house.

The house was quiet. Amara went to her room, showered, put on her pajamas, and grabbed her laptop. She had a lot to think about. Molloy and Mr. Dumont were at the top of her list to contact tomorrow. It was a waiting game for now.

She needed to do something to take her mind off the situation. Amara tried to work on the article about the foster children, but was at a standstill. Perhaps it was time to consider another tack. Amara yawned, closed her laptop, and slipped under the covers.

When her alarm buzzed the next morning, she felt exhausted. Thoughts of Casey's murder and the death of the lawyer kept her awake most of the night. She'd also thought about the little girl who'd been given up for adoption nearly a decade ago. Why was it such a huge issue now?

In the kitchen, she breathed in the aroma of fresh brewed coffee and something scrumptious baking. Her mother removed a breakfast casserole from the oven. "Mm, that smells wonderful!" Her mother signaled for her sit down at the kitchen table.

Cora poured her daughter a cup of coffee and prepared a plate for her and carried her own mug of coffee and casserole to the table.

"Did you and Terrance make up?" she asked.

Amara shoveled casserole into her mouth to keep from answering. "Ouch!" she cried, and waved her hand in front of her mouth.

Cora smirked and went to get a glass of cold water. She handed Amara the glass. "Serves you right," she chastised. "You saw me take the casserole out of the oven!" Cora sat down, picked up her fork, and waved the tines in Amara's direction. "Okay, I won't press the issue. You're grown and I'll stay out of your business."

"Mom!" Amara protested.

Her mother peered over the brim of her cup, but remained silent. The ticking from wall clock was the only sound in the kitchen.

Amara ate the rest of the casserole and drank the last of her coffee. "Thanks for the breakfast. It was delicious as always." She carried her dishes to the sink, grabbed the paper sack from the counter, and rushed out of the kitchen.

"Uh, huh. You're stubborn, just like your daddy," Cora griped.

Amara opened the front door and yelled, "No, I'm just like you!" She dashed out the front door before her mother could provide a retort.

Cora's shoulders shook as fought the laugh bubbling inside her chest.

Chapter 37

Amara combed through her emails and was surprised to receive one from a young woman who was a former foster care recipient. The email wasn't favorable and she wanted to meet with Amara. She picked up the phone and contacted the case worker's supervisor. It was time to get some answers. As she ended the call, her cell phone chimed. She stood and hurried to the hallway. "Hello Mr. Dumont," she answered. Her voice was low and soft.

His deep voice resonated through the receiver. "Good afternoon, Amara. I was wondering if you wouldn't mind stopping by after work this evening."

Amara swallowed hard. "Sure thing, Mr. Dumont."

"Call me Rolanzo," he said.

"Is there a certain time you'd like me to arrive, Rolanzo?" She typed seven o'clock in her phone calendar and thanked him. Amara felt nervous about seeing him. Would he share good or bad news? She walked to her desk and grabbed her lunch. The gray clouds had burned away and the sun shone bright through the office windows.

Remy leaned in her direction as she passed and asked, "Good news?"

Amara grabbed her lunch bag. "Yes, good news. I'm headed to the park. See you in a bit." "Enjoy your lunch with your new girlfriend," she teased.

Remy grinned despite trying to keep a straight face. He typed faster. Amara was right. He was excited to have lunch with the flight attendant who was becoming his girlfriend.

Amara walked down the paved path and stopped in front of her favorite bench. She was pleased to find it empty. Legs stretched out on the bench; she removed the turkey sandwich her mother had made for lunch and water bottle. It felt nice to be taken care of.

Eyes closed; she tilted her head toward the sun. It warmed her face. She bit into her sandwich and thought about the recent sequence of events. So much had happened in a short period of time. Her relationship with her boyfriend was strained. The caseworker for her foster care article continued to elude her.

How was Pradeep tied to the murders? His VP seemed to be making all the moves. According to Terrance, there was a new suspect in the mix. When would it all end? She released a ragged breath as she unscrewed the top of the water bottle and took a sip. If Mr. Athy hadn't asked her to help, she wouldn't be involved. At least she believed that to be the case.

Suddenly, the sun was blocked by a large male form. Amara dumped her sandwich in her bag, whirled her feet to the ground, prepared to fight or flee. When she looked up, her breath caught. It was Terrance. "What are you doing here?" she croaked.

He gave a sheepish grin. "I wanted to talk. Remy told me where you were. I didn't mean to startle you."

She sat down, shaded her eyes with her hand and looked into his handsome face. "You found me, what do you want?"

Terrance sat beside her; his gaze steady. "I'm an idiot. I acted rashly and I'm very sorry."

Amara felt her resolve weaken. "Okay, what does that mean for us?"

Terrance's shoulders relaxed a bit. "It means I promise to do better. I'll listen before I jump to conclusions. I didn't give you a chance to speak. I just reacted. I was wrong." His fingertips touched the sleeve of her blouse. "I miss you; miss us."

Amara clutched her lunch bag and water bottle. "You really hurt me. The fact I needed to defend myself angered me more. If we're going to be a serious couple, we must communicate better and trust one another. I wasn't even at the apartment when those guys broke in!"

Terrance stood and pulled her up from the bench. "You're right. Can we start by having dinner tonight?" His eyes sparkled as he asked. He gestured to her lunch bag. "Especially since I interrupted your lunch."

Amara's cheeks dimpled when she smiled. "I'd love to, but I'm meeting with Mr. Dumont after work." She paused and added, "You're welcome to accompany me."

Terrance held her hand. It felt warm and reassuring. "I'd like that. How about a late dinner afterward?"

She agreed as they walked to her office in companionable silence.

Chapter 38

Amara glanced at Remy when she entered the office. She thought about making him suffer for telling Terrance where she'd gone, but decided against it. "Thank you," she whispered as she walked to her desk. He winked and continued to work on his current article.

She and Remy hadn't always been so tight. When they first met, she thought he was gorgeous, of course. His sun-bleached blond hair, year-round tan, strong features that seemed to be symmetrically perfect and sea blue eyes turned women's heads of all ages. She'd disliked him on sight.

Her hasty assumption was that he was a rich, spoiled man who was full of himself. This was one of the few times she was pleased to be wrong. He'd been there for her and had her back on more than one occasion. He was a true friend.

Amara called her mother to let her know she planned to have a late dinner with Terrance. Instead of the expected elation, her mother's voice sounded strained. Amara immediately became alarmed. "Mom, what's going on?! Are you all right? Is someone there?!"

"You have a visitor. Someone from your past. I need you to come home now." When her mother's voice quivered, a chill ran down Amara's spine.

Amara nearly ran to Matt's office and knocked on the doorframe. "Matt, would it be okay if I left early? I need to do some research out of the office before I meet with the caseworker tomorrow. That's if she doesn't stand me up."

Matt's attention remained on the computer screen as he shooed her away.

Amara stopped at Remy's desk and hissed, "My mom might be in trouble. She told me to come home right now. I had a visitor. I'll call you if there's a problem."

"Do you want me to come with you?"

Amara shook her head. "Just keep your phone close by."

Remy watched her dash out of the office. He hoped everything was okay. So much had happened since Casey's death.

Amara sped down the interstate and drove up the slanted concrete driveway. The front of her car scraped the concrete as she stomped her brake to a stop. There was a late model Mercedes coupe convertible parked in the driveway. She shut off the engine, sprinted up the drive, and rushed through the front door. "Mom!" she yelled as her eyes surveyed the immediate area.

Her mother rushed from the kitchen, wiping her hands on a dish towel. 'I'm sorry I scared you. When you called, I'd just answered the door. I was shocked by the visitor."

"Who is it?" Amara asked.

Cora jerked her head in the direction of the kitchen. Amara followed and halted. A stunning, well-dressed woman sat on a stool at the kitchen counter. She swiveled to face her.

"Hello, Mari."

Amara couldn't seem to move. She stared, speechless.

Divya stood and swept a wayward strand of her perfectly styled bob into place. Amara took in the Ralph Lauren fuchsia silk camisole, cropped blazer and black tapered designer slacks that hugged her slender frame and black Prada wedge sandals. Amara was certain the outfit cost more than she made in a month. A vintage designer purse with a gold chain shoulder strap hung on her right shoulder. It was as if she'd walked off the pages of Vogue.

Amara felt self-conscious dressed in her off-the-rack navy wide legged pants from Nordstrom with its matching blazer and cream-colored polyester shell beneath. She took a deep breath and replied, "Hello, Divya. What are you doing here?"

"Can we go somewhere and talk?" Divya asked.

Amara pointed outside to the deck. It was a lovely, sunny day. She needed the warmth only sun could provide to ward off the sudden chill she felt. Divya was absolutely the last person she'd thought would show up at her parents' house.

Cora carried a tray with fresh squeezed lemonade in frosted glasses and wordlessly set it on the round, glass table. Amara motioned for Divya to take a seat. She was glad her mother was so fastidious. The glass table gleamed and the chair cushions were dust free.

Tall evergreen trees provided a nice barrier from the neighbor's backyard. She and Divya sat facing each other. Divya was still beautiful. Her unblemished skin was the color of eggnog. Her wide, expressive eyes were carefully lined with long lashes coated with mascara. She wore fuchsia lipstick on bowed lips. Large diamond stud earrings glittered in the sunlight.

"I didn't know where you lived, but remembered the location of your parents' house." Her eyes skittered around the deck and back towards the kitchen. "It's just as I remember it."

Amara didn't reply. She watched as Divya clasped her ringed fingers on top of the table. Her manicured nails were painted fuchsia to match the rest of her ensemble. "I found your number and tried to call. I even left a message." Amara's expression remained unreadable. Divya's voice trailed off as she looked around. "I'm relieved your parents hadn't moved."

She'd been so busy with the case and latest break-in; she hadn't listened to the voicemail. At least that solved the mystery call she'd received from the restricted number.

Divya gave an exasperated sigh. "You're going to make this hard for me. I get it."

Amara sipped her lemonade. She'd wait until Divya revealed the reason for this unannounced visit.

Divya bit her lower lip and veered her eyes from Amara's steady gaze. When she spoke, her words came out in a rush. "My husband told me you've been asking questions about his businesses, taking up where that dead girl left off; digging into his personal life." Her eyes narrowed when she added, "You've also been asking questions about a little girl you met at the lending library box."

Amara took another sip of lemonade. Her mother had coated the rim of the glass with sugar crystals. It tasted extra sweet on her tongue. She placed her glass on the table and allowed Divya's question to remain unanswered.

Divya tapped her manicured nails impatiently against the glass top table and stared at Amara.

Amara took another sip of lemonade. There was no way she'd offer an explanation to someone who'd callously ended their friendship, hadn't contacted her in nearly a decade, and showed up unannounced.

Divya clasped her hands beneath the table as she leaned forward; her voice desperate. "My husband had nothing to do with the allegations of drugs and weapons being shipped with his merchandise."

"Okay," Amara drawled. "By the way, the dead girl's name is Casey Athy."

202

Divya sat back hard and replied, "Yes...sorry." Amara noticed a slight tremor when Divya picked up the glass of lemonade. She absently rubbed condensation from the glass. "Look, I know we didn't reconnect after I returned from India."

Amara snorted, but said nothing. A strong breeze rustled her curls as nearby birds chirped their annoyance and flew off.

Divya looked away. "I know it was my fault. When I returned from India, I was a different person." Eyes ablaze, her cheeks reddened as she confessed, "I was very angry with my parents for sending me away."

Amara crossed her arms and asked, "Is that why you lied and told your parents I supplied you with drugs and allowed you to use my house to see your boyfriend?"

Divya's eyes widened. Wha-...you know about that?" Her chin lifted defiantly as she explained, "I had way too many responsibilities for a girl my age. I wasn't allowed to have fun." She lowered her eyes and added, "I'm sorry for lying. You were a good friend and didn't deserve that." Her hands gesticulated in the air as she continued. "Please understand; I couldn't attend school activities. I had to cook, clean, and take care of my two younger siblings."

"O-kay," Amara drawled. "That's all in the past. Why are you here now?"

"I want you to back off my husband and the little girl."

"You mean Ella," Amara replied.

"H-how do you know her name?" she stammered.

"Is she Pradeep's?" Amara asked. "Or is she Samesh's love child? I know he's single and continues to follow me around town." She'd shocked her old classmate. Good.

When Divya replied, her voice was so soft, Amara strained to hear her. "Ella was mine. I got pregnant in middle school by the guy I was sneaking around with. My parents sent me to India to have the baby. She was adopted by distant relatives and brought to the U.S."

It took Amara several seconds to regain her bearings. "Does Ella know you're her biological mother?"

Divya shook her head as a tear rolled down her cheek and splashed against her silk camisole.

Amara handed her a napkin. "What about the father? Does he know about Ella?" Divya looked away and didn't answer. Amara took a deep breath and asked the last question. "Was the lawyer who recently died involved with the adoption?"

Divya hiccupped and nodded.

"Damn," Amara whispered. She told Divya about the break-in at her apartment. "Were you or your husband responsible for that?"

Divya balled the napkin in her fist. "No!"

Amara pointed at Divya. "If your husband is innocent as you say, he'd better watch his back." Amara shared what she'd learned about Samesh living well beyond his income.

Amara noticed Divya's expression changed as she took it all in. "I don't plan to do anything more involving your husband. But, if his VP continues to harass me, I will continue to dig. He'd better be careful. I'm damn good at finding dirt," she warned.

Divya murmured she understood. "I will have my husband talk to him."

Amara stood. "If you decide to discuss this situation with your husband, I hope you'll advise him to beware of the man he's allowed into his inner circle."

Divya's voice cracked as she said, "Thank you for agreeing to see me. I really am sorry for how our friendship ended."

Amara gave a sad smile. "Yeah, me too." She led Divya through the patio door into the kitchen.

Amara watched Divya get into her convertible, put on designer sunglasses and back out the drive. She checked up and down the street before she closed the door and returned to the kitchen.

Cora stood at the counter and looked expectantly at her daughter. Amara motioned for her mother to join her outside on the deck.

"Well, what did Divya want?"

When Amara told her, Cora patted her daughter's hand. "Be careful. I don't trust Divya. She's never made any effort to contact you until now. Do you think she'll tell her husband what you two discussed?"

Amara saw the apprehension in her mother's eyes. "I'm not sure what she'll do. You're right about not trusting her. Divya came here on a fact-finding mission. She wanted to know what I'd discovered and warn me to back off her husband." Amara splayed her hands and admitted, "Maybe I shared too much. I guess I'll find out soon."

"Be careful around that woman," her mother cautioned again.

Amara promised and picked up her cell phone. "I need to let Remy know everything is okay." She sent a quick text. Remy sent a thumbs up emoji.

Chapter 39

Amara pulled into the circular drive of Rolanzo Dumont's mansion and parked beside Terrance's car. They walked up the path and were met by Dora Lee. She hugged them both and pointed a thumb down the hallway. "He's in the library."

Rolanzo's gray eyes lit on Amara. "I discovered news about Ella," he said. He picked up a single sheet of paper from his desk.

Before he could launch into his spiel, Amara announced, "Divya, a childhood friend came to my parents' house this afternoon. She informed me Ella is her biological child. I also know Ella is unaware of Divya's existence."

The room was silent for several seconds. Amara could feel Rolanzo's gray eyes bore into her, as if he saw her differently. She sat erect under his scrutiny.

"You are one sharp woman. That is exactly what I discovered. I also discovered the identity of the father. His name is Connor."

Amara waited anxiously for him to continue.

Terrance cleared his throat. "We questioned a guy by that name at the station earlier today. We believe he's responsible for sending those interns to Amara's house to plant listening devices."

Terrance glanced in Amara's direction. She hadn't told him the information regarding Divya. In the past she'd call right away with her news. Is this how he made her feel when he failed to tell her something and she learned about it through other people? He vowed to do better. He missed the ease of their relationship before the misunderstanding.

"According to my intel, Connor forfeited all parental rights before Ella was born. He has no claim on the child. I don't believe he even knows about the child," Rolanzo said.

"Then why is he so interested now?" Amara asked.

Rolanzo smiled. His teeth were even and white. Amara thought he looked even more handsome. "Ella will turn ten next month. At that time, she'll inherit a trust set up by her biological mother." He held up the sheet of paper. "When Divya became a widow; one of the first things she did was set up a trust for biological daughter. It's enormous. Ella will have limited access to these funds once she turns ten. There are strict stipulations and a conservator over the funds so she can't be swindled or spend money recklessly."

"Those records are usually sealed. How did you get access?" Amara asked. Rolanzo didn't answer. Amara burst out laughing. She couldn't help it. This was the icing on one hell of a day.

Rolanzo waited patiently until she gathered herself. He knew she'd been through a lot lately.

Amara took a deep breath. "Do you think Ella's father is trying to get to her money?" She lifted her finger as another thought arose. "I know Samesh is living well beyond his means. Do you think he's trying to get to Ella? Would he harm her?" Her voice rose as she asked the last question.

Rolanzo shrugged. "I'm not sure. You're right about one thing. Samesh is several million dollars in debt and will have to do something soon. Otherwise, the façade of his wealthy life will crumble."

Rolanzo thumbed through sheets of paper on his desk before he continued. "Connor is financially stable and lives within his means. I'm not sure what he's trying to find out or if Pradeep's VP is blackmailing and using him to get to Ella or Divya's money."

Rolanzo held up another sheet of paper and added, "He got in trouble as a teenager. When he turned twenty-one, he turned his life around. According to the report, he attended college and earned a business degree. He's enrolled in a graduate program at UW earning his MBA."

Amara tugged one of her curls and asked, "What does he want from me?" Slowly, the pieces of the puzzle began to come together. As Rolanzo speculated, it was all about money. The question now was whose money? Divya's, Ella's, or money from the illegal shipments?

"I'm not sure," Rolanzo replied. He picked up another sheet of paper before he continued. "I can tell you Divya was smart. She added a codicil to the trust. If anything happens to Ella, the money from the trust goes to an Indian orphanage she's supported for decades."

Amara's face beamed with approval. She prayed nothing happened to that sweet little girl.

Rolanzo placed the paper on the stack with the others. He sat back in his chair and gazed at Amara and Terrance. Terrance stood. Amara joined him and thanked Rolanzo. He gave a slight nod as they walked out the study.

Dora Lee met them in the foyer and walked them to the door.

Amara followed Terrance to the restaurant. Once they were seated, Terrance glanced nervously at Amara. She was usually a chatter box. Tonight, she was subdued, contemplative. He was at a loss of how to return their relationship to where it was before his bonehead move at her office. "You're awfully quiet," he said in a gentle tone.

A waitress carrying a round tray with two plates of burgers, fries and drinks appeared. Amara placed a straw in her cup and shrugged. "I was thinking about what Mr. Dumont, I mean Rolanzo, told us tonight." She placed the paper napkin on her lap and continued. "When I met Ella and her brother, she seemed happy and well-adjusted. I'd hate to learn anything bad happened to her."

"Molloy plans to monitor her biological father. We'll find out what he's after." Terrance bit into his burger and chewed thoughtfully. He took a sip of his Coke before he continued. "According to Rolanzo, the guy sounds like he's on the right track and doing well." He shrugged and added, "Perhaps he's being blackmailed."

Amara changed the subject. She needed a mental break from the case. "I'm thinking of taking Italian so I can understand what you and Rolanzo are talking about," she teased.

Terrance grinned and reminded her he spoke five different languages.

"I guess I have a lot to learn," she countered.

Terrance spoke in Italian as he picked up her hand and kissed it.

"Yes, I'll definitely start with Italian," Amara joked.

Amara turned down Terrance's offer to stay at his place. She needed space and time to think about the situation she was tangled in. There was no doubt Samesh orchestrated this chaos.

She entered her parents' house and headed up the stairs to her old bedroom. When she heard the television in her parents' room, she smiled. Her mother had waited for her to return. As she undressed and put on her favorite pajamas, she thought about Divya, Ella, and Samesh.

Divya could claim Pradeep was innocent all she wanted. He'd allowed bad things to occur right under his nose. He spent six months out of the year in India. How much control and oversight did he have in the day-to-day business of his Seattle office? Did Samesh have free rein during Pradeep's absence?

Amara crossed her legs on her childhood bed and began to surf on her laptop. She returned to a site where Divya posed with children at an orphanage in India. She enlarged the photo to check out the other adults in the background. Several men in suits and one woman dressed in a sari stood in the background. Amara examined the group. In the very last row, almost concealed behind a larger man, stood someone who resembled Samesh.

"What are you doing at an orphanage in India with Divya?" she asked aloud. Why wasn't her husband with her? Were Divya and Samesh having an affair? Or had Pradeep sent his second in charge to keep an eye on his wife? She shook her head. That made no sense. Pradeep lived in India at least half of the year.

Amara checked her watch and texted Remy. She asked him to meet her at the office thirty minutes early. She had a couple things to discuss.

Remy offered to call and talk now. Amara assured him the conversation needed to be conducted face to face. Remy started to type. The little bubbles formed in the corner of her text screen and halted.

"OK...TTYL—talk to you later," he typed. Amara turned off the light and fell fast asleep.

Chapter 40

Remy sat at his desk with a bag of pastries and two cups of hot coffee. Amara rushed inside, took off her coat and grabbed one of the cups.

Remy sipped his coffee and snatched a bear claw from the bag. "What couldn't you discuss over the phone?"

Amara removed a copy of the photo she'd printed and handed it to him. He immediately recognized Samesh in the back of the photo.

"He pointed at Samesh and Divya. "Do these two have something going on?" he asked.

Amara shrugged. "That's what I'm wondering." She told him what she'd learned about Ella's trust and her biological father.

Remy's blue eyes widened. "I feel like I'm in a soap opera. This is too much!" He took another bite of his pastry and considered the implications of this new information.

Amara fished a glazed donut from the bag. She licked her fingers. "Yep. According to Mr. Dumont, Divya included a codicil. If anything happens to Ella, no one gets the money. The entire trust goes to charity."

Remy's expression darkened. "Do you think Ella's biological father would try to harm her?"

Amara shook her head. "No, but I'm not so sure about Samesh. Let's not forget he's followed me all over town after I took photos of Ella and spoke to her at the library box." Though she didn't have proof, Amara was positive Samesh was involved in the deaths of Casey and the attorney. She kept her theories to herself. It would only cause Remy to worry.

Remy wiped his fingers and typed rapidly. He pointed at the page from the Samesh's social media site. "Take a look at this."

211

Amara glanced at Remy's monitor. "Oh, my goodness! He's planning to buy a plane! This man is millions of dollars in debt. Where is he getting the money to buy a jet?"

Remy clicked on another website with private planes for sale. "Good question. The point is, he's obtained enough money from someone or somewhere to purchase a plane." He gestured to the monitor screen. "That's a midsize twinjet aircraft! They run over a million dollars!"

She stared at the screen. "This makes it even more interesting. He's confident enough to show the world the plane he's in the process of buying." Amara tapped the table to emphasize her next words. "Something big is getting ready to go down. I think we need to check the date of Pradeep's next shipment."

Remy returned to the VP's social media page. They stared at the plane Samesh planned to purchase a few seconds more as the rest of the staff entered the office.

Chapter 41

The following morning, Amara contacted Mr. Dumont and asked if he knew when Pradeep's freighter would dock that week. She heard papers rustle before he told her the freighter was due to dock tomorrow evening. Good, that gave her time to plan.

Rolanzo broke into her thoughts. "I don't know what you're planning, but you'd better be careful. This man has you on his radar."

Amara sighed. "Yes, I know. What do you think he believes I have or know?"

It was Rolanzo's turn to sigh. "I wish I knew. Casey had some damning information on him and possibly his company. I believe Casey planned to meet with my friend at the wedding. When she saw the impostor sitting in his seat, she took photos of him and tried to send it to someone at the newspaper to check out his identity. After she was escorted off the property and her photos were deleted; her investigation into this guy and my friend was thwarted.

Amara picked up the thread. "I believe Casey's killer wanted everyone to think she'd been attacked, kidnapped, and robbed. Her purse was empty. The problem was her missing car. Whoever attacked her, didn't know where she'd parked it."

Amara thought about the video Molloy had received. Why hadn't the Port Police intervened when she was attacked? Someone had to be monitoring the security screens. Had they been paid to turn a blind eye?

Rolanzo's voice boomed through the receiver. "Are you still there?"

"Yes, sorry Rolanzo. I was thinking about the video footage from the pier. I believe Casey went there to video whatever was going on with Pradeep's shipment. My question is, why hadn't the Port Police seen her or the altercation between her and her attacker? Do you think Pradeep or his VP paid the night security to turn a blind eye to whatever occurred at the dock?"

Rolanzo paused a few seconds. "The thought crossed my mind."

When he didn't elaborate, Amara said, "I'm going to talk to Molloy. Based on what I learned about the video, Casey knew how to skirt most of the cameras at the port. Fortunately, she'd been caught on one." She exhaled. "Whoever attacked her didn't have to kill her."

Rolanzo measured his words. "Going to Detective Molloy is a good idea." He could sense her smile when he ended the call.

Amara left work early and drove to the police station to see Molloy.

Chapter 42

Molloy grunted when he spotted Amara. He wished he'd kept that awful chair. It ensured she'd never stay long. Her determined look gave him pause.

"I know you're busy, but I have a theory I want to run by you."

He reluctantly motioned for her to take a seat.

She wasted no time. "Would you check to see who was monitoring the cameras during the times we know Casey visited the pier?" Molloy glared at her. "I think Samesh paid off the patrol officer who monitored the security camera feed that night. Do you think that's a possibility?"

Molloy squinted. "It's already being checked out." His nostrils flared in anger. "If someone isn't doing their job or worse, receiving payment not to do their job, then they don't deserve to wear the uniform."

Amara stood. "I figured you'd you say that. Thanks for seeing me." There was a bounce in her step as she left Molloy's office.

When she returned to work, there was a recording on her office phone from a young woman who'd been in the foster care system. She wanted to meet. Amara returned the call and left a message. While conducting research for her article on the foster care system, she received an email that the caseworker she was supposed to interview was on vacation. Frustrated, she packed her things and left the office.

On her way to her parents' house, Terrance called and invited her to dinner. She agreed.

Terrance's face lit up when he saw her. He pulled her into his arms and kissed her deeply.

Amara was breathless when he released her. "Wow, now that's a hello!"

Terrance gave a shy grin and confessed, "I've missed you." He took her hand and led her to the sofa.

She told him about her visit with Molloy and phone call with Rolanzo. Her expression was resolute when she told him of her plans to return to her apartment. "I don't know what the heck Samesh and Divya think I have. But I know I can't continue to be afraid or live with my parents." A tear slid down her cheek.

Terrance put his arm around her shoulders and pulled her close. She rested her head against his chest. The steady beat of his heart calmed her. "Molloy is on top of this case. I think it's safe for you to go home," he said.

Amara sighed with relief. She sat up and faced Terrance. "You're off tomorrow, right?" He nodded. "You have a special delivery arriving at noon."

Terrance nuzzled her neck. "Could that special delivery be you?"

Amara giggled. "No, but I like what you're thinking," she said and nipped his ear gently with her teeth.

He lifted her from the sofa and carried her to his room. She looped her arms around his neck and rested her head in the crook of his neck. "What about dinner?" she asked.

Amara relaxed in Terrance's arms. She hadn't realized she'd been so tense. He ran his fingers through her curly mane and kissed the back of her neck, traced a path on the outside of her arm, and kissed her again. She turned to face him. Her breath caught as he and kissed her closed eye lids, nose, and lips.

Her limbs felt like limp noodles. Covered with sweat, she lay on her back and caught her breath. She smiled as her fingertips trailed along her man's muscular, naked torso. "I wish I could stay, but my parents are expecting me." She sighed and heaved herself upright in bed.

He began to protest, but stopped. He pulled her close and gave her a passionate kiss. "I'm glad you came over. Do you have time for dinner?"

Amara shook her head.

Terrance watched her dress. His eyes travelled along the shadowed outline of her body. He was in love with this woman and didn't want anything to happen to her. Once she was fully dressed, he swung his feet to the floor and grabbed his robe. He walked Amara to the front door and gave her a final kiss before opening it. Terrance watched her back out the driveway and head down the street before shutting and locking the front door.

Amara couldn't help but smile as she drove to her parents' house. She hoped he liked her surprise. She'd taken three chairs that belonged to his parents from storage. They'd been reupholstered, and would be delivered to his house tomorrow.

Amara walked to the doorway of the kitchen where her parents were eating dinner. Her mother eyed her suspiciously. "Your dinner is in the oven."

Uh, oh...Amara knew that look. Feeling self-conscious, she rushed upstairs to her bathroom to check her appearance. It was dark when she dressed and wrapped her hair in a bun. Was it too messy? A smile played across her lips at the memory of how her hair got mussed.

She glanced in the mirror. Damn. She had raccoon eyes from smudged mascara and a bun that was messy, not in a cute way. She quickly washed her face, smoothed the errant curls, and adjusted her bun.

"Did you have a good time at Terrance's house?" her father wisecracked when she entered the kitchen. Amara blushed and her mother kicked her husband beneath the table. "Ow!" he yelped. Cora shushed him and continued to eat as if nothing happened.

Amara carried her plate to the table. Yep, it was time to return to her apartment.

Chapter 43

Amara hummed a cheerful tune as she packed her duffle and stripped the linens from her childhood bed. She'd slept better last night than she had the past week. Hopefully, the investigation would soon be over and her life returned to normal.

She felt certain Samesh was somehow responsible for Casey and the lawyer's death. She wouldn't want to be in his shoes when Rolanzo's men got a hold of him. Rolanzo had a way of setting people up by using their own greed against them. In this case the catalyst was money. What she wouldn't give to be a fly on the wall when that occurred.

She wondered how Connor, Ella's biological father fit in all of this. Divya had to be aware he was employed at her husband's company. How awkward was that?

Amara tossed the linen into the washer and carried her duffle to the car. As she locked the car and walked up the drive, a ride share car screeched to a halt in front of the house.

When her name was called, Amara glanced over her shoulder and saw a disheveled woman get out of the car. Her designer clothes looked as if she'd slept in them. Her normally coiffed hair stuck out at odd angles. There were dark circles beneath puffy, red eyes.

She stared in disbelief. "Divya?" she croaked.

The woman rushed up the drive and grabbed Amara's bicep. Her momentum caused Amara to jog up the stairs and propelled them through the front door she'd left slightly ajar. Once inside, Amara extracted her arm. "What is going on? Why are you here?!"

Divya's eyes were wild. "They took her! They stole Ella!" she shouted. Her head swayed from side to side. "Her parents found her bike near the library box. She was supposed to go straight to school, but made a detour to get another book. Her brother rode to school alone. She hasn't been seen since," Divya sobbed.

The commotion caused Amara's parents to rush into the room. Jackson closed the front door while Cora led a sobbing Divya to the sofa.

Jackson's voice was calm. "Start at the beginning. Who took Ella?"

Divya's hand shook as she produced a crumbled piece of paper. Jackson carefully held the computer-generated note by its edges and read it aloud. "Ella will die unless you pay her ransom of $30 million. If you call the police, Ella dies," he read.

Amara considered the man who couldn't afford his expensive homes, cars, trips, and new plane. Thirty million would be enough to take care of all his debts. Her tone was urgent. "Is it possible Samesh kidnapped Ella?" she asked.

Divya stared at Amara. "What? No! Why would Samesh kidnap Ella?"

Amara sat next to Divya. "Is he aware of Ella's parentage?"

Divya bolted upright. "No!"

"How about Connor? He works at your husband's company under Samesh."

Divya began to pace. "What are you talking about!" she screamed. "Connor lives in Ohio! The only thing he knows is I got pregnant and my parents sent me to India. My parents made sure Connor signed over his parental rights before she was born. He doesn't know if I had the baby or got an abortion." Her chest heaved with heavy sobs. "If anything happens to Ella because of me, I...I don't know what I'd do!" she wailed.

"Divya, we need to contact the police," Jackson reasoned.

Her head swiveled from side to side. "I can't! You read the note! No police or Ella dies!"

Amara frowned. "If Ella's parents found her bike at the library box, wouldn't they have already called the police? How many people know Ella is your biological child?" Amara wanted to know how Divya had discovered the details of the child's last location before she went missing, but kept that question to herself.

Divya shrugged. "Including everyone in this room; no one else knows I'm Ella's biological mother. I don't know why the letter was sent to me."

Liar. Samesh knew. Possibly, the biological father as well. "What are Ella's parents saying? Do they know about the ransom demand?" Amara asked.

Divya bowed her head. "I...I don't think so."

"Does your husband know about this?" Cora asked.

Divya plucked a tissue from the box on the table and dabbed her eyes. "Yes. He's out of town, but on his way back."

Amara pressed on. "We need to locate Samesh. I believe he has Ella or is part of this kidnapping." There was no way she'd reveal she knew Ella would become a very rich girl in a few days. She turned to face Divya. "Did you know Samesh recently purchased a new plane?" Divya stared at Amara as if in a trance. Amara pressed, "The police need to be involved."

Divya blinked rapidly. "No, no police! Please stop with all the questions!"

Amara remained quiet. If Divya agreed to pay the ransom, would they ever see the sweet little girl again? She gave Divya's disheveled appearance a once over. If Ella had been missing for only a few hours, why did she look so bedraggled? She looked as if she'd slept in her clothes; as if she hadn't slept at all. Had she received some type of warning of what was to come last night? If so, why hadn't she acted then? More important, why bring this personal issue to her parents' house? Especially if she didn't want the police involved.

Amara called her office and took a vacation day. So many unanswered questions swirled in her mind. Instead of voicing them she asked, "When will your husband arrive?"

Divya checked her watch. Her voice quivered when she replied, "Sometime this afternoon." Tears streaked her face as she began to sob.

Convenient timing for Samesh, Amara thought.

Jackson left the room and called Molloy. This was too much for him and his family to handle. He was certain Molloy would contact the FBI.

Divya shrieked when Molloy knocked on the back door and entered. He'd driven through the alley to their backyard. "Who is that man?!" she cried.

Amara's stiff shoulders relaxed when she saw Molloy. "It's going to be all right," she said.

"No one knows I'm here. I drove my personal car and entered through the alley and back door." Molloy held out a gloved hand. "Let me see the note."

Jackson handed Molloy the note. He doubted the lab would get the culprit's fingerprints from the paper. The perpetrator most likely wore gloves.

Amara headed to the kitchen. She needed to tell Molloy about Ella's trust. "Detective Molloy, may I get you some coffee?" She motioned for him to accompany her.

"Yes, thank you," he said and followed her.

Amara removed four mugs from the cabinet, poured coffee, and quickly told him about Ella's trust. She handed the detective a mug of coffee before he returned to the family room.

Amara followed the detective carrying three mugs of coffee. She handed one to Divya and her parents. Divya set her cup on the table. Her body seemed to fold within itself as she rocked back and forth.

Molloy approached Divya. He held up the note. "Is there something you haven't told me? Something that would cause someone to kidnap Ella now?"

Divya hesitated before telling Molloy about the adoption and how Ella would become very wealthy when she turned ten in a few days.

Molloy raked stubby fingers through his thick hair. His green eyes held Divya's soft brown, teary eyes. "We need to bring the FBI in on this."

"No!" Divya cried as she covered her face.

"We don't have a choice if we want to get Ella back alive," Molloy reasoned.

There was a flurry of activity in the Mackelroy household. A nondescript sedan drove down the alley through the backyard gate. Two agents pulled Divya aside for questioning. Another sedan was already at Ella's adopted parents' home.

Amara stared in Divya's direction. Why hadn't she hired professionals to search and find Ella? She could certainly afford it. And why involve her and her family? Amara's lips pursed as she watched Divya sob uncontrollably.

Chapter 45

Amara's phone chimed. It was Terrance. She answered, and before she could speak, Terrance exclaimed, "I love them! These are the chairs that once belonged to my grandmother! They were also my mother's favorite." There was a catch in his voice as he prattled on. "I can't believe you did this for me. Thank you."

He fingered the fine upholstery of one of the chairs as he continued to gush over their beauty. "You knocked this out of the park!"

Her voice dropped to a whisper as she confessed, "We're dealing with a situation here."

Terrance heard the familiar squelch of a police radio and men conversing in the background. "What's going on?" He listened intently while Amara explained Divya's frantic appearance and Ella being kidnapped. Terrance heard Molloy's voice boom in the background when he called Amara's name.

"Listen, I've got to go. I'm happy you're pleased with my surprise. I'll talk to you soon."

Terrance stared at the phone for several seconds before he tucked it in his back pocket, grabbed his car keys, and headed to Rolanzo's.

He parked in the curved drive and knocked on the massive front door. He was greeted by Dora Lee. She wrapped him in a hug and pulled him inside. She looked around and teased, "Where's your trusty side kick?"

Terrance ducked his head to hide a smile. "You know you're wrong Dora Lee," he chastised. Dora Lee laughed and pointed in the direction of the library.

Rolanzo sat at his desk with papers covering the entire surface. He looked up from the spreadsheets and waved Terrance over. "I can't believe you came to visit me alone."

Terrance rolled his eyes and took a seat beside the huge mahogany desk. His hand automatically gravitated to the carved rail on the side of the desk, to a small button that unlocked a hidden compartment. It was something he'd done whenever he was worried or frustrated.

So, to what do I owe this visit?"

Terrance told him about Ella's kidnapping.

All joking ceased. Rolanzo turned his attention to Terrance. This was connected to his friend's suspicious death. "What do you know?"

Terrance shrugged. "Not much. Divya is at Amara's parents' house. I heard the police radios and people talking. Cian Molloy is there and I assume the FBI is as well."

Rolanzo sat back in his chair and was quiet for several seconds. "This is all somehow connected. The New York police caught the guy who broke into my friend's apartment the day before the wedding." He didn't add it was his and Amara's tip that led police to the impostor and possible killer of his friend.

"I have a buddy on the police force in New York. According to him, the guy who showed up at my wedding is Gerard, a professional thief. He claimed to have coordinated a meeting with my friend before he was scheduled to leave for Seattle to attend my wedding. When he didn't answer the door, he got worried and broke into the apartment. He found my friend on the floor. He'd been hired to steal certain legal documents. Since he had a criminal record, he got spooked and ran."

Terrance frowned. "Isn't that just a Swiss cheese of a story! I don't buy it for one minute!" He thought about the doorman and concierge that he and Amara had discussed. "If he'd come through the front door as he claimed, why hadn't the concierge called up to the apartment to make sure he was expected? Also, once he discovered your friend on the floor of the apartment, why hadn't he called 911 or anonymously informed the front desk of the man's death?"

Terrance wagged a finger. "Why perpetrate your friend at the wedding? What was that about?"

Rolanzo leaned back in his chair and replied, "According to the police, this guy claimed he'd met my friend in Europe. We were able to track the last phone call between the two numbers. It lasted ten minutes. I agree. Something isn't right. Especially since we know this guy is a criminal."

Terrance threw up his hands. "This is getting worse by the minute. Let's say the thief and your friend had spoken to one another. How had he known about the wedding and what had he hoped to discover?"

The conversation was cut short when a slight man entered the room. He spoke barely above a whisper as he gave Rolanzo an update. Terrance strained to hear.

The head of security confirmed that Connor was at the office. "He's gone to work every day." He handed Rolanzo a sheet of paper. "Connor attends night classes at the University of Washington to earn his Master's Degree in Business. He's dating a librarian who works at the Central Library downtown."

Rolanzo glanced at Terrance. "I don't believe he's aware Ella is his daughter."

Terrance scratched his head. He still questioned how or why Connor started working at Pradeep's company. He had to know Pradeep was married to Divya.

The head of security tapped his tablet and continued. "As for Samesh; he did not show up for work this morning. He left his apartment at dawn and we lost him downtown. I assume he made our guy." He looked at both men. "What's happened?"

"The little girl, Ella has been kidnapped. The kidnapper is demanding $30 million. The FBI are involved. That's all we know right now," Rolanzo said.

The head of security frowned. "You think Samesh is involved?"

Rolanzo gave a slow nod. "Along with everything else that's occurred."

"What do you want to do?"

"Check around. Let's start at with the airport where he keeps his new plane and the little lake house he purchased in Olympia."

The head of security scowled. "The one he purchased under his mother's maiden name?"

Rolanzo gave another slow nod. "Also, keep a guy on Connor today."

The head of security hurried out the room. He tapped the side of his right ear and spoke in a low, deliberate tone.

Rolanzo steepled his fingers beneath his chin. "If he took Ella to either of those locations, we'll know soon enough. I believe Samesh is responsible for the death of my friend. He needs to be stopped."

"I agree. Samesh may have hired the man who impersonated your friend at the wedding. The question is why? What had he hoped to learn or gain?"

Rolanzo pursed his lips, uncertain how much to reveal. "We learned the impostor received $50,000 in his account the day he visited my friend. I think he was sent to find adoption documents regarding Ella. My friend's law office was broken into as well."

Terrance grinned. The thief didn't stand a chance. Rolanzo was part owner in a security company that always layered their systems. There would have been motion detectors, silent alarms, cypher locks on the file cabinets and a hidden safe in the floor or wall. "So, where's the safe located?"

Rolanzo smirked. "Floor, in the storage room. The intruder set off the silent alarm and the police along with guards from the security company arrived before he had a chance to break into any of the offices. My friend's law partner was contacted and went to the office to make sure nothing was taken. Everyone assumed my friend was at my wedding."

Terrance was relieved. "Do you still think this guy killed your friend?"

Rolanzo stroked his chin. "Originally, yes. But I recently learned my friend had a bad heart. When this guy broke into his apartment, he could have caused him to have an attack. If that was the case, I just wished he'd called the EMT. He may not have been dead, just unconscious."

"I'm so sorry," Terrance whispered.

"Let's return to Ella. I'm certain Samesh either personally kidnapped or arranged for someone to kidnap the child. We know he lives well beyond his means. What better way to get money than to ransom the little girl." Rolanzo picked up the phone and called Molloy.

He answered on the first ring. Rolanzo shared the information regarding the plane and the lake house in Olympia.

Chapter 46

Molloy rushed over to the FBI agent in charge, who notified the field office in Olympia. He thanked Molloy and assured him they'd send an agent to the lake house.

Amara was surprised that Samesh owned a home in Olympia under his mother's maiden name. He was one slippery character. She'd grant him that. She checked her watch. Three hours had passed since Molloy and the FBI arrived.

Out of the corner of her eye, there was movement. Divya eased the door open and slipped out. She'd left the door partially open. Amara followed and softly called her name. Divya halted. "Where are you going?" Amara asked.

A car screeched to a stop in front of the house. Pradeep behind the wheel.

Divya raced to the car as the passenger door swung open.

"Divya, wait! Please, don't leave!" Amara stared as Divya jumped inside. She rolled down the window and spoke through clenched teeth. "If he took Ella, I swear he'll pay. Pradeep and I know of a few places Samesh might be."

"Tell the FBI what you know! Don't try to find him on your own. He's probably armed. Samesh could hurt Ella if he sees you," she reasoned. "Let the FBI and police do their jobs. They are better equipped to handle this situation!"

"That asshole will never see a dime of that ransom money!" Divya hissed. "I will see him in hell first!" she yelled as the car roared down the street.

Amara felt helpless as the car sped away. She memorized the license plate and sprinted up the drive into the house. She caught her breath and yelled for Molloy.

Molloy's head snapped in Amara's direction. He saw the alarm on her face and strode in her direction. His words were clipped as he asked, "What is it? Where's Divya?"

"She's gone. Her husband picked her up. They plan to look for Samesh on their own. Divya said they knew where Samesh might have taken Ella. I think Pradeep may be armed." She gave Molloy the license plate number.

Molloy nodded. He knew Pradeep had several weapons registered. Molloy thanked her and spoke with the FBI agent in charge.

Amara felt disheartened as the FBI packed their equipment. The room fell eerily silent as the last agent departed.

Molloy thanked Amara's parents for the use of their home. He pointed toward the back yard. "They're headed to their office. It's not over. They'll find Ella."

Amara and her parents sat on the sofa in a daze. Amara massaged her temples. "This ordeal has given me a headache. I'm going to take a couple aspirin and rest."

Cora accompanied her daughter. She retrieved the aspirin from the medicine cabinet and walked to the bedroom. "Let me help you put fresh linens on the bed."

The events of the day caught up with Amara all at once. Cora removed the quilted blanket from the foot of her bed and placed it over her daughter. Amara inhaled the fresh scent of the pillowcase and closed her eyes. Gentle fingertips stroked her hair and temples until she fell asleep.

Amara awoke with a start and checked her watch. She rushed to the bathroom to wash her face and comb her hair. Her feet thumped against the stairs as she took them two at a time.

Her mother hurried from the kitchen; eyes wide. "It sounded like an earthquake! What's going on?"

Amara was breathless. "Mom, I think the kidnapping is only part of the plan." She pointed to the sofa and sat down. Cora dried her hands and sat beside her. "I have a bunch of random notes from Casey's storage unit. One of the notes indicated Samesh had snuck aboard the ship while it was docked to remove the drugs *before* the cargo was inspected. Although Divya said the shipment was rescheduled, I think it's still arriving this afternoon. I believe the kidnapping was a diversion!"

Cora stared at her daughter. "Call Cian right now!"

The detective answered after the first ring. "What's up, Amara?"

She explained the information about the scheduled shipment. "Everyone is focused on the kidnapping, not the shipment!"

"I've already spoken with the Port Police Commander. We've got a plan. Stay far away from the pier young lady!" He disconnected the call before Amara could argue.

Chapter 47

Connor checked his watch and rushed to a nondescript car parked in the back of the building. His fingers shook as they trailed over the ridges atop the front tire on the driver's side. He clutched a dark object, aimed it at the car, and pressed the button. The lock clicked and he opened the car door.

He'd managed to avoid the police and FBI in their office suite as they questioned the employees. He heard a voice behind him as he opened the door.

"Going somewhere Connor?" He jumped, whirled around, and came face to face with a large, angry looking African American man, dressed entirely in black. His long braids were held at bay by a thick leather band.

Connor's eyes darted wildly around the parking lot. "How do you know my name? What do you want?"

Rolanzo's security pointed at the car. "Where are you going in such a hurry?"

Connor avoided the question and quickly slid into the driver's seat. Rolanzo's man got into the back seat. "I-I need to get to the pier! If I don't go, I'll lose my job!" He pleaded for understanding as he stared at Rolanzo's man in the rear-view mirror. "Please, let me go! If I don't do what he says, I'll lose everything I've worked so hard to achieve!"

Rolanzo's man placed a finger to his lips to quiet the man. He pressed the side of his earpiece and asked, "Did you get all that?" He listened intently to the voice transmitted through his earpiece. He nodded and glanced at Connor. "Okay, go to the pier. We'll be watching you," he warned and got out the car.

Terrance thanked his godfather and headed to the door. He glanced at his phone and noticed several missed calls from Amara. Once he was inside his car, he returned her call. When she asked where he was, Terrance explained he'd gone to see Rolanzo.

"Terrance, what's going on?" she asked. There'd been no updates since the FBI and Detective Molloy left. When she told him about the scheduled shipment, he warned her to stay away from the pier.

"Does Rolanzo believe Samesh had something to do with his friend's death?" Several seconds passed in silence. "Hello? Terrance?"

"I'm here. Yes, he suspects there might be a connection but doesn't know for sure. The thief who broke into his friend's apartment is in custody. He remains adamant he had nothing to do with Rolanzo's friend's death."

"Then why did he pretend to be him at the wedding?" She didn't give Terrance a chance to answer. "I'll tell you why! Samesh wanted eyes on Casey. He wanted to know what she was up to and what she'd planned to ask the lawyer. Unfortunately, the impostor made a mistake. Casey had done her homework and knew what the lawyer looked like. Remember when she took those pictures? She'd spotted him sitting in the lawyer's seat and had taken pictures. He must have told Samesh and he killed, or had Casey killed."

"You're probably right. Casey got too close. He needed her out of the picture so he could continue to ship illegal cargo."

Amara's voice grew agitated. "How could Pradeep not know? Is his head so far in the clouds he doesn't realize what's going on in one of his companies?"

Terrance pulled into the police parking garage and turned off the engine. "The operative word is companies. He owns companies overseas, in California as well as here. He probably doesn't keep close tabs on the day-to-day activities in all three companies."

Amara considered the FDA investigation into his contaminated face creams and Casey's photos of the malnourished workers from his tea plantations.

"Terrance headed to his desk. "I'm at the station. I'll give you a call if I learn anything. Stay away from the pier!" he reiterated.

She tossed her phone on the table and picked up the TV remote. When she tuned to one of the news stations, she hollered for her parents. Cora and Jackson rushed to the family room. Amara pointed a shaky finger at the television screen. A reporter spoke while a photo of Ella appeared accompanied with a red banner that read, she was missing.

Amara was surprised it was on the news. She turned to her father. "Will the publicity put Ella's life in jeopardy? How will this affect the investigation?"

Jackson placed an arm around his daughter. "I don't believe anything will happen to Ella. She's worth more alive than dead."

She leaned against her father and whispered, "Unless the kidnapper feels he no longer needs her."

Cora covered her mouth to smother a gasp.

Amara stared at her mother. "We both know desperate people do desperate things."

Chapter 48

Molloy watched the news report and cursed. Hands on hips, his lip curled in disgust. "Who in the hell leaked the information?!"

This blatant move gave credence to Samesh's ulterior motive. The kidnapping was a diversion. Molloy grabbed his jacket and strode to the elevator. He contacted his buddy; a detective in the Narcotics Unit, and told him what was going on. The detective agreed to accompany him to the pier. Molloy told his buddy what he knew as they headed to the detective's vehicle.

Amara felt helpless. She grabbed her phone and examined the photos of the slips of paper she'd taken from Casey's storage unit. One of the sheets of paper had numbers on it. She stared at the numbers and laughed aloud. They were latitude and longitude numbers. Amara raced to her father's study and plotted the coordinates on the oversized Atlas map he'd had since she was a child. She jumped when Jackson entered the office.

"What are you up to, Pumpkin?" he asked.

Amara pointed at the map. "Casey had these coordinates in one of her notes. I plotted them and look where they lead!"

Jackson stared at the map. "Hmm, Mercer Island," he murmured.

"Divya's mansion is located on Mercer Island. The press doesn't know Divya is Ella's biological mother. What if Samesh hid Ella somewhere on her property?"

Jackson frowned. "Mari, how on earth did you surmise that from those coordinates? Casey didn't know anything about the planned kidnapping. Maybe she discovered the link between Divya and Ella and plotted the coordinates instead of using Divya's actual address."

Amara's eyes twinkled. "Can we at least check it out?"

"No, we cannot! Have you lost your mind? If Samesh is there, he's most likely armed, and as you said earlier, desperate." He held up a finger to cut off whatever she'd planned to say. "I will contact Cian and let him handle it."

Amara's shoulders slumped. Though he was right, it was nerve wracking standing around, unable to help. It would be dark soon. She hoped the FBI would find Ella and reunite her with her family.

Amara joined her mother on the sofa. They were discussing the kidnapping when her phone chimed. The call was from a restricted number. It had to be Divya! Amara took a deep breath to calm her nerves before she answered, "Hello?"

Divya's voice was high pitched, her words rushed. "We found Ella. I need your help. Pradeep is hurt and I can't get to Ella by myself. I need you to come to my house." She gave her the address and security code to the gate at the entrance of her driveway. "Tell no one and come alone!"

"Wait! Did Samesh take Ella? How did Pradeep get hurt? What do you need from me?"

Divya sounded manic. "I'll explain everything. Do not tell anyone! Ella's life depends on it."

"What about the FBI?" Amara cried, but the line went dead. Amara told her mother about the call.

Cora called Jackson into the room. Jackson rushed into the room. Amara knew her parents wouldn't allow her to go.

She looked at her parents. "Something wasn't right about her story and her voice sounded strange; desperate. I'm going to call Terrance," she said.

"Amara, I'm in the middle of something right now. I'll call you right back!" He'd ended the call before she could respond. Her fingers trembled as she made the next call. Molloy answered on the first ring.

"What 'cha got?" he queried. She told him about Divya's call. "I'll contact the FBI. I have an officer I can send to the mansion in your stead if the FBI agrees."

"Divya expects me to show up! If law enforcement arrives, something might happen to Ella. She sounds unhinged and claims Pradeep is injured!"

Molloy sighed and explained, "Remember the police officer who pretended to be you at your apartment when you researched those two Russian women?" She told him she remembered. "If the FBI approves, we'll use her again. It will be dark and Divya won't know it's not you until it's too late. If she found Ella, I need to notify the FBI now."

Amara paused. Though there was a strong resemblance, the officer didn't sound like her. "I'll send you a recording of my voice calling Divya's name. My mom said the police officer doesn't sound like me." She had to agree; the darkness of night worked in their favor.

"Send the recording and stay put. Thanks for the call, Amara."

Jackson hugged his daughter. "You did the right thing. You haven't had any contact with Divya in years. She shows up at our house unannounced, not once, but twice. Now she's asking you to come alone to a possible hostage situation." He shook his head. "She was untrustworthy as a child and I believe she's untrustworthy as an adult."

Amara made the recording and forwarded it to Molloy.

Chapter 49

An officer stood at the pier entrance and directed Connor to stop. The officer was dressed casually in pants, t-shirt, and a reflective vest with a logo on the back. Connor braked and rolled down the window. He swallowed hard after the officer removed an orange cone from a front parking space and directed him into the space.

A trickle of sweat rolled down Connor's back and formed above his top lip. The officer asked Connor to follow him. Connor followed the officer and was relieved his car was out of view from the port and freighter.

Detective Molloy motioned for Connor to join him. Gone was the self-assured man who'd strutted out of the interview room without a backward glance. The detective from the Narcotics Unit introduced himself and explained his presence.

Molloy signaled for the technician who asked Connor for his smartphone. He quickly installed an app and returned the phone. "Your phone will enable us to hear whatever Samesh says. We know he's blackmailing you," Molloy said.

Connor shook his head in protest.

Molloy swatted the air. "We're not interested in what you did as a juvenile. Don't worry, we'll be with you every step of the way."

Connor gripped his phone tight. "Okay, okay," he replied shakily. He jumped when his phone buzzed. He stared at the detective with wide eyes. "It's him," he whispered.

"Answer it," Molloy said. He noticed the tremble in Connor's hand. "Take a deep breath, son; we're here."

Connor sucked in a deep breath and released it. When he answered, his voice was calm and steady. "I'm here," he said.

Molloy motioned for him to place the call on speaker. They listened to Samesh's instructions and his threat to expose Connor if he didn't comply.

"I understand," Connor answered through clenched teeth.

Molloy scowled as he listened to Samesh's pompous tone. He looked forward to having him arrested. When the call ended Molloy said, "Once the merchandise is offloaded and you meet with him, we'll intercept the goods and arrest both of you. Don't worry, you'll be released. We want Samesh to believe you were following his instructions and nothing more. Got it?"

Connor's head bobbed up and down as he swallowed hard.

The other detective signaled the men in overalls. "Let's do this."

Connor signed the documents for the cargo, and men began to offload the cargo. Connor watched as a man drove a forklift to pick up the pallet and place it inside a nearby truck. It was well organized. He'd never been privy to this part of the process. His phone buzzed again with Samesh's instructions to accompany the driver to the warehouse. Molloy stood partially hidden in the shadows and gave a nod of encouragement.

Connor stepped on the side rail of the truck and hoisted himself inside the cab. His breath came out in staccato bursts. The driver muttered a few words to calm him.

"I can do this," Connor told himself. His heart began to beat wildly when the warehouse came into view. He glanced out the side window and noticed that the detective and police officers dressed in coveralls were gone.

As the truck lumbered over the last speed bump and entered the warehouse. Two men stood ready to offload the shipment from the pallet. Connor hoped Samesh would finally get what he deserved.

When Connor saw Samesh swagger from the shadows, he threw open the heavy passenger door and hopped out the cab. Fist balled; he strode toward Samesh. He was immediately surrounded by workers in coveralls. One whispered, "Stay cool. Don't blow this."

Samesh clapped his hands and waved the men away. His large teeth gleamed in the dull lights of the warehouse as he directed the man driving the forklift to unload the pallet.

The driver eased into position and lifted the pronged fork. A scraping noise and thump echoed in the cavernous warehouse as the forklift picked up the pallet from the back of the large truck. "Careful!" Samesh shouted.

The beeping sound of the forklift resonated as it backed away from the truck. Once the pallet was removed, the officer dressed as a worker drove out of the warehouse.

Samesh pointed at Connor. "Help unload the pallet." He directed the other two men to place the large boxes into a smaller truck parked in the far corner of the warehouse. "Connor, unload the boxes wrapped in red cellophane and put them in my truck." He gestured in the direction of the black Maserati SUV.

Once the packages were loaded in the SUV, Samesh opened the driver's door. Before he could get in, the police surrounded the vehicle, weapons drawn, and began to shout instructions.

Samesh's man driving the forklift turned off the vehicle. It shook and rattled to a stop. The police yelled for him to get down and took him into custody.

Molloy enjoyed the sound of handcuffs being ratcheted around Samesh's wrists. The metal scraped against his Rolex watch.

Connor walked from behind the truck to where Samesh stood and punched him hard in the face. A slab of light brown latex material fell from the man's face onto the concrete floor. Connor stared; mouth agape. "This is not Samesh!"

Molloy's eyes blazed. Spittle flew from the detective's mouth. "Who the hell are you and where's Samesh!"

The FBI agent spun the man to face him. "Answer the detective. Where is Samesh? Where is Ella?"

The man's voice shook as he held up his hands. "I-I was told this was to be a prank for a f-friend! Samesh...Samesh told me he was playing a joke on his friend Connor. He paid me $500 to impersonate him!" The man raised his chin defiantly. "I'm an actor." He pointed at the latex on the ground. "That was my work! Ha! You all thought I was Samesh."

Molloy couldn't decide whether to throttle or release him. For the time being, he removed the handcuffs.

The actor rubbed his wrists and clucked his tongue. "Geez, Samesh didn't pay me enough for this gig."

"This is not a game!" Molloy growled. "You'd better start talking or the cuffs go back on!" He dangled them in front of the actor's face.

The man grew serious. "Oh my God, you guys are real police officers!" He quickly peeled away the rest of the latex prosthetics from his face and removed the fake teeth and wig. He was younger and fairer than Samesh. He wasn't Indian, but Latino.

"Where is Sam-esh?!" Molloy bellowed.

The man waved his hands frantically. "Honest, I don't know!"

Guns were raised and aimed in the actor's direction when he shoved his right hand inside his left breast pocket.

He yipped and held up both hands, palms faced out. "I'm just reaching for a letter! Geez." The actor looked at Molloy for

241

permission. The detective gave a sharp nod. He reached in his pocket and produced beige envelope with Connor's name. The FBI agent donned gloves, snatched the letter, and tore it open. A sheet of expensive linen stationary with Samesh's initials embossed at the top was inside. The letter read, "We're even- S."

Connor's shoulders relaxed as he exhaled.

Molloy and the FBI walked over to the Maserati. The agent opened one of the packages wrapped with red cellophane. They contained pills, heroin, and cocaine. The FBI agent picked up the sheet of paper that accompanied the packages. Divya's home address was carefully printed on the paper. "Can you communicate with the agents at Divya's home?" Molloy asked.

Chapter 50

Sydney Palmer, the officer impersonating Amara, punched in the code to the gate of Divya's mansion. The unmarked police and FBI sedans entered the estate. The grounds were dark and eerily quiet.

Sydney and one of the FBI agents followed the paved path that snaked around the spacious, modern home. The huge structure had floor-to-ceiling windows. The other FBI agents went to the front door of the mansion.

Lush grass muted the officer and agent's footsteps as they crossed the lawn to the front door of the guesthouse. Shadows from tall hedges bordered the edge of the property. From this vantage point, they could see twinkling lights from boats and larger vessels on Lake Washington.

The guesthouse was a miniature version of the main house, with angular walls, sharp contour lines and skylights instead of the large windows. The front door was made of tinted glass in a rich wood frame. Several port hole windows surrounded the house.

They peered through the glass door. The interior of the small house was dark. The FBI agent stood aside as the officer whispered, "I'm going in."

The FBI agents notified the lead agent they were inside the main house. Sydney knocked on the door and played Amara's recorded voice. "Divya!" She played it once more, "Divya!"

The door slowly opened, and she stepped inside. It took a few seconds for her eyes to adjust. Sydney's hand rested on her pistol, concealed beneath her jacket. She quickly surveyed the space. The layout worked in her favor. It was a studio dwelling with a bathroom shielded behind a wall. A white marble island separated the living room/bedroom from the kitchen area.

Shafts of moonlight shone through the skylight window in the kitchen.

The familiar click of a pistol caused Sydney's head to snap in the direction of the sound. "I needed to get your attention. You've always been a bit slow, Amara." Divya's words were clipped and harsh. "You are as dumb and gullible as you were in high school."

The words hung in the air, unrefuted. "Oh, no comment or quick comeback? You were so full of comments and suggestions earlier when my only child was kidnapped!"

The officer cautiously stepped back and used her thumb to unsnap her holster. Divya waved the pistol in the air carelessly as she shouted, "Say something!"

"Where's Ella," she asked, barely above a whisper.

"Ella! Ella!" Divya shouted. Suddenly, she burst into a fit of laughter. The laughter ceased. "Don't worry, she's safe."

Her next words were spoken as if she was sharing a secret. "Thanks to my dear auntie in India, I can no longer have children. Did you know that?! The monster had me sterilized after I delivered Ella. She resented the way I was raised and accused my parents of being too lenient." The gun waved in the air as she screamed, "That bitch made a life-altering decision without consulting me or my parents! In the end, she got what she deserved." She tsked and drawled, "She died of carbon monoxide poisoning while asleep. The stupid woman left the gas stove on after cooking dinner for her daughter's family."

Sydney remained quiet as Divya ranted on. "I didn't know until I tried to have children with my first husband. He wanted, no needed, at least one heir to carry on the family name. His father was dead, and he was an only son." Her voice trembled. "Imagine my shock when the doctor informed my husband and me that I'd been sterilized and could not bear his children."

She sighed dramatically as she waved the pistol in the air. "He'd demanded a divorce. There was no way I was going back to Seattle destitute, discarded, and divorced. I'd signed a prenup. I would get nothing." The barrel of the pistol clinked against the side of her head. "It was stupid to agree to the terms, but I did. We were so much in love, and he was rich and I was...well, I was not. My husband's family blamed me when he died. If they find out what I've done..."

"Divya, where is Ella?" Sydney interrupted.

"Where is Ella?" Divya mimicked in a whiny voice.

"Divya," the officer warned.

Divya aimed her pistol at the officer's head and shouted, "Shut up, before I shut you up permanently! You're too nosey for your own good. You just wouldn't stop digging into my life, my husband's life." The pistol glinted in the pale moonlight as she flipped off the safety and placed her finger on the trigger. "You know too much, and I need to get rid of you!"

In one fluid motion, the officer drew her pistol, aimed, and fired. Divya screamed as her pistol clattered onto the wood floor. The FBI agent rushed inside as Sydney kicked the pistol beyond Divya's reach.

Sydney and Divya blinked when the agent turned on the lights. Divya's eyes grew wide when the officer flung the curly wig to the floor and aimed her weapon at Divya. "Where the hell is Ella?!" she shouted.

Divya struggled to sit upright as the agent ripped the sleeve of her blouse to inspect her flesh wound. Blood trickled down her right arm.

Officer Palmer kept her pistol trained on Divya while the FBI agent secured her wrists with a zip tie. "I could have killed your ass, but I need to know what you did with Ella."

Sirens sounded in the distance. The FBI agent radioed the gate code to the ambulance driver.

Only then did he notice the unconscious man slumped in the corner. He raced over, placed his finger on the side of the victim's neck, and felt a weak pulse. The man's skin was clammy, his breathing shallow.

"What did you give him?" the FBI agent demanded.

"Just a little something to slow his heart wa-ay down," she drawled. "The heartless bastard got exactly what he deserved!"

The agent patted Divya down. He found a bottle of procainamide tucked in a side pocket of her trousers. He returned to the unconscious man and spotted an empty syringe on the floor. The agent cursed and spoke into his mic. He glared at Divya and asked, "Does this man have a heart condition?" Divya shrugged. He located the man's identification. It was Samesh. "Where is your husband? Where is Ella?" the agent shouted.

Divya stared vacantly at Sydney Palmer. "I guess Amara isn't so dumb after all." An EMT rushed inside to retrieve Samesh's unconscious body. Divya was escorted to the front of the mansion. Her torn right sleeve exposed her bare arm streaked with blood.

Molloy and FBI agents raced up the drive. Sydney Palmer made her way to the front of the house and spoke to the detective. "Ella isn't in the guesthouse. Pradeep is missing as well. Samesh was drugged. They're taking him to the hospital."

As the FBI agent handed off Divya, he spotted movement in mansion front window. He looked at Molloy who'd seen it too. "We have agents inside," he said.

Pradeep wrung his hands and slowly inched to the side of the large, floor to ceiling window. Flashing lights illuminated the police officers and men in windbreakers that read FBI. They'd gathered in front of the house and on the lawn. An ambulance raced down the drive onto the street. Pradeep peered over his shoulder at the child sitting on a high stool, munching sugar cookies, and drinking milk at the round glass bistro table. She wore headphones and watched a cartoon on an electronic tablet propped against the milk carton.

Pradeep jumped when two armed agents crept into the room. One gestured for him to remain quiet. The other beckoned him to move in their direction. Eyes wide, he quickly complied. The agent reached out and whisked him from the room without making a sound.

The remaining agent holstered his weapon and approached the young girl. He tapped her on the shoulder. She snatched the earphones from her ears. Hazel eyes stared up at the man dressed in dark clothing and windbreaker.

"Hello Ella, are you ready to go home?"

The young girl stared at the stranger. A milk mustache coated her upper lip as she nodded. She wiped her mouth with the back of her hand and carefully placed the headphones on the table next to the tablet. Her eyes remained on the agent while she debated whether to trust him.

"How do you know my name?" she asked. The agent identified himself. Ella shook her head and announced, "I need to talk to my mom. The other man wouldn't let me talk to my mom. He brought me here and left me. Is my auntie here? The man told me my auntie was coming to get me."

The agent removed his phone and handed it to Ella. "We don't know anything about your auntie."

Ella dialed her home number. Her face lit with delight at the sound of her mother's voice. She ended the call and jumped from the chair. Her sneakers landed on the wood floor with a loud thump. "I'm ready," she declared, and accompanied the agent out of the mansion.

Chapter 51

Ella sprang from the sedan and raced to her parents and brother. They met in the middle of their front lawn, hugging and kissing. Molloy was pleased Ella seemed unfazed by her ordeal.

Molloy sat at his desk and pondered the day's events. Unbeknownst to Ella's parents, Samesh had made contact with Ella and her brother several times at the library box. She'd grown comfortable with him.

Ella never saw Divya, who'd been alerted by her housekeeper and gone directly to the guesthouse with the briefcase filled with money. The promise of the $30 million ransom convinced Samesh to leave Ella with the housekeeper and meet her in the guesthouse.

Once Samesh was out of the house, Pradeep made sure Ella was safe and unharmed. He sent the housekeeper home and remained with the little girl.

Focused on the briefcase filled with money, Samesh neglected to notice the syringe in Divya's other hand.

He'd blackmailed so many people. This time the joke was on him. Only the top bills of the ransom money in the briefcase were real. Though Samesh was in the custody of the FBI, the investigation was far from over. Molloy couldn't wait to question him about the murder of Casey Athy and the family law attorney in New York.

His attention was drawn to the door when Sydney Palmer entered the office. He motioned to the chair in front of his desk.

Her brown eyes twinkled with mischief as took a seat. "I don't know whether to thank Amara or kick her ass for the messes she continues to get into."

Molloy leaned back in his chair. "At least you didn't get slapped or shot at this time."

The police officer barked a laugh. "Oh! You've got jokes huh?"

A timid voice broke into their jousting. Amara slowly entered the office. "Am I interrupting something?"

Officer Sydney Palmer turned and gave Amara a thorough once over. Amara didn't flinch or squirm under the scrutiny. "Well, well, we finally meet," the officer announced. She introduced herself.

"I can't thank you enough for all you've done for me and my family," Amara said. Except for the short, dark, spiked hair, they could pass as sisters.

"Uh huh...how about we not make this a habit?" the officer wisecracked.

Amara chuckled and shook her head. "I'd love to make that promise but..."

Molloy laughed and gestured to the vacant chair.

Amara sat down. "I'm dying to know, is Ella, okay? What about Divya and that awful Samesh?"

Molloy assured her Ella was home safe with her parents. He told her as much as he could since it was an ongoing investigation. Amara slapped her jean-clad thighs and stood. "That's great news! Thank you for telling me." Without warning, she hugged Sydney. "Thank you!" she whispered in her ear. Amara straightened and left with a bounce in her step.

Officer Palmer couldn't help but chuckle. She stuck her thumb in the direction of the doorway. "She's a force all by herself, isn't she?"

Molloy tilted his head back and gave a raucous laugh. "Welcome to my world." Officer Palmer stood, shook her head, and waved as she headed out the suite.

Terrance intercepted Amara as she exited the elevator. He stepped close and asked, "How are you?" He hadn't noticed Officer Palmer as she stepped out of the second elevator and glanced in their direction. Amara had his full attention. "Sorry I didn't answer your calls. I was helping Lanzo with something."

Amara's brow lifted. "I won't even ask what you two were up to."

"Good idea."

"Will you have time for dinner tonight?" Amara asked.

"I just got off duty. I need to speak with Molloy. Will you wait for me? I won't be long."

Amara nodded. "I'll be in my car."

Terrance squeezed her hand and pushed the button for the elevator. The doors slid open and he pushed the button for Molloy's office. He sat in the chair in front of Molloy's desk. "I heard everything went as planned and Samesh is in custody. Is it true Divya is in the psyche ward?"

Molloy pursed his lips and shrugged. "Yep. I guess she lost it after the arrest. Samesh knew about Ella's parentage and blackmailed Divya for millions. He'd purposely hired Connor, Ella's biological father, to maintain control. Pradeep hadn't known about Ella until the kidnapping." He tapped his desk and added, "Luckily, everything turned out all right. Ella wasn't harmed and doesn't know Divya is her biological mother. I don't believe Connor has a clue about Ella." Molloy held up a document from the file. "Connor had signed over guardianship before Ella was born and is engaged to be married."

Terrance leaned forward in his chair. "I came to talk to you about Rolanzo's friend who was found dead in his apartment. Evidence was discovered in Gerard's New York apartment."

Molloy squinted. "Who discovered the evidence? The police or one of Rolanzo's men?"

Terrance looked away. He was torn between his loyalty to Rolanzo and Molloy. The truth was always the best policy. He took a breath and replied, "Rolanzo's men, but they were careful and contacted the police."

Molloy held up a hand. "Don't tell me anything more." He picked up the phone. "I'll contact my buddy and get an update."

Terrance visibly relaxed while Molloy was on the phone.

Molloy ended the call and explained, "The NYPD followed up on the tip provided by Rolanzo's guys. The thief received a sizeable deposit the day the lawyer died. It looks like it came from Pradeep's company account."

Terrance exhaled. Rolanzo had shared that information as well.

Molloy stood and grabbed his sports jacket. "I think I need to speak to a certain accountant in Pradeep's company." Molloy patted Terrance's shoulder. "Thanks for the info."

They walked together to the bank of elevators.

Amara jumped when Terrance tapped the driver's side window. She rolled down the window and placed a hand over her heart. "You scared me!"

"Sorry. Hey, where do you want to go for dinner?"

"My parents invited us over. They're anxious to hear about what happened with Ella." Amara recalled Divya's mental state when she'd been at her parents' home. "Have you seen the news?" she asked. Terrance shook his head. The child's reunion with her family had been captured by a neighbor and sent to a local news station.

Terrance frowned. "Did the news report reveal who was responsible for the kidnapping?"

Amara smirked and replied, "The family claimed it was a misunderstanding involving a relative. Samesh, Divya, or Pradeep wasn't mentioned."

"Good. Ella doesn't need to know about Divya until her parents are ready to tell her."

Amara thought that might be sooner than later due to her inheritance. "So, do you want to follow me to my parents' house for dinner or just go for dessert later?"

Terrance placed his hands on the roof of the car and leaned in close. "Let's do dinner. I have another idea for dessert."

Amara thumped his stomach gently with her fingers. "You're so bad!" Her smile relayed otherwise and Terrance laughed aloud.

He tapped the hood of her car. "It's settled, dessert at your place," he called over his shoulder.

"I'm going to hold you to that," she teased.

Amara watched as he strode to his car. No, she wouldn't mind being his dessert one bit.

Terrance had everyone's attention as he described what he knew transpired at Divya's home and in the warehouse at the pier.

Amara's head swam. Though Molloy had basically told her what had occurred, she'd underestimated the ramifications of Samesh's actions. Casey had been right. He'd been sneaking drugs into the country and most likely selling them to maintain his over-the-top standard of living.

Samesh was like a tornado. A trail of wreckage and destruction remained wherever he went. Casey, Rolanzo's lawyer friend, Connor, Divya, the thief who left Rolanzo's friend for dead, the accountant, the actor who'd pretended to be him at the pier warehouse...God only knew how many others.

It gave Amara great pleasure to picture Samesh dressed in prison garb, devoid of all the glitz and glamour.

Chapter 52

Molloy sat across from the young accountant. Her face was flushed and eyes welled with tears as she pulled open a desk drawer and removed the blackmail photos. In a quiet voice, she explained what Samesh had forced her to do. Molloy studied the pictures and was certain she'd been unconscious when they were taken. The whole thing looked staged. She printed out the invoice for the transfer of funds to Gerard, the con-man's account.

He felt bad for her. She'd likely lose her job and face possible jail time if Pradeep pressed charges. When Molloy shared his opinion regarding the photos, the accountant broke down and sobbed with relief. Before he left, she told him about Samesh's overseas personal account in his mother's maiden name.

The detective contacted the FBI and told them about the funds transferred to Gerard who'd allegedly murdered the attorney in New York. The FBI agent assured him they'd contact NYPD and continue their investigation. He also told the agent about Samesh's personal overseas account that was in his mother's maiden name. The agent invited Molloy to join them at Samesh's condo.

Molloy and the FBI agents entered Samesh's plush condo that overlooked Lake Washington. The place was minimally furnished and felt sterile. If Molloy hadn't known better, he would have sworn no one lived there. There wasn't a speck of dust or piece of furniture out of place. The marble kitchen countertop gleamed and looked as if a dish had never graced its surface.

Molloy opened one of the solid white wooden cabinets and found white plates, mugs, bowls and two expensive crystal Waterford Lismore water glasses.

One of the agents whistled as another voiced Molloy's thoughts. "Did the guy actually live here or what?" FBI agents continued to search the kitchen cabinets and drawers. Most were empty. There were no pots or pans in the cabinets. Evidently, Samesh dined out or ordered takeout.

Molloy sank on his haunches and checked the cabinets beneath the sink. They were bare as well. Where was the dishwashing liquid, sponge, or dish towel? Had Samesh planned to leave the state if not the country?

"I found something!" yelled one of the agents from another room. Molloy followed the voice into Samesh's stark bedroom that contained a hand crafted, king-sized platform bed. The FBI agent lifted the mattress encased in plastic.

Molloy stared at the folder and disposable cell phone. The folder contained a passport with a dated photo of Ella. Molloy's shoulders relaxed with the knowledge Ella was safe.

The FBI agent in charge received a call regarding Samesh's yacht. There were photos of Casey at the pier, Ella, and her brother at the library box, and a picture of Amara. They'd also discovered altered passports that contained false names for Divya and Samesh. Why hadn't those items been discovered during the FBI's previous search?

The detective walked to the closet as the agent continued to list the evidence discovered on the yacht. The closet was empty save for expensive wooden hangers and dry-cleaning tags that had been removed from suits, slacks, and shirts.

He stooped and shined a flashlight in the corners of the carpeted floor of the closet. His flashlight illuminated paper wrappers that once held bundles of one-hundred-dollar bills.

An agent appeared and whistled as he photographed and gathered the wrappers. "There must have been over $4 million in this closet!"

Another agent called out from the bathroom where sealed plastic packets of heroin, cocaine and bright colored pills were taped inside of the white porcelain toilet tank with waterproof duct tape. Had he forgotten to retrieve his stash or didn't care if the drugs were discovered?

Once the evidence was photographed and accounted for, the agents collected each piece and departed.

The manager of the exclusive condo met them outside the door and ensured the place was properly secured. He turned to Molloy and the FBI agents and explained Samesh had given notice and sold the condo to include the contents.

Molloy smirked. Samesh had planned to flee the country and hadn't cared what they discovered in his condo. The plane was a decoy. That was why he'd flashed it all over his social media sites. He'd planned to slip away on his yacht. What had he planned to do with Ella and Divya? The thought sent a shiver down his spine. Molloy was certain Samesh knew about Ella's trust fund.

As they headed to their cars, Molloy learned $6 million worth of empty wrappers were also discovered inside the storage compartments on Samesh's yacht. He'd hidden $10 million between the two locations. That didn't include the $30 million ransom he'd planned to get from Divya. Where was all that money now, Molloy wondered?

As Molloy drove home, he pondered Pradeep's roll in Samesh's blackmail schemes. Had he really been clueless to Samesh's blackmail schemes and the millions stolen from his company? Was Samesh blackmailing him also? Pradeep had admitted he'd given Samesh too much control.

There was more to the story, but Molloy didn't have time to dig through the minutia and learn what it was. He called his NYPD buddy to learn if there was new information about the death of the attorney. Was it murder or death by natural causes?

When the call ended, Molloy phoned Rolanzo Dumont. Molloy enjoyed the irony of it all. A few months ago, he considered Dumont a foe. Though they weren't exactly friends, they'd reached a truce and mutual respect.

Rolanzo thanked the detective and ended the call. He'd known most of the information Molloy provided. Samesh had hired a thief to break into his friend's apartment and steal information regarding Ella's birth and adoption. The part of the story that didn't make sense was that Samesh had blackmailed Divya for millions to keep her secret. If Samesh knew about Ella's parentage, what had he hoped to learn from the family lawyer Divya hired? Then it dawned on him. Samesh was looking for the trust paperwork. He wanted to know how much money Ella would inherit and when. The man had zero scruples or principles.

Rolanzo wished his men had gotten to Samesh first. He'd have told them everything. It was clear Samesh spent an inordinate amount of time and effort in manipulation and blackmail. He looked at the document from his head of security. The autopsy report confirmed his friend died of a heart attack. What happened to cause the attack in the first place? Rolanzo closed his eyes and placed the document on the desk. "Rest in peace my friend," he whispered.

Chapter 53

Amara lay tangled in the sheets next to Terrance who slept peacefully. She turned to look at his shadowed face. Those long lashes, sexy lips and little button nose took her breath away. They'd enjoyed their special dessert and then slept soundly. It was well after midnight and she couldn't dismiss thoughts of Divya. Even though the FBI had access to all her devices, Samesh had communicated Ella's location and instructions for the ransom to Divya without it being intercepted. Had he given her a burner phone? Whatever the case, he'd been thwarted and Ella was home safe with her family.

Amara wasn't stupid. She knew Divya had played her and doubted they'd ever speak again.

It was clear Samesh was responsible for Casey's death and hoped Molloy would uncover evidence soon. What was Divya's role in all this? The photo from Casey's storage room showed Samesh partially hidden in the background with a group of men at the orphanage in India. Why had he attended Divya's charitable event? Were they having an affair?

Amara scowled. Samesh was like a carton of sour milk; perfectly fine on the outside until you opened the carton and smelled its putrid, curdled contents.

Her thoughts turned to Pradeep. He was twenty years Divya's senior. Was he more ornament than partner? Someone who fit nicely on the crook of her arm like one of her expensive designer handbags?

Had Samesh forced Divya to contact her to determine how much or what she knew? At this point, she wouldn't discount Samesh or Divya's motives.

Terrance's strong arms pulled her close. His voice was deep from sleep when he said, "Turn off your brain and go back to sleep." Her body went slack in his embrace. He was right. There was nothing she could solve right now. As her eyes closed, she wondered if this case kept Molloy up late as well. Terrance gently stroked her hair until she fell asleep.

Detective Molloy rubbed his tired eyes. It was well after midnight. The information he'd received from the NYPD homicide detective wasn't what he'd hoped. They could only charge the suspect with breaking and entering. There'd been the ten-minute phone call between the victim and suspect. The police had no evidence he'd caused the lawyer's death. Maybe they could charge him with negligence since he hadn't called for help when he'd found the victim on the floor.

Doubt niggled inside of Molloy's brain. Something wasn't right. The man was paid $50,000 dollars to pretend to be the deceased lawyer at Dumont's wedding. Was the money an incentive for him to learn what Casey knew or for killing the lawyer? He sighed, clicked off the lamp, pushed himself up from the chair and went to bed.

Chapter 54

Amara sat at her kitchen table and checked the morning news feeds on her laptop. Ella's kidnapping and Samesh's involvement hadn't been in the newspapers or broadcasted on the news. Ella's parents stuck to their story of a misunderstanding with a family member. Amara guessed that was partially true.

Pradeep's company distanced itself from Samesh and the illegal shipment of drugs confiscated by the police and FBI. Divya had been released from the hospital and was home on bail. How in the world had she gotten bail? The power of money, Amara thought.

Though she was certain of Samesh's culpability in the death of Mr. Dumont's friend and Casey; she wondered if it would be proven. She guessed that's why Molloy and the FBI took an oath to solve crimes such as these.

She considered the coordinates to Divya's home in Casey's notes. What did they mean to Casey? Amara sighed. Maybe she was making way too much of Casey's scraps of paper. Except Casey believed they were important enough to secure in her storage unit.

Terrance placed a mug of coffee beside her laptop and kissed her cheek. "What are you working on?"

Amara sipped her coffee. It allowed her a few seconds to form her response. She wasn't ready to let this go. Though Terrance would worry, she wanted to see this thing through for Casey's parents. Amara pointed at her computer screen and replied, "I'm catching up on the news. I guess I shouldn't be surprised Ella's kidnapping wasn't mentioned." She tapped the screen with her forefinger and added, "Pradeep's company downplayed the illegal drugs found in the tea shipment by the FBI and Port Police."

Terrance rested his chin in the curve between her neck and shoulder and read the screen. He breathed in her freshly showered scent. Suddenly the aroma of burning toast permeated the air. He juggled the nearly burnt English muffin to a plate and slathered it with butter and jam. "You're not surprised, are you?" he asked and fed her a piece of his English muffin. Terrance placed her half on a plate next to her computer.

"No, just a little sad," she replied. The authorities had yet to unravel all the evidence and clues of who killed Casey and if Mr. Dumont's friend's death was solely due to heart failure.

Terrance popped the last of his English muffin in his mouth, gave her a quick, buttery, kiss and headed out the kitchen. "I need to go home and change for work. What are your plans for the day?"

It was Friday and she needed to get to the office. Amara couldn't take another day off without raising questions. She gulped the last of her coffee, took a bite of her muffin, and rushed to the bedroom to grab her satchel.

When Terrance opened the front door, Amara was at his heels. He reset the alarm and secured both locks.

Amara jogged to her car, backed out and waved to Terrance.

Chapter 55

Amara entered the office and sat at her desk. She noticed Matt's office light beneath the closed door. The staff hadn't arrived, and she used the time to gather her thoughts and organize the day without distraction or interruption.

Matt opened his office door and stuck his head out. He wasn't wearing his glasses. The sight of his pale face and deep-set blue eyes reminded her of a character from a horror movie. The thought made her laugh.

"Amara, a moment please?" His expression was serious. Her smile evaporated as she heaved herself from the chair and braced for what was to come. He pointed to one of his chairs. Amara sat down and waited. "So, how was your day off?" he asked.

"It was fine, thank you. I appreciate the extra time. My parents and I had a busy morning."

Matt picked up his glasses and cleaned the lenses. He had a faraway look as he glanced in her direction. When he put on his glasses, intense blue eyes focused on her.

She waited for him to speak. When he didn't, she broke the silence. "Is there a problem? I used authorized leave time. Did you receive negative feedback on one of my articles?"

His hands remained busy straightening papers and pencils on his desk. "Actually," he drawled, "I want to know what the heck is going on. You're always knee deep in some type of drama!" He grabbed one of the pencils and tapped it rapidly against his desk.

Amara held his steady gaze and the impulse to tell him off. Her boss had stepped over the line.

Matt leaned back in his chair. "A news reporter called the office yesterday. He wanted information regarding the possible kidnapping of a young girl. I did a bit of research. It was the same girl you photographed for your library box article! What do you know about that?"

Amara waited a beat before she replied, "Not much. I heard something about that in the news this morning. Though it wasn't a kidnapping. The girl's parents said it was a miscommunication with a family member."

She frowned at Matt. "You know the photos in my article were of the backsides of the boy and girl as they faced the box. They were also wearing helmets. I made sure not to use their names in the article. Where are you getting your information?"

Matt broke eye contact. He avoided her question with one of his own. "Is there anything you want to tell me?"

Amara looked at her watch. "No. Is there anything you want to tell me?" It was a struggle to maintain a calm demeanor. What she did on her day off was her business.

Matt waved in the direction of the door. "You're worse than Remy. Get back to work. I know there's more to the story." Amara didn't respond as she stood and left his office. She couldn't divulge Divya's secret. The FBI was investigating, and it wasn't her information to share; no matter how much she disliked the woman.

Amara scowled and sat down hard in her chair. He had a lot of nerve pouncing on her like that. Drama, really? The subscription numbers had doubled since she'd been hired. Readers liked her investigative pieces. Though she hadn't been putting much effort in her blog lately, she was doing a great job at the office with the magazine articles. He could take that drama and...

Before she could finish the thought, Remy bounced into the office whistling another French tune. Amara smiled despite her residual anger. "Wow, you sound happy," she teased.

Remy winked. "My flight attendant was here for the weekend. She left this morning."

"Oh, so now she's your flight attendant, huh?"

He smiled wide and walked to her desk. "Yep. Hey, what happened yesterday? Matt went ballistic after some reporter called. He said it had to do with the girl in your photograph." He lowered his voice and leaned close. "Is this connected to the Casey Athy case?"

Amara shrugged. "Like I told Matt. I have no idea." She pointed at her boss' office door. "Why did he think I had something to do with it? The photo I used in the magazine was of the kids' backside. I didn't include their names. Why did the reporter call this office? The kid in the magazine could have been any little girl."

Remy held up his hands, palms facing out. "Whoa! I don't know what Matt said to you this morning, but that reporter got a tip from someone. They were told our magazine had information about the girl who'd been kidnapped." "What's going on?" he whispered.

Amara blew a stray curl from her face. "I wish I knew." She closed her eyes, hating the deception, but there was no way she could tell him what happened yesterday. Ella would suffer and might be put in danger if the truth got out. Especially if the truth included information about her inheritance. This was Divya's mess, and she needed to clean it up. Remy returned to his desk.

Matt came out of his office and headed in her direction. She attempted to hide her displeasure when he sat in the chair beside her desk. Amara glanced in his direction as her fingertips rapidly tapped computer keys.

"I was out of line this morning. I know better than to make suppositions without concrete evidence. I apologize."

It took all her willpower not to tell him where he could stick his apology. Amara loved her job and felt Matt was a fair boss, until this morning. She gave a quick nod and continued to type. Matt returned to his office while she ignored Remy's attempts to get her attention.

When the clock signaled the end of the workday, Amara couldn't get out of the office fast enough. She packed her things and left with the rest of the staff. Remy glanced up in surprise but continued typing. It was a comfort Remy knew her well enough to allow her some space.

Once the staff was gone, Remy headed to his brother's office.

Chapter 56

The next morning, Amara completed her article and submitted it to Matt for review. She'd kept her distance. His actions still stung. How could a phone call from some reporter prompt such behavior? Samesh had something to do with the reporter calling the office. Had it been his final attempt to keep the attention on the kidnapping and away from the pier? What better way than to put the spotlight on her and the magazine?

At the end of the day, she and Remy left the office together. They joked back and forth before heading to their respective cars. She'd persuaded Terrance to take her to the bar downtown where police officers hung out. She wanted to speak with Sydney Palmer.

People stared when she entered the bar with Terrance. She wasn't sure if it was because she was with her police officer boyfriend or that she resembled Sydney, who was tucked away in a back booth nursing a beer. Amara slid across the vinyl bench seat in the booth. Terrance ordered two beers and a couple of appetizers.

When the beer and appetizers were almost gone, Sydney stared at Amara. "Why are you here and what do you expect me to tell you?" she asked bluntly.

Amara ate the last appetizer and drained her mug of beer. "I want to know what Divya said to you in her guesthouse." She paused. "When she thought you were me."

Sydney tilted her head as if to decide how much to tell. "It's not pretty." Sydney shrugged and added, "In fact, I was hurt for you."

Amara clasped her hands and leaned forward. "What did she say?" Her words held a bit more force than intended.

Sydney glanced at Terrance, who nodded. She placed bills on the table and announced, "Amara and I are going to step out for a minute."

They faced each other beneath the dim light a few feet from the door. Amara tucked her hands inside her jacket to keep out the chill. She waited patiently until Sydney was ready to speak.

Sydney leaned against the building and repeated the names Divya had called Amara. "She pointed her pistol at me, and I shot her." The officer decided not to repeat Divya's confession regarding her first husband's death that was possibly murder. That information might be dangerous for Amara if she knew.

Amara placed her hand on the woman's forearm. It felt hard and muscular. "Thank you for telling me. I know it's your job, but I appreciate what you did for me. Believe it or not, I didn't pursue Divya. We hadn't spoken in years. Casey's father asked me to look into his daughter's death. Out of deference to him, I did."

"Trouble seems to follow you. Try to stay out of trouble, okay?"

Amara shrugged. "I can't make any promises. You're right about one thing; trouble seems to follow me whether I want it or not." She saw a twinkle in the officer's brown eyes. Amara knew Sydney hadn't shared everything that had transpired between her and Divya.

"Nice car!" she called as the officer dug in her purse for her keys to her classic 1980 Dodge Charger. The car was in mint condition and looked to have its original paint job. Amara checked her watch. It was late; time to head home. She turned and headed back inside.

Terrance stood and escorted Amara out of the pub. "Do you feel better knowing?" he asked.

Amara nodded. "Divya never considered me a true friend. I guess she involved me because she believed I knew too much and would tell someone. Though there's a problem with that theory. My parents, Molloy and the FBI knew as well. What was her plan for them?"

Terrance gripped her hand tight. "Thank God, we will never have to find out. The police brought Divya in for more questioning. She may be out on bail, but her problems with the law are just beginning."

Amara turned to stare at her boyfriend. "What aren't you telling me?"

Terrance shook his head. "If I could tell you, I would."

"Did she have something to do with Casey's murder?"

"At this time, she's being charged with the attack against Samesh and pointing a loaded weapon at a police officer." He led the way to his car.

Amara leaned against the car door. "What's happening with Pradeep?"

Terrance unlocked the door. "It seems he was in the dark about the entire situation until Divya called him, hysterical about Ella. He hadn't known about the child." Terrance shrugged and noted, "I hope the major shakedown at his company helps. That accountant who was blackmailed by Samesh was reassigned, which was benevolent."

Terrance paused when he saw Sydney's Dodge Charger in the parking lot. He wondered why she hadn't left. He began to look around while he continued updating Amara. "I heard Samesh's assets have been frozen. Divya hired a lawyer to get her money back. He'd blackmailed her for millions." Terrance didn't tell Amara about the cash wrappers from Samesh's apartment and yacht.

Amara whistled and opened the car door. "I wish Divya luck." Her thoughts drifted to Ella's birth father. How had he fared?

She looked over the hood of the car and asked, "What about Connor? What's happened...?"

Before she could complete the last question, Terrance turned and sprinted down the sidewalk. A figure dressed in dark clothes raced away from a crumpled form next to Sydney's car.

"Dial 911!" Terrance yelled as he chased the attacker.

Amara punched in the emergency number and screamed for help.

Adrenalin pumped as Terrance caught up with the attacker. He'd played football in college and was still in top shape. He used the attacker's momentum and shoved them to the ground.

"Stay down," Terrance ordered as he pinned the suspect to the ground. The side of the assailant's face was smooshed against the pebbled asphalt.

He glanced over his shoulder as several officers raced in his direction. The first to arrive handed Terrance a plastic zip tie. He bound the attacker's hands and hoisted them upright as the emergency lights from a police sedan lit up the area. Sounds of an ambulance siren echoed in the night air. When Terrance saw the suspect's face, his breath caught.

Chapter 57

Amara shivered as she followed Terrance inside at the police station. The violence of the evening felt like a damp, wool blanket on a frigid, winter day.

The young officer at the front desk stared and blurted, "Has anyone ever told you that you resemble Officer Palmer?"

Her eyes filled with tears. It was clear the news hadn't reached this officer. "Yes, I've been told that," Amara choked out.

When Terrance explained about the attack against Sydney Palmer, the young officer turned crimson. He became all business as he took Amara's statement. Terrance sat in the chair at the vacant desk next to Amara and typed his statement.

The station fell silent when a police officer escorted Divya into the precinct. Several officers glared in her direction. There was a slight bruise on the right side of her face. Mud stained her expensive black Natori stretch ankle pants and matching Natori sweater where she'd collided with the muddy pavement.

Amara's fists balled instinctively. Divya had attacked the wrong woman...hadn't she? The realization nearly took her breath away. Her gaze swiveled in Terrance's direction. His square jaw was locked tight and fists clinched as Divya passed. It was a comfort that her man fought the same impulse.

Terrance texted Molloy about the attack. As they left the precinct, Amara suggested they head to the hospital to visit Sydney.

"Yeah, I was thinking the same thing," Terrance said.

Once they were inside their car, Amara faced him. "Terrance, I don't think Divya meant to attack me. I believe her target was Officer Palmer all along."

Terrance's eyes grew wide. "What! Why-why do you think she was the target?"

Amara pursed her lips. "When I asked Sydney what Divya said in the guesthouse, I could tell she'd held something back. I've been around Molloy and you long enough to know when something is not being said. Sydney knew something, but was unable or unwilling to share it with me."

"Wow, it must have been something pretty bad for Divya to come at her like that."

"There's no way Divya could have known we'd be at the bar. That place is a popular cop hangout." Amara tapped his hand. "What if Divya followed Sydney to the bar? Remember, she was already there when we arrived. I never discussed my personal life with Divya. She doesn't know where I live! That's why she kept going to my parents' house." Amara pointed at her chest and said, "Terrance, I'm fairly certain I wasn't the target tonight."

"If you're right, I need to speak with Cian. I'm sure Sydney told him everything Divya said in the guesthouse." He dialed Molloy's cell. He answered on the first ring.

Terrance explained Amara's theory. The line was silent for so long Terrance thought the call had been disconnected. "Hello?"

Molloy finally spoke. "Amara may be right. Meet me at the hospital."

Terrance cut his eyes in Amara's direction. "Gloating is not a good look."

Amara stared out the passenger window as a knowing smile spread across her face.

Terrance and Amara entered the curtained area where Sydney Palmer sat partially upright on a gurney. Bloodstains marred the front of her blouse. A white bandage peeked through the bloodied tear at the knee on the right leg of her slacks. Another white bandage covered the back of her head. An angry bruise marred the right side of her face, close to her temple.

Amara remained silent. She knew anything she said at this point would be taken the wrong way.

Terrance let go of her hand and inched forward. His voice was filled with concern as he asked, "How are you doing?"

Sydney grimaced. "I've been better. I was cracked in the head from behind and hit the edge of the car mirror as I went down."

Terrance leaned close and spoke quietly into Sydney's ear.

The surprised look on Sydney's face as she stared at Amara was priceless. "Damn," she muttered.

Amara shrugged. "I could tell you were holding something back and figured whatever it was, you were either investigating, or had provided the information to Molloy or the FBI to investigate."

Sydney struggled to sit upright. Terrance stepped forward to help, but she waved him away. Before she could speak, Molloy broke through the curtained area. "Can you give us a few minutes?" he asked.

Terrance parted the curtain and Amara followed. She slowed to eavesdrop on the conversation between Molloy and Sydney. Terrance grabbed her hand and pulled her away from the curtained area. "You are so nosey," he chastised.

Busted. Amara followed Terrance to the waiting room without uttering a word of protest.

Terrance pulled her close and whispered, "Now you're too quiet. What are you up to Amara Mackelroy?"

Amara sighed. "I just wanted to hear what the big secret was." She folded her arms over her chest. "If I had been at Divya's instead of Sydney, I'd know," she rationalized.

Terrance snorted. "Good try. You'd also most likely be dead."

Molloy joined them in the waiting room before Amara could provide a retort. He motioned for them to follow him outside. Once they were a fair distance from the hospital entrance, Molloy began to explain, "Divya confessed something in the presence of Sydney. I believe she made the confession because Divya thought she was speaking to Amara and planned to kill her." His green eyes swept in her direction as he apologized.

His statement confirmed what Terrance had said. To hear it from Molloy felt like a punch in the gut. Though she'd known Sydney grazed Divya's arm in the guesthouse, she hadn't considered Divya's intent.

Molloy used the toe of his shoe to move loose gravel. "I plan to phone my contact at the FBI. Apparently, this is more serious than I initially believed."

Amara's eyes grew wide. What in the world had Divya confessed? She recalled the photos and scraps of paper found in the box inside Casey's storage unit. Why had Casey included Divya's first husband, his siblings and mother-in-law? She'd also included Pradeep's children. She needed to review all the information gathered from Casey's storage unit. Her eyes slid in the detective's direction. There was no way she'd tell him about her copies of the photos and notes. At least not tonight.

Terrance thanked the detective and led Amara back into the hospital. They parted the curtain in time to see Sydney attempt to stand. Terrance rushed to help as she swayed and nearly toppled to the floor.

A nurse rushed into the curtained area. "Whoa! Where do you think you're going Officer Palmer! You're still under observation. You took a hard hit to the head." The nurse checked her watch. "The doctor will check on you in thirty minutes or so." She helped Terrance put Sydney on the gurney. "Sit tight until the doctor arrives."

Sydney griped but did as she was told. She looked at Terrance and held out a set of car keys. "Would you pick up my car and drive it to the hospital? I should be released soon."

Terrance took the keys and shook his head. "Nope. But I will take the car to your apartment and get you home when you're ready to leave."

Sydney's nostrils flared with frustration, but there was nothing she could do. The doctor would not allow her to drive with a possible concussion. She sighed and compromised. "How about this; return my keys, I'll call my roommate, and she can drive me home."

Terrance gave her a hard stare and removed his phone. "What's her number?"

Sydney cursed, turned, and stared at the curtained partition. She glared in Amara's direction and groused, "I guess you're enjoying this."

Amara didn't respond. She might need this woman in the future and wasn't about to burn any bridges. She parted the curtain and left as Sydney gave Terrance her roommate's phone number. "I'll get your car, drive it to the hospital and leave the keys at the nurse's station," he said.

Amara chuckled. Did Sydney think she'd con Terrance into giving her the keys? The stubborn woman had intended to drive herself home.

Terrance joined her in the waiting room, and they returned to the pub where Sydney's car was parked. He pulled into the slot beside the Dodge Charger and unlocked the door.

Amara followed in his car to the hospital. As promised, he left the keys at the nurse's station. When Terrance exited the hospital, Amara got out and sat in the passenger seat. She yawned and reclined the seat as he got behind the wheel.

Terrance gave her shoulder a gentle push. Amara awoke with a start. Bright lights bathed her apartment building. She opened the door, and Terrance placed his hand on her arm to stop her. The cold air jolted her wide awake. Amara turned and was surprised by Terrance's troubled expression. She closed the car door. "What is it?" she asked.

"I need to tell you something about Sydney."

Amara pushed curls from her face. "What, the fact you two dated in the past?"

"Y-yes, how, how did you know?"

Amara shrugged and said, "The way she looks at you and the ease you seem to have around her. I figured she was someone from your past. Do you still have feelings for her?"

"No!" he barked. His voice became gentle as he continued. "We went out a couple of times but agreed to remain friends."

Amara shrugged. "Okay. You know my next question. Were you attracted to me because we resemble one another?"

Terrance laughed and shook his head. "You two slightly resemble one another, but that's where the similarities end. I was attracted to you; all of you. Your tenacity, kindness, and ability to love with your whole heart." He kissed her and added, "I just wanted you to hear it from me. She and I went out on a couple dates and that was it."

Amara kissed his cheek. "I'm glad you told me." She opened the door and got out. The cold air energized her as she jogged up the steps and opened her door. She waved and closed the door. A few seconds later, she heard Terrance's car as he drove away.

Amara was too exhausted to research anything. She made her way to her bedroom, peeled off her clothes, put on her favorite pajamas and crawled into bed. Terrance was a good man. She was glad he told her about his past relationship with Sydney. Her eyes closed and she fell asleep in minutes.

Chapter 58

Amara was awakened by pounding on her front door. She brushed back a mass of red curls and fussed at herself for not wearing her sleep cap. She grabbed a thick headband and pushed back her long, tangled curls from her face. Phone in hand, Amara stumbled to the front door and yelled, "Coming!" The image on her phone caused her to groan.

Amara opened the door to a freshly showered and shaved man holding two cups of steaming hot brew. She grabbed one of the cups. "What are you doing here?"

Remy stepped inside. "Well good morning to you, sunshine." He pointed his cup at her hair. "Nice hairdo."

"Shut up!" she snapped.

"Hm, we're in a mood this morning."

Amara sighed and apologized. "I haven't been able to tell you something. It involves Divya. She was arrested last night for attacking an officer at a downtown pub."

Remy pulled the folded newspaper from his jacket pocket. "Oh, you mean the one who looks like your twin?"

Amara snatched the paper. "How, why, who...?"

He pointed at the paper and remarked, "Isn't she the one who pretended to be you when that big Russian broad broke into your apartment and held your mom hostage?"

"Please, don't remind me."

"What in the world is going on?!" Remy demanded.

Amara couldn't say, not yet anyway. Not until Casey's killer was discovered. "Something happened the day I wasn't at work. I'm not at liberty to talk about it. When I can, you will be the first person I tell."

Remy plopped down on one of her kitchen chairs. He started to laugh and took another sip of coffee. "Never a boring moment Mackelroy. If nothing else, you keep my life exciting."

She held up her cup. "Thank you for the coffee. I hope you didn't forget I'm coming into the office late today."

Remy shook his head. "No, Matt told me you'd be in later and were pissed at him. In his defense, he feels bad. Cut him some slack, okay?"

"Right now, I'm feeling a bit salty towards your brother." She saw his confused expression and raised her hand. "I promise, when I can, I'll tell you everything."

"You'd better. You know I always have your back."

Amara smiled and nodded. "Who knew we'd end up being such good friends?" she joked.

Remy laughed and headed to the door. "Later, Mackelroy."

"Later, Remy." She followed him to the door and held up the cup. "Thanks again for the coffee and checking on me. I appreciate it and you."

Remy blushed. "Don't go getting all mushy. It's just coffee." He pointed at her hair. "Now do something with that rat's nest you call hair."

She made an obscene gesture and closed the door. Remy laughed all the way to his car.

At the office, Amara put the finishing touches on her article and sent the draft to Matt. She'd decided to focus on young adults who'd aged out of the system. This is going to be a great article, she thought.

When it was time to leave, Remy caught her eye and asked her to wait for him. He didn't want her to walk out alone.

Chapter 59

Amara changed into comfortable sweats and grabbed the pages she'd printed of Casey's notes and photos from the storage unit. Terrance was at work and her parents were out with friends. Her apartment was quiet and she could give the task her full attention without interruption. She spread the random pages and pictures on the carpet.

She had to give Divya her props. Her first husband was extremely handsome. His sisters had beautiful faces. They wore the customary Muslim hijab and abaya. She noticed there were no pictures with Divya dressed in an abaya, though she'd been photographed with a scarf loosely covering her hair.

Amara set the note with the coordinates to Divya's house aside and read each note carefully. One had "Pier" written on it, another the number of the freighter that carried Pradeep's merchandise. A third note read "Sammy". Was this a nickname she'd given Samesh?

She grabbed her laptop and went to Samesh's social media account. There it was, *Sammy*; the name of his yacht! Did his yacht have some type of significance? Amara shifted her attention to a photo of Samesh with a woman. She was a bit heavier than the women he usually posed with and had shoulder-length, dark, straight hair. The woman's back was to the camera. Why hadn't she paid closer attention to this photo before? The woman was smartly dressed in a designer outfit. The couple stood in a loose embrace. His hands rested on her hips while hers were positioned against his chest.

Amara examined the photo closer. Perhaps they weren't embracing. Maybe she was pushing him away. She scrutinized the background. They were near a body of water. The Puget Sound? She'd seen him photographed with many beautiful women. He was not the steady, one-woman type. Why did Casey believe this woman was significant?

She read the words from the note pages aloud, "Sammy, 47.574585° N - 122.22207° E, pier, theft, drugs, fake, Nhava Sheva Port, Ella, Divya." Amara picked up each sheet and tried to arrange them in a meaningful order. She put the first note that read "Sammy" on the carpet. The second was the coordinates to Mercer Island; the pier was where Samesh was shipping illegal drugs. What does the word "fake" mean? She shook the sheet as she considered what could be considered fake? Amara placed the remaining notes on the carpet, grabbed her laptop and typed Nhava Sheva Port in the search engine.

"Okay," she said aloud. It was a popular port east of Mumbai, where Divya and her husband's second home was located. So, Samesh was transporting illegal drugs in the freighter from the port in Mumbai to the pier in Seattle. She stared at the sheets with "Divya" and "Ella" printed on them. Had Casey learned or suspected Divya's relation to Ella? Or was it something else?

Was that why she'd planned to speak with the lawyer at the wedding? Had he broken a confidence? Otherwise, there was no way he'd reveal information regarding the adoption, Ella's biological parents, or Ella's trust fund.

Amara paced as she tried to understand the remaining words; "theft" and "fake". She was sure the word theft was somehow related to Samesh. What was fake?

The knock at the door startled Amara. She grabbed her phone and saw a woman standing at her front door.

Amara hesitated a beat before opening the door. "Hey, w-what are you doing here?" she stammered. Inwardly chastising herself for her lack of manners, she opened the door and allowed the woman to enter her apartment. She glanced at the small bandage on the side of her face. "How are you feeling?" she asked.

Sydney Palmer gently touched the bandage and shrugged off her jacket as she entered. When she spotted the sheets of paper on the carpet, Sydney smirked. "You just can't leave it alone, can you?"

Amara took Sydney's jacket. "Apparently, neither can you. Why are you here?"

Sydney pointed at the pages of photos and notes. "Where did you get those?"

Amara collected the sheets and placed them on the kitchen table. She motioned for Sydney to take a seat on the sofa. "May I get you something to drink?"

"Red wine if you've got some," Sydney replied.

Amara lifted a brow, removed two bottles of water from the refrigerator and handed her one.

Sydney accepted the bottle of water and took a drink. "I guess I'm here out of curiosity. Why are you so interested in this case? It's apparent Divya can't stand your ass and Casey, well, we both know you and Casey weren't exactly friends."

Amara took a seat and schooled her expression. "What can I do for you Sydney?"

Sydney set the bottle of water on the table and leaned back against the cushions, making herself comfortable. "I think you know more about this case than you're letting on. What haven't you shared? Do you think you're going to crack this case all by yourself Nancy Drew?" Sydney picked up the bottle and took a sip; her eyes never leaving Amara.

Amara stood. Her chest heaved and her nostrils flared. "I think it's time for you to leave!"

Sydney stood and held out her hands. "Hey, I'm sorry. Sarcasm is how I deal with uncomfortable situations. That woman planned to kill me without a second thought. I want to know why. Was it because of her daughter or something more? She called you for a reason and asked you to come alone. What does she think you know?"

Amara sighed and told her about Mr. and Mrs. Athy's request. "I worked with Casey for two years and knew she never threw anything away. I went to her storage unit and found notes and pictures from a box marked, "Divya". I gave Molloy all the originals." Amara crossed her arms over her chest. "So, does that answer your questions about Nancy Drew's great detective work?"

Sydney flushed. "I guess I deserved that. What else did you learn?"

Amara pointed a finger at Sydney. "You're the one who's holding something back. Does it have something to do with Divya and her first husband?"

Something flickered in Sydney's eyes and quickly disappeared. "All I can't say is this case is dangerous and you need to leave it alone."

Amara handed Sydney her coat. "Yeah, you're right. Thanks for your concern."

Sydney chuckled. "You're not going to let this go." It was a statement rather than a question.

Amara shrugged.

Sydney put on her jacket. Her mouth snaked into half a smile. "Just so you know, Terry and I went out a couple of times. Nothing came of it."

Terry? Amara kept her expression neutral. "I know, Terrance told me."

"Of course you do." She held up the bottle and followed Amara to the door. "Thanks for the water." Amara opened the door and watched Sydney jog down the steps to her Dodge Charger. She had to admit, that was a pretty car.

Amara tucked away the photos and notes. Sydney's visit ruined her concentration. What was the real reason for her visit? Her phone rang. It was Terrance. Sydney hadn't wasted any time; tattletale.

"Hey, I just got a call from Sydney. She said she dropped by your apartment."

"Yeah, she did. She was fishing and I was the trout."

Terrance chuckled. "Okay, I was just checking. She told me you had some pictures and notes regarding the case."

"Yep, I do. Molloy has the originals. They're from Casey's storage unit. Her father gave me permission to go through the boxes, remember?" She didn't need to be interrogated. Molloy had the originals! Did it occur to him that she could have kept it all and not provided anything?

"I understand," he said slowly. "I was just checking. She seemed really concerned that you had them."

Amara's words had an edge when she replied, "Molloy has the originals. There's nothing but photos of Divya, Samesh, and Pradeep's family as well as pages with random words on them. It's not like I kept something I hadn't given Molloy."

"All right then. I'll leave you to it. Dinner tomorrow?" he asked.

"Sure," Amara replied. It was time to end the call. "Hey, I'm about to go for a jog, thanks for calling." She hung up without waiting for a reply.

Terrance stared at the phone and groaned inward. When would he learn?

Sydney passed and quipped, "Trouble in paradise Terry?"

Terrance glared at her. She knew he hated being called Terry. He smirked and replied, "No Cindy...no trouble at all." His brow furrowed as he watched Sydney head to her desk. She was supposed to be on paid leave due to the shooting. Why was she in the office?

Sydney gave him a sideways glance as she grabbed an object from her desk and walked out the station.

Chapter 60

After her run, Amara wanted to call Remy, but couldn't without telling him the whole story. She decided to text her mother. "When are you coming home? I need to talk to you about something." Her mother's response was immediate. "Come over in about one hour. Is everything okay?"

"Yes. Just need to vent and get your opinion on something." Her mother texted an emoji and Amara laughed. "Go, mom!"

As Amara headed to her car, she was pleasantly surprised it was still warm out. When Sydney visited, she'd worn a jacket. Strange, she thought.

Cora opened the door and pulled her daughter inside. "Your dad is in his office talking with one of his old law buddies. They're going to be awhile." She gave an exaggerated eye roll and Amara grinned.

She followed her mother to the deck and sat in the comfortable chair. The clear night sky was sprinkled with twinkling stars. She grabbed the glass of lemonade her mother had set on the table.

"What's going on?" Cora asked.

Amara took a sip of lemonade and told her about Sydney's unexpected visit, the photos, and notes. "Mom, you know I only have those things because Mr. and Mrs. Athy begged me to look into their daughter's death. I gave the original copies to Molloy." Cora rubbed the condensation from her glass with her finger. "I knew there was something about Sydney, I just couldn't put my finger on it."

Amara fought the impulse to smile. Her mother always knew the right words to say. "That's exactly how I feel! Also, she told me she and Terrance used to date." She wrinkled her nose. "Then she tattled to Terrance about the notes and photos."

Cora gasped. "No, she didn't!"

"Uh, huh. Terrance had already told me they'd gone out a couple of times and decided to remain friends. Why do you think she came over? And why did she run and tell Terrance about the pictures and papers?"

Cora sat back in her chair. "I think she wanted to cause a little discord between you and Terrance. I don't believe she knew you guys were dating the first time she pretended to be you. This time she saw you two together. Maybe she was curious why Terrance chose you over her?"

Amara sipped her lemonade and smiled. "I really like Terrance."

Her mother swatted her arm and said, "Of course you do, and from what I've seen, the feeling is mutual. Truthfully, I think whatever Divya shared in the guesthouse and the attack at the pub rattled Sydney."

Amara pursed her lips and replied, "I've been thinking about what Divya told Sydney in the guesthouse. It might have had something to do with her first husband or Ella." Amara handed her mother her phone with the photos and the random notes Casey had written. "What do you make of it all?"

Cora examined each picture and the notes. She handed Amara her phone and replied, "I think you're on to something. Why would Casey have photos of Divya's first husband and his family?" She raised a finger. "Also, that woman posing with Samesh looks a lot like Divya."

Amara reexamined the picture on her phone. "The hair is all wrong and her figure is different. She's heavier than Divya."

Cora shrugged. "It depends on when the photo was taken. She may have had longer hair and gained a bit of weight. You know Divya was a chubby child."

Amara sat back hard against the cushioned chair as she remembered her previous assumption. "Mom, do you think Divya and Samesh had an affair?"

Cora lifted a brow and shrugged. "I don't know, but you need to call Cian and tell him about those photos first thing tomorrow. He doesn't need to hear it from Sydney."

Her mother was loyal to the core. "Amara stood and kissed her mother's cheek. "Thank you for listening. I'll contact Molloy first thing in the morning."

Cora stood. "Mari, don't pay that woman any attention. Sydney just wants to cause trouble." She collected their empty glasses and looked at her daughter from head to toe. "You and Sydney may resemble one another, but that's where it ends. Sydney is not you."

Amara wrapped her mother in a hug before they walked inside. She stuck her head in her father's office and mouthed, "Goodbye," before heading home.

Terrance's car was parked in front of her apartment. She checked her watch. It was after ten. "Hey, I didn't know you were coming over. Is something wrong?"

Terrance shook his head and clasped her hands in his. "I didn't like the way things were left during our last conversation. Sydney is trying to start trouble. I know I can be overprotective at times, but I trust you. I came at the situation all wrong. I'm sorry."

Amara looked at him a long time. "Do you want to come up?" He nodded and she led him up the stairs.

Chapter 61

Amara woke up feeling much better than yesterday. She and Terrance had a good talk, among other things. When she walked into the kitchen, there was a note propped against the coffee cup. She read it and giggled. Apparently, she wasn't the only one who enjoyed last night. She hummed as she poured a cup of coffee.

On her way to work, she called Molloy. He sounded preoccupied. Amara got right to the point and confessed to keeping a copy of the photos and random notes from Casey's storage unit.

"Uh huh...I already knew that. I saw your phone remember? I knew you'd photographed a copy and emailed it to yourself. Why are you telling me this now?" She could hear his fingers tapping against the keyboard.

Her second confession was a lot harder. She told him about Sydney's visit and how she'd tattled to Terrance about the photos and notes. The line went silent. "Are you there?" she asked.

Molloy thanked her for telling him. "I would tell you to destroy them, but we'd have never gotten them as quickly without your help. Just stay out of the fray!"

When the call ended, Molloy ran a hand through his hair. What had Sydney hoped to learn from Amara, and why tell Terrance and not him? He knew Sydney had been affected by Divya's confession and her attack at the pub. Divya should have remained in jail the first time she was taken into custody. He wondered how she finagled getting released on bail.

He contacted Sydney's counselor. She'd missed her counseling session. He dialed her sergeant's number.

The sight of Sydney sitting in his chair with her feet propped on his desk, gave Terrance pause. "What are you doing at my desk?"

She sat up straight and narrowed her gaze. "You'd better be nice to me. I could have your little girlfriend thrown in jail for tampering with evidence." She snapped her fingers for effect and leaned back in his chair. "You couldn't have me, so you got a substitute; sloppy seconds."

Terrance's jaw rippled as he bit down on his molars. "Get up," he growled. His tone brokered no compromise. She tried to make a joke of it, but he wasn't having it. His eyes never wavered from hers.

She stood and raised her hands in a mock apology. "Geez, I was just playing around. Can't you take a joke?"

"Let's get one thing straight, Sydney. Don't you ever threaten or disrespect me or my girlfriend." He pointed down the hall. "You have your own desk and you're not even supposed to be here."

"Oooh...I'm shaking in my shoes," she sneered.

"That's it!" Terrance grabbed her arm. "We can settle this right now."

Sydney tried to pull away. The harder she pulled the tighter he gripped. If she continued to struggle, she'd have a bruise. "Hey, I'm sorry. Can't you take joke?"

Terrance didn't slow his pace or look at her. His jaw was clinched tight to prevent him from saying something he'd regret. Other officers stared as he knocked on the door with his free hand, shoved Sydney inside and shut the door.

The sergeant looked up from his document. He motioned for them to sit down and faced Sydney. "I've been trying to reach you. Why haven't you returned my calls or texts? I called your counselor; you didn't attend your session."

291

He pointed at Terrance and the door. Terrance stood and left the office. The sergeant returned his attention to Sydney. "Start talking, Palmer."

A half hour later, Terrance glimpsed Sydney as she left the sergeant's office. Head held high and posture erect, she ignored the stares of curious onlookers. His phone buzzed. It was the sergeant.

Terrance left the sergeant's office relieved. Sydney had been ordered to see the psychologist. He knew she was going through a rough time after being involved in a recent shooting and recuperating from the attack. He hoped she'd get the help she needed. Sydney was a good cop.

Chapter 62

Amara returned from lunch humming a happy tune.

Remy caught sight of her. "Someone is in a very good mood. What did you do during lunch?"

Amara ignored the gibe. Most of the staff was still out. She was tempted to stick out her tongue, but fought the urge. It would be her luck that Matt would walk out of his office and catch her in the act. Right now, she didn't need anything to cause her boss to question her professionalism.

She placed a cupcake on his desk with flourish."

Remy grabbed the cupcake and took a huge bite. He finished the rest with the second bite. It was vanilla with cream cheese frosting, his favorite. "Thanks. How's your article on the foster care system coming?"

Amara's eyes twinkled as she removed her jacket and tucked her satchel below her desk. She returned to Remy's desk and sat down in the adjacent chair. "It's coming along fine. Though I must admit, initially I wasn't feeling this assignment. Writing this article helped me understand what some of our young people in the foster care system have gone through. What are you working on and how is your flight attendant?"

Remy told her about his latest article and smiled when he talked about his new relationship. "I really like her. We get along and I trust her. I don't feel that insecurity creeping up from that college debacle involving my best friend and ex-fiancé."

Amara gave Remy a high five. "Good for you. When do I get to meet her and give my seal of approval?" she joked.

Remy chuckled. "She'll be in town next weekend. How about you and Terrance come to my place for dinner next Saturday?"

"That sounds great! Let me text Terrance to make sure he's off."
She raised her phone and announced, "He's available. We'll be
there!"

Remy typed a quick message to his girlfriend and grinned.
"We're all set. It's a date."

Amara returned to her desk and thought about Divya and
Samesh. The police and FBI remained mum about the two cases.
She wondered if Samesh had confessed to killing Casey. Though
it was plausible, she didn't believe he'd done the deed. If he was
responsible, she felt certain he'd hired someone. He seemed
more focused on blackmail, amassing as much money as
possible, fleeing the country, and living a luxurious life.

Although, she couldn't discount him. He'd followed her around
and visited her apartment under the guise of being a private
investigator. He'd also hired people to follow her. He was
always getting others to do his dirty work, like the impostor at
Rolanzo's wedding.

A man escorting Casey at the pier had been caught on video.
The man in the video was tall and Samesh was short. That led
her back to her suspicion he'd hired someone to remove Casey
from the pier and take her to Schmitz Park. The DNA found
beneath Casey's nails might help the police to identify her
attacker.

Her thoughts returned to the photos and random notes she'd
discovered in Casey's storage unit. The photos of Pradeep's
children, Divya's first husband and his sisters, along with Ella
bothered her. Why did she have photos of those particular
people and why store them in the storage unit instead of inside
her journal or pages of notes she'd given her father for
safekeeping? What was the connection?

Amara's brows knitted together. They meant something…she
forced herself not to dwell on it. It would only cause trouble if
she dug into it. Except, Casey's killer might still be out there.

She thought about Divya and Sydney in the guesthouse. Something monumental had occurred between the two ladies. Amara struggled to wrap her brain around the fact Divya meant to kill her and Samesh. How had Divya planned to cover up her murder? Accuse Samesh of attacking and killing her before Divya killed him? What had Divya told Sydney she'd intended for her to take to the grave? Why was it so important for Ella to remain a secret?

Perhaps Divya blamed her for involving the authorities which led to more people to knowing her secret. The thought made her shiver. The truth was somewhere in between. One thing was certain; she didn't owe Divya anything.

Amara combed the news websites and the local newspaper. There'd been a tiny article about Divya's arrest for her latest attack. There was no mention of Sydney's name. Amara hoped to never cross paths with Divya again.

Samesh wouldn't be released from jail any time soon for kidnapping Ella. She'd also heard Pradeep remained in town to quell bankruptcy rumors regarding his company as well as Samesh embezzling millions of dollars. A brief article in the business section revealed the contamination in Pradeep's company's face cream had been resolved. Maybe things were looking up for Pradeep. At least with his businesses.

Chapter 63

As Amara and her mother cleaned the kitchen after dinner, their conversation was interrupted by a knock at the door. "Are you expecting Terrance?" Jackson called over his shoulder as he strode to the front door and turned on the porch light. Amara told him Terrance was working late.

A well-dressed man with dark eyes, ebony hair, and a handsome face stood on the porch. He clutched a bundle of thin blue envelopes in one hand. The man cleared his throat and spoke with a slight British accent. After he quickly introduced himself, as Nasir, he asked, "Is this the Mackelroy residence?"

Amara and her mother joined Jackson at the door. Amara inhaled sharply when she spotted the bundle of envelopes. She could see her name scrawled on the edge of one. "Where did you get those?" Cora put a protective arm around her daughter's shoulder.

Nasir held up the bundle of letters and replied, "This is why I'm here." He informed them he was Divya's first husband's best friend and was in town on business. "This address was on the envelopes." He pointed at Amara. "I'd hoped you or your parents hadn't moved."

After everything that had happened, Jackson was hesitant to allow Nasir into their home. But Amara had to know why and how he'd gotten her old correspondence. Jackson led the gentleman to the family room, while Cora offered him coffee.

Amara observed Nasir's attempt to present a pleasant demeanor as his dark eyes took in the room. She wasn't fooled. This had something to do with Divya. After he accepted a cup of coffee, he began his spiel. "I was with Divya's husband the day of the accident. He and Divya weren't getting along. They'd been trying to have a child, you see."

Amara held her tongue and allowed him to continue. "He was the only son and needed an heir to carry on the family name." He held up the bundled envelopes. The fragile paper crinkled in his grasp. "My friend's mother found these letters during the renovation of her home. Divya was very secretive."

Amara fought the impulse to roll her eyes when she interrupted the man's spiel. "What exactly do you want to know and what did you read in those letters that prompted you to search me out after all these years?" It had been nearly a decade ago when she and Divya had corresponded.

The visitor exhaled. "My friend's mother prompted this visit." He fidgeted with the faded velvet green ribbon that held the letters together. "I didn't pursue it immediately because Divya returned my friend's inheritance. She invested wisely and quadrupled the money she'd been given as a gift from my friend during their marriage. I heard she remarried."

When Amara and her parents didn't respond, he shrugged. "I was told Divya sold pieces of her jewelry and maintained the three overseas properties she received during their marriage." He ran a hand over his well-coiffed hair. "After my friend died, we learned she'd set up a trust for one of the children at the orphanage in India where she'd volunteered." He held up the bundled letters. "There are two letters addressed to you that were never mailed."

Amara and her mother exchanged quick glances. They were finally getting to the crux of this impromptu visit. Amara was about to ask a question when her mother lightly tapped the side of her leg. It was apparent the man was unaware the little orphan girl he spoke about was Ella.

The puzzle pieces began to come together. It was possible Divya never spoke with the adoptive family when Ella was kidnapped. They probably didn't know Ella is Divya's biological child. Ella never saw Divya at the mansion. The inheritance piece would most likely be handled anonymously. Amara forced her attention back to Nasir as he droned on about Divya and his best friend's dysfunctional relationship.

"For the sake of my best friend's mother, I'm attempting to learn more about the woman my friend married." He patted the bundle and said, "These letters are addressed to you. Whatever you can tell me would be greatly appreciated."

Amara held his gaze. "Why not question Divya?" The man's laugh was harsh as his eyes blazed with something Amara could only describe as deep hatred.

After several seconds of silence, the man pleaded, "Whatever you can tell me would mean the world to my friend's mother."

Amara gave an exaggerated sigh. "Unfortunately, our friendship didn't withstand the test of time." She raised two fingers. "I had the opportunity to see Divya twice before she married your friend. A couple weeks ago, she came to see me."

Nasir leaned forward. His eyes glistened with something Amara couldn't quite gauge. Hunger for information, hostility, hatred? "What did she want?" he asked.

"What do *you* want?" she countered.

His eyes turned to slits. "I want to know why she killed my best friend!"

"Do you have evidence to support this claim?" Amara countered. If he had, he wouldn't have come to her parents' house asking these questions, she thought.

"No, I do not," Nasir admitted.

"I'm sorry about your friend. I don't know anything about Divya's current life. You should have this conversation with her," she said softly.

The man stood and slapped the envelopes against this thigh. "She wrote a letter to you about a child and never mailed it. Does she have a child?"

Amara and her parents stood. "As I said, I don't know anything about Divya or this letter. If you want to know the truth, I suggest you go directly to the source. I'm sure you're aware she has a home here."

He handed Jackson his card. "Thank you for your time. That is my card in case you remember anything. I apologize for the intrusion."

Jackson escorted Nasir to the door. By the sound of the tires squealing against the damp pavement, he wasn't pleased with the outcome of his visit. "What in the world is going on?!" her father demanded.

Amara shrugged. "Why would Divya write such a revealing letter to me and leave it for someone to find?"

Cora took the card from her husband and added, "He wanted information from us, but he wasn't forthcoming with everything he knew."

Amara checked her watch and yawned. "I think I'll stay here tonight." Her parents agreed. She headed to her childhood bedroom and conducted a hasty internet search on their visitor. She typed Nasir's full from the card and waited as her search engine churned. As suspected, he was extremely wealthy and well connected. He was a businessman who owned hotels in Dubai and a few in other countries. He wasn't married, which surprised her. There were several dated photos on his social media site of him and Divya's first husband. Two very rich and handsome men, Amara thought. She made a mental note to research Divya's first husband more thoroughly in the morning.

Chapter 64

Amara felt sluggish as she gulped the last of her coffee and hurried out the door. She'd returned to her apartment to shower and dress for work. Her sleep had been fitful. Ella and the death of Divya's first husband invaded her thoughts the entire night.

She couldn't shake Nasir's visit. It prompted more questions than answers.

Divya's life seemed to be a labyrinth of questions. Did Divya know the couple who adopted her child? Though Ella didn't resemble Divya, she resembled Connor, her biological father.

Amara wasn't sure what to believe when it came to her old classmate. She'd lied to her parents to cover her misdeeds as a teenager! The words of her father came to mind. If she lied on you, who's to say she's still not lying about this entire situation? Why had she roped Amara into her drama? Especially regarding the kidnapping?

Amara thought about Nasir's accusation against Divya. Killing or attempting to kill seemed to come easy for Divya. How many other times had she tried or succeeded? Was she personally involved in Casey's death?

Yes, the puzzle was coming together. Samesh probably told Divya she'd been looking into Casey's death. Was that the reason Divya had showed up the first time unannounced? Amara was thankful she hadn't divulged too much information. That possibly saved her life.

Amara was disgusted with the thought of Divya having an affair with Samesh. How else would he know about Ella? Divya's own husband hadn't known. Although she couldn't deny Samesh was an expert at ferreting out useful information about a person and using it for financial gain.

The fact Samesh was in jail gave Amara hope this ordeal might be over soon. He'd go to prison for fraud, stealing money from his company, and kidnapping Ella. He'd made Pradeep look stupid and nearly bankrupted him.

Amara phoned Terrance and told him what happened at her parent's house. He was alarmed and told her to remain alert. "Don't talk to that guy alone!" he warned. "In fact, I'll meet you in the parking lot at your office after work tonight. I've got to work tonight so I'll be in uniform.

The work day seemed to drag on. Everyone was busy trying to meet the magazine deadline for the issue. She was grateful for that. It was a challenge to focus. She peeked over at Remy's desk. He was totally focused and hard at work. When it was time to go home, Amara packed quickly and followed the rest of the crowd out the door. Remy was still typing away and hadn't looked up when she bade him goodnight.

Terrance was in the parking lot as promised. She tilted her head toward the tall, impeccably dressed man who'd gotten out of his rental car. When Terrance joined Amara, Nasir looked startled, but quickly recovered. He introduced himself to Terrance, who simply nodded. The man held out a faded blue envelope. "You had asked to see the letter. This is it."

Amara took the letter and quickly read the familiar cursive handwriting. She felt a lump in her throat as she handed the letter back to him. "As I told you last night, I wasn't aware of any of this. When she returned, she ended our friendship. It wasn't until I began looking into the death of a college classmate that Divya visited my parents, asking questions."

"What? What type of questions? Did it have anything to do with the death my friend or this child?"

Amara shook her head. "No, it had to do with Divya's second husband and someone who worked at his company."

The man's expression darkened. "I read something about that in the paper. Divya was arrested for trying to shoot a police officer at her home. Why was the police officer there in the first place?"

Terrance spoke up. "That involves an ongoing investigation. What is it you want to know from my girlfriend?" he asked.

"I just want to know what's going on. My best friend's mother asked me to look into this inheritance Divya provided for a child after the death of her son. She believes Divya was having an affair while married to her son," he sputtered.

Amara crossed her arms over her chest and didn't bother to hide her disbelief. Ella was ten years old which meant she was born during the timeframe they were in middle school. There's no way he was telling the truth. Amara arched a brow and retorted, "Want to try that again?"

The man had the good manners to blush for being caught in a lie. "Okay, okay. She wants to know more about the child and her connection with Divya."

Amara shrugged. "Why? Didn't you tell me Divya returned her husband's inheritance minus the money and gifts he'd given her? Why does it matter what she does with the things given to her by her husband?"

The man's eyes narrowed. Amara could tell he wasn't used to be challenged in this manner; especially by a woman he felt superior to. Amara and Terrance remained silent and waited.

"I can see I've made a terrible mistake approaching you in this manner. Please forgive my rudeness." His hands fluttered in Amara's direction. "Your father has my card. I would appreciate a call if you recall anything regarding the matter of the child and Divya."

Amara's eyes never left his. She watched him take a step back, turn and get into the rental car. They didn't move until he was well down the road. Amara exhaled and said, "Thanks. You were right about him attempting to ambush me at work."

Remy interrupted their conversation. "Hey, what was Nasir doing here? He lives in Dubai. Terrible what happened to Nasir's best friend a few years back." Amara and Terrance faced Remy.

Terrance stuck a thumb in the direction the visitor traveled. "You know that guy?" he asked.

Remy nodded. "I've been on his yacht a couple of times. Nice guy, though his friend was nicer. His friend's mother was a real...tyrant. He'd married a gorgeous Indian woman who used to live here." He snapped his fingers. "I can't remember her name."

"Divya?" supplied Amara.

Remy stared at Amara. "Yes! Oh my gosh!" He slapped his forehead, chastising himself for not putting it all together sooner. "She was my friend's widow. We met briefly, but I didn't know her."

Terrance kissed Amara goodbye. Once he was gone Remy faced Amara and growled, "Start talking, Mackelroy!"

"Let's go to your place," she suggested. "It's time I told you the whole story. Plus, I'm hungry. Maybe your chef can whip up one of his famous meals for us?"

"Follow me," he said.

Amara sat with Remy on his deck sipping wine and eating canapés topped with salmon mousse and crab. When she finished telling Remy the entire sordid, story, he stared, aghast.

"I couldn't tell you!" she cried. The next words rushed out in one long stream. "Casey's death is still under investigation and I was sworn to secrecy about Ella. That was until Divya thought the police officer was me and tried to kill her! I'd learned about

Ella by accident while writing the article about the library boxes."

Remy stared at Amara. "So, the day you took off from work was the day Samesh, who works for Divya's husband, kidnapped Ella for ransom?"

Amara nodded; her voice low as she leaned close. "Nassir believes Divya had something to do with her first husband's death. Also, Divya confided something to Officer Palmer at the guesthouse. Whatever it was, she didn't want anyone to know and tried to kill her at a pub after the kidnapping."

Remy's mouth dropped open as he snapped his finger. "Now it's all coming together. I knew there was more to the story than what was in the newspaper!"

Amara nodded. "Divya intended to kill me because I knew about Ella."

Remy rubbed his face. "Damn! I see why you didn't share any of this. Do you think she's connected with Casey's murder?"

"I do, I just don't know how. Casey had photos and random notes in her storage unit. She hadn't put them with the other notes given to her father for safekeeping. I'm not sure why she kept them separate."

Her eyes were shiny with unshed tears. "I've been wanting to talk to you about this for a while, but I couldn't. Now, I feel I can. Especially since that crazy cow tried to kill both me and Officer Palmer."

"What do you plan to do?"

Amara wrapped a curl around her finger. "I don't know yet. The person on the video with Casey at the pier was built like a man." She closed her eyes. "Remy, what if it wasn't? What if the person who took Casey from the pier was a woman disguised as a man? There was a reason she had photos of your friend, Ella, and Pradeep's kids in that box. I just can't figure out why."

"Do you want me to talk to my friend?" Remy asked.

"If you think he'll tell you more than he's shared with me. I say go for it." She checked her watch. "He mentioned he's here on business. I don't know when he'll return to Dubai."

Remy removed his cell phone. "Leave that to me." He dialed Nasir's number and invited him over for dinner. "He's coming for dinner tonight. I'll let you know what I find out."

Amara thanked Remy as he walked her to the elevator.

Chapter 65

Amara entered her apartment and looked around. Her place seemed tiny and dark after Remy's spacious place with the view of Puget Sound. She opened the blinds over the sliding glass door that led to her tiny deck and allowed the last of the late afternoon sun to shine as she went to her bedroom to change clothes.

It was time to research Divya's first husband. The weather was nice, and she carried her laptop outside to the deck.

A knock at the door broke her train of thought. Her phone showed Sydney standing at her door with a bottle of wine. Amara ignored her. There was nothing more to discuss. She was glad she'd parked on the far side of the apartment in case Nasir tried to ambush her at home. After a few more knocks, Sydney left.

As she watched the late evening news in her pajamas, her phone chimed. It was Remy. She picked up after the first ring. "What did you find out?" she asked.

She could hear the excitement in his voice. "You are not going to believe it! This can't be told over the phone. I'm in your parking lot."

Amara threw on sweats and removed the sleep cap from her curly mane. She pushed her curls away from her face with a thick headband and texted Remy to come up. When she heard the knock, she opened the door.

Remy rushed inside. His blue eyes shimmered with excitement.

"What!" she screeched and motioned for him to sit down.

Remy sat down and grabbed her laptop from the coffee table. He navigated to a site where there'd been a photo of him, Divya, Omar, her late husband, Nasir, his best friend, and

Nasira, the woman who'd been a childhood friend. He pointed at the woman and explained Nasira had been chosen by Omar's mother to be his future wife. He explained how Divya had met his good friend at the yacht club.

"Nasir hit on Divya first, but she chose Omar instead," Amara said.

"Stop high jacking my story. Yes, you're right. I should have recognized Divya with all the publicity circulating." Remy shrugged. "Truthfully, Nasir never got over the fact Divya hadn't chosen him. He began to dig into her personal life and interfere with his friend's budding relationship."

Amara frowned. Divya wasn't rich or well connected, why would Nasir care, she wondered.

Remy grinned and pointed. "You're asking yourself why would Nasir care?"

Amara nodded.

Remy explained Omar and Nasir were in constant competition over everything; to include women. Omar had brought home Divya, a non-Muslim, Indian woman he'd already married.

"Once Omar moved Divya into the family residence, his mother treated her terribly. It got so bad Omar moved his mother to the wing on the opposite side of their palatial home." Remy navigated to a site on her laptop and showed her the home.

"Oh wow!" Amara whispered. The home resembled a royal palace. "Okay, so this couple was madly in love until..."

Remy resumed his story. "Until Omar learned Divya couldn't have children. Before they married, he asked Divya to sign a document that assured him she didn't have any children." Remy shrugged and explained, "For whatever reason, this was important to him. I believe his mother was the reason he was so adamant about this. Omar also told me on more than one occasion he didn't want any children not sired by him to be able to claim any of his wealth." His voice was low when he announced, "Divya signed the document."

Amara gaped at Remy.

"You can close your mouth Mackelroy," he teased.

Amara did, too stunned to speak. She now understood Divya's over-the-top demand for secrecy, to the point she was willing to kill for it.

"Divya left Ella a sizeable inheritance that's scheduled to be delivered once she turns ten. I'm sure the trust will be given to her anonymously," she said.

Remy brows knitted together. "For whatever reason, my friend's mother is afraid this child is going to demand part of her son's inheritance, which is crazy. Divya's child isn't related to her son."

Amara held up two fingers. "First, what does your friend hope to learn and why is this so important?"

Remy closed the laptop. "Divya's ex-mother-in-law believes Divya may have used her son's money to pay for the child's inheritance."

Amara shrugged. "She kept only the gifts of money, jewelry, and property given to her by her first husband. Who's to say she didn't use Pradeep's money?"

Remy scrubbed his face. "This entire situation smacks of revenge. I'm sure you heard his family blamed Divya for Omar's death."

He explained how they had gone out on his yacht for a guys' weekend and there was an accident with a drunk who was driving a speed boat. "Initially, Nasir planned to divorce Divya. His mother was really pushing the issue. Believe it or not, it was

308

Nasira, his childhood girlfriend, who persuaded him to rethink the divorce. It was clear he still loved Divya."

Omar's decision not to divorce Divya had caused him to nearly go to blows with Nasir on the yacht. "I had to intervene. Divya's husband announced he needed to get away from Nasir and went water skiing."

Amara wanted to know the truth. "How was her husband killed?"

"A boat careened into Omar while he was water skiing," Remy said. "Nasir spun a false story and blamed Divya to remove the spotlight from him. He was the reason Omar had gone water skiing."

Remy looked at his shoes and shook his head. "I wasn't there to refute his story. By the time I'd heard, the damage was done; everyone blamed Divya." He threw up his hands. "She wasn't even on vacation with us." His voice was low. "I learned she left Dubai after the funeral and returned to Seattle."

"Do you think Nasir has paid Divya a visit before now?" she asked.

"What? Why? Do you think he threatened her in the past?"

"If what you say is true, he resented her and needed her to feel guilty for something that was partly his fault. Divya is facing possible prison time for attempting to shoot a police officer who she thought was me," Amara replied.

Remy's mouth went dry. "What?!" he croaked.

Amara revealed what had happened at Divya's mansion.

Remy closed his eyes and massaged his temples. "I didn't realize what you've been going through. How are you coping with all of this?"

Amara shrugged. "In the beginning, I was angry." Her voice shook as she explained, "I didn't ask to be part of this. I wasn't friends with Casey, but her father asked me to help uncover who killed her and why. I hadn't spoken with Divya since high school."

She told Remy how Divya showed up at her house unannounced twice. Amara filled him in on Samesh, now in jail.

"Ah, so that's why Terrance was in the parking lot earlier."

Amara's eyes glistened with tears. "It's been a lot."

Remy got a napkin from the kitchen table and handed it to her. Amara dabbed her eyes. "I just want it to be over. To make matters worse, I still don't know who killed Casey. I initially thought it was Samesh. Now, I'm not so sure."

Remy paced in front of Amara and returned to the sofa. "You think it's Divya, don't you?"

"I do," she whispered.

Remy folded his hands and said, "Let me help."

The tense muscles in Amara's neck and shoulders slowly relaxed. "By the way, is Nasir aware you know me?"

"No way!" Remy laughed. "He leaves for home early tomorrow morning. There's no way he could prove Divya used money from her first husband to finance Ella's inheritance. For all they know, Ella is a child she met in one of the orphanages."

Amara shook her head. "It's not over yet. If Divya murdered Casey, we need to learn how. I think we have the why."

Remy's checked his watch. "Agreed. It's late. Let's meet tomorrow after work and discuss a game plan." He wore a sly smile.

"You're enjoying this way too much," she accused.

His eyes danced with amusement as he opened the door. "Never a dull moment, Mackelroy, never a dull moment."

Amara walked Remy to the door. Once he was gone, she locked the door and set the alarm. She yawned and headed to the bedroom. It felt good to discuss the situation with Remy. Terrance worried too much and was overly protective. She had to agree with Remy. Her life was anything but dull.

Chapter 66

Molloy stood so quickly his chair rolled back and crashed against the wall. He looked around and slowly pushed his chair to his desk and rushed out the office. He'd received the results of the DNA taken from beneath Casey's fingernails. It came from two individuals. He contacted the NYPD detective on the way to Mercer Island.

Pradeep opened the door and looked at the detective warily. Molloy's green eyes gleamed with harnessed energy as he produced the warrant. "We're here to search the premises."

Pradeep stared at document. "What is this all about? Why do you need to search our home?!" He removed his phone and called his lawyer as three additional officers entered. He watched as the officers headed in different directions of the sprawling mansion.

Molloy's phone rang. It was the NYPD detective regarding the DNA evidence from Casey Athy's fingernails. He was on his way to question the thief who'd broken into the dead lawyer's apartment. "I got the lab report. Your timing is perfect."

Molloy learned the suspect in the lawyer's death was scheduled to be released. The detective promised to keep Molloy informed of the outcome of the interview. Molloy exhaled heavily and thanked the detective.

The detective stood in the dining room when one of the police officers called him. He'd found something in the master bedroom. Molloy jogged up the stairs. A pair of black pants was positioned on the bed. The officer unzipped the pocket and exposed a long, slender object that flared at the base with a black tip on the end. It was a heel to a woman's dress shoe. Molloy donned gloves and removed the heel from the zippered pocket of the black pants. He held the object up to the light before placing it inside an evidence bag.

Pradeep stood at the door and stared at the heel sealed in the evidence bag. Molloy faced the man. "Sir, does your wife own a pair of shoes that match this heel? Have you seen this heel before?"

Pradeep's expression remained stoic. "I'm not sure. My wife owns many pairs of shoes."

As Molloy and the officers left, Pradeep called his lawyer once more.

Chapter 67

Molloy entered the interview room. Divya looked calm and self-assured. It took all his willpower to tamp down his excitement. "I found something very interesting inside your home," he said.

Divya acted as if she was bored until the detective placed the plastic bag with the heel on the table. Her show of bravado and confidence quickly evaporated. "I demand to have my lawyer present!" she squawked.

Molloy gave a careless shrug. "As you wish." He stood, picked up the evidence bag and left the room. The heel fit perfectly to Casey's shoe.

When Divya's lawyer had arrived an hour later, a smile crept across Molloy's lips as he returned to the interview room. "Game time," he murmured.

Molloy placed a document on the table. "The heel retrieved from your residence matches perfectly with Casey Athy's shoe. Her DNA is on the heel as well. How do you explain this item being in your possession?"

"I found it," Divya replied.

"Where?!" Molloy snapped.

Her lawyer leaned over and whispered in her ear. Divya's mouth clamped shut.

Molloy glared at the lawyer. "She's already admitted to finding the heel. I need to know where she found it. It will help with the murder I'm investigating."

Her lawyer whispered in her ear once more before she replied. "I found it at the pier. Casey phoned and asked me questions regarding my husband's shipments. It was then I'd discovered Samesh had shipped illegal goods with my husband's legal merchandise. I'd confronted him and he began to blackmail me for money and my silence."

She'd followed him the night Casey went missing and discovered the heel on the ground at the pier. "I kept it for insurance. I knew Samesh had something to do with that woman's disappearance."

Molloy stared at her for several seconds. He leaned forward and inquired, "Why didn't you turn the heel over to the police? Samesh is in jail. Why didn't you tell us what you knew?"

"I couldn't! He threatened to expose information about my child. If it got out that I had a daughter, she'd lose her inheritance." She choked back a sob. "It took years to find her. I made sure my first husband's family never learned about her."

Molloy sat back and waited. "Are you saying you had nothing to do with Casey's murder?"

Divya glanced down at her manicured nails. "I-I didn't kill her. I only wanted to speak with her and try to convince her not to write the article. She was going to expose my secret and ruin my husband!" she wailed. She bowed her head and pressed her lips together as tears splashed against the surface of the table.

Molloy waited until she'd composed herself before asking, "When did you approach her?"

Divya seemed anxious to answer. "I never got the chance to speak with her. I was behind the wall at the pier. Samesh grabbed her! She kicked him and got away. I saw her stumble and fall." Her voice was barely above a whisper. "I don't know what happened after that." Divya raised her eyes to meet the detective's. "I didn't follow them."

"You drugged her!" Molloy said. "You waited in the shadows, out of the view of the camera and drugged her. She scratched your arm and got away!"

Divya instinctively covered the scratch on her arm. She tapped her throat and requested a cup of water. Molloy left and returned with it. She gulped the water until it ran down her chin. She wiped her mouth and chin with the tips of her manicured fingers.

"Samesh forced me to do it! I...I didn't give her the full dose. That would have knocked her out. She tripped and fell! The heel of her shoe was on the ground! I swear it!"

Molloy squinted at her. He'd watched the video numerous times. Divya never appeared on the video...unless she was the one who had attacked Casey and gotten kicked. The person who picked up Casey's shoes.

Molloy pointed. "It was you. You were the one who fought with Casey after you drugged her!" He shook his finger in her direction. "You chased after her!"

Divya shook her head. "No, no," she whispered. Her lawyer advised her not to say anything more.

Molloy stood and left the interview room.

Terrance sat stunned on the other side of the interview window. Divya was complicit in Casey's murder. She'd wanted to protect her daughter's identity. He headed down the hall to his desk.

Molloy returned to his office and contacted the detective in New York. He leaned back in his office chair and squeezed a rubber stress ball as he listened to the latest update. Gerard sang like a bird and confessed to taking Casey to the woods at Schmitz Park. She'd fought him and ran further into the wooded area of the park.

He'd been hired by Divya, not Samesh to steal the files of Ella's adoption. Gerard remained adamant he hadn't killed the lawyer or Casey. He'd knocked on the door to make sure Dumont's friend had left for the wedding before he entered. Gerard found the man on the floor. "His body was cold to the touch and there wasn't a pulse. I left." He explained the fear of being accused of the man's death since he'd broken in. Gerard admitted going to the lawyer's office, but was unable to get inside. Divya paid him to impersonate the lawyer at the wedding to learn what Casey Athy knew. When Casey took his photo at the wedding, he knew he'd been discovered.

Gerard assumed it was only a matter of time before he'd be tied to the dead lawyer. He confessed Divya paid him an additional $100,000 to get rid of Casey Athy's body. He swore he hadn't killed her. He'd left her drugged and staggering around in the woods.

The New York detective had located the additional funds in an off-shore account in the Cayman Islands. He had traced the money back to an account from Pradeep's company. The thief confirmed that Divya drugged Casey and chased her until she reached the spot where he'd hidden and waited. He grabbed Casey and knocked her out with chloroform.

He also confessed Divya helped tie her wrists and feet together before he drove Casey in the trunk of a stolen car to the park, where he untied and carried her from the car. They were inside the park when Casey came out of her drugged state. Gerard panicked and dropped her. She'd rolled off the path and staggered into the woods.

The drugs hadn't allowed her to run fast or far. Since she hadn't seen his face, he'd left her wandering in the woods. Divya told him she'd handle the situation.

Through hours of questioning, he never wavered from his account of what happened and the fact Casey Athy was alive when he left the park.

Molloy ended the call, closed his eyes, and rubbed his temples with his fingertips. Someone, possibly Divya, had murdered Casey, though he didn't think she could carry the victim to the alligator tree. Casey was taller and outweighed her by at least twenty pounds. Also, they hadn't located the murder weapon.

He needed the final piece of the puzzle. Where was the braided rope or belt used to strangle Casey Athy?

Chapter 68

Amara spotted Molloy at his desk with his eyes closed. Was he asleep or deep in thought? She rapped lightly on the door jamb. "You got a minute? There's something I want to share with you."

Molloy opened his eyes and waved her inside. A torrent of words rushed from her mouth. Amara told him about her visit from Nasir.

"Divya's mother-in-law from her first marriage blamed her for her son, Omar's death, but it wasn't Divya's fault. This whole thing with Divya has been about keeping the paternity of Ella a secret. Especially from Omar's family and Pradeep."

Molloy listened without interrupting. Amara explained how Divya signed a contract with her first husband regarding having no children. The trust she'd established with Omar's money, and her fear of losing the money and assets if his family discovered the truth about Ella. "I believe Divya killed Casey in order to keep her secret!"

Molloy stared at Amara for several seconds. "What in the world am I going to do with you, Amara Mackelroy?"

"I suggest you lock her in the cell with her buddy, Divya," Terrance suggested. He leaned against the opened door and shook his head.

Molloy barked out a laugh. "That's not a bad idea."

"Detective Molloy! I didn't go snooping around. I got the information from a mutual friend of Divya's first husband."

"I'm guessing the mutual friend is Remington Walters," Terrance added.

Amara shot him an annoyed look. "Remy had dinner with Nasir, after he'd accosted me in the parking lot at my job."

She explained Remy's relationship with Nasir and Omar. "During their dinner, he told Remy the reason for his visit. He'd contacted her at the behest of Omar's mother. She blamed Divya for Omar's death and wanted revenge. I also learned Omar had decided not to divorce Divya. I'm sure she doesn't know that. Would you please tell her?"

The detective made a shooing motion with his hand and picked up a document from his desk. Amara stood and followed Terrance to the bank of elevators.

Terrance took Amara's hand. "It's almost over. Samesh and Divya are going to prison for a long time."

Casey's death was so unnecessary. Fear makes people do awful things, she thought. She squeezed Terrance's hand. "I hope this brings Casey's family a bit of peace."

Terrance released her hand and headed to his desk.

"I hope the rest of your shift is quiet," she said and walked to the exit.

Terrance gave a crooked grin. "Me too."

Amara exited the station and encountered Sydney. She groaned inward and forced herself to maintain a neutral expression.

Sydney paused at the door. "Hey," she said.

"Hello, Sydney."

"I want to apologize for my behavior. I've been going through a tough time." She looked down at the ground before lifting her gaze to Amara. "I haven't handled it very well," Sydney explained.

Amara managed a slight smile. "I hope things are better now," she replied.

Sydney held a large envelope in her left hand. She pointed at herself and Amara with her free hand. "Are we cool?"

Amara gave a genuine smile. "Yeah, we're cool." She watched Sydney enter the station and hoped she never gave that woman a reason to pretend to be her again.

When Amara arrived at her apartment, she went out on her deck. The dark sky was clear and the stars seemed to twinkle a bit brighter than usual. She rubbed her arms to ward off the chill as she contemplated what she'd learned about Divya.

Chapter 69

The Athys called and asked Amara to come over. Mr. Athy stood at the door. He looked much better. They'd never get their daughter back, but at least they now knew what happened and why.

Mr. Athy gave her a quick hug. "Thank you for coming," he said and led her inside. Mrs. Athy brought a tray with warm slices of banana bread and coffee.

"That smells heavenly Mrs. Athy," Amara gushed.

Mrs. Athy smiled and handed her a plate and a mug.

Before she could speak, Mr. Athy said, "Amara, we want to thank you for not giving up. This was not an easy case to solve." He pointed in her direction and added, "You helped Cian. He even said so himself, but swore us to secrecy." He winked and Amara chuckled.

Amara sipped her coffee. "I'm glad we caught the people responsible for your daughter's death. Casey was smart and tenacious."

Mrs. Athy swiped at a tear as her husband removed his glasses and dabbed at his eyes. Amara ate a piece of the warm banana bread. "Oh my gosh! Mrs. Athy this bread is wonderful!" She took another bite and sipped her coffee. They spoke a few minutes more before Amara stood to leave. Mrs. Athy handed her a loaf of banana bread wrapped in cellophane. She caressed Amara's cheek and whispered, "Thank you."

Amara took the bread and fought the tears that threatened to spill over. "You're welcome," she replied hoarsely.

Amara waved at the couple and got into her car. Terrance had invited her to dinner. The banana bread would make a nice dessert.

Chapter 70

On Saturday evening, Amara and Terrance went to Remy's apartment for dinner. Terrance looked around the opulent foyer as the concierge greeted Amara by name. Once the elevator closed, Terrance smirked and whispered, "Oh, so you got it like that, huh?"

"You don't know the half of it," Amara replied as the elevator swooshed up to Remy's penthouse apartment. She told him how the concierge dissed her the first time she visited until he discovered she was good friends with Remy.

"Damn!" Terrance whispered as they entered Remy's apartment from the elevator. He took in the expensive, hand-woven Persian carpets in vibrant colors in the hallway, along with stunning oil paintings on the walls. Further down the hall, through the open door, he could see the spectacular view of the Puget Sound.

Amara sighed and quipped, "I know, right?"

Remy and his girlfriend appeared from the kitchen hand in hand. Amara had to admit; she was gorgeous. She wore her shoulder-length, thick blond hair loose. Her style was simple and classy. Her sky-blue eyes matched Remy's and her welcoming smile lit up her beautiful face with its slight upturned nose and high cheek bones.

The way she looked at Remy made Amara's heart melt. She was happy for her friend. He'd had a rough time not only finding, but trusting a woman he could possibly spend the rest of his life with. He beamed as he let go of his girlfriend's hand to shake Terrance's hand and hug Amara. He introduced Brooklyn, who went by Brooke and led them to the elegantly set table in the formal dining room. "Fancy," Amara teased.

Brooke clapped her hands. "I thought it would be fun to dress up the table and have dinner in here. Remington told me he rarely uses the space and I know you two are close friends of his...so..."

She gave a brilliant smile while Amara's brow raised in question. Remington? He answered her unspoken question with a blush and a shrug.

Remy's housekeeper served them an exquisite meal, starting with cucumber cups filled with fresh crab, shallots, and lime zest. Amara took a bite and closed her eyes. "This is fabulous," she moaned." Courses of Vichyssoise and chicken breast stuffed with Boursin cheese and noodles followed.

Amara enjoyed the banter and relaxed atmosphere. It had been a while since she'd relaxed in the company of friends.

Brooke kissed Remy on the cheek, leaving an imprint of red lipstick before she got up and headed to the kitchen. She returned with a dessert with browned peaks of fluffy meringue frosting.

Her cheeks flushed with pride. "I made this myself!" she bragged as everyone clapped. "Baked Alaska!"

"Compliments to the chef!" Terrance and Amara cheered. It looked scrumptious.

It was quiet while everyone enjoyed the dessert. Terrance pointed his fork at the dessert. "This is really good Brooke!" Brooke glowed with pride. Remy gave her hand a quick squeeze.

They played a game of charades, men against the women. The women won by a landslide. Terrance draped his arm around Amara's shoulders as they thanked their hosts for a wonderful evening. When Amara hugged Remy she whispered, "Brooke is definitely a keeper." Remy nodded as Terrance hugged Brooke.

In the car Terrance whistled. "Remy's place is off the chain. He gave me a quick tour of the house while you were talking to Brooke. That view is spectacular!"

Amara leaned back in her seat and closed her eyes. "I really like Brooke," she said.

Terrance agreed as he drove them to his place. "Yes, they make a fine couple," he replied. He glanced in Amara's direction when she didn't respond. She was fast asleep. He couldn't blame her. It had been rough dealing with Divya and Samesh's drama.

Chapter 71

Amara awoke with a start from a nightmare about the random cards from Casey's storage unit. The word "fraud" kept appearing in her dream. Who or what was a fraud? Terrance's side of the bed was empty. The clock read eight a.m. She yawned and raised her arms high over her head in a feline stretch.

During the kidnapping investigation, they'd discovered Samesh owned property in Olympia in his mother's maiden name. What if...A smile crept across her face as she pondered the idea further. She picked up her phone and tiptoed to the bathroom, and shut the door.

She called her girlfriend who owned a real estate company. It was early and Amara was relieved she was in the office. Amara skipped the pleasantries and announced, "I need a favor."

"Well, good morning to you." Her girlfriend sighed dramatically and continued. "Yes, my family is well as am I. Thank you for asking."

Amara blushed. "Girl, I apologize. Please forgive my behavior, but this is important. Would you please tell me if these people own any properties in the area?" She gave her friend Pradeep's children's first and last names.

"Hm...one of the names sounds familiar. Just a sec," she said. Soft jazz music played while Amara was on hold.

She paced back and forth on the bathroom tile, quickly washed her face, brushed her teeth, and tamed her wild curls. As she put on deodorant, her friend returned.

"Amara Mackelroy, I swear, this is the absolute last time! Do I make myself clear?"

Amara punched the air with her fist. "Yes, I understand. What did you find?"

Her friend read off the address. "This better not come back to me," she warned.

"It won't!" Amara reassured her as she thanked her profusely. She opened the bathroom door and nearly collided with Terrance. She let out a high-pitched yelp.

Arms were crossed over his chest, Terrance squinted. "Amara what are you up to and what won't you do?"

"I had a bad dream last night. It was about the note cards, papers, and photos I discovered in Casey's storage unit. One word continued to baffle me along with the photos of Pradeep's children. The word is "fraud"."

Before Terrance could comment, she continued. "I believe Pradeep was aware of what was going on in his company. We already know Samesh blackmailed a lot of people." She cocked her head to one side and blurted, "Where's the missing money? If Molloy or the FBI had discovered the money, it would have been broadcast all over the news." Her curls swept across her face as her head shifted from side to side. "Not a peep. So that tells me the money is still hidden."

She told him about the address provided by her friend. "It's a two-story beach house on Bainbridge Island." She paused for effect. "The house belongs to Pradeep's children." Terrance stared at Amara and asked to see the address. He typed it in his phone and contacted Molloy.

"This better be good," Molloy growled. Terrance quickly explained what Amara had discovered. "I know, I'm looking at the house right now," Molloy said.

Terrance shoved the phone in his back pocket and faced Amara. "Cian is there now. He's waiting for Pradeep or someone to show up. You may be right about this one." He looked over his shoulder and asked, "Are you ready to go?"

"Give me a couple of minutes!" she exclaimed and quickly dressed.

Molloy shook his head in amazement. He should have known Amara would stick with this until the end. Last night, he'd reread a portion of Casey's journal and reviewed the cards and photos from Casey's storage unit. After he spread out the cards on the carpet in his den, he was able to cancel out each word and photo until he came across photos of Pradeep, along with his children. Like Amara, "fraud" was the only word he couldn't attach to a specific act or person. He was certain the money was hidden in a location close enough for Samesh to retrieve it quickly and disappear. When one of his techs discovered the property on Bainbridge Island under the name of Pradeep's children, he figured he'd found the missing link. Casey had been one clever woman.

Molloy knew there was no way Pradeep was oblivious to the disappearance of millions from his company. There was only so much camouflaging and shifting of money that could be done before the missing funds impacted the company.

His assumptions were confirmed when Pradeep hadn't fired the young accountant Samesh blackmailed to do his bidding. She'd revealed something to Pradeep. How much, he'd never know. But it was enough for her to keep her job.

The detective parked his sedan behind a large tree, out of view from the road and house. He rolled down his window and felt the cool breeze from the Puget Sound less than a mile away. He itched for a cigarette, but settled for one of the mints he kept in his pocket. The rattle of a vehicle caught his attention.

Molloy scooted low in his seat as an expensive SUV made its way along the dirt road peppered with oversized potholes.

Molloy texted Terrance and directed him to pick up a document for him. He could have the warrant emailed to him, but since he was out of his jurisdiction, Molloy wanted a paper copy. He'd already coordinated with the Bainbridge Island Police Department; BIPD. As the car door slammed, he notified the BIPD of the vehicle.

A man dressed in expensive slacks, shined leather shoes and long-sleeved dress shirt got out of the car. His clothing was incongruent with the wooded area and seaside surroundings. Molloy picked up his camera and photographed the driver as he hurried inside the rustic house with its sagging, wrap-around porch.

Molloy noted that the house stood alone, deep in the woods. The neighboring home was a half mile away; its grounds were better maintained than Pradeep's. The neighbor's house sat closer to the edge of a rocky beach that led to the Puget Sound.

There was only one way in and out of Pradeep's property; a narrow, dirt road that curved from the paved street. It was clear that the house, once tan, now faded to a light beige color, had been grand when purchased.

The maroon paint on the door had begun to peel from neglect. Clumps of weeds choked out the lawn and vines had over taken the wooden spindles and wrap around porch. The decorative shutters were coated with dirt and had rusty hinges.

Nearly a half hour later, Pradeep returned toting two large duffle bags. He stumbled several times as his dress shoes snagged on high weeds. Molloy watched Pradeep attempt to remain upright with the oversized bags draped over each shoulder.

His chest heaved when he reached the SUV. His thick hair was shiny with sweat and stuck to his forehead. Rivulets of sweat ran down his cinnamon-toned face. The back of his shirt clung to his damp skin.

Molloy wondered where the money had been hidden to elicit such a level of exertion. He watched Pradeep open the trunk of his vehicle by sweeping his foot beneath the sensor. The wide trunk door swung upward.

Pradeep looked around before he heaved the duffle bags into the back of the SUV. As the automatic trunk closed with a loud click, Pradeep slid into the driver's seat and rested his sweaty forehead against the steering wheel.

Once he'd caught his breath, he started the SUV and slowly backed away from the house. The car swayed from side to side as he drove over large potholes.

When Pradeep braked to drive around the last oversized hole, Molloy sped down the street and blocked the driveway. Gravel and dust spewed when Pradeep slammed on the brake and put the SUV in reverse.

The engine roared as he steered off the path across high grass and sharp rocks. The tires of the vehicle slid to a stop when its path was blocked by two BIPD vehicles.

Molloy waited for the local police to get out of the car and approach Pradeep. He watched them remove Pradeep from the car. Molloy couldn't help but give Pradeep and Samesh their props. They chose the perfect place to hide millions of dollars in plain sight; his ramshackle house on Bainbridge Island.

As Terrance and Amara stood on the upper ferry deck headed toward Bainbridge Island, news reports began to pop up on social media sites. Amara was glad Terrance overheard her conversation and allowed her to accompany him to Bainbridge Island.

Mist sprayed from the Sound as she leaned against the dark green, mesh rail of the ferry, deep in contemplation. Her curls whipped across her face when she turned to look at Terrance. She wanted to ask him if he thought they'd be able to see inside the house, but didn't dare. The local news station broadcasted $40 million had been confiscated from two duffle bags discovered in the trunk of Pradeep's SUV by the BIPD.

Chapter 72

Terrance and Amara were allowed access and wove through reporters, cameras, and curious residents. Molloy met them before they crossed the yellow caution tape. He looked sincere when he thanked Amara for her hard work, and handed her a lanyard with a placard that allowed her to remain on the premises. "You won't be able to come inside the house since we're still investigating."

Amara felt privileged. She placed the lanyard around her neck and headed to the edge of the property, away from reporters. She found a spot that allowed her a clear vantage point inside the house. She watched Terrance hand Molloy the document as they walked up the steps.

Reporters clamored to get in the best position to see as much as they could and speak with the officers. Amara scoped out the backyard and took in the view of the Sound. She heard footsteps tearing through the high grass behind her and turned. A reporter had managed to get past the barrier and was headed in her direction, microphone poised. Amara jogged toward the house as a police officer ushered the reporter back behind the yellow tape.

She walked as close as she dared and peered through the back door. It was slightly ajar. She could see Molloy and Terrance. Amara inched a few feet closer, careful to remain out of the way and eavesdropped on the local police officers as they searched the main floor.

Molloy looked around the first floor. It was surprisingly dust free and modestly furnished. Photos of Pradeep's children at various ages hung on the walls. There were also photos of a woman he assumed was Pradeep's first wife. Her long face and sad eyes matched those of his two children. He knew she'd died in India, but didn't know the cause. There were no photos of Divya and only one of Pradeep with his first wife and young children. They were dressed in traditional Indian clothing and appeared very serious.

The overstuffed sofa and chairs were outdated but clean. The pine coffee and side tables were bare; free of knick knacks or books. The bright colored drapes that covered oversized windows had been pulled open by the police to let in sunlight.

A bookcase filled with works by Indian authors took up the wall at the opposite end of the room. Two officers opened and shook each volume to ensure Pradeep hadn't hidden anything in the pages.

Terrance made his way to a guest room and meticulously ran his hand along the bottom of each drawer of the dresser. The last drawer had a small white envelope taped to its underside. He felt the impression of a key inside and called Molloy.

The detective entered the room and snapped a photo of the envelope before he removed it. It contained a key and a business card with the name Coppertop and a set of numbers

One of the BIPD officers peered over Molloy's shoulder. "I know that place. It's a local storage unit," he said. He pointed at the card. "The numbers are likely the combination to the lock or gated entrance. "It's about fifteen minutes away."

Amara craned her neck and saw Molloy climb the ladder to the attic. Terrance waited at the bottom of the ladder; his head tilted upward.

The detective stood in the cavernous space and shined his bright flashlight. He was struck by the intense heat, even with the hatch opened. A bald bulb hanging from the rafters was the only source of light. Molloy leaned his torso against the attic wall and ran the flashlight throughout the cluttered space. Two oblong prints on the dusty floor were exposed, as well as a box that looked new. He cursed as he ducked and walked further into the attic. He grabbed the box and moved it to the attic opening. The simple effort caused sweat to drizzle down his face and burn his eyes. He understood why Pradeep was covered with sweat and dust when he left the house. He tossed the box through the opening to Terrance and climbed down the ladder. Molloy mopped his face with his handkerchief.

"What did you find?" one of the BIPD officers asked.

Molloy wiped his face once more and replied, "I'm not sure." He gestured to the box. "I believe the box was recently placed up there." He waved his handkerchief in the direction of the attic. "It's dusty and hot up there, but as you can see, this box is dust free. Are you guys finished with photographing everything in the attic?"

The officer assured Molloy they were. A BIPD detective approached holding several items. "These have been photographed and cataloged. He opened the three passports and handed them to Molloy.

Two of the passports belonged to Samesh and Divya; the third one caused his breath to catch. It was for a little girl with beautiful, hazel eyes. This changed what he'd assumed during the ordeal of Ella's kidnapping. Had Divya been involved all along? Had she planned to leave the country with Samesh and Ella? Samesh must have betrayed Divya at the last minute and demanded more money.

There were financial papers from Pradeep's company as well as bank account information for the location where the stolen funds had been deposited. Molloy grunted. Most of the accounts belonged to Samesh. Though the FBI knew about them, he'd make sure they received copies of the documents.

Molloy and Terrance stared at the envelope at the bottom of the box. There were photographs inside an envelope. They pulled out the first picture and were speechless. It was a younger, shirtless Pradeep in a loving embrace with a beautiful, young woman. She was not the woman in the portrait.

The second was a recent photo of the same woman and Pradeep kissing in a large pool with a mansion in the background. The woman was topless. Terrance nudged Molloy. "That's Pradeep's mansion in Mumbai. Amara showed me photos of it."

Molloy popped a mint in his mouth as the pieces of the puzzle came together. It appeared Pradeep was having an affair during both marriages. Samesh had used the photographs to blackmail him. It was the reason Pradeep never reported Samesh's embezzlement to the authorities.

Chapter 73

When the BIPD released Pradeep to the Seattle Police Department, Molloy had his opportunity to question Pradeep.

Pradeep was placed in a stark interview room. The stench of sweat and dirt filled the small, windowless room. His clothes were rumpled and dirty from the trip to the attic. Pradeep's red rimmed eyes were sunk deep into a tired face; his mouth downturned in defeat.

Molloy entered and took the seat across from him. The intensity of his stare was unnerving. Pradeep's shoulders slumped and he lowered his gaze to the scarred table.

Molloy's calm demeanor eroded the man's self-confidence and control as the minutes silently ticked past. He'd requested his lawyer be present and refused to speak until he arrived. After thirty minutes, Pradeep began to fidget. "You have no right to keep me here! I've not broken any laws!"

Molloy leaned forward; his voice quiet. "You had $40 million hidden in your attic. You claimed $30 million was stolen from your company. Did you embezzle money from your own company?"

Pradeep confessed he knew Samesh was syphoning money from the company. Pradeep's housekeeper had told him where Samesh had hidden the money.

Pradeep's lawyer arrived and stopped the interview. He requested time to speak privately with his client. Molloy stood and left the room.

When he returned, the lawyer's face was flushed. "Against my advice, my client has agreed to speak with you and answer your questions."

Molloy's expression remained unreadable. He waited patiently for Pradeep to speak.

Pradeep admitted his companies hadn't been doing well and he'd "borrowed" money from one of Divya's personal accounts. He'd hired a private investigator and discovered Divya and Samesh had been together on several occasions while he was out of the country.

Initially, he suspected they were having an affair until Ella was kidnapped and Divya confessed that Samesh had been blackmailing her. Once Samesh was arrested, he'd gone to the house, climbed up the ladder into the attic and found two black duffle bags tucked in the corner. There were stacks of one-hundred-dollar bills bound with rubber bands.

Molloy smirked. He was sure Pradeep used his friend's greed to his benefit. He'd planned all along to have Samesh take the fall and keep all the money for himself.

Pradeep swore he had no knowledge of Divya or Samesh's involvement in Casey's murder. Molloy believed him. He'd verified Pradeep was in India at the time. Plus, Divya never told him she'd had a child until Ella was kidnapped. She'd told Pradeep she was unable to have children and he had no desire to father more children.

Molloy believed part of his statement. If Pradeep hired the private investigator to investigate his wife, Molloy thought it was likely he knew about Ella. Though he may not have known she was Divya's daughter.

After an hour of questioning, Pradeep admitted he'd confronted Samesh about the money stolen from the company. Samesh promised to return half of what he'd taken and Pradeep would recoup the remaining amount through an insurance claim.

"Samesh planned to take his share and start a new life in another country. Once he was arrested, I went to get the money," Pradeep said. He shifted in his seat. "It was mine since he'd stolen it from me in the first place! I didn't believe I was doing anything wrong!" He stuck a thumb at his chest and reiterated, "The money came from my company! It's mine!"

The lawyer tilted his head in Pradeep's direction and whispered softly in his ear. His client gave a curt nod and looked at Detective Molloy. He sat erect in his seat and met Molloy's steady gaze. "On the advice of my lawyer, I do not wish to continue this interview."

Molloy leaned back in his seat. "We discovered a box in the attic that contained passports for Samesh, Divya, and Ella. Did you know about that?"

Surprise appeared on Pradeep's face before quickly schooled his expression. He shifted in the uncomfortable chair. It was as if he and the detective were playing a game of chess.

Molloy's tone was quiet as he delivered the final blow. "We also discovered photos of you and a *friend*." Molloy added emphasis on the last word.

Color drained from Pradeep's face and perspiration appeared at his hairline. "Those photos are my personal property. I'd like them returned please." The tremble in his voice revealed the detective had struck a nerve.

"Who is the woman?" Molloy asked.

Pradeep spoke barely above a whisper. "She's my best friend's wife. Divya can't know about this!" He bowed his head. His voice was barely above a whisper. "What else do you want to know detective?"

Molloy's expression was confident as he asked his last questions.

Pradeep and his lawyer left the interview room. "Remember your promise," Pradeep called over his shoulder. Molloy assured him the photos would be returned.

Chapter 74

Amara and Terrance rode the return ferry to Seattle from Bainbridge Island in silence. They stood alone as the cold wind whipped across the stern of the ship. Terrance had remained after Molloy left to view the evidence. Nothing of interest was uncovered after the key taped to the bottom drawer was discovered.

He placed his jacket around Amara's shoulders and rested his chin in the crook of her shoulder. "You were right about Samesh and Divya," he said.

Amara kept her eyes trained on the water, too choked up to reply. The thought of those three passports turned her stomach. Had Divya intended to steal Ella from her parents? The image of Divya and Samesh together made her skin crawl. Amara couldn't imagine what attracted her to him. Had he somehow forced her to be with him? That wasn't such a farfetched idea.

Terrance bumped her shoulder. "I see the wheels turning. What are you thinking about?" When she told him, he gave a tired smile. "Casey had pretty much figured it all out. Though I don't condone what they did to her, I understand why they feared having her article published."

Tears pricked Amara's eyes and Terrance wrapped his arms around her. Several minutes later, Amara faced Terrance. "I overheard a conversation about a key to a storage unit. Is Molloy going to check it out?"

Terrance nodded, but gave no explanation.

Amara knew he couldn't discuss it further. She'd have to wait and learn about its contents later.

Terrance peeked at his phone and laughed aloud. "We're on our way back to Seattle and Molloy is headed to Bainbridge." He showed her the text. "It's going to be a late night for the detective."

It was nearly dusk when Molloy pulled into the Bainbridge Island police department. They gave him an inventory of what they'd found inside the Coppertop storage unit. "There's just a bunch of boxes filled with photographs and financial documents," the senior officer reported. "You're free to look at them." He pointed a one of the younger officers and added, "I'll have one of our men accompany you."

Two hours later, Molloy shut his eyes and rubbed his face. The officer who'd accompanied him didn't hesitate to leave when the detective told him he could manage on his own. It was tedious work.

There were thirty boxes that belonged to Samesh. Each box had carefully labeled folders with the individual's name, date and a ledger with figures that spanned weeks, months and sometimes years, along with documents, photos, and videos that Molloy was sure Samesh used to blackmail wealthy individuals.

Samesh had easily amassed several hundred million dollars by blackmailing people. The man had a serious racket going. It was a wonder no one had killed him. Molloy snapped photos of the bank information from several boxes and requested custody of the items from the BIPD. He planned to destroy them once the case was completed.

Molloy scratched his head. Who killed Casey Athy? Samesh, Divya, or both and where was the murder weapon? If the suspect's statement in New York was true, Casey was alive when Gerard left the park. Divya told him she'd take care of Casey. He needed to put all the facts together, locate the murder weapon, and finalize the case.

Chapter 75

Sleep eluded Amara as she tossed and turned. She sat up, rubbed tired, bloodshot eyes, and placed her bare feet on the floor. Dawn shone through the sheered window. Gray sky and puffy clouds made Amara feel more depressed. The information Remy shared about Nasir during the time of Omar's accident bothered her.

There was something she needed to do, she decided. After work, she'd go to the police station and have a final conversation with Divya. She opened her laptop and filled out the online request for the visit.

Amara's head throbbed and her mouth was dry. If she didn't know better, she would swear she'd been out partying all night. She hoped a hot shower would make her feel better.

Remy was busy at work when she leaned over and asked if he'd meet her for lunch at their favorite Thai restaurant. She suggested they go early to beat the lunch crowd.

Amara got to work on her next article. She needed to clear her mind and concentrate on something other than the investigation of Samesh and Divya.

The restaurant was nearly empty when Amara took a seat across from Remy. The waitress considered them regular customers and brought over soft drinks and a crab ragoon appetizer. They laughed when she recited their order before they spoke.

Amara waited until the waitress was out of earshot and told Remy what had happened at the lake house on Bainbridge Island.

His mouth formed a small circle as he stared at his friend and shook his head. "Never a dull moment Mackelroy," he teased.

"I couldn't go in, but Molloy gave me a special pass and I was allowed to stand a short distance from the house. From there I got to see and hear quite a bit. Terrance was inside for several hours."

"I'm glad she's in jail," Remy said. "Divya doesn't need to be anywhere near that little girl."

Amara took a deep breath and launched into her plan. "I'm going to visit Divya after work today. I want to share what you told me. She needs to know her first husband hadn't planned to go through with the divorce and still loved her. She needs to know she wasn't responsible for his death."

Remy puckered his lips and narrowed his gaze. "After everything she put you and your family through? Are you crazy?"

Amara broke eye contact and fiddled with her chopsticks that rested on her napkin. "It's the right thing to do," she said softly.

"I'm sure Terrance doesn't know about this," he said a bit louder than necessary.

Amara ducked her head once more. "Nope, though I plan to tell him before I see her."

"Please reconsider," he implored. "That woman planned to kill you in that guesthouse! You don't owe her anything! Write her a damn letter!" He threw his napkin on the table and excused himself.

Amara watched as Remy strode to the restroom. His suggestion to write her a letter was the smart thing to do. Except she needed to look Divya in the eyes and ask about the passport for Ella.

When he returned, Amara attempted to reason with him. "You're right. I should just write a letter, but I want to know one thing about Ella." Her red curls wobbled back and forth as she shook her head. "I won't ask any other questions. After the question I will relay the information about Omar and leave."

Remy ran a hand through his hair. "I'll go with you. I'm the one who was there and heard the conversation between her husband and his best friend. I don't want you near that woman alone. I don't care if she's in jail. She's evil and can't be trusted."

Amara knew Remy had a point, but she had to know the truth about that sweet little girl.

As they drove to the office, Amara glanced at Remy as he wrestled to maintain his composure and keep his opinions to himself. She admired his efforts and appreciated their friendship that much more.

She texted Terrance and told him of her plan to visit Divya. Amara was relieved and a bit surprised when she received his one-word response, "Okay."

Chapter 76

Molloy made his way to the evidence room, signed out several boxes from the Coppertop storage unit, stacked them next to his desk and donned gloves. He focused on Divya's box first. He retrieved photos of Ella and Connor, the child's biological father. The letters threatened to expose Divya's secret to the first mother-in-law regarding Ella if she didn't pay what he'd requested, and he threatened to harm Ella if Divya refused to comply with his demands. According to the financial spreadsheet, Divya had already paid Samesh $13 million over the span of three years. He found a note that demanded they meet at Pradeep's house and the repeated threat against Ella if she didn't comply.

It was clear Divya wasn't having an affair with Samesh. Molloy shook his head in disgust and wished Divya had gone to the authorities with this information instead of trying to handle the situation herself.

"Extortion at its finest," Molloy murmured and called his friend in the FBI.

The phone rang as Molloy wrapped up his report. It had been a long day and he wanted to finish and head home.

Terrance told him Divya had two visitors and Molloy cursed aloud when he learned their names. He stood abruptly and headed to the elevators. If Terrance had pulled strings to make the visit happen, he'd deal with him later.

Amara and Remy sat side by side when the door opened and Divya was escorted into the room. Amara was taken aback at the sight of her old classmate. Gone were the makeup, expensive clothes, and expertly styled hair. In their place was a woman with dark circles beneath tired eyes and unkempt hair that framed a gaunt face.

She took one look at Amara and Remy and scowled. "So, you came here to gloat, huh?" Divya's cuffed wrists jingled as she gestured to her slim frame clothed in inmate attire. "What do you want and who is he?"

Amara took a deep breath. "I've come because I have something to tell you. This is Remy. He was a classmate and good friend of Omar. He was on the yacht the day your husband was killed."

Divya gasped as her eyes filled with tears. "What?! How…" She didn't finish, but continued to stare as recognition hit her. "Wait! Yes! We met at the yacht club in Seattle!"

Remy sat erect. "Yes." He paused before he spoke again. "I was good friends with your husband. We attended boarding school together. I was there when the accident occurred."

Before he could continue, Amara interrupted. "Before we get into that, I have one question. Were you planning to take Ella when you and Samesh left the country?"

Divya's eyes blazed. "What?!" She shook her head. "I wouldn't have gone anywhere with that pig! Ella? No…she's with a good family. I would never take her away from her brother and parents. Why would you think such a thing?"

Amara told her about the passports found in Pradeep's house.

Divya gawked at the pair. "Ugh! I hate Samesh! I had no plans to take Ella anywhere. I love my husband, even though our marriage is a bit unconventional. He's a good man and good to me."

Although Amara didn't believe her, she'd asked the intended question. She told Divya what she'd learned about the day her husband died and wanted her to know everything that occurred.

Divya inhaled sharply. She blinked away unshed tears. "What are you talking about?"

Amara motioned for Remy to speak. "Before Omar was killed, he'd decided not to go through with the divorce. He loved you and wanted to remain married."

Tears streamed down Divya's face. "Oh my God...no...you can't mean..."

"Nasir didn't agree. They got into a terrible argument. You see Nasir wanted Omar to go through with the divorce. He never got over the fact he'd met you first and you chose Omar over him."

Divya croaked a harsh laugh. "Nasir is a self-indulgent, pompous ass. I never liked him and the feeling was mutual."

Remy nodded. "Omar was really upset after their argument. He'd decided to water ski to get away from Nasir. A drunk, driving a speedboat clipped him. We thought Omar was joking around. As you know he was a big kidder. But when he didn't get up, we knew it was serious."

Remy blinked away tears. "I wasn't aware of the lies Nasir told your mother-in-law and friends. When I learned of it, the damage was done and you'd returned to Seattle. I'd only met you briefly and didn't feel it was my place to tell you what really happened. I'm sorry for that." He gestured in Amara's direction. "Amara wanted you to know the truth."

Divya's chest heaved as she brushed away tears with the back of her hand. "You don't know how much this means to me. Nasir told me my refusal to agree to the divorce had pushed him over the edge. All this time I believed I was responsible for his death. That I was the reason Omar was dead. I had killed him because I wouldn't let him go."

She shook her head as if to clear away old memories. "You have given me a special gift and I will give you one in return." Amara and Remy exchanged a look. "Go to my house on Mercer Island. There is a false wall inside my closet. You'll find an indentation and a small lever. Push the lever. Once the wall opens, the combination to the safe is 4917. I think you'll find what you're looking for regarding Casey Athy's murder. I was saving it for another day, but this is my gift for the one you've given me." She tilted her head up toward the ceiling as tears streamed down her cheeks.

Amara thanked Divya in a quiet voice.

"I've treated you horribly and am very sorry, Amara," Divya said. "You're a better friend than I'll ever be...to anyone." She motioned to the guard to return her to her cell.

Molloy listened to the exchange in awe. He immediately requested a warrant, contacted the Mercer Island Police Department, and sent a unit from their station.

Amara and Remy were intercepted by Molloy in the hallway. They stopped in their tracks; eyes wide like two children who'd been caught by their parent after breaking curfew. He pointed an index finger in their direction. "You should have told me you'd planned to speak to my suspect."

Amara shrugged. "I came with the sole purpose of sharing the truth about her first husband. We had no idea she'd reciprocate with that information! Did you hear the entire conversation?"

Molloy was irritated over Amara's lack of remorse. But if he was being honest, he wouldn't have received the vital information that might lead to the missing evidence in Casey's murder. No matter how hard he may have pushed or cajoled the suspect, she wouldn't have divulged the information. Divya had nothing to lose. She'd go to prison for her part in Casey's death as well as attempted murder against a police officer.

"We have a unit going to her place right now." He shook his finger in their direction. "You two stay far away from that house!"

Amara and Remy grinned and quickly left the building. Amara knew Terrance was out on patrol and sent him a text on what transpired. She was pleasantly surprised when he replied with a thumbs up emoji and invited her to dinner to hear all about what had happened.

Chapter 77

The detective stood with an officer from the Mercer Island Police Department and a patrol from Seattle in Divya's walk-in closet. It was the size of a small studio apartment. Pradeep sat in the living room; the warrant clutched tight in his hand. Several suitcases were in the hallway, next to the front door.

Molloy slid hangers with expensive, designer outfits aside and felt along the edge of the far wall until his fingers swept over a slight indentation. He pressed the indentation and the wall slid to expose a safe. The numbers 4917 were pressed on the keypad and it opened with loud click.

The safe contained several legal documents, cash and a man's leather braided belt carefully rolled, inside a plastic bag, tucked in the corner. His gloved hand removed the belt. The pattern of the belt matched the braided welts he'd seen on Casey Athy's neck. He could see dried blood and slivers of tree bark stuck inside the weave. His smile widened when he spotted a thin strand of blond hair stuck to the buckle with a drop of blood. Bloody fingerprints were on the buckle.

Molloy was certain it was used to strangle Casey Athy. How had Divya gotten the belt? He searched the entire contents inside of the safe and found nothing else pertinent to the murder. He clutched the plastic bag, closed the safe, pushed the button. The wall slowly slid into place. Molloy joined the officers and left the mansion.

Amara was dumbfounded as she and Terrance sat on his sofa and watched the evening news. A photo of Samesh appeared on the screen. He'd officially been charged with Casey's murder in addition to several other felonies the FBI was investigating.

Divya's photo appeared next. She had been charged as an accessory to Casey's murder in addition to the charges for attempted murder of a police officer. There was no doubt she'd serve time.

Reporters chased after Pradeep as he left the mansion and sprinted to an idling car in the driveway. They yelled out questions as the car sped away. As promised, Molloy had returned his photos.

The company spokesperson reported Pradeep planned to return to India. His son would run the company based in Seattle until further notice. The spokesperson went on to say the property on Mercer Island would be sold. It held too many painful memories for Pradeep and his family. They'd already received several offers.

Amara rolled her eyes and turned down the volume on the television and faced Terrance. "It's finally over," she said.

Terrance kissed the tip of her nose. "Yes, it is," he replied.

Amara watched with interest as Terrance stood abruptly and walked to the front door. He'd been fidgety all evening. She assumed he was a bit upset because she'd gone to visit Divya in jail. "Where are you going?" she called.

When Terrance returned, Amara was surprised to see her parents. His expression was serious as he placed his hand inside his pant pocket and brought out a black velvet box.

Before he could utter a word, there was a rapid knock on the door. Jackson quietly excused himself and answered the door.

Terrance froze as a beautiful woman and a child who looked like him entered the room.